Also by

Lizzy Shannon

A Celtic Yearbook
(Original and Journal)

Tales from Erin

Time Twist

Tempest Raised

Short Stories

Through the Dolmen

Ashes

Lizzy Shannon

A Song of Bullets

A NORTHERN IRISH THRILLER

Sheffield Publications

Sheffield Publications

10 9 8 7 6 5 4 3 1

A Song of Bullets

ISBN 10: 069279655X

ISBN 13: 9780692796559

Printed and bound in the United States of America.

TEXT WRITTEN IN AMERICAN STANDARD ENGLISH

For "Mike"

Prologue

I struggled fiercely until he forced the pistol barrel into my mouth. Galvanic shock reverberated through my teeth followed by the tang of blood from a split lip. My throat closed against the metallic incursion, and I tried to resist the urgent gag reflex.

Wind slapped me in the face, throwing dust in my eyes and whipping my hair banshee-wild around me. A black shape blurred the inkiness of the indigo sky as something unfurled silently from above. I thought I was hallucinating. A surreal white semicircle pulsed overhead. It took me a moment to understand it was the whirring of 'copter blades. I could only see a glittering fan shape as they caught the light from the beam on the palace roof. Four dark, almost invisible figures silently slid down ropes and landed in graceful readiness, like stalking panthers on the cobblestones.

1
December 1978

When you grow up in a place like Northern Ireland you know who belongs where at a glance. Behind me on the Ulsterbus heading out from Belfast city center huddled a young mother with two toddlers. Catholic, from the guarded expression I caught crossing her face as we wound through an obviously Protestant area. Gaudy red, white and blue Union Jacks flapped from lampposts on both sides of the street.

Across from me slouched two teenage boys in indigo denim jackets, eyes angry and watchful. Definitely Prods, by the bold plaid scarves proclaiming loyalty to one of the violent Tartan gangs of Belfast. The very sight of those would get them badly beaten or shot in a Catholic neighborhood. The driver, also a Prod from east Belfast based on his accent.

I could say where everyone belonged, except for me. My parents, good devout thou-shalt-not Presbyterian farmers who wanted me to get a college degree in managing cow shit so I could marry a local farm boy. And my best friend Deirdre, a Roman Catholic Irish Nationalist.

Which left me. Twenty-plus, unmarried, an Ulster Protestant girl who loves to play traditional Celtic music on my violin. Talk about a fish out of water. I just got rejected from the local music college I'd seen as a ticket to a better life away from the 'Troubles' as we called the conflict in Northern Ireland. I alone did not belong anywhere or to anyone. I expected my life would be like riding this bus till I died - through neighborhoods and towns where every single person knew who and what clan they belonged to. But I could never get off the bus and join them.

I shook myself out of my self-pity. Maybe I should just try to relax. But it was difficult, considering this journey was likely the proverbial calm before the storm when I met my parents at the station in Newcastle. I'd decided to finally tell them I could no longer pretend to want to get a degree at Queen's University in farming, or that I had any interest at all in squeezing out future generations of loyal Prod farm stock. All I wanted was my music and someplace I could play.

I focused on the steamed-up window. Shit, I couldn't see a thing. Had I missed it? Cold permeated my fingers as I swept the glass clear. We'd left Belfast far behind, but not quite there yet. The brakes huffed as the driver drew up to an old-fashioned concrete stop with the words 'bus stage' carved into it. Exhaust steam whirled and the doors sighed open, letting in a blessed rush of frigid air. An elderly man in a tweed peaked cap hauled himself on board, pausing by the driver to fumble in a coat pocket. Not so easy to tell his religion or politics, but probably a Prod in this area.

"Yer all right, mate." The driver waved him past and hit a lever that hissed the doors closed.

As we pulled away the newcomer edged over to one of the empty front seats. Clearing his throat like a revving engine low on oil, he hawked and spat into the aisle. I grimaced, averting my gaze to look back out of the window.

There. It finally came into view: Slieve Donard, Ulster's highest peak, soaring into the troubled, achromatic winter sky. Its vertex was overlaid with hoary snow, stark and unreal, a frozen ice cream cornet upended in a river of mercury.

Now I'd seen my mountain, all would be well.

We drove through 13th century Dundrum without stopping, its Church of Ireland pointed steeple standing vigil at one end, and Catholic chapel twin spires at the other; bookends on each side of the village. Dad always joked that there was no difference between them, with all the 'Popery-like rituals' the Church of Ireland employed.

The ancient keep of the Norman castle watched over the bay as always from the hill above. Just a few miles further and we'd reach my destination.

My heart plummeted. Not that I wasn't glad to be shot of Belfast for the Christmas holidays, but it wasn't going to be a particularly happy homecoming. Not once my parents heard what I had to tell them.

Newcastle town council had done its best to make the season-bleak seaside town look cheerful. Multicolored Christmas lights glowed softly in the afternoon twilight and an array of plastic Santas, holly wreaths, and candles hung from lampposts, criss-crossing above the main street. A huge fir had been plonked near the bus station, festooned with oversized lights and tinsel, and topped with a shiny star. Branches violently dipped and waved in the unforgiving wind sweeping off the Irish Sea. The star looked precariously in danger of toppling and decapitating a passerby.

The bus pulled up to the curb outside the terminus, its exhaust sighing as though fatigued after the thirty mile trip from Belfast. I waited until the other passengers had shuffled by before clambering to my feet to retrieve my violin case from the baggage net overhead. Grabbing my rucksack from the carry-on space behind the driver I hauled it over my shoulder and descended the steps. The driver huffed warm breath on his fingers, chapped and sore where they poked out of his fingerless woolen gloves.

I smiled, making eye contact. "Thanks."

His face lit up. No one else had acknowledged him. "Bye, love. Happy Christmas."

I shifted along the pavement to the adjacent petrol station where I could gaze down the length of Newcastle Main Street. Even after six months, weather-torn red-hand of Ulster flags and Union Jacks flapped from some of the lampposts, the remains of the 12th Holiday in July. A source of great irritation to the Roman Catholic community in Newcastle. You'd think the council would take the flags down to make room for the Christmas decorations, but no. The wind whipped them into ugly frayed rags until their replacements next July.

A familiar grimy two-door Jeep turned onto Main Street and I couldn't help but grin. Mac, our border collie, had his head thrust out one of the windows, tongue lolling, black and white ears streaming in the wind. Mum and Dad sat in front, Dad myopically peering around for a parking space. I placed the rucksack and violin at my feet and windmilled my arms until they spotted me. The Jeep veered over and clanked to a halt. Dad looked the same as ever: farmer stalwart, hair a bit wispy on top like scattered iron filings, and the perpetual pipe drooping from his mouth.

Mum fought to open the stiff passenger side door. With an effort she triumphed and scrambled out. Having not seen her since September I fancied she had a few more silver strands amid her chestnut hair. I took after her in looks minus the gray, with brown hair and blue eyes. She seemed ageless to me, the kind laughter lines around her eyes only marginally deeper with each passing year. She lunged forward to make a grab for my rucksack and faltered at its weight.

"What on earth is in here, Jennifer?" Her gentle, cultured Anglo-Irish accent sounded so welcome after the harsh, broad tones of Belfast.

I yanked the rucksack back. "No peeking. It is Christmas, Mum."

She bent to tip up the passenger seat so I could climb into the back. I noticed she wore her best pearls, even though in comic contrast she had on one of the sack-like mud-spattered farm overcoats. Mac pounced on me, exploding into a flurry of wriggling limbs and darting tongue.

"Stop it, Macaroni, wet noodle mutt!" I gave him a gentle shove and he settled next to me, tongue lolling and tail quivering. I petted him while he regarded me intently, one blue eye and one brown.

My father peered over his shoulder as Mum got back in. "Has your hair always been that color?" he demanded.

"Course it has," I lied. I'd used lemon juice to bleach some lighter streaks through it. "Must have caught the sun."

He raised a shaggy eyebrow and turned back. The Jeep's gears squawked in complaint as he forced it into first.

"Wait, John," objected Mum, slamming the passenger door shut and reaching for her seat belt.

He sighed heavily and braked, ground the gear back into neutral and took his foot off the clutch. Resting both hands on the steering wheel, he waited with exaggerated attention until her belt clicked into place. Then he jerked back into gear and set off down Main Street. In a vehicle at least fifteen years old the engine rattled unmercifully. I braced myself as we left the town and headed up the narrow, winding road that led into the mountains. The track higher up wasn't maintained very well, and the lack of suspension in the Jeep jarred every bone in my body. Conversation rendered impossible over the racket, I contented myself with watching the houses grow sparser, giving way to ragged hedgerows and stone walls built with granite boulders. Close to Mourneview Farm, Dad clanked the Jeep back down to first gear as we toiled up a steep incline. From this angle gun-metal sky met the gritty tarmac brow of the hill.

Sudden darkness blotted out the horizon. We ducked instinctively, including Mac.

"Bloody hell!" shouted Dad, slamming on the brakes. The Jeep stalled.

A British Army helicopter swooped up from the other side of the hill, almost colliding with us. The 'copter circled so close I could make out the pale oval of the pilot's face peering down. Dad shoved the sliding window open and shook his fist. "Watch where you're going, you bloody moron!"

"John!" admonished Mum, even though he couldn't possibly be heard over the roar of the 'copter blades.

Mac turned fearful eyes on me and I cuddled him, pulling on his tufty ears. Dad restarted the Jeep and we reached the apex of the hill to see the helicopter lurching toward Mourneview, still dangerously near to the ground.

"Bloody army," grumbled Dad.

Mum watched the pitching aircraft with concern. "They must be in trouble."

I held my breath as the 'copter barely cleared the farmhouse roof and chimney tops. We watched in helpless disbelief as vacuum caused by the whirring blades snapped the antique cockerel weathervane, Dad's pride and joy, from the top of the barn. It tumbled down out of sight into the farmyard.

"God Almighty!" Dad floored the accelerator and we bounced over the rutted track leading to Mourneview. He shuddered the Jeep to a halt in the farmyard, sending up a flurry of mud. The weathercock had narrowly missed landing in the pigsty, and Sadie, the huge sow leveled belligerent pink eyes on us, as though we'd deliberately attempted to assassinate her and her drove. The vane poked out of a pile of manure, the tip of its arrow pointing west. Mac ran in circles around it, barking a Lassie-type warning as though we'd been invaded by aliens.

"Quiet, boy!" bellowed Dad. Mac immediately dropped to a crouch, tail quivering. Dad's pipe had gone out but he didn't seem to notice as he puffed furiously. "I'm not standing for this." He strode to the farmhouse, Mac at his heels. I realized they hadn't bothered to lock the door when he thrust it open and marched right in.

Mum gave me a little shrug and followed. Grabbing the rucksack and violin from the Jeep I trailed after them. A familiar scent of lemon furniture polish engulfed me as I stepped into the hall, and as childhood memories rushed back I felt my worries slip away. Nothing ever changed here. A row of brass hooks along one wall held an assortment of ancient coats, jackets, and rainproof wear. Dad never threw anything away while it retained a semblance of utility. On the floor below the coats piled a huge jumble of all kinds of footwear, including Wellington boots and threadbare slippers. Glimpsing a yellow plastic wheel, I couldn't believe he'd kept my old roller skates from ten years ago. Under the stairs, I knew a Tilley-lamp and Monopoly and Cluedo lay in wait for the next time we had a power cut and couldn't watch television.

Three doors opened off the hall into the kitchen, dining and sitting rooms. A wooden staircase covered with a worn royal blue carpet led upstairs, and to the right of the stairs nestled a half-moon oak table piled with a horde of unopened mail that spilled onto the floor. The table also held the ancient family Bible bound in black leather, beside which the antique black telephone squatted.

My father had the receiver in his hand. I listened to the tail end of his blustering as I dropped my rucksack at the foot of the stairs and shucked off my anorak. "I don't care if you send a bloody general. Just get someone over here to fix my weathercock at once!" He slammed down the receiver.

"Sherry?" inquired Mum from the kitchen doorway, coat in hand.

"Absolutely," I agreed, taking the coat from her and hanging it up.

Dad shot us a disapproving look and stomped back out into the yard. I brought my violin case into the kitchen and laid it on the solid pine table in front of the window that overlooked the yard. This was the heart of the house. It was the second-to-largest room, after the dining room. An avocado-green metal monstrosity dominated one wall of the kitchen - Mum's prized 1950's Aga cooker. Mac loved to curl up against its ever-present warmth. Our tinsel-decked Christmas tree sat in the bay window opposite that afforded a view of the overgrown garden at the back of the house. The old plastic doll that was supposed to be the Christmas fairy but looked more like a madam at a bordello, perched at the top of the fir. Ridiculous to anyone outside the family, but my father's mother had given them that fairy on their first Christmas together and it had topped the tree for as long as I could remember.

A cork popped. I turned to see Mum pour her favorite Amontillado into two of her Tyrone crystal sherry glasses. She handed one to me and we settled at the table. "Welcome home, Jen."

It was all so comforting and familiar. When to tell her my news - should I just blurt it out and get it over and done with?

Mum sipped from her glass and sighed deeply, contentment smoothing her features. "That's better." She reached down to lift something from underneath the Christmas tree, and placed a long narrow festively wrapped package on the table in front of me. "Early Christmas present."

With a grin I felt it between my fingers, suspecting what it was. I carefully peeled the sticky tape away and gently unwrapped the gift. Many years of being yelled at not to rip off the paper made it second nature. A brand new set of violin strings. My mother knew me well. Even though both she and Dad made it clear they thought playing a musical instrument was nothing more than a pleasant hobby, she had always encouraged me to keep at it.

I got up and dashed round the table to envelop her in a hug. "Thank you, Mum."

Never one for physical demonstrations of affection, she patted my back, extricated herself and stood. "Better see about those Cornish pasties for lunch."

"Need some help?"

She waved me away. "Not at all, sweetheart."

Most people would grab a frozen package of ready-made pastry from the freezer and toss it on a baking tray, but not Mum. As she busied herself with bowls, lard, flour and eggs, I clicked open the violin case and drew out my beloved musical friend. The strings were pretty worn, showing rough spots in places where I now found it hard to move my finger across. I swiftly untwined them and set to threading through and tightening the new ones. I found tuning brand new strings always a challenge as they were so tight, but I kept refining and tweaking until they stayed in tune, sounding rich and full. What a difference to the tinniness of the old strings! I drew the bow from its place in the lid of the case and torqued at the tension. Tucking the violin under my chin, I raised the bow and drew it gently along the strings. Almost of their own volition my fingers picked out the notes to *A Coventry Carol*, one of my favorites. With the scent of the fir Christmas tree so close by, I lost myself in the plaintive, haunting tune.

On the last note, I opened my eyes to find Mum standing motionless, watching me. Pride shone on her face but once she realized I saw her she turned back to her kneading. "I hope you've been studying your Economics, too," she said with a sniff.

A pang of anxiety thrust through me and I set the violin and bow on the table. I didn't want to spoil the lovely Christmassy mood. But it had to be done, and as she'd brought it up this was as good a time as ever. "Yeah, I wanted to talk to you about that, Mum."

A thundering rumble intruded.

"What in the name of God?" Mum hurried to the window.

I joined her to watch two large British Army Land Rovers roar up and crunch to a halt in the yard. "Weathercock cavalry's here," I said, relieved at the interruption.

"I don't see your Dad anywhere." She wiped her hands on her apron, too late realizing she hadn't put it on. She looked aghast at the pale smear of raw pastry all down the front of her skirt. Soldiers spilled out of the Land Rover and I knew Mum would rather face a firing squad than be seen all messy like that.

"I'll go," I offered.

She smiled in relief. I started toward the hall and had to pause as she tore past me. Her feet thumped on the landing above as I headed to the front door. Stepping outside, I almost collided with a very tall soldier wearing an olive green pullover with shoulder and arm patches. Fortunately he wasn't carrying a rifle.

I took a step back. "Sorry."

He carried a dark beret in hand, which he tucked into a leg pocket in his green trousers. Towering over me, about six-one, he sported a thicket of curly black hair, barely tamed by his military haircut. The wind had tousled it back from his face, revealing elegant cheekbones and really striking dark eyes. No one this exotic had ever set foot in Mourneview; he looked like he'd walked off the set of *Lawrence of Arabia*.

I realized I'd been staring and felt my face flush at his quizzical look.

He probably thought I was some kind of halfwit.

"Sergeant McLeod, Miss," he said, maybe for the second or third time. To my surprise he wasn't English, he had the rich tones and elongated vowels of an American.

I floundered. My brain and vocal chords couldn't seem to connect. Feeling the incredulous scrutiny of the rest of the soldiers I forced myself out of my fugue.

"Cock's over there," I blurted. The squaddies burst out into loud guffaws and I flinched.

The sergeant raised an elegant eyebrow. "Excuse me?"

I thought I'd shrivel up from mortification. "The *weather*cock." Hurrying over to the heap of manure, I vehemently pointed to it.

"The weather*vane?*"

Was he deliberately trying to be obtuse? "We call them weathercocks here."

I swear his lips twitched as he turned to address the soldiers. "Get to work." At once they snapped into action.

They looked different, somehow, from the soldiers I was used to seeing at checkpoints and such. I realized it was because they didn't wear bulletproof flak jackets over their uniforms. Two of them drew an extension ladder from the back of one of the Land Rovers while a third produced a soldering iron and jammed a welding helmet over his head. Two others got to sweeping the yard. Dad would be happily mollified - they were cleaning out a week's worth of rain-congealed mud and manure.

Mum appeared in the farmhouse doorway wearing an impeccable Sunday-best dress with a white lace collar. "Would you like a cup of tea?" she called to Sergeant McLeod.

"Thank you, Ma'am." He turned to me and held out an open palm, indicating that I should precede him.

Face still blazing, I led the way into the kitchen. Mum had brought out her best Staffordshire bone china with the Elizabethan design of delicate pink roses. On the table by my violin I saw three teacups and saucers with silver teaspoons, matching china milk jug and sugar bowl, teapot stand, a two-tier cake stand with sandwiches on the bottom plate, and her famous cherry loaf on the top. How the hell did she have the time to put all this together?

"Please, Sergeant." Mum positively simpered, gesturing that he should sit.

I gaped, my own embarrassment forgotten. I'd never seen her act all flirty and silly like this before. She fetched the teapot from the Aga, while McLeod lowered his tall frame onto one of the pine chairs. I noticed three dark stripes on his right arm. He kept his uniform in immaculate condition - green shirt collar and trousers crisply ironed, his black leather boots gleaming with polish. Mum placed the teapot on the stand on the table, nudging my violin out of the way. Hot liquids and musical instruments do not go well together so I snatched up the violin and bow. I saw McLeod's gaze alight on them for a moment, then he smiled at Mum as she poured tea into his cup. His white, even teeth would have done a movie star proud.

"Thank you." He used the sterling silver tongs to add two lumps of sugar.

"You're welcome." Then she tittered. There no other word to describe the girlish tinkle, her cheeks glowing pink.

God Mum, get a grip! I bent my head and ran my fingers along the neck of the violin, quietly picking out the opening notes to Simon & Garfunkel's *Mrs. Robinson*. McLeod lifted both teacup and saucer and raised the cup to his lips. His long graceful fingers made the cup diminutive. Our eyes met over the rim and I faltered mid tune, speared by his gaze. Dipping my head, I busied myself with torquing the bow. He really was extraordinarily good looking. No wonder Mum acted like a star struck groupie. So was I, minus the tittering.

"Would you like a sandwich, Sergeant?" she trilled. "Or some cake?"

"Thank you, cake will do nicely." He reached for the cherry loaf.

"What a wonderful accent, you have," Mum said. "What part of America are you from?"

"Virginia, Ma'am."

My fingers began to pick out *I Wish I Was in Dixie*. Judging by the amused look McLeod shot me, that definitely appealed to his sense of humor. It hadn't occurred to me that a soldier might have a sense of humor. How daft was that? It's just that I'd never met any that weren't on duty out on roadside checkpoints. They'd only ever come across as professional and efficient, not showing any personality.

Mum looked flummoxed. She had no idea where Virginia was.

"That's - nice." Her mainstay when she had nothing else to say.

I could see she was on the brink of asking something else. Probably a totally inappropriate question like what his religion was. I spoke quickly, to head her off. "What's an American doing in the British Army?"

His eyes crinkled attractively at the corners as he smiled. "Do you sing, too?"

I frowned. "Sorry?"

He put the teacup on the table and nodded toward the violin.

"Oh. Yes, a bit."

"She's very good," interjected Mum, refilling his cup.

I realized he'd deftly avoided telling me how someone from the States came to be in the British Army.

He kept his gaze on me. "What do you sing, Irish traditional?"

"We don't hold with that sort of thing, here." Mum sniffed

disapprovingly. "Not in a good British household–"

"I do," I interrupted. "And modern stuff, too."

I heard Dad's voice in the yard and glanced through the window. The soldiers were putting everything back into the Land Rovers.

McLeod got to his feet. "Thanks for the tea." He held Mum's hand briefly between both of his.

She gazed adoringly at him, blushing. *Good grief.* He pulled his beret from his trouser pocket and fixed it on his head, the darkened badge perfectly aligned over his left eye. Not shiny in case it made a good target, I suppose. He turned to me and nodded toward the violin in my hand. "I'd sure like to hear you play sometime."

He looked right into my eyes and my stomach did a sort of flip-flop. I bit my lower lip and watched his gaze settle on my mouth. "That could be arranged," I managed.

A grin lit his face, then he spun on his gleaming black heel and strode out of the kitchen. Through the window I watched as he exchanged a few words with my father and they shook hands before he got into one of the Land Rovers. Moments later the vehicles rumbled to life and roared out of the yard. I took one look at Mum's blushing face and rescued our glasses. We sat back at the table and I poured us both another sherry - for medicinal purposes, of course.

2
Reunion

Out of the summer season the only two places worth going to at night in Newcastle were the opulent castle-like Slieve Donard Hotel by the sea or the less impressive Ben Crom Lodge at the foot of the Mournes. My best friend Deirdre worked as a receptionist in the Donard, so she point blankly refused to hang out there. I couldn't blame her. I'd only been in it a few times for afternoon tea and scones with Mum, and felt uncomfortable with the snooty attitude the waiting staff gave us, treating us like the common farming folk we so obviously were. The place wasn't that clean, either, and after Dee told me how hit or miss hygiene was in the kitchen, I vowed never to eat there again.

The Ben Crom was only a few miles up the mountain from Mourneview, so I talked Dad into giving me a lift up there to meet Dee at eight. Once a grand manor house, the Ben Crom sat in solitary splendor above Newcastle amidst a patch of fir trees. It sported a massive, old-fashioned gilt ballroom, complete with a mirrored disco ball suspended from the ceiling. To my despair, the resident band played nothing but

American country and western songs, surreal-sounding when sung with a broad Northern Irish accent.

I got there early enough to snag one of the tables by the dance floor just as the band was setting up. The Ben Crom had gone all out for Christmas. Scallops of holly and colored lights swathed the walls wherever I looked. A white imitation tree had been squished into a corner by the bar, its tinselly branches around the bottom looking a bit worse for wear.

When I shrugged off my coat and claimed a table, the waitress strolled over. "Are you gettin'?" she demanded. She meant had I already ordered, but as she'd seen me pass the bar, she knew I hadn't.

"Two pints of Double Diamond and two Piña Coladas, please." Knowing the Ben Crom, once the dancing was under way we'd have more chance of water skiing in the rings of Saturn than getting another round of drinks.

On stage guitar music blasted through the speakers, making me cringe. The lead singer, wearing a shiny white leisure suit with painfully tight trousers, broke out in a loud Ulster-American twang, "'*Well, I left Kentucky back in forty-nine an' went to Detroit workin' on a 'sembly line—'*" The evening officially began.

By the time Dee appeared I was halfway through one of the pints. She paused in the main doorway to scan the ballroom. Everyone in the place turned to look at her, resplendent in black skinny trousers with leopard spotted high-heeled ankle boots under an imitation leopard-skin coat. Rhinestone clips glittered in her Marilyn Monroe hair. She looked so glamorous and I felt frumpy in my bell-bottomed denim jeans with moderately low-cut sweater. She spied me and waved, trotting over. Shirley Bassey singing *Big Spender* came to mind as she sashayed toward me.

"Thank God that's over fer another day," she announced.

I often envied her soft regional accent. I felt like I stuck out here like the proverbial sore thumb with my pseudo-Anglicized tones, beaten into me at school. She slipped off her coat, revealing a black sequined tube top underneath. Several guys turned as one and leered as she tossed her coat carelessly across the back of her chair before sitting down.

"Donard still as bad as ever?"

She rolled her eyes. "Oh, God, isn't it just. That bloody Mr. McKimmon is a psycho megalomaniac."

"The manager?"

"Aye. He lives in an apartment just down the corridor from reception. This morning he lumbered out and bellowed, 'Where's my orange juice?' I had to scramble to get it to him, even though I'm not a bloody waitress. And then he took one look at me and told me I dressed like an Albert Clock hooker. Ignorant git. I mean, do I look like a fuckin' prostitute?"

I bit my lip. "Did you wear that tube top to work?"

"Course not!"

"Well, then. You look like you stepped off the cover of *Cosmopolitan*." I pushed one of the two frothy, bulbous glasses toward her.

She raised her glass and I clinked my pint against it. "Fuck the Queen," she riposted with a wink.

"Fuck the Pope," I parried, after checking no one around could overhear.

We'd been toasting like that since we were old enough to drink. Even before that, imitating our parents and their Pimm's No. 1 cocktails. She took a sip, then a gulp, and fluttered her eyelids in ecstasy.

"Totally yummy." She scowled at my pint glasses. "You still on the Double Diamond? Can ya not drink a good Irish beer like Guinness?"

I laughed. "Yuck, I hate stout - I'd rather stick wasps up my nose! Besides, you know Mum and Dad would only hold with me drinking good Protestant English ale."

Her parents had the farm across the valley from Mourneview, so we were the rural version of next door neighbors. We'd been best friends since before going to our respective Catholic and Protestant schools and stayed friends despite being separated by religion and politics.

The ballroom quickly grew crowded, smoky, and loud. I recognized a Kenny Rogers song as the lead singer whined, *'In a bar in Toledo, across from the depot, on a bar stool she took off her ring.'* His lackluster, nasal twang as he mournfully tried to imitate an American accent made me want to lay my head down on the table and give up on life.

Dee broke into my self-pity. "So, what's so urgent that we couldn't talk about at home?"

I took a deep draft of my ale. "I need to tell Mum and Dad about Queen's."

"Made up yer mind, then?"

"Yeah. I hate it, Dee. Agricultural Technology has to be the most soul-destroying, boring course at the university. It might be different if I had a head for mathematics, but I haven't a bloody clue."

"Ach, Jen. You only started in September, for fuck's sake."

I bit my lip. I hadn't expected her to react like my mother. "But what's the point? I simply can't grasp any relevance between what they're teaching in class to the day-to-day running of a farm." Worse, since term began I had scarcely touched the violin.

"You don't know how lucky you are, Jen. Lucky bitch. Sure, who cares about the course! Just have a blast with all the parties and everything."

"Well, that's the other thing. Being a mature student, I don't get invited to parties."

"You're only twenty-two, hinny. Two months younger than me."

"I'm four years older than pretty much everyone else in my class."

Dee gave me a shrewd look. "This isn't about the course, is it?"

She knew me so well. "The violin."

"Ach." She gave me a sympathetic look. "You still on that?"

"I don't want to be a farmer!" I banged my pint down on the table, spilling some. "I want to apply to the Belfast City School of Music again."

Dee licked at her hand where beer had sploshed. "What's the point of that?"

"They teach all kinds of classes. Piano, guitar, choral singing - even harp, I think. Thing is, if I did go there for violin, I'd automatically be in their orchestra. And the classes would only be a couple of days a week, and a few evenings now and then for concerts."

"I get it. You could do both, and keep yer Ma and Da happy."

"Yes! And who knows after that. But at least it'd get me out of Queen's and into playing music again."

She raised her glass and we clinked. "If you get yer driving license you can borrow my car," she promised. "And if yer Ma and Da don't go for it, maybe I'll just move to Belfast and share an apartment with you. I could work in any of the hotels."

"Why don't you, anyway? You're wasted out here in the sticks, missus."

She beamed. "Maybe I just will. You know, if you want to work in a band, there's always my brother, Seamus's. You still doin' the *céilidh* on Boxing Day?"

Shit, I'd forgotten it in all the drama. "Of course."

She gave me a wink. "Told your Ma and Da about that?"

"Jesus, no. They'd blow a gasket! Me, playing in a Nationalist town in a traditional Irish band?"

"Aye, shockin'. A good Ulster Orange Protestant like yourself."

"Shut up. One day the Troubles will settle down and it won't be so *out there* for someone like me to play in a band like that."

"Exactly. When we have a United Ireland it'll be perfectly normal for everyone to play in a band like that."

I sucked in a sharp breath. "Don't start, I'm not rising to the bait."

She laughed. "All right, all right. I'll spare you as it's yer homecoming."

Thank God. "So, when do you think I should tell Mum and Dad about Queen's?"

She pondered. "Wait till after Christmas. They're going to be royally pissed off with ya, so better not spoil it."

I agreed. "Good thinking, Batwoman. Thanks."

"No problem. Anything else ya need sorting out? Dr. Dee is in."

I took another swallow of beer. "Well, since you ask." I launched into how I met the exotic and sexy Sergeant McLeod earlier.

She gaped at me across the table as though I had fifty snakes coming out of my hair. "A *squaddie*?"

"Non-commissioned officer, if you're splitting hairs."

"In the *British Army*?"

I rolled my eyes. "No, the Imperial Stormtroopers."

She tsked loudly and drained her second cocktail. "Have you completely lost your fuckin' mind?" Her hazel eyes widened, pupils huge in the dim ballroom light. She tossed back a wisp of blonde hair that had escaped from under the jeweled clips. "You'll get fuckin' done for seeing a soldier, Yank or not."

"Shush!" I glanced round, but no one had heard. "For God's sake, Dee, I only said he was gorgeous, not that I'm going to marry him."

"I don't know what you're thinkin', Jen." She sounded as disapproving and judgmental as my mother. "Why can't you go out with someone from round here?"

The waitress chose that moment to ask if we wanted another round. I figured I'd better start saving for my trip to Saturn. Dee ordered us two Harvey Wallbangers and yanked her handbag up from where she'd stashed it under her chair.

"You know why, Dee," I answered when the waitress was out of earshot. "Anyone I've gone out with - it's like they're from a different planet. I can't find a single thing in common with them, except farming."

Out came her purse, then a packet of Silk Cut cigarettes, followed by her stainless steel Zippo Venetian lighter engraved with an elaborate swirling design. "What about Clancy?" she demanded.

I sighed heavily. Clancy was one of Dee's five brothers, fourteen months older than she. I'd never confessed to the one date I had with him a year ago. Nurturing a wee bit of leftover teenage crush, I finally plucked up enough courage to ask him out. I had an extra ticket for a play at the Lyric Theatre in Belfast, and invited him to accompany me.

The evening did not start well. He drew up in a rattling old Volkswagen Beetle and parked in the yard at Mourneview. I heard the car but waited for him to come knock on the door, as was usual when someone came to pick you up. Besides, I didn't want to look like I'd been waiting for him, even though I had. When several minutes passed, I finally went out. Apparently he'd expected me to come out as soon as he pulled up and barely concealed his impatience at being kept waiting.

As we pulled out of Mourneview a rabbit scurried from a hedgerow and got pulped under one of the front wheels. "I just killed a *wab*bit!" he crowed at the same time that I yelped, "Oh, poor bunny!" So we settled into an uneasy silence until we reached the Lyric. In my haste to buy the tickets I hadn't actually checked out what the play was. It turned out to be *Facing North* by John Boyd, with some blazingly anti-British sentiments. Clancy warmed up considerably, obviously agreeing with them judging by his lopsided grin and fervent head-nodding.

At the very least it gave us something to talk about on the trip home. Except we got into an argument about the Troubles.

"What hell kind of a name is the 'Troubles' for a fuckin' civil war, anyway?" he demanded. "Oh, how 'troubling' those Irish micks are over there," he scoffed, imitating someone from the House of Lords. "How about telling it as it really is: the 'Rages' or the 'Frenzied War' of Northern Ireland as we fight to be freed from fuckin' tyrannical British oppression."

Tyrannical British oppression? Had he forgotten who was in the car with him? Through gritted teeth I tried to keep my voice even. "All right, Clancy. Explain this to me: how can Ireland be 'freed' from the British, when every generation born after the vote of 1925 knows only a British Northern Ireland?"

"Kill off every last Brit if that's what it takes."

I stifled a gasp. "Well, thank God for the British Army, then! If they're the only thing stopping us from being killed off by arseholes like you." I wanted to demand he stop the car, but he was my only way to get home at this time of night.

He sputtered and glared at me. I thought he might crash the car, he looked so angry. His Adam's apple bobbed up and down a few times, then he neither looked at me nor spoke the rest of the thirty miles until he pulled the car into our farmyard.

I gathered up my handbag and unclipped the seat belt. Years of Mum bashing good manners into me made me blurt, "Did you want a cup of tea?" *Shit!* The last thing I wanted was to spend another moment in his murderous, bigoted company.

He gave me an incredulous look and actually scoffed, making me want to ram his head into the steering wheel. "Afraid?" I snapped. "That we'll poison you with our tyrannical British Earl Grey instead of Tetley teabags?"

Actually, that saved the day. He gaped and then burst out laughing. After a moment I saw the funny side and joined in.

"I'm sorry, Jen. I didn't mean to say what I did. It came out all wrong."

I wanted to believe him. "I'm sorry too."

"Look, let's try this again. We'll go somewhere neutral, okay?"

I agreed. But it never happened.

Dee jerked my thoughts back to the present as she clicked her Zippo several times, lighting up a long, elegant cigarette. "Well?"

"Clance is okay. But we'll never be anything more than friends."

"So you say. He's at Queen's too, you know."

"I know."

"Have ya not seen him?"

"No, it's a big place. What's he studying?"

She shrugged. "Somethin' to do with farming, like you." The waitress delivered our drinks and we clinked glasses. "Fuck the Pope."

For once it aggravated me, remembering her brother's outburst. But I dutifully responded, "Fuck the Queen," in a neutral tone.

The Harvey Wallbanger hit the spot. The Galliano liqueur gave the orange juice and vodka just the right amount of sweetness and zing. On top of the two pints of Double Diamond, I settled into a pleasant, mellow fog. My thoughts kept returning to Sergeant McLeod, but I didn't dare bring him up again.

Dee groaned. "Oh, shite."

"What?" Following her nod I saw two beefy guys, ogling us from across the dance floor, pints in hand. They looked ruddy and well-nourished, and not at all comfortable in the dark suits they both wore. The larger of the two offered a toothy smile and raised his pint to us. Dee lifted her glass and mimicked him. "Don't!" I hissed, but too late. Encouraged, the duo made their way across the dance floor and presented themselves side by side at the table. I couldn't help but think of Tweedledee and Tweedledum from Lewis Carroll's *Through the Looking Glass.*

"'Bout ye, girls," said the larger of the two. "I'm Dennis. He's Philip."

Philip nodded somberly. "We just came from a funeral."

I fought an impulse to laugh. "I'm sorry," I managed, my voice unsteady. I didn't dare look at Dee.

"Oh, don't worry," Dennis assured me. "We didn't really like him."

I could see Dee's shoulders shaking out of the corner of my eye. "That's all right, then," I responded, my voice wobbly.

Philip placed his pint down on our table and reached both hands under his suit jacket to vigorously flap the armpits of his starched white shirt. "Can ya smell me? I'm all sweaty."

That was it. There was a limit to how much self-control I had. Unfortunately, I'd just drained my Harvey Wallbanger and ended up alternatively choking and spitting as citrus painfully stung my sinuses. Dee pealed with laughter, and the two farmers joined in, presumably thinking she was laughing at me.

"We have t'go, fellas," she said.

I looked at my watch. It was only twenty past nine.

Dennis' face fell. "Would you's not stay and have a drink?"

"Ah, no, thanks." Dee handed me my handbag from under the table as we stood and gathered up our coats. "You can have our seats," she told them grandly as though offering a worthy consolation prize.

We took off, dodging through pairs of undulating couples and escaped into the Ben Crom's reception area. I glanced over my shoulder to see the guys sitting side by side at our table, looking crestfallen.

Dee led the way across reception toward the public bar. "We can get a drink in here in peace."

I don't know why we hadn't done that in the first place, could have saved myself from the country and western torture.

We found a free table right in the middle. "My round," I said putting my coat over my chair. "I need a beer."

"Nah, sit down, I'll get it. Yer homecoming celebration, and all that."

Waiting for her to come back, I glanced around with interest. This was my first time in the Public Bar. It was just your basic tavern, with cement floors, hard wooden pews and chairs, and tables with ashtrays. The windows gave me pause, though. They were blacked out completely, with wooden shutters on either side.

Dee returned with another Harvey Wallbanger for herself and a pint for me. "This is Harp," she announced. "Give it a try, you'll like it."

"Made in Southern Ireland, I take it?"

"Brewed by the illustrious Guinness and sons."

I rolled my eyes and took a sip. I hated to admit it but I think I liked it better than Double Diamond. "It'll do," I admitted grudgingly.

She produced a couple of packets of salted peanuts. "To soak up the alcohol," she explained with a laugh.

The bar began filling steadily and it was standing room only by last orders at 11 o'clock. But no one showed any sign of going home. At 11.20 a frisson of excitement swept through the bar and suddenly everyone went very quiet. One barman crossed to the door that led to reception, pulled it shut and locked it, while a second locked the front door and closed over the shutters on the windows.

"What's going on?" I asked Dee, trepidation filling me.

She laughed. "Don't panic. It's a lock in."

"How come?"

She shrugged. "Who needs an excuse?"

The feeling of camaraderie in the bar was great. People grinned in collusion at each other, apparently pleased to get one over on the authorities. The noise level increased as more drinks were ordered. Now I understood why Speakeasies did so well in the days of prohibition.

The barman rapped the counter. "Shut yer traps!" he hissed, "the Fuzz is outside".

Those of us who'd heard 'shushed' the people next to us and it went round the bar like a wave. The *'ssshhhhhhing'* was so loud I thought the cops couldn't help but hear. But at last an engine revved, pulled away and then silence.

"All clear," declared the barman.

Everyone burst into excited chattering, and more drinks were ordered. I stole a glance at my watch.

"Ya want to go?" asked Dee.

"Yeah, morning comes early on a farm."

We asked the barman to let us out and he unlocked the door. In reception we pulled on our coats before braving the night air and checked our reflections in the wall-length mirror by the door. I looked like a hobo in my navy anorak compared to Dee's flamboyant leopard spots. She couldn't stop giggling, which set me off. Through snorts of laughter I met her reflected gaze in the mirror.

"Can ya smell me?" I gulped, flapping at the underarms of my anorak.

She shrieked, drawing a malevolent glare from the night porter. Rendered useless, we made it out to the car park and staggered over to her little blue Austin Mini. I leaned on the passenger side of the car, laughing so hard I had to hold my sides. All the beer I'd drunk was making itself felt in more ways than silliness, and I wished I'd stopped at the Ladies' room before leaving. But the trip to Mourneview was only a few minutes. I could wait.

Hindered significantly by her mirth, Dee fumbled in her handbag for the keys. I hopped from foot to foot. "Hurry up!" She finally extracted them, then promptly dropped them. I sighed loudly as she bent to retrieve them, sobering up fast at the sight of ice glittering on the road. I grimaced as the keys thunked to the ground again. "Maybe you shouldn't be driving in this state." I could phone Dad to come get us. He'd rather do that than find our frozen corpses in a ditch in the morning.

"Ach, who'll know?" She got the key in the lock and opened the car door. Sinking into the driver's seat she leaned across to unlock the passenger side for me. "I'll take the back roads home, Jen. There're never any checkpoints there."

"That's not the point."

I'd forgotten what a maniacal driver she could be, even without several drinks in her. She puttered the Mini sedately enough out of the hotel car park while she thought people might be looking. But once the night engulfed us, she put her foot to the floor. In the moonlight I glimpsed a few inches of snow along the sides of the looping, narrow road. She took a corner way too fast, making the car slide.

I checked my seat belt was properly fastened. "Dee, for God's sake, slow down!"

We quickly descended below the snowline and I began to breathe easier. In the distance I could see the Irish Sea glinting in the moonlight. Then a hairpin bend in the road loomed and my foot instinctively slammed down on a non-existent brake. Too late, Dee hit the real brakes, hauling the steering wheel round. All four wheels locked with a screech, and the hedgerows spun terrifyingly.

Although it felt like a lifetime, in seconds we came to rest in a ditch by the side of the road. My prophecy had come true, except fortunately we weren't dead. Dee and I looked at each other in shock. The Mini sat cock-eyed off the road, facing the wrong way up the mountain.

A wide grin spread across her face. "That was fun."

I snorted. "Thrilling."

She turned the key. The engine sputtered to life and she began to maneuver us out of the ditch but the wheels spun in vain. Leaving the Mini idling we got out to investigate. The back end was totally bogged down in mud. I watched our breath streaming, mingling fog-like with the exhaust from the car. Even through my thick anorak I already felt the icy night air chilling my bones. And neither of us wore footwear suitable to walk any distance in, even though Mourneview couldn't be more than a mile away.

"Trouble, ladies?" inquired a male voice in a clipped English accent.

I just about jumped out of my skin. An army Land Rover had rolled up, coasting with both the engine and headlights off. The open passenger side window revealed a fair-haired man with gray-blue eyes and an aristocratic aquiline nose. He had deep furrows between his light eyebrows even though he looked to be in his early thirties.

The door opened and the man stepped out. "Captain Charles Stratton, at your service," he announced with such exaggerated flourish I expected him to bow and present an ankle. "Private Cooper!" he barked over his shoulder. "Help out the young ladies."

A hefty young soldier in his late teens scrambled out of the back. He gripped a Self-Loading Rifle that got stuck sideways, blocking him. He jiggled it impatiently and it swung unrestrained, the barrel pointing alternately between Dee and me. We both gasped and jumped apart out of range.

"Give me that!" snapped Stratton.

The private handed the weapon over and approached the Mini, aiming a flashlight at the rear wheels.

"One of you get in and press the accelerator when I tell you," ordered the captain. I noticed two of his fingers automatically hovered over the rifle's trigger.

"Right then." Dee climbed back into the Mini.

I watched as the private brought all of his considerable weight to bear on the bumper, raising up the rear of the car.

"Now!" shouted Stratton, and Dee floored the accelerator.

As though in slow motion an arc of mud flew up from the back wheels, instantly coating the private and splattering Stratton from beret to boot. I clamped both my hands over my mouth, wanting desperately to laugh. But I was afraid to. Stratton's face was a picture of fury. And you don't laugh at people who carry guns.

"Oh, God," I heard Dee say. She peered over her shoulder at Stratton, her eyes wide.

Loud hoots of laughter came from the back of the armored Land Rover and its suspension rocked as four more soldiers jumped out. My stomach and heart did all the kinds of things you read about in romance novels when I realized one of them was Sergeant McLeod. I addressed Stratton. "I'm so very sorry, Captain."

He mustered as much dignity as he could. "Think nothing of it," he said graciously, and retreated back to the passenger seat in the Land Rover.

McLeod and the other squaddies physically lifted the Mini free with Dee still at the wheel, and carried it onto the road. I could only see the white-toothed grin of Cooper through his coating of mud.

"Thanks!" I called and one of them tipped his beret at me. McLeod approached me as the others climbed back into the Land Rover. I wanted to drag him over to Dee and say, "See? Told you he was gorgeous!" But by her astounded expression I knew she'd already determined that for herself. "Thank you very much," I said, shyness flooding back as he smiled at me.

"No, thank *you*. Best laugh we've had in months." He tilted his head toward Stratton, who glared through the window. "Gotta go." Walking over to the Mini, he leaned down to look Dee in the eye. "Slow the heck down, Miss." Straightening, he shot me a wink. "We'll follow you down the mountain, make sure you're all right."

"*That* was yer gallant squaddie?" demanded Dee as I got back into the Mini. "Yum. Now I see why he's got ya all in a tizzy."

A frisson of something akin to jealousy shot through me. "Just drive."

"Wonder what they were up to, out here like that?"

"What do you mean?"

"Officers don't go out on patrol. At least, not busy-brass ones like captains, as far as I know."

I gave her a skeptical look. "How do you know so much about how the British Army operates?"

The Land Rover headlights came on and the engine revved impatiently behind us.

Dee put the Mini in gear. "Ach, I hear Seamus and m'brothers talk." She turned her attention to the road as she drove decorously down the winding hill.

The Land Rover headlights blinded us in the rear view and side mirrors. It stayed behind us all the way down to the lane that led to Mourneview, but when we turned left at the junction it continued straight on, speeding up until the red tail lights were out of sight. I slumped into my seat. Now what? McLeod hadn't asked for my phone number or anything.

3
Behind Enemy Lines

On Boxing Day I watched from the hall window as an orange Honda Civic pulled into the yard just after seven. I shrugged on the lovely new leather aviator's jacket my parents had given me for Christmas.

Mum came out of the kitchen. "Where is that Seamus O'Neill taking you?" she demanded.

I'd been hoping she mightn't have seen him. "Giving Deirdre and me a lift."

"I don't want you going anywhere with that man, young lady. He's a bad lot. Keeps the wrong kind of company, if you know what I mean."

I grabbed my violin case from where I'd set it on the bottom stair. "No, I don't know."

"He's IRA, Jennifer. You don't want to be seen anywhere with the likes of him."

Fuck, she'd go spare if she knew where I was headed. So would Dad. The *céildh* was in Ballyben, about five miles away. A real Nationalist stronghold, where they flew the Irish green, white and gold tricolor flag and spoke Gaelic. But not IRA, to my knowledge.

"Well, we need the lift tonight. But only this once, okay?" Feeling like a total heel for lying, I edged toward the door, hoping to intercept Dee before she knocked.

"I suppose so. But don't you be alone with Seamus, okay?"

I bristled. Sometimes she forgot I was twenty-two and not a child anymore. Grabbing my violin I charged out into the frosty night. Fortunately, taking it to all kinds of places wasn't unusual so Mum didn't question me. Opening the back door of the Honda I slid into its cigarette-musty warmth. Dee sat shotgun in the passenger seat.

"Aloha," she greeted me. Presumably because of the riotous blue and pink Hawaiian hibiscus comb she wore in her hair.

"'Bout ye," said Seamus. He shot a grin over his shoulder as he drove out of the yard.

Dee and he looked very alike, except he hadn't dyed his copper hair to her signature platinum blonde. "Great, thanks," I replied. "How about you?"

"Grand, grand."

Typical mountain Northern Irish guy, not very forthcoming in conversation. That would be all I'd get out of him.

"Ready for this, Jen?" asked Dee.

"Think so. Been practicing all day." That was true, and I'd even attempted *Paganini's Caprice No. 5*, way beyond my capability. It required a lot of lightning-quick finger and bow work. If I could even perform it at half speed, I'd do all right at the *céildh* with the Irish reels and jigs.

Dee turned in her seat and gave me a wink. "She might be lookin' for a full time job as a fiddler, Seamus."

"That so?" He smiled at me in the rear view mirror. "Ya should talk to the band playin' after us. They might need someone."

"Who's that?" asked Dee.

"Some fellas from Belfast."

"Maybe I will," I said, but knew I wouldn't. Better take it one day at a time with Mum and Dad, and tell them about leaving Queen's first.

Seamus knew the back lanes to Ballyben, and we were there in less than twenty minutes. The roads were pretty icy in places. Would the army come rescue us again if we got bogged down in a ditch? Didn't think so, somehow. Well, not the *British* Army, anyway.

At the thought of meeting the IRA on the deserted Mourne lanes, a sliver of fear touched my heart. Was Mum right about Seamus? I remembered Dee saying how her brothers seemed to know how the British Army operated.

He parked in a little space of concrete behind a tavern called Mooney's, which flew a huge tricolor over its front door. My stomach automatically lurched in a mixture of offense and fear. It was so hidebound a reaction to seeing this flag flown in British Northern Ireland.

I trailed behind Seamus and Dee through the back door of the pub. A rush of warm air greeted us and a cheer went up at the sight of Seamus and his one-sided drum, the bodhrán. Mooney's open fire gave off a rich scent of burning peat bog, along with a heady sherry aroma from the various casks and barrels behind the bar. Seamus led the way through the length of the bar and under an archway, which opened out into a large oblong room with a wood dance floor. A small stage with an upright piano on it stood at the far end, and a separate entrance from the street led in at this end. Here tricolors were pinned all over the walls and ceiling. I averted my eyes from posters declaring such things as *'THE NORTH IS IRISH. No collaboration with Brits. KILL THE BILL.'* One in particular drew my eye: *'Loose-talk costs lives'* it proclaimed along the top, with a picture underneath of a ski-masked, machine gun-toting terrorist to the right of the poster. Beside that was:

> *'In taxis, on the phone*
> *In clubs and bars, at football matches*
> *At home with friends ANYWHERE!*
> **Whatever you say - say nothing.'**

Several framed black and white photographs of balaclava helmeted men in army camouflage hung prominently. Oh my God. How could I have been so naïve as to think this wasn't an IRA place? Of course it bloody was! Nationalism and IRA seemed to go hand in hand. I tried to pretend the photos weren't there. They scared the fuck out of me. Dee didn't seem concerned, nor seemed to realize how uncomfortable I felt. She'd been coming here with her family for years and I suppose thought nothing of it. I, on the other hand, felt extremely vulnerable and exposed. How stupid I'd been.

Seamus turned out to be less oblivious than I thought. At the stage he took me by the arm and drew me aside. "Listen, thanks for doin' this. It's only us - you know, the family who knows who you are. And we'll say nothin' to nobody about ye, okay?"

"Thanks." I smiled, greatly relieved. "But what about the rest of the band?" I'd jammed with them a few times in one of the McNeill's barns.

"They only know yer from a neighboring farm," he assured me.

At ten past eight the rest of the band showed up. Gavin on flute and tin whistle, Johnny on the uilleann pipes, Patrick on the bouzouki and guitar, Eileen on a Celtic lap-harp, and Seamus on the bodhrán. Both he and Eileen sang lead. I spotted a drum kit at the back of the stage. "Whose are those?" I asked Seamus.

"The band that's after us. They're more modern, like."

We got wood and metal chairs from the stacks along one side of the dance floor and put them in a semi-circular row on stage. He made me sit on the far right hand so I wouldn't bonk anyone with my elbow while 'sawing' with the bow, as he put it. We got everything tuned and I took the opportunity to run a few warm up scales.

"So, do what ya did with us in the jam," Seamus advised. "Follow Mickey and Eileen, and if the spirit moves ya, improvise with the fiddly bits."

I laughed and the others grinned knowingly. 'Fiddly bits' was a good description. I could do that, all right. That's where the classical training came in handy.

A few people trickled in just before eight thirty. Seamus gave us the nod and I referred to the handwritten list of tunes he'd handed round. First one was to be *Sliabh Russell*. That featured tin whistle and bouzouki with the rest of us backing up, so an easy beginning for me. One by one, we joined in several stanzas apart and I began to feel more relaxed as I got into the swing of it. A ton more people thronged into the dance room once the music got under way. I recognized three of Dee's brothers with various girls but didn't see Clancy.

I was amazed at how much fun everyone was having. These people really knew how to have a great time and I'd never seen anything like it. The room became a seething mass of bobbing heads, flurrying limbs, and loud, jubilant 'heys!' as they got into it. Why didn't the Protestants have anything like this? It was wonderful and I felt privileged to be part of it. How I envied Dee and her family that they considered themselves Irish and belonged to a specific heritage. I never had this feeling of cohesion in my own community. My glance shifted to one of the photos of the ski-masked IRA terrorists and I flushed with shame. I felt like a turncoat.

We played one more piece and then took a break. Dee appeared and handed me a vodka and orange juice and I perched on the edge of the stage to take a grateful gulp.

With a grin she raised her rum and coke. "Fuck the Queen!"

I went ice cold. If she thought I was going to come back with, 'Fuck the Pope' in here she had another think coming. "Yeah, fuck the Queen!" I returned, louder than I meant to. A cheer went through a group of people close by. Oh, Jesus, if I hadn't felt like a turncoat before, now I definitely did. I narrowed my eyes at Dee, who roared with laughter.

A good-looking guy with a mustache, goatee and long hair the color of espresso coffee came up behind her and apparently goosed her. She squeaked and spun round. "Gerry!" He lifted her off her feet and swept her toward the bar. "Be right back!" she called over her shoulder.

I smiled and nodded, nervous at being on my own. I sipped at my drink and surreptitiously watched the crowd. Raised voices drew my attention. A group of guys stood in a semicircle with their backs to me. I could tell by the set of their shoulders that they were angry.

"Who the fuck are ye, anyway?" One of them challenged, his fists clenched tightly at his sides.

People around them eased out of the way and I got up to retreat back onto the stage. I caught a glimpse of the man the guys were provoking and my heart just about went into arrest. He was the image of Sergeant McLeod, wearing jeans and a black leather jacket. I almost dropped my glass as I looked closer. It fucking was Sergeant McLeod!

"I'm here to see a friend," he said, his American accent prominent. He didn't look afraid, but he should be. What was he doing here of all places? That accent must allow him access to where other soldiers couldn't go, but coming here was sheer insanity.

Adrenaline coursed through me. They hadn't worked out who he was yet. I'd moved before I knew it and pushed my way between two of the guys. McLeod locked eyes with me, his expression unreadable. "Hey, you made it!" I forced gaiety into my voice. A muscle moved in his right cheek, betraying his anxiety. With drink in hand I embraced him as though I knew him well. He went along with it. "I was gettin' worried you weren't comin'." I affected a more regional accent, like Dee's. Keeping an arm around McLeod's waist, I turned toward the lead guy and glared. He looked less certain, his fists no longer clenched. "What d'you think you're doin'?" I demanded, "This is my friend–" Jesus, what was his first name? "Mickey," which is all I could come up with from 'McLeod.' "We're at university together." McLeod laid a casual arm across my shoulders, looking relaxed but the tension coiled in his muscles told me otherwise.

The guy looked from me to my abandoned violin on stage and back.

"Is this any way to treat a visitor from America?" I continued. "I invite him to come see me play and all ya can do is threaten him? That's fuckin' brilliant, that."

He addressed McLeod. "Sorry, mate. Ya could've been anybody. How the fuck were we supposed to know? No hard feelings, right?"

"No problem," McLeod assured him. "Don't worry about it." His accent sounded much thicker than I'd heard before, a lovely rich drawl.

The guys backed off, heading for the bar. McLeod kept his arm around my shoulders and we stood side by side until the posse had disappeared through the archway.

Noticing that people still watched us, I turned to him, removing my arm from his waist. "Took ya bloody long enough to get here. Thought ya'd stood me up."

He dropped his arm from my shoulders and took a step back. "Yeah, sorry, I had trouble finding it."

I pretended to be placated. "Well, you're here, now. Better late than never, s'pose." I realized I still gripped my drink with white-knuckles. And now that disaster had been averted my hands began to shake. I held the glass even tighter to counteract it and took a swallow.

McLeod bent his head close to mine. "I didn't expect to run into you here. Sure glad I did."

My heart and stomach felt like they performed a few somersaults around each other. For a moment I thought he'd been about to kiss me.

Seamus appeared beside us. "Break's over," he told me, giving McLeod a friendly nod before heading for the stage.

"You need to leave," I said quietly. "You're not at all safe. Are you going to be all right getting back–" Shit, I almost said 'to base'. "Getting home?"

He smiled, showing those beautiful pearly teeth of his. "I'm good. Thank you again."

Adrenaline no longer giving me courage, I felt tongue-tied once more. "Okay, well. Be careful." I gave him an uncertain smile and joined the band on stage.

We checked to make sure we were still in tune and retook our seats. I scanned the crowd looking for McLeod but he had vanished. I felt a bit cold and shaky, like I was in a state of shock or something. Dee returned with Gerry and gave me a wave as they found a space on the dance floor.

Whiskey in the Jar was next, with Seamus singing heartily. That got even more people crowding onto the dance floor. I was glad McLeod had left while he still could. What had he been thinking? It couldn't have been anything to do with me, he'd said he hadn't expected to run into me. I thrust him from my mind and concentrated on the song. My feet couldn't stay still, it was so fantastic to be making music with others like this. I felt so giddy and free I wanted to leap to my feet and dance as well.

Then I noticed five guys standing in a row at the back of the crowd. Their stillness drew my eye, making my heart lurch. They looked like one of the groups of terrorists in the photos on the wall. However it wasn't machine guns two of them held, but guitars. I relaxed. They must be the band up next. The guy in the middle was distinctive, with a blaze of fiery red hair that reached his shoulders.

Virginia Reel was up next, a fast one that featured the fiddle. Seamus must have a lot of faith in me to include it. It would have been great if McLeod had stayed for this, coming from Virginia. I gave myself a mental shake. *Get. Him. Out. Of. Your. Mind.* I think I did all right with *Virginia*, and in no time we thundered to a rip-roaring crescendo. Applause and cheers filled the hall.

Seamus leapt to his feet. "And let's say a big thank you to–" He glanced back at me. "To Fionnuir, who stepped in at the last minute on the fiddle to save our arses tonight!" He gestured for me to get up. I stumbled to my feet and he pulled me by the elbow to the front of the stage. "Fionnuir's Irish for Jennifer," he whispered. "As good as, anyway." He pronounced it 'fenoor'.

We all jumped as the door to the street crashed open and in flooded a squad of British soldiers. Screams erupted and the dance floor parted like the Red Sea. I saw some enter by the back door, too. They targeted two men on the dance floor. Squaddies held the crowd back at gunpoint, allowing four of them to rush the two men, grabbing them and bodily hauling them out of the front door. It was done so fast no one had time to react.

Seamus recovered first. "Bastards!" he shouted.

"Yeah, fuckin' Brit bastards!" yelled a man in the crowd, and then individual words got lost in a stream of babbling hatred. I froze in place, front center stage, not able to believe my eyes. I needn't have worried about McLeod at all. He'd had back up close by all along.

"Stay back!" shouted an authoritative voice with an English accent.

Seamus turned to us and hissed, "*The Men Behind the Wire.* Quick!" He gave me a shove back toward my chair.

"I don't know that one–" I began, but was drowned out as Johnny loudly banged the opening notes on his accordion.

I looked on as Seamus, still on his feet, sang:

"*'Armored cars and tanks and guns, came to take away our sons,*
But every man must stand behind the men behind the wire–'"

Oh my God. I felt sick. I wanted to vanish, but what could I do? I watched the squaddies peel out, all keeping a watchful eye and SLR muzzle on the livid crowd.

I wasn't surprised that no one felt like dancing after that. Seamus wrapped up the song, which I did attempt to play along to, once the soldiers had gone. He was so rattled by the interruption that he insisted on sending 'us girls' home right away.

"Ach, Seamus, for God's sake," complained Dee. "They won't be back."

"It's not safe, not even on a holy day like *Lá Fhéile Stiofáin*. We can't even gather in our own country and celebrate without the fuckin' Brits harassing us."

"La Fey what?" I whispered to Dee.

"St. Stephen's Day. Boxing Day."

Oh. I'd heard the carol where it mentioned 'on the feast of Stephen' but never knew it meant today.

"Come on," she said with a sigh. "No point in arguin' with him once he's got his dander up. We can have a drink back at ours."

Her youngest brother Frankie, a laconic freckle-faced young man of few words, drove us back. I didn't mention anything about McLeod being there to Dee. What must he think of me, being in the middle of a bunch of IRA supporters?

Of all the gin-joints in all the world.

4

A While Longer

I scarcely slept that night, the *céildh* careening through my head. The good and bad. If playing with that band hadn't convinced me that Agricultural Technology was entirely the wrong path for me to take, then nothing would. And I couldn't help reliving the moment McLeod had looked at me with such admiration when he leaned close. And then my heart would race at how blindingly stupid I'd been rushing to his rescue. If those guys hadn't believed me, we'd both be dead by now, shot as spies.

I found Mum and Dad just finishing breakfast when I came down to the kitchen. I got a cup of tea and joined them. Mac lifted his head from his nest by the toasty Aga, but went straight back to sleep when he understood I wasn't about to take him out for a walk.

"What time did you come in last night?" interrogated Mum.

"Not sure. Ended up over at the O'Neill's and had a few drinks." I nodded at the Christmas tree, attempting to distract her. "Looks a bit bare round the bottom now without the presents, doesn't it?"

Dad lowered his newspaper so he could peer over it and wink. The

Peterson pipe I'd given him for Christmas drooped from his mouth. "Very nice pipe," he mumbled around it. He began to fold up the paper and I realized he was readying to head out into the yard.

"I've something to tell you," I blurted. Both of them froze and stared. God, they probably thought I was pregnant. "Queen's just isn't working out." My words came in a rush. "I'm not going back. I'm reapplying for the Belfast City School of Music instead." They continued staring. "To study violin part time," I added, "while working here on the farm."

Mum busied herself with pouring tea, milk, and adding sugar to her teacup. "John?"

"Thanks."

She did the same for him while I waited for a response. Dad dropped in four lumps of sugar, one more than usual, and stirred clockwise. He kept slowly stirring for several seconds, studying the depths of the cup.

Weren't they going to say anything? "Why you thought I'd be any good at Economics beats me." I knew sounded like a sulky child. "I've never had a head for math."

"Sure, didn't I say it all along?" said Dad at last. "All she needs to learn about a farm is right here."

"No, John!" Mum snapped. "It's important she gets a proper agricultural degree."

Dad harrumphed. "What good is that to a farmer's wife?"

"She's not a farmer's wife, yet. Or anyone's wife, the way she's going."

I went hot. "I can hear you, you know."

Mum carried on as though I hadn't spoken. "Mrs. Whitman in the farm up the road has a doctorate in psychology."

"But what use is that to a farmer's wife?" insisted Dad.

She rested her forearms on the table and leaned forward intently. "I'll tell you what use it is, John. It means she will have choices that I did not. She'll have a solid education that will take her anywhere. And," she added, "she'll have more to talk about than the price of oats or foot and mouth disease. That's what."

"Humph." I could tell Dad suspected he'd been insulted.

Mum straightened in her seat. "Listen Jen, I know it's been difficult, you being used to working here since leaving school and then having to adjust back to being in a classroom. And I know Belfast is very different to Newcastle. Tell you what, just give it until Easter, dear. Only another couple of months, not long at all. If you still feel the same way you can leave Queen's then, with our blessing."

I hesitated. What she asked was more than reasonable. How hard would it be to get through another couple of months? I sighed in resignation. "I suppose so."

⌘

The week after New Year Dad drove me back to Belfast to commence the winter term. I'd have been happy to take the bus but he wouldn't hear of it. He insisted he had farm supplies to pick up on the outskirts of Belfast, but I think he felt sorry for me having to go back when it was obvious I didn't want to.

The poor man had just developed shingles after Christmas and he found sitting for any length of time very painful. Another reason both Mum and I remonstrated with him but he was on his high horse after her foot and mouth disease speech.

Mum baked a batch of my favorite potato bread, a peace offering. I piled my rucksack and violin into the Jeep's back seat beside Mac and then got into the front with Dad. She came running to the door in her slippers, brandishing something wrapped in tin foil. I'd forgotten the bread.

Dad realized he'd left his pipe behind and stormed back into the farmhouse. He returned, plonking himself in the driver's seat, then rocketed upward with a sharp yelp. I stifled an unsympathetic laugh, feeling guilty. He'd obviously forgotten about his shingles. Mum waved until we were out of the yard and heading up the lane. At the brow of the hill behind Mourneview I turned to look over my shoulder until the tip of the weathercock was out of sight. Easter wasn't far off, I reassured myself. I'd be back before I knew it.

The ancient radio in the Jeep was habitually tuned to Radio Ulster. I smothered a groan as some dreary country-type song about corncrake birds all disappearing from Ireland started playing. It was going to be a long trip. Dad, a careful driver at the best of times, was even more so on the icy January roads. He drove a painful twenty-five miles an hour through Dundrum, Clough and Seaforde villages. I tried not to notice the long traffic cavalcade gathering behind us.

We reached open road after crawling through market town Ballynahinch, and one by one the cars behind overtook us. Dad remained oblivious to the scouring glares and fists shaken at him as they sped past. I kept my gaze resolutely on the road ahead.

On the radio the cheery Radio Ulster news jingle played. But nothing was cheerful about the news headlines. Dad turned up the volume as the polite Anglo/Northern Irish voice of the newscaster announced: "*Last night in the predominantly Catholic Falls Road area, a Protestant man was found in an alley viciously beaten to death. It is thought to be another sectarian killing by the Irish Republican Army, who has also recently increased bombing activities across the Province. On Friday two members of the Provisional Irish Republican Army were killed in the Ardoyne in Belfast, when the car bomb they were transporting exploded prematurely.*"

Dad snapped the radio off altogether. "You be careful in Belfast," he said with a reprimanding finger wag. "Stay away from trouble, you hear?"

"Of course," I assured him. The university area was pretty safe, although admittedly what the IRA might target next was anyone's guess. He pulled up to the curb outside my apartment and I unclipped my seat belt. "Would you like a cuppa, Dad?"

"Best not. Snow's on the way." The forecaster hadn't mentioned anything on the radio but I nodded and opened the door. Dad's farmer's instinct was rarely wrong. He reached over and patted my hand. "Don't you worry, love. I'll talk to your mother. Make her see sense. It'll be grand to have you back on the farm."

I felt a mixture of gratitude and guilt. How could I tell him I had no interest in being a farmer at all? I gathered my rucksack and violin case, gave Mac a hug, and climbed the three steps from the pavement to my front door. Painted dark blue, it had a semi-circular window above with *Botanic House* engraved on the glass. It stood in the middle of a row of houses exactly alike, all badly in need of paint and repair. The rent for my cramped little apartment at the top in the converted attic cost a lot less than the others.

I slipped my key into the lock and opened the door. Dad waited to make sure I got in okay and I paused to wave. He honked the horn and the gears ground as he pulled away. My chest grew tight, tears threatening as the Jeep merged with traffic and disappeared.

⌘

After a frigid night curled up in my bed under every blanket and coat I could pile on it, I woke to find that snow had indeed fallen. It was fast disappearing from the pavements and roads but clung to the bushes and grass. The Botanic Gardens looked like CS Lewis' *Narnia* in its magical eternal winter. I detoured through the park on my way to class, just to marvel at the pristine fairy-like world.

I emerged on University Road on the far side of the park and walked down to the front gates of the campus. No matter how many times I approached the ornate Elizabethan-inspired structure built by Sir Charles Lanyon in the late 1840's, I felt awestruck. For a hundred and thirty years, generations of men and women with all their young hopes and ambitions had come and gone through those massive double doors.

My arms ached from hefting five heavy economics books. I wished I'd been sensible and brought them in my rucksack but I hadn't been awake enough to think of that when I set out. I'd also forgotten gloves so my fingers felt stingingly numb.

The Lanyon Building looked like a fairy palace inside a snow globe. Frost sparkled on the grass outside and clumps of icy snow lined the walkway to the entrance. Hordes of warmly-wrapped students and faculty milled about, wearing festive scarves and hats, a fallout from Christmas. As

I passed through the open gates my books slipped from my frozen grasp. I clutched desperately to hang onto them but gravity won.

"Bugger it." I stooped to pick them up.

"Let me." Clancy appeared at my side and helped me retrieve them. I'll bet Dee told him to keep an eye out for me.

He looked healthy and ruddy, cheeks Robin-red from the cold. His sandy hair grazed his shoulders, and he wore a snazzy tan leather jacket with a striped green and white scarf around his neck. Celtic Football Team colors. He wouldn't dare wear those in Newcastle lest he piss off the British side of the mixed community.

"Thank you, Clance." I automatically used his old childhood name. "Good to see you."

He piled the books back into my arms. "You too."

As he accompanied me to the entrance the silence between us grew a little awkward. He probably remembered our disastrous date too.

I cleared my throat. "Did you have a good Christmas?"

He shrugged. "Okay. How 'bout yours?"

"The usual family pantomime. Next year I think I'll go abroad instead."

He cocked a sandy eyebrow. "No more consortin' with the army for you, then?"

My heart leapt. Dee couldn't have been stupid enough to tell him about Sergeant McLeod, could she?

"Yer mud-covering captain stunt," he continued. "You know how it goes. This country's like a village."

He must have heard it from Dee for how else would he know? I just hoped that was all she'd told her family.

"Want to meet up later?" he asked.

My spirits lifted. "That'd be lovely." We made arrangements to meet in the Students' Union bar at four-thirty when we'd both finished for the day.

Just my luck, my first lecture of the term was on economic trends within agriculture. I found my brain zoning out, my thoughts returning to how Clancy knew about Captain Stratton and then on to obsess about Sergeant McLeod. I was probably never going to see him again, I should just forget about him. No doubt since he'd seen me in a Nationalist pub in Ballyben he'd avoid me like the proverbial plague.

The guy sitting next to me in class shot me a frown. I realized I was humming *Going To Get Along Without You Now* by Skeeter Davis and shut myself up.

I looked forward to meeting up with Clancy. At least he was someone familiar from home. And a couple of years older than me so he knew what it was like to be a mature student.

Not surprisingly, he ordered a Guinness in the Students' Union and I had Harp. Dee had succeeded in converting me. The late afternoon crept into evening, so we ordered sandwiches and a few more rounds from the bar. One beer led to another, and soon I found myself confiding in him like he was my brother.

"I don't know what I'm going to do, Clance," I blurted, biting back tears.

Concern swept across his face. "Jen, what's wrong?"

"It's this place. I hate it. I don't belong." Through sniffles I confessed my stupefaction and despair over the agricultural course. I even shared how lonely I felt, having been unable to find any friends my age at Queen's.

"Sure, I'm the same. Bunch of bloody wankers, so they are."

I smiled. "I thought it was just me. I've tried to make friends but they're all kind of cliquey in my class. We're only a few years apart in age but I feel like a bloody dinosaur."

"You're not alone in that."

A catch in his voice made me look closely at him. "But surely you have no trouble fitting in?"

"You don't know the half of it." He got up, lifting both our glasses from the table. "Let me get another round."

He leaned on the bar as the glasses were refilled, his shoulders slumped as though he carried a great weight. There was comfort in knowing I wasn't the only one having trouble fitting in, but I didn't like to think of him unhappy.

He returned with two frothing pints. "I know what you mean about the course," he commiserated. "I'm doin' it, too, but have Dr. Steane, the prof who came down from the New University in Coleraine. I'll tell ya, he's the only reason I'm gettin' through it."

I brightened. "Why's that?"

"Ach, he makes the effort to make it interestin' and relevant." He grinned. "And he throws chalk at you if he thinks you're not concentrating."

"That's exactly what I need."

"I can throw chalk at you if that'd help."

I laughed. "I wish."

"But seriously, why don't you switch?"

"Can I?"

"Don't see why not."

⌘

Switching lecturers turned out to be simple. Suddenly my days at university improved exponentially and time no longer dragged. It was so much easier when one had a 'buddy' to hang out with. Clancy and I settled into a comfortable, easy routine, sitting next to each other in lectures and in the canteen. He regularly came to my apartment when I needed extra coaching in exchange for me cooking dinner for him. He was so good at stripping the subject down to brass tacks, to the point where I could actually grasp what it all meant. It finally dawned on me how to apply it to modern farming and then it wasn't so mind-numbing. Still boring but tolerable now. Especially when I only had to endure it for another couple of months.

To an outsider Clancy and I looked like we were in a deeply committed relationship. But only in friendship. He'd become the big brother I never had. I managed to think less and less about Sergeant McLeod. He only came to mind when I saw army patrols go by, or the time Clancy and I went to see *The Deerhunter* in the Odeon downtown. Any uniform made me think of him. And come to think of it, there were quite a lot of uniforms worn in Belfast. Particularly after the beginning of February when a former prison officer and his wife were shot dead at their home in Belfast by the IRA. It was in Oldpark in the Crumlin area - nowhere near Queen's, but there was increased military activity all over the city.

Dee phoned early one evening, and the very attractive single male neighbor from downstairs came up to knock on my door. He obviously didn't think the same about me. He scarcely gave me a look as he mumbled that someone was on the phone and retreated back down the stairs.

I ran down to the hall and picked up the receiver. "Hello?"

"Hiya, mucker! Just phoned for a gab."

I perched on the bottom step and we chatted about nothing in particular. I'd wondered fancifully on the way down if the call could possibly be from McLeod, but of course it wasn't. When I got a word in edgeways I couldn't help but ask, "Have you seen Sergeant McLeod anywhere about there, at checkpoints or anything?"

"Nah," she replied after a fairly significant pause. "Just the usual squaddie. Not quite as spiffy as your gallant sergeant." I heard her Zippo clicking and she inhaled. "How's it goin' with Clance?"

"He's great. Helping me with the course." I remembered something I'd meant to ask her since January. "Hey, how come Clancy knew all about Captain Stratton? The officer we covered in mud up in the Mournes?"

"He did?" I listened as she exhaled smoke. "Well, I don't see how he knew."

"You must have told him."

"I didn't, I swear. Jen, I didn't tell no one at all, least of all m'brothers." That rang true, particularly now that I knew most of them hung out in Nationalist IRA Ballyben. "Anyway, ya got Clancy now. What ya need that Yank for?"

I sighed heavily. "Talking of whom, Clancy's on his way over so I'd better go."

"Ooooh!" she undulated suggestively.

"Fuck's sake. Good*bye*." Exasperated, I hung up and headed back to the attic. I wish she'd get it into her head that there would never be anything between her brother and me.

My kitchen comprised of a cramped narrow strip along part of one wall with a Formica counter-come-dining bar separating it from the living room. While I prepared dinner I put on my new Yehudi Menuhin record, a Christmas present ostensibly from Mac. Emptying a packet of ground meat in a pan on the gas stove to brown, I put noodles in water to boil, and began quartering tomatoes and chopping onions for spaghetti sauce. I already had water, Oxo stock cubes, tomato paste, mixed herbs, and dried garlic mixed in the measuring jug to pour over the meat when it had browned.

The doorbell shrilled. I put down the knife, grabbed my keys and went to the window. Clancy stood on the pavement below, leaning back so I could see him from the window. Forcing the sash up I yelled, "Incoming!" and tossed my keys down. I took a tin of the Guinness I'd bought for him out of the fridge and waited until I heard him clunking up the stairs. As soon as the door opened, I yanked the ring pull off and presented him with the tin.

"You'll make somebody a wonderful wife, one day," he remarked, kicking the door closed behind him.

"Ha." I returned to the kitchen. "Your bloody sister has us already married and committed for life."

The meat had browned so I added the sauce mixture, threw some salt on it and put the lids on the pans. Clancy stood at the window, gazing out. He raised the Guinness to his mouth and emptied a substantial amount down his throat. Then he leaned heavily on the sill, staring at the street below.

I joined him at the window. "Anything wrong, Clance?" He shifted away like I was infected with bubonic plague or something, so I grabbed him and tried to ruffle his hair. "What's the matter, don't you want to marry me?"

He ducked, annoyance flashing across his face. "Stop it."

I poked at his ribs, trying to find a tickly spot. "Come on, it wouldn't be that bad, would it?"

"Jennifer, quit!" He grabbed at my arms, spilling beer onto the worn carpet. "I mean it, okay?"

God, he hadn't taken me seriously, had he? "All right, for goodness sakes. Stay a bachelor, then. See if I care."

My bantering tone was lost on him. He stared at me as though he were a cat about to be steeped in a tub of water. "Listen, there can never be anything between us, Jen."

I gave an incredulous laugh. "Jesus, I was only kidding. Did you leave your sense of humor at the door or something?"

"But do you know why?"

"Well–" I hesitated. I thought I did, but maybe not. "Why?"

He twisted away from me and roamed over to the fireplace where he swallowed the last of his beer. "Ach. It's not easy."

"What isn't?"

The empty tin made a rattling sound as he crumpled it in his hand. "Jesus Christ." He aimed the tin at the rubbish bin. Bullseye, it went in first time. Going to the fridge he pulled out another Guinness and handed it to me. I didn't like stout but took it, not wanting to distract him. I held my tongue, wondering what the hell he was going to say.

We snapped off the church keychains in synchronicity, tossed them into the bin, and clunked our tins together. I automatically opened my mouth to utter 'Fuck the Pope' but stopped myself in time. Clancy would not get the joke at all.

"Jen, ever wondered why I never made a move on you?"

"'Cos your Mum would skin you alive for shagging a manky Protestant?" He didn't laugh. "Okay," I continued, "maybe at first. But not now. You're like my brother." Where was this headed?

"Exactly. Look, we're pretty good mates, right? I can trust ya."

"You know you can." I was getting really worried.

"Ya have to keep this to yourself. Promise me. My sister Dee, m'brothers - none of them back there can ever know."

Oh, God, what had he done? "I promise, Clance. Come on, tell me."

He screwed his eyes tightly closed and spoke in a rush. "Do you remember when we went to see *Grease*?"

I nodded. The film had come out a year ago but as neither of us had seen it, we'd made a point of going last month when a local youth club screened it to raise funds.

"Remember how you got all mushy over John Travolta?" he continued. "I felt the same way."

"I remember. You said how sexy Olivia Newton-John was."

"You weren't listening. I said how sexy *he* was."

I gaped. "What do you mean?"

"Do I have to spell it out for ya?"

"You're - gay?"

"Duh."

Oh. Holy shit. He hid that well, I'd never have guessed. In my ignorance I thought all homosexual men acted like John Inman's flamboyant character on the television show, *Are You Being Served*. The O'Neills would be devastated. And his intolerant brothers were totally capable of beating the living crap out of him.

He watched me, his face drawn and lined with worry. I pasted on a smile. "Is that all? Fucking hell, I thought you'd cancer or something."

His jaw dropped, then we burst out laughing.

"Did you always know you were gay?" I asked after a moment.

"No. I thought I wanted to get married and have kids like anyone else." He gave a bitter laugh. "Holy mother of God, I *do* want to get married and have kids like anyone else. To be what I am goes against everything in the Catholic church. I'm going to die with a mortal sin on my soul." His voice cracked. "I'll spend eternity in hell."

I stepped forward and clamped my hand across his mouth. "You shut up *now*, Clancy." His eyes were bright with unshed tears. "You're not going to hell. That's rubbish. Come on, you can't believe that, can you?"

He gently pushed my hand away and shrugged. How I hated religion more than ever for making this man ashamed of who he was. "Look, I've been to Mass with Dee enough times to know the Catholic thing about 'God loving you and offering a wonderful plan for your life'. If that's the case, then this is all ordained - part of the 'plan', right?"

He blinked. "You've been to Mass?"

I guffawed, startling him. "*That's* what you got out of that? Yes, I've been to Mass. Many times."

"A good Orangewoman like yerself? What would your parents say?"

"We all have our secrets, Clance." I held out my tin so we could clank them together again. "Feel better?"

"Yeah. Thanks." He raised a sandy eyebrow. "Fuck the Pope?"

I gave him a playful thump on the arm. "You know about that?"

"Hard to miss, when you and Dee only do it when yer stocious. And loud."

"That's not true, but okay. Fuck the Queen, then."

We took a drink. "So much for Dee's wedding plans for us," he said. "She'll kill me."

"No, she won't. Why would she care, anyway? *She's* not exactly conformist, is she?"

"Aye." He took another long draft of beer. "But I don't want her to know, okay? I doubt she could keep it to herself."

"Okay." I don't know if he was right or not. She'd kept quite a few of my secrets over the years.

The lid on the noodle saucepan rattled loudly. Returning to the kitchen I used a fork to secure a noodle from the pot and sharply flicked my wrist. The noodle flew off and hit the wall over the sink where it stayed stuck.

Clancy looked at me like I'd lost my senses. "What the fuck are ya doing?"

"If it sticks it's cooked," I explained, turning off the heat under the pot. "All part of the Great Plan."

He rolled his eyes and leaned his elbows on the counter. "You're all right about it, aren't ya? About me bein' - you know."

I came round the counter and gave him a bear hug. It was the first time we'd ever touched with any sense of intimacy. "Of course I'm all right about it, Clancy." Letting him go, I went to the china piggy bank that I kept on a shelf by the bathroom door for the electric meter. Upending it, I emptied out almost five pounds in change. "You stay here and watch the stove. I'll be right back." I grabbed my anorak and opened the door.

"Where ya going?"

"Bubbly. We need to celebrate your coming out."

The smile that spread across his face made me hurry out the door before he saw tears well up in my eyes. How had he expected me to react? Probably with hate and condemnation. He'd get a lot of that in this country.

5

Then There Were Two

After Clancy left I sat by the fire and finished the cheap sparkling wine I'd bought. My piggy bank savings didn't stretch to proper bubbly, but it had made Clancy happy.

I glanced at the clock. Almost nine. He'd come over to help me with a course paper but that had fallen by the wayside. I felt hyper and wound up. Maybe I could have a go at writing the paper myself. If I got a draft done then I could head off for the weekend to Mourneview for Dad's birthday on Saturday.

It felt warm in the apartment for a change as I'd banked the fire up for Clancy's visit. I had about five big pieces of coal left. If I could make them last till the weekend I'd be able to nick some more from Dad's shed at Mourneview. And do my laundry.

I pulled the shabby, worn armchair up close to the fire and tucked a blanket round my legs. Resting a ring binder on my lap I made some notes, outlining the paper. If I did manage to get it drafted I'd have time to run it by Clancy before the weekend.

After an hour and a half I couldn't see the pages for yawning. Setting the binder and pen down on the floor, I stretched. The glowing fire still had plenty of heat. I should bring in my mattress and bedding from the bedroom, use the last of the coal and sleep in warmth for a change.

To hell with economizing. I dragged everything off the box spring and out to the living room. Pushing the armchair and sofa out of the way I let the mattress flop to the floor. Kneeling down I put in the last five lumps of coal in the fireplace. Luxury.

A sharp rap on the door made me jump. I waited, hoping they'd go away. But the knocking increased in volume and intensity. I jumped up and ran over. It's a wonder the door hadn't burst open. The lock could be temperamental and sometimes the door slid ajar even though I thought I'd locked it. I yanked it open, ready to ream out whoever was making the racket, but stopped dead in my tracks. Dee stood on the landing, an improbably huge suitcase by her feet. She was bundled up against the cold, with a scarf, wool hat and gloves along with her leopard coat.

She struck an attitude. "Took ya long enough."

Something awful must have happened to have her show up at this time of night.

"Come in, quick." I leaned down and dragged her case inside, nearly dislocating a shoulder. My God, did she have a body in there? "What's the matter, Dee?"

She laughed. "Nothin'. You've been on at me long enough to ditch Newcastle and come to the Big Smoke, so here I am."

I blinked. "But it's so late."

"I knew you'd be up."

"Why didn't you mention this on the bloody phone earlier?"

"'Cos I didn't decide to fuckin' come until after we hung up. Is it a problem?"

"Course not. It's just so sudden."

She spotted the abandoned dishes with the remains of spaghetti Bolognese on them. I watched as she surveyed the glasses and empty sparkling wine bottle on the coffee table. Her eyes widened at the sight of the mattress in front of the fire. "No way! You and Clancy? Have ya finally lost yer virginity? The ice princess has fuckin' melted at last - with my big brother?"

I rolled my eyes. "It's *melteth*. And no. The bed's there because I'm so freaking cold."

"If ya say so." She threw herself onto the sofa, still wearing her coat. "Really though - you guys done it, yet?"

If only she knew! "Don't be disgusting, Dee. We're just friends. How many times do I have to tell you?"

Eyeing my meager fire she reached over to drag her suitcase closer and unzipped it. Drawing out a large grocery plastic bag, she handed it over. I almost dropped it, it was so heavily jam-packed with coal. "There's another two bags in the car, we can get 'em tomorrow. So where do I sleep?"

"In the bedroom, now that there's enough coal to heat the whole apartment. But there's only my single bed. I'll sleep on the box spring and you take the mattress."

"No need." She went to the door, pulling it open. From the landing outside she hauled in a folded metal contraption. "I stopped by Mourneview and got that old camp bed from yer room."

"How the hell did you get it up the stairs?"

"Yer neighbor was very obliging." She twinkled.

Funny, he wasn't so obliging to me. We dragged my mattress back into the bedroom and then snapped the cot open, setting it up on the other side of the room. "What did my parents say about this?" I asked as I scrounged up fresh sheets, blankets and a pillow.

"Didn't see them. They were at that Newcastle community thing with my Mum and Dad."

I laughed incredulously. They'd apparently once again forgotten to lock the farmhouse. "So you just went in and stole this?"

"And this." She returned to her suitcase and produced a bottle of Dad's homemade plum wine.

I shook my head. "Jesus, Dee." She had some nerve, she really did.

⌘

Helping Dee to move in was a great excuse for me to play hooky the next day. She had another huge suitcase and two boxes of stuff piled in the Mini. They took no time at all to shift from where she'd parked in the side street.

She took one look at my charity shop utensils in the kitchen and grabbed both of our coats from the back of the sofa. "Come on. Housewares shopping. Now. I need to buy you a house warming present for letting me move in."

"What's wrong with what I've got?"

"If ya have to ask that."

She bundled me outside and we caught a bus into downtown Belfast. There wasn't any point in driving down. The center was cordoned off to vehicles and we'd never get parked anywhere without a long walk. Our destination was the British Home Stores, a huge department store in Corn Market. "Let's get some lunch in the Bodega Bar afterward," I suggested. "It's close by."

The bus dropped us at the main terminus beside the City Hall, with Queen Victoria's statue in front of it. On the far side, an old church with pillars had a massive sign up that counted the death toll of people killed in the Troubles. I averted my eyes, not wanting to know.

Crossing over the street to the main thoroughfare of Donegall Place, we lined up to go through the security gate cordoning off the city center. We opened up our handbags and held them ready for the on-duty police officers to look inside. Armed British soldiers oversaw it all. I automatically scrutinized their faces, looking for Sergeant McLeod, even though there was as much chance of the Queen abdicating tomorrow for Prince Charles than McLeod being here.

As we approached the main entrance to the British Home Stores, a big red cardboard heart in a shop window on the other side of Corn Market caught my eye. "Shit, I forgot it was Valentine's Day tomorrow." No cards for me this year. Or any year, except when Mum remembered to put one in the post and then act all surprised when it arrived. Her copperplate handwriting was distinctive, no matter how well she attempted to disguise it.

Dee shot me a sideways glance. "Maybe Clancy's sent ya one."

I ignored her, diverting across Corn Market and heading into the shop. Clancy would have to tell her he was gay, just to get her to shut the hell up.

The shop interior was festooned with crimson hearts and balloons, displaying every kind of card you could think of. In the far corner I found the *'For Him'* section and selected a birthday card for Dad. It showed a man in a peaked tweed cap smoking a pipe, with an adoring sheepdog sitting at his feet. Perfect. The dog even looked like Mac. Dee waited as I paid at the cash register, an old-fashioned brass one with huge keys. The drawer opened with a loud *ka-ching*.

"Why don't you come back with me for the weekend?" I asked. "We could get the rest of your stuff."

She shook her head. "Can't. I'm auditionin' for a part in a play on Saturday."

I did a double take. She tried to look nonchalant as though she auditioned for plays every day of the year.

The girl at the register slid Dad's card into a little paper bag with flowers printed on it and handed me my change. I thanked her and we made our way to the door.

"So that's why you came to Belfast," I teased. "Nothing to do with seeing me at all."

Dee laughed, looking a little shamefaced.

"Which play?" I asked as we stepped out into the street.

"*Shadow of a Gunman*. By Séan O'Casey."

I blinked. "That's a bit—" I hesitated.

"Irish?" she finished for me.

I flushed. *Anti-British* was what I'd been about to say.

A rack of impossibly high stiletto boots caught my eye, saving me from having to reply. We were both drawn like sirens to the McManus shoe shop display.

Dee grabbed a calf-length purple suede boot. "Come here, you beauty." Bending to haul off the leopard spot ankle boot on her right foot, she pulled on the stiletto. Leaning a hand on my shoulder to balance she used the other to zip it up. Teetering on the absurdly unmatched heel sizes she studied her reflection in the shop window.

"'Fuck me' boots," she proclaimed. "That's the only thing these're good for."

A shadow fell across us. I looked up to see a guy with a shock of thick, red-gold hair passing by. He wore a maxi-length black leather coat, the back tails flying behind him like the dark wings of a fallen angel. I narrowed my eyes. I'm sure I knew him from somewhere. A weaselly-looking short guy with spiky black hair scurried behind, scuttling to keep up. They both moved fast and with intent, their heads down.

"Help me get this fuckin' thing off," demanded Dee.

I grabbed hold of the fuck me boot tightly encased around her calf and yanked hard. It came away after the third pull and I returned it to the rack while she replaced her own boot. Leaning against the shop window I waited as she rummaged through the rest of the boots on display, checking the sizes printed on the soles. A brick of four British Army soldiers wearing flak jackets walked in measured steps toward Corn Market, SLR's held at the ready. They guarded two armed Royal Ulster Constabulary officers on patrol. Both policemen had an unhealthy pallor and looked uncomfortable wearing heavy black bulletproof vests over their dark green uniforms.

A lone white delivery van with its back doors open was parked outside Woolworth's just along the street. The only vehicle around as regular traffic wasn't allowed into the city center. A man carrying a clipboard came round the side of the van and slammed the doors shut. The sound reverberated loudly, making me flinch. Everyone else on the street, including the soldiers and policemen, looked at the van.

Oblivious, the driver started up the engine and eased away from Woolworth's. I hadn't realized how silent it had fallen in the street until chatter between people began again. I heard relieved laughter and a child's voice demanded, "Mummy, what happened?"

Dee abandoned her boot pilgrimage and we headed back toward the British Home Stores. On the right was where the Abercorn Restaurant had been bombed by the IRA in '72. Every time I thought about it, I felt such anger. A ghastly carnage. They'd given no warning and over a hundred and thirty innocent people had been horrifically maimed. I shivered and yanked my thoughts elsewhere.

As we neared the Stores a sudden and violent pressure roared. I found myself face down on the pavement, protecting my head with my arms as a million hurtling shards exploded into the air. Cascades of debris pummeled me, thudding into my back and legs and stinging my bare hands.

The avalanche stopped. Ears ringing, I tentatively raised my head. Dee mirrored me. Murky smoke and dust billowed from where the British Home Stores front windows had been. Fire crackled nearby.

"You okay?" she asked.

"Think so."

Streaks of crimson cuts and scratches lacerated the back of my hands and my heart felt like it had been blasted out of my chest. If we hadn't dawdled in the shoe shop we'd have been caught directly in the bomb.

We picked ourselves up from the pavement. Police and soldiers were already in action, triaging. More arrived and began herding people to a safe distance. Sirens wailed, steadily getting louder. Dee had broken one of the heels on her boots and balanced unsteadily. Livid scratches lined her face. Mine too, judging by how much my right cheek burned.

An RUC officer appeared beside us. "Anyone badly hurt?" I shook my head. He assessed us with an expert glance and gestured toward Donegall Place with compact precision. "Please clear the area."

I spotted the flowered paper bag with Dad's card in it a few feet away. Picking it up, I brushed it free of ash. It had been crumpled but otherwise undamaged. We obediently moved over to where a crowd clustered behind another RUC officer. Something white in the smoldering ashy rubble caught my eye. I couldn't quite register what it was. A thin, pale thing, black and glutinous-smeared at one end. Like bramble jelly on a loaf of French bread.

Bile rose in my throat. I finally recognized a severed, bloody arm, bent at the elbow and palm raised as though pleading. I couldn't breathe. Then I heard a terrible screaming, a desperate keening like nothing I ever wanted to hear again. A woman threw herself toward the arm, followed by a policeman who tried to drag her back. She had survived while the person she was with had not. Oh, God. A child, judging by the smallness of the arm. I gulped in air. My lungs and throat burned but tears refused to spill.

A fleet of vehicles streamed into Corn Market: fire engines, ambulances, and army Saracens. In a flurry the badly injured were taken immediately while medics triaged and attended to the less wounded. What was left of the rest would be removed, silently and deliberately.

Listening to the chatter around us, I found out who was responsible for the atrocity. The IRA. No warning phoned in. No chance to get anyone out in time.

Fucking murdering Fenian bastards. They should be lined up against a wall and shot.

⌘

The phone in the hall was ringing when we got back to the apartment. Some sixth sense told me it was for me. Apparently my mother had called over and over since the bomb had been reported on Radio Ulster.

"I know you were at class and wouldn't have been anywhere near it, Jen, but we wanted to make sure you were all right, anyway."

I tried to lie and reassure her, but I burst into tears. Dee and I huddled side by side on the bottom step as in between gulps I told Mum all about it.

"What were you doing downtown, anyway, Jen? Why weren't you at class?" Trust her to manifest fear into confrontation. I heard Dad's voice rumbling in the background. "Your father's on his way to pick you up," she relayed.

"No, tell him it's okay. We're coming back home as soon as we've packed a bag." Neither of us felt like staying in Belfast tonight.

"Who's we?"

"Deirdre and me."

She paused while she took that in. "All right, love. See you soon."

⌘

Dee dropped me at Mourneview and headed straight home. Mum went into fuss mode. I had to allow her to dab iodine on the cut along my cheekbone before I could lock myself in the bathroom. All I wanted was a long, hot bath in the old tarnished enamel claw foot tub. After that I went straight to bed. Dear Mum had just put fresh sheets on it and laid a clean pair of flannel pajamas out for me. My lower lip trembled when I saw she'd left a mug of *Horlicks* on my bedside table with a saucer over the top of it to keep it warm. She swore by that drink. She took a cup every night to bed with her, convinced it helped her sleep, like they advertised it did. The sweet, oatmealy liquid felt comforting in my upset stomach, and despite the recurring image of that bramble jelly arm I fell into a deep sleep.

I felt better in the light of day, having slept for almost ten hours. The abrasions on my face and hands were superficial and would heal fast enough. But the cut on my cheekbone had bruised, making it look a lot worse than it was.

Clancy phoned that afternoon. "Jen, I just found out. I'm so sorry."

"I'm all right," I reassured him. "If we'd been a few seconds earlier–" I couldn't finish the sentence. And I couldn't help but remember how much he lauded the IRA's cause against us British.

He cleared his throat. "Listen, you haven't said nothin', have you?"

"About what?" Then I remembered. I'd forgotten all about his confession. "No, course not."

"Cheers. When you coming back?"

I bit my lip. "I don't know. In a few days. Oh, listen, Dee's going to be by herself in the apartment at the weekend. Will you call by and make sure she's all right?"

"The apartment?"

"She's moved in with me."

"When did that happen?" He sounded a bit put out.

"Yesterday, but I've been asking her to since September."

"Okay. Yeah, sure. I'll check on her."

After he hung up I called the bursar at Queen's and okayed it with her to stay a few more days at Mourneview. She promised to make arrangements with my lecturers so that I'd be able to catch up after I got back, without any penalty. I spent the next three days in a sort of trance. All I did was eat, sleep, and watch mindless television. And cry every time I thought of that woman losing her child. But by Saturday I felt considerably better. Life went on, regardless of tragedy.

Dad seemed delighted with his card and the pouch of tobacco I'd hastily bought in Newcastle. Mum baked a Victoria Sponge, his favorite cake. We scoured the kitchen but could only find one leftover yellow striped birthday candle. She stuck that in the cake so he could blow it out and make a wish. For his present she gave him a brand new Burberry raincoat. It rather resembled a duster from the Wild West and he looked quite imposing sweeping around the farm in it. That's if you ignored the mud-encrusted welly boots. He kept reminding me of something and I finally put it together that it was the red-haired guy with the long leather coat I'd seen in Belfast.

Awful things were happening all over Northern Ireland. On Valentine's Day a soldier was shot by an IRA sniper in Londonderry, further up north. I knew McLeod was nowhere near Derry, but I couldn't help thinking about him and hoping he was all right.

⌘

After a week of Mum's home cooking I felt like I'd put on half a stone in weight. I decided to return to Belfast tomorrow. Then I could spend Thursday and Friday catching up with my studies and start afresh on Monday.

Plastered all over the news was the life sentencing of the Shankill Butchers. Eleven Loyalist Protestants had lost their fucking minds and had horribly cut up and murdered nineteen people. Mostly Catholics. I couldn't believe the stories plastered all through the *Belfast Telegraph*. It read like *The Texas Chainsaw Massacre*, a film I wished I'd never seen.

The sun shone brightly for a February day, albeit intermittently between gaps in the clouds. I decided to take Mac for a walk on the Mournes. Selecting an old waterproof anorak in the hall, I slipped it on and zipped it closed. The pocket bulged and I found one of Mac's rubber balls from the last time I'd taken him out. I grabbed his leash from another hook and went out to the yard, jingling it. "Mac!"

He came bounding, yipping with excitement. Dad emerged from the barn. I waved the leash at him and he nodded, heading back inside. Mac dashed in front of me as I left the yard and headed up the hill behind Mourneview. He covered three times as much ground as me as he snuffed for rabbits in the gorse.

Up high enough I could see all the way across Dundrum Bay to where Ballykinlar Army base nestled. The only evidence that it was there at all was a row of little red flags flapping in the wind to warn of live fire target practice. A regular *rat-a-tat* sound carried across the bay. I imagined Sergeant McLeod overseeing a squadron of men as they lay prone, aiming big automatic weapons at paper targets. I hadn't thought about him for a while. I wondered if he were even still over there.

Drawing Mac's ball out of my pocket, I yelled, "Hey!" He charged at me, bouncing up and trying to snatch the ball from my hand. I hurled it through the air as hard as I could. "Go get it, wet noodle-Macaroni!"

He raced away, all four paws seeming to lift from the earth at once. I ducked behind a gorse bush to hide, a game we'd played since he'd been a puppy. Loud whirring thumped suddenly overhead and the branches around me shimmied violently. Mac dropped the ball, barking furiously at the sky as a British Army helicopter descended. The wind caused by the blades whipped my hair around me like Medusan snakes. Keeping hold of Mac's collar with one hand I used the other to keep the hair off my face. The helicopter lowered to the moor about fifty feet away and hovered a couple of feet off the ground. A door slid open and out jumped a soldier.

I blinked. It couldn't be. Sergeant McLeod ducked under the blades and approached, fixing his already precisely-placed beret on his head.

"How's it going?" he greeted me.

After a stunned moment I found my voice. "This gives a whole new meaning to just dropping in, doesn't it?"

He grinned, showing his even, white teeth. "Been kinda hoping I'd run into you again." He spotted the cut on my cheek and his smile faded. "What happened there?"

I put a hand to my face. "The British Home Store bomb in Belfast."

"You okay?"

"Yes." His intense scrutiny had robbed my ability of speech again. I bit my lip and felt my face flush. I should tell him what I'd been doing at that *céilidh* in Ballyben in case he thought I was a Nationalist. "Look, about Boxing Day–"

"No need to explain," he interrupted. "Thanks again for what you did."

A sharp whistle came from the helicopter and he glanced over his shoulder. Reaching into a trouser pocket he pulled out a battered red envelope. "Here." Shoving it into my hand he raced away, leaping gracefully back through the door. The 'copter rose up and whirred off at a low trajectory toward the mountains. And Mourneview.

"There goes the weathercock," I said to Mac, who wagged his tail uncertainly. I imagined my father's wrath should the beloved antique be felled again.

I smoothed out the crumpled envelope. If I weren't holding it I might have thought I'd just had a wishful-thinking hallucination. Mac bounced in front of me, giving little yips of impatience and tried to snatch the envelope. I kicked the ball away to distract him and carefully peeled open the glue flap of the envelope, drawing out a much-rumpled card with the words *Happy Valentine's Day* printed in a red satin heart on the front. Oh, goodness. The printed inscription inside read *'May your every heart's desire come true for you today.'* McLeod had scrawled 'Mike' underneath with a phone number and extension.

6
A Trip North

I took the bus back to Belfast the next morning, having spent yesterday in a state of high anticipation. Thing was, should I talk to Dee about it or not? Now that she actually lived with me she'd need to know if I were seeing McLeod. It's not something I could easily hide.

I filched another big bottle of plum wine from Dad's stash in the pantry, for medicinal purposes and to butter her up. Poor Dad. Did he ever wonder why the wine disappeared so quickly?

By the time the bus dropped me off on the Ormeau Road it was already after one. It took me about twenty minutes to cut across to Botanic Avenue. Dee was out somewhere, and had been gone for hours as the apartment felt frigidly cold. I lit the fire before heading into the bedroom to change out of my jeans into a tracksuit. I think Americans call them *sweats*, which sounds much better. I never used mine for exercising, just slopping about when I wanted to be comfortable.

Dee had brought more items from home. A gilt-framed mirror propped up on the mantelpiece of the fireplace, along with a little moss-green Wade porcelain trinket dish that I'd given her years ago for her birthday. A picture had been painted on it of Finn MacCoul, the legendary giant of Ireland, about to throw a great chunk of earth.

I stopped in my tracks when I saw what she'd put up on the wall between the fireplace and the window. A Sacred Heart of Jesus picture in a gold frame, complete with red lamp in front of it. The nail wounds of his crucifixion showed vividly on his hands, and he had perfectly coiffed wavy brown hair. I think I'd seen this in the O'Neill's farmhouse. Her mother probably gave it to her to protect her from the evils of Belfast and having to share an apartment with a nasty heretical Protestant.

I didn't like how his eyes seemed to stare at me, following no matter where I moved in the room. I pointedly turned my back and settled in the armchair by the fire to finish the paper I had started last week. Before the bombing.

When I looked up the apartment had been blanketed in darkness. I'd been straining my eyes working by firelight and the streetlamp slanting in from outside. I got up and snapped on the table lamp that sat on the edge of the kitchen counter. My stomach rumbled, reminding me I'd missed lunch. I remembered the potato bread and Tupperware container of Irish stew that Mum had sent me off with. I'd transported them along with Dad's wine in the rucksack and had meant to put them in the fridge when I came in. I retrieved them from the rucksack by the door and discovered the Valentine card. How could I have forgotten that?

I read it one more time, then slipped it into my sweats pocket. Snapping open the Tupperware, I emptied the stew into a saucepan to warm it on the stove. Like magic it conjured Dee. She came in and sniffed the air like a bloodhound. "That smells amazing." The scratches on her face were almost healed.

"Just in time." I got a couple of bowls down from the kitchen cupboard, filled them with stew, and put them on plates with a piece of potato bread beside them.

"Your Mum's wonderful." She shed her coat, opened a drawer and pulled out two round spoons.

I held up the bottle of plum wine. "Dad's pretty wonderful, too."

"Ah, yes he is, the dear." She rescued a couple of glasses from the dish rack by the sink.

We dined in style at the coffee table, sitting on the rug in front of the fire. The coal scuttle on the hearth overflowed in abundance thanks to her.

"How did your audition go?" I asked, realizing I hadn't spoken to her since she dropped me off last week.

She beamed. "I got the part."

"Really?"

She eyed me. "Don't sound so surprised."

"Sorry, I didn't even know you could act. Who you playing?"

"Minnie Powell, of course."

"The lead?"

She struck a pose. "Female ingénue."

I laughed. "Of course, silly me. Wow. Well done." I pushed our used dinner dishes aside and poured her another glass of wine. "When did you decide you wanted to be an actress?"

"Ach, it's somethin' I've thought about trying for a while."

"First I heard of it."

"Well, I don't tell you everything, do I? When I saw the ad in the *Irish Times* last Saturday that the Lyric was holding auditions, I thought, why not?"

"Many up for the part?"

"A few. I think I impressed the buggers with my scratched up face. Gave me a good story. And maybe 'cause I was the only one there who knew how to do an Irish jig."

She leapt up to demonstrate, skipping and clopping a couple of steps in place. She looked glorious, platinum hair flying and skirt swirling as she swung her legs in a rhythmic beat. Frantic pounding came from below. I don't know who lived directly beneath us, I'd never seen them. But whoever they were they seemed allergic to noise of any kind. If I dropped something heavier than a ballpoint pen they'd pummel the ceiling.

Dee stopped mid step. "Mean old gits." We giggled and she sat back down with a thump.

I once again envied her Irish heritage. "You're lucky. Wish I'd had the chance to take lessons."

"Jesus, yer joking. The nun who taught us was a bloody sadist. I kept looking at my feet when learning the steps so she pinned holly on me so it'd scratch my chin if I didn't keep my head up."

"That sounds extreme."

"All nuns are extreme. You Prods have it easy."

I snorted. "You Catholics don't have the monopoly on sadistic teachers, you know." I thought back to the all-girls' private school I'd attended in Newcastle. The English teacher, Miss Anderson, whose looks unfortunately resembled a popular comedian, Frankie Howard, had been particularly vicious. Not for the first time I wondered why someone like she took up teaching. Nurturing and encouraging were words she had no understanding of, yet her heart must have been in the right place at one time for her to embark on it in the first place.

"I blanked it all out the day I left school. Except for stupid stuff. All I remember about geography for instance, is how potholes are formed. And that's only because I kept imagining water rising and drowning any people potholing there."

"Cheerful."

I noticed our glasses had evaporated again and poured us both another refill. Bringing up the subject of Sergeant McLeod was proving more difficult than I expected.

Dee tilted her head to the side. "You must have remembered more than potholes or ya wouldn't have made it to university."

I made a non-committal *hmph* and leaned my back against the armchair. My hand brushed the card in my pocket. "Can I talk to you, Deirdre?"

"Uh-oh. Sounds serious." She rested her elbows on the coffee table. "Sure, as long as it's nothing about arsin' potholes."

"Men business." I pulled out the card and handed to her.

She took it out of the envelope and read it. "Mike?"

"Sergeant McLeod."

Her brow furrowed. "I didn't know you'd seen him again."

"I hadn't. Not until yesterday." I described how he had literally dropped in on me up on the Mournes.

She thrust the card back. "That's quite the grand gesture. Bloody selfish, if ya ask me."

My eyes widened. "What do you mean?"

"What if someone had seen him with you?"

"What if they had? He might have just been asking directions."

She snorted with laughter. I did too when I realized how absurd I sounded. "We were far enough up the Mournes so that even if someone did see the helicopter, they wouldn't have known I was anywhere near it."

She drained her glass and took her time pouring us another.

"Say something, Deirdre," I entreated.

"Looks like you've already made up yer mind." She relented with a lopsided grin. "I never thought I'd see the ice princess all gooey over a guy like this. Go on, then. Just don't invite him here."

"I have to! I can't very well have him come to Mourneview. Or should I just prance into Ballykinlar and let everyone and their grandmother see me going in?"

"We'll be tarred and feathered for having an English soldier in the apartment!"

"He's American, actually."

She considered this, twirling the stem of her glass round and round on the table. I waited, biting my lip so hard it hurt. She gave a heavy sigh. "All right, put yourself out of your misery. Go call him."

I scooted round the table and grabbed her, giving her a hug. She patted my back just like my mother did when I embraced her. "I hope he's worth it, Jen. If the 'RA doesn't kill me, me brothers will if they find out."

"No one will find out. Not if we don't tell."

"What'll your parents say?"

"Fuck, I'm just going to meet up with him, not marry him. I'm supposed to marry a farmer anyway, remember?"

She snorted. "Yeah, and I'm to marry the Pope."

Laughing, I grabbed the china piggy bank by the bathroom door. Taking a handful of coins, I stepped out onto the landing and located the timed light switch our thrifty landlord had installed to save on electricity. A bleak yellowish bulb blinked on, exposing the shabby stairway. I only had so long to get to the next switch at the landing below before the light went out, entombing me again. I charged, pressing each switch as I passed until I reached the downstairs hall. The switch there was just inside the front door, across the passage from the payphone attached to the wall. I laid McLeod's card open on the top of the rotary phone to read the numbers. I dialed the first few only to be plunged into darkness again. For fuck's sake, I mustn't have hit the switch properly. Holding the receiver in one hand I stretched across the hall and reached with my other hand for the switch. Slamming my fist against it I stepped back to the phone but had lost my place. Hanging up, I started to redial. *Plunk.* The hall light went off again.

Fucking hell. At this rate I'd lose my nerve completely. I contorted myself all over again to turn the light back on and hurried to finish dialing. After a few whirrs it rang on the other end. The light clicked off but I could see the coin slot glinting in the street lamp through the skylight over the door. A woman's voice answered but her greeting was cut out by the loud pips interrupting. I shoved in a ten pence piece.

"Extension 346, please."

The line transferred immediately and I listened to a crackly recording of McLeod's American accent. *"Mike McLeod. Leave a name and number where you can be reached."* A prolonged beep sounded and I took a breath.

"Hello. It's Jennifer. From the farm with the–" I couldn't resist. "With the cock. You can call me at this number." I recited it, enunciating clearly, then hung up.

I climbed all the way up to the apartment, barely making it to the top step before the phone shrilled. I hurtled back down in the dark. Light flooded the hall as the ground floor neighbor threw open her door. She wore only a towel wrapped around her ample girth, and water dripped from her hair. I hurled myself down the last of the stairs as she reached for the phone. "That's for me!" I howled. She shrugged and went back into her apartment. I grabbed the receiver, my heart pounding. "Hello? Jennifer Hamilton," I added, attempting to sound nonchalant.

"Hey," came McLeod's voice. "Need any weathervanes fixing?"

I had more courage on the phone when I couldn't see him. "Not here, but judging by your flying there'll be several in the Mournes in need of attention."

He laughed. The first time I'd heard it, a rich, deep sexy sound. "You want to go for a drive Saturday?" he asked. "How about the north coast? There's a giant's roadway up there is supposedly the eighth wonder of the world."

I laughed. "The Giant's Causeway? Well, I wouldn't go so far as to say that, but yes, it's about the only big tourist attraction we have in Northern Ireland."

"Oh, I wouldn't say that," he replied, a bantering tone in his voice. While I racked my brain for something witty to retort he continued. "So, you interested?"

Was I interested? *Strewth.* "I'd love to, thanks. I could show you my most favorite place if you like. It's just up the coast from the Causeway."

"Where's that?"

"Dunluce Castle. A ruin. It's just - it looks so - well, beautiful." God, why couldn't I put a coherent sentence together?

"Sounds like a plan. We'll picnic there first and hit the Causeway on the way back. Pick you up at ten?"

"Okay, Sergeant."

"And Jennifer?"

"Yes?"

"Call me 'Mike'."

⌘

On Saturday I woke up just after six, well before the alarm. I crept stealthily out and gently shut the door behind me so I wouldn't disturb Dee in her warm cocoon across the room. It felt bitterly cold so I laid the fire and lit it. I dug into the piggy bank for a fifty pence piece so I'd have plenty of hot water. I wanted to take my time with a proper bath and wash my hair. We didn't have a shower but made do with a forked rubber hose that had a showerhead on the end. It attached by two nozzles to the taps in the bath. Not being air tight, we had to wind washcloths around the top of each nozzle to stop water spraying all over the place. More often than not one of the nozzles would slip completely off, alternatively scalding or freezing us.

The living room felt lovely and warm when I emerged from the steamy bathroom. Wearing my old bathrobe I boiled up the kettle to make tea. Dee joined me in the kitchen, sleepily putting two slices of toast under the grill while the tea stewed. Buttering them both, she slathered marmalade on top, and held one out to me.

I shook my head. "No thanks." My insides felt tied in knots.

"Ya got to eat, young lady," admonished Dee, parroting her mother. "Can't have ya fainting all over the place, can we?"

I gave in and we sat by the fireside. The toast stuck in my throat and I had to wash it down with the tea. I felt ridiculous being so nervous about seeing McLeod. I couldn't work out if it was because he was a British soldier or because I wanted so much for him to like me. Maybe I should cancel the whole bloody thing. Except by now he'd be on his way from Ballykinlar.

Dee took our plates to the kitchen. "Go get dressed. I'll make yer sandwiches."

Bugger, I'd forgotten I meant to do that first thing! "Oh, you darling, thank you."

"Anything to stop ya having a nervous breakdown."

I went to the bedroom to put on the outfit that had taken days to carefully select. Clinging bell-bottom jeans and tight chocolate brown sweater that nicely defined my curves. The north coast in February would be absolutely freezing, so over the sweater I pulled on a heavy Aran cardigan that my mother had knitted. Then I rethought the jeans. They'd be no match to the frigid temperature so I pulled them off, yanked on a pair of woolen tights and slipped the jeans over them. By nine-thirty I was ready to go and kept vigil by the window, nipping back repeatedly to the mirror to check my reflection.

"For God's sake," complained Dee. "You're making me dizzy." She opened a cupboard in the kitchen and pulled out our emergency bottle of Bushmills whiskey. She unscrewed the cap, took a swig from the bottle and handed it to me.

"Get this down yer neck. Better than Valium any day."

I gulped a mouthful that scorched its way down my gullet. If someone lit a match I'd breathe fire like a dragon. *God,* I couldn't meet Mike stinking of whiskey! I thrust the bottle back and ran to the bathroom to scrub my teeth. A great rumbling approached from outside.

"He's here!" called Dee. And you're never going to believe the state of him."

I dashed back to join her at the window. A leather-clad biker on a powerful red shiny motorbike pulled up at the curb outside our building. People passing by turned to stare. The roaring abruptly stopped and the biker reached up to remove his matching red helmet. The thicket of dark hair confirmed it was Mike.

"Discreet, isn't he?" she remarked.

I felt like running and hiding under the covers of my bed. Mustering my courage I slipped my leather aviator's jacket on over the Aran cardigan and sweater. "God, with all these layers I feel like the fucking Michelin man."

Dee rolled her eyes and shoved me toward the door. "Piss off before he thinks you've stood him up." She bent to retrieve a discarded black anorak from the floor. "Better take this if you're going to be on a bike."

Now I really would look like the Michelin man. Or a massive, charred marshmallow. I didn't recognize the anorak. "Where'd this come from?"

"Clance forgot it. He came by at the weekend."

I'd forgotten I'd asked him to. Lucky for me he did, I guess. A large thermal glove was stuffed in each pocket, and I found his Celtic Football scarf tucked into one of the sleeves. I laid the scarf on the arm of the sofa, slung the anorak over my arm and picked up my shoulder bag.

Dee handed me a foil-wrapped package. "Don't forget these."

I slipped it into my bag and gave her a hug. "Thank you. I don't know how I managed before you moved in."

"Just remember when it's my turn." She opened the door and laid a hand on my arm, halting me. "Be careful, okay?"

7
Ghosts, Seagulls, and Giants

In the hall on the ground floor I paused, taking a deep breath before opening the front door. McLeod stood on the bottom step, pulling off a glove. I intercepted him before he could ring the doorbell. He looked even more stunning than ever, dressed in head-to-toe biking leather, and tousled hair. The epitome of some designer aftershave advertisement. Once again the ability to think of one single coherent word left me.

"Hey. You look gorgeous." His eyes crinkled attractively at the corners as he smiled.

I immediately felt better even though I knew the Michelin man wasn't gorgeous. "Thank you." I resisted adding, *So do you.*

Out of the corner of my eye I noticed movement and caught sight of the ground floor neighbor peering out from behind her grubby net curtain. Bypassers took notice of us, too. I flushed, suddenly feeling an overwhelming sense of dread. Mike stood out like the proverbial sore thumb. "Maybe this wasn't such a good idea."

His eyes softened. He put a hand out and his thumb lightly brushed the fading scratch on my cheek. I bit my lip. It's the first time we'd actually touched since the Boxing Day *céildh*.

He took the anorak from my grasp and held it out so I could slip my arms in. "It'll be all right, Jennifer. No one will suspect your Yankee biker dude is in the military, trust me."

How did he know that's what I'd been thinking? But he was right, of course. In his leather gear he couldn't look more *un*like a soldier. He led me over to the bike and opened up the trunk attached to the back. The name 'Suzuki' shone in silver on the sides of the bike, and the number 1000 further back. Powerful indeed.

Mike lifted out a second red helmet and handed it to me. I slipped it over my head and with his help fastened the buckles. Putting his own back on he climbed onto the bike. I pulled on Clancy's gloves and took the hand Mike offered to help me clamber on behind him. My first time on a motorcycle! I felt a mixture of excitement and terror as the engine gunned into life under me.

"Hold on tight!" he shouted.

I placed my hands on either side of his waist. All hard muscle. Vibrating with laughter he reached back, grasped my wrist and pulled my arm all the way round his middle. He patted my other hand and I obediently clasped my hands together around his waist. It was astonishingly intimate, holding him against me with the powerful throb of the bike between my thighs. I'm glad he couldn't see my burning face, which probably matched the shade of the helmet.

I caught a glimpse of platinum hair at the attic room window and took one hand off Mike's waist long enough to wave. Dee returned it as we launched down Botanic Avenue toward Belfast city center. The bike was sturdy enough under me but I still felt exposed. If we got into an accident there was nothing to cushion the impact. I tried not to imagine the skin ripping from my body on the rough tarmac of the road. But by the time we'd reached the bottom of Botanic Avenue and traversed the bottleneck junction at Shaftesbury Square, I felt less apprehensive. Mike confidently navigated the traffic, obviously knowing what he was doing.

We rumbled downtown and past Queen Victoria's statue outside the City Hall. Just beyond sat the black taxi stand, an island of curving pavement. I did a double take. The fiery-haired guy in the long leather coat I'd seen the day of the bombing stood there. He and the smaller guy were hunched together attempting to light cigarettes behind sheltering hands. Beside them a cabbie loaded what looked like an amp and an electric guitar case into the back of the taxi. That explained the glamorous and distinctive look. He must be with a local band. Come to think of it, I wondered if he could have been the guy I'd seen at the *céildh*? How many guitar players from Belfast had long glorious red locks like that?

I expected Mike to take the motorway but he turned toward the ferry town of Larne. The bike made short work of the winding coast road, the North Channel glistening to our right. At times it felt like we literally flew. We sped through Larne and on past the supposedly haunted Ballygally Castle, now a hotel. At a particularly sharp bend in the road, terror-struck, I thought we'd careen into the ocean. But we passed safely through the town of Cushendall and braved the tiny, twisting lane along the coast to Ballycastle. The words of a song I'd learned at Sunday school choir came to mind: *'The wee road, the sunny road, the twisting winding mountain road–'* Cringing, I realized I was humming out loud. With a bit of luck the noise of the bike had drowned me out.

Neither tractors nor wandering sheep on the road could hold us up. In what seemed like no time at all the bike climbed the brow of a hill, the other side revealing Dunluce Castle in its dramatic, rugged beauty. It jutted out on its own promontory, silhouetted against the sea. I don't know what it was about this place that I loved so much. If I believed in reincarnation maybe I could have been someone who lived here in the past.

Mike turned the bike into the narrow lane that led up to the car park at the castle. After the racket of the engine the contrasting quiet was almost overpowering. My legs felt unsteady as I dismounted and I continued to feel the vibration of the engine thrumming under me as I got my bearings.

Mike surveyed the castle. "Your favorite place, huh?"

"Yes."

He nodded. "I can see why."

It delighted me that he liked it. I hadn't realized until now how important it had been that he did. He tipped open the bike trunk and pulled out a bulging canvas bag.

"I brought some sandwiches too," I said, although they had probably been crushed by now in my shoulder bag.

The National Trust owned the castle and it was open to the public all year round. But in February we pretty much had the place to ourselves, with maybe four other people wandering through the ruins. I led Mike down a great many stone steps to the shore at the foot of the castle, where a sheltered grassy area gave way to rocks that guarded the sea.

Mike looked all around him, turning in a circle before unfastening the canvas bag. He produced a rolled up rug, which he shook out and spread on the ground. Taking my hand he helped me down and folded himself down beside me. Then he took out a bottle shape wrapped in multiple plastic bags, two plastic saucer-shaped glasses, and three Tupperware boxes, which held smoked salmon, a brie-like cheese with blue stuff in it, and crackers.

I needn't have bothered bringing the sandwiches at all. "You've thought of everything!"

He grinned. "Hope so."

I removed Clancy's gloves and opened up my bag. The foil package was indeed squished but not as badly as I'd feared. I unwrapped it and placed my offering on the rug by the rest of the food. "My roommate Deirdre made these. No idea what's in them."

He fumbled with the plastic bags. "Shoot," he muttered. "No nails." He held the bottle out to me.

I picked at the plastic until a *Moët & Chandon* label was revealed. I looked at Mike in delighted surprise. I'd only ever had champagne at my eighteenth birthday dinner, and even then only a glass.

He reclaimed the bottle and uncorked it. The pop made me jump even though I'd been expecting it. A man and woman in their twenties appeared at the bottom of the steps. They gave us and our picnic a cursory glance, saw the champagne and strolled on. They headed a discreet distance down to the shore to climb onto one of the big rocks overlooking the sea.

Mike filled the two plastic glasses with bubbly and handed one to me. "What'll we drink to?"

"Deirdre and I usually toast the Queen or the Pope, in no particular order." I didn't tell him exactly how.

"Her Majesty then." He tipped his glass against mine.

"And the Pope. Let's not take sides."

His eyes glinted. "Not today, anyway."

The golden liquid tasted cool and fresh. I loved the feel of the bubbles on my tongue. I felt like a Hollywood star, drinking champers in the middle of the day by the ocean's side. And with perhaps one of the most handsome men in the world.

Mike speared me with an intense look making my heart skip a beat. "Jennifer, I never had a chance to thank you properly. For helping me out in Ballyben."

I felt a rush of pleasure. "You already thanked me. Anyone would have done it in my place."

He barked a laugh. "No, they wouldn't. You got me out of quite a jam."

"Not really. You had back up ready, didn't you?"

He took a sip of champagne, his expression giving nothing away. "You were quite the smooth operator, fitting into that IRA place. Impressive."

His praise thrilled, yet embarrassed me. Self-conscious, I replied, "A lifetime growing up with my Roman Catholic best friend Deirdre obviously paid off. Not that the religion makes any difference," I added quickly. "I mean because of her I'm comfortable in–" I cast about for the right word. "Nationalist situations." Crap, that wasn't what I meant, either. I was babbling.

"I sure hadn't expected to run across you there of all places."

"Same here," I countered. "The last place I expected to see you."

"You're pretty proficient in playing traditional Irish tunes would you say?"

"I take it you didn't stick around to hear me play *Virginia Reel?*"

"So that's yes, you are proficient?"

"Yes." No point in being diffident about it. I was.

"You play in traditional bands often?"

"That was my first time in public. Jammed a few times before." I watched him swirl the champagne in his glass. He'd hardly touched it.

"And exactly how did that transpire?"

This felt like the Spanish Inquisition. "It's Dee's brother Seamus's band."

"And you were helping out."

Was that a question or a statement? "That's right."

He raised his glass toward me. "You're a lady of many hidden talents." He downed the champagne in one swallow.

I flushed crimson and followed suit, so he poured us a refill. Then we got started on the picnic. The salmon, cheese and crackers tasted amazing washed down with the *Moët*. Investigating the sandwiches, they turned out to be ham. I offered one to Mike.

"No thanks. I don't do ham."

"Why not?"

"I'm Jewish."

Oh. I hadn't even wondered about his religion. How exotic. I'd never met anyone Jewish before. A thought occurred to me and I tried to suppress a smile.

"What?" he demanded, catching me.

"With this country the way it is if you were walking down the Falls or Shankill Roads, they'd ask if you were a Catholic Jew or a Protestant Jew."

He grinned. I was glad he got the humor. My insecurities played havoc with me. Was this outing merely his way of thanking me or was it a bona fide date? I wished he weren't so difficult to read.

We polished off most of the picnic and reclined on the rug to watch the sea. Neither of us dared take off our coats it was so fiercely cold. We probably looked ridiculous, behaving as though it were summer and not deep winter, but I didn't care. The day was magical. Waves crashed against the rocks, shooting flecks of foam into the air. I found the sound soothing along with the intermittent keen of seagulls soaring above. Mike sat up and inspected the remnants of our picnic. There were a few crackers left and I'd torn off the thick crusts from the sandwiches. He broke them up into pieces, tossing them toward the seagulls. With the uncanny sense that birds have, at once two dozen or more appeared out of nowhere, squawking overhead and scuttling on the ground. I peered up at the castle walls high above us to see another stream of gulls zeroing in from the furthest promontory. "Looks like you've disturbed the kitchen maids," I warned.

Mike looked round inquiringly.

I pointed. "See how the cliff is shaved away at the edge? In the sixteen-hundreds when Dunluce lost its kitchens to the sea in a storm, the maids working there fell to their deaths. Nowadays they say the cries of the seagulls are the cries of their ghosts."

One elegant dark eyebrow shot up. "Cheerful lot, you Irish, aren't you?"

Irritation flashed through me. "I wouldn't know. I'm British."

He looked away and watched the sprays of foam spurting up from the nearby rocks. I regretted snapping.

"That your kitchen maids?" he asked, indicating the foam.

Relieved I hadn't caused offense, I laughed. "Oh, that's supposed to be Neptune making love to his queen."

Mike turned the full headlights of his compelling gaze on me. "Is that a suggestion?"

I blushed. Now I had no doubt that this was a date. "Behave yourself, Sergeant!" I teased.

Tensing, he looked swiftly toward the couple on the rock but they were totally absorbed in each other. He bent forward and spoke softly. "Try not to mention my rank in public, if you don't mind."

I bit my lip. "Sorry. Wasn't thinking."

His gaze dropped to my mouth. I held my breath as he leaned closer and our lips touched. I felt like electrical currents coursed through me. My head swam, probably from holding my breath, and I had the sensation of falling. Gasping, I pulled back. His beautiful dark eyes under their thick lashes met mine, then he slid a hand behind my head to draw me back. I closed my eyes and gave in. And just hoped he'd catch me if I fell.

⌘

After the picnic just enough daylight remained for us to stop by the Giant's Causeway. I didn't really think it was worth the effort.

"Isn't the Causeway a big deal?" he asked, seeing my diffidence.

I felt quite clever as I quoted his countryman, Samuel Johnson: *"It's worth seeing, but not worth going to see."* But we were so close to it and it'd be a shame if he didn't at least see where the Giant's 'stepping stones' began. By this time the car park was deserted, so he drove on down the little track to where the Causeway rose out of the ocean. Basalt columns formed hexagonal stepping stones that led from the cliffs, disappearing under the water. Further along the cliffs, certain columns took the shape of a huge throne and a pipe organ set into the cliff. They were a bit of a hike away and best left for another day.

"So, what's the story about this place?" Mike asked.

I parroted what Mum told me. "There's a fun legend about Finn MacCoul who lived here. He was fighting with another giant in Scotland, and grabbed a chunk of Ireland to toss at him. If you look at a map of the British Isles and see the shape of the Isle of Man between here and the mainland, it's about the same shape as Lough Neagh. That's the bit he tore out of the earth."

Mike chuckled. "Kitchen maids, seagulls, and giants. What next?"

"Finn MacCoul's said to be sleeping in Black Mountain above Belfast, waiting for Ireland's direst hour so he can come to the rescue."

"Bit late, ain't he?"

We both laughed and he turned the bike around, heading inland to the car park.

The whole way back from the north coast, all I thought about was Mike. Kissing him, holding him, our bodies pressed tightly together.

Even the speed at which he drove the bike down the M-2 couldn't divert my thoughts. If that couple hadn't been close by on the rocks at Dunluce, who knows how far we might have gone. I believe I'd have gladly ripped off all my clothes and let Mike take me there and then. Which is saying a lot considering my virgin state.

The amber T-shaped fog lights down the motorway central divider blurred as the bike raced toward Belfast. My lips felt raw and chapped. Not just from the wind but from our extended, passionate kissing. I must have lost all reason. I'd never felt nor acted like this before. I'd secretly always wondered why Dee made such a big deal over sex. My very few - actually two attempts had been ungainly and embarrassing. If this powerful, aching need that consumed me was anything to go by, I finally understood. *The ice princess melteth indeed.*

Back in Belfast he had to park the bike on the side street closest to the apartment as the front was chock-a-block with parked cars. I dismounted and almost fell. My legs had stiffened up from being in the same position for so long. As Mike stowed my helmet back in the trunk I shifted my weight from foot to foot until the circulation got going again.

Keeping his helmet on he walked me the few yards to my front door. He was so silent he unnerved me. Would he ask me out again or not? Had I made a complete fool of myself, getting so worked up over our kissing?

When all else failed, one could always fall back on good manners. Behind the attic curtain a soft light glowed, indicating that Dee was home. I took a deep breath. "Would you like to come in for a cup of tea?" If she hadn't been there I'm not sure I'd have had the nerve to ask.

His manner relaxed and he unclipped his helmet. "That'd be cool, thanks."

Did he feel as awkward as I did? I found that hard to believe. He pulled the helmet off as I fumbled in my bag for my key. I unlocked and pushed open the door, feeling along the wall for the timed switch. Light flooded the dingy hall. I gave Mike a smile as I led the way upstairs, trying not to show how uncertain I felt. Halfway up the second flight, the stairway plunged back into darkness. Typical.

An arm slid round my waist and lifted me off my feet. I gasped, dropping my bag. Mike's helmet fell with a thud and rolled away as he set me down on the step above him. I glimpsed his smile in the light cast by the skylight, then his mouth claimed mine. I almost lost my footing and he steadied me, pressing me up against the wall. My arms slid around him and we kissed as ravenously as at Dunluce. God, he was incredible. Lips soft and teasing one moment, hard and supple the next. The tip of his tongue tantalized mine until I thought I'd spontaneously combust.

The sound of a toilet flushing in the first floor apartment made both of us freeze. Mike laughed, his breath warm on my neck. "I couldn't help myself," he whispered. Stepping back he stooped to the landing to locate his helmet.

Heart pounding, I retrieved my bag and we continued on up to the attic. A slant of light filtered vertically from our door. Obviously the lock had not caught again. I pushed it open and halted in surprise. Mike just stopped short of colliding into me. Clancy and Dee sat cozily by the fire, sharing a pot of tea.

"Hello you two," I said. They both turned their heads.

I felt Mike's body tense up behind me and glanced over my shoulder. His gaze was fixed on Clancy, his face taut. Mug in hand, Clancy stood so quickly he spilled tea on the floor.

"That bloody door." Dee grabbed the closest thing to hand, Clancy's Celtic scarf on the arm of the sofa, and knelt to mop at the tea. The two men seemed frozen in place.

"Do you know each other?" I asked.

"No," mumbled Clancy. He bent to put his mug on the coffee table. "I should get going." He moved toward the door.

"Oh!" I remembered his anorak and shrugged out of it, making sure the gloves were in the pockets. "Kept it warm for you. Thank you." He took it and I shifted to let him pass. To my astonishment Mike didn't move and Clancy was forced to dodge around him. He clattered down the stairs without switching on the timed light.

"I should go, too," said Mike.

"What about tea?"

"Next time, beautiful." He gave me a chaste peck on the cheek. "I'll call you when I get leave - in a couple of weeks."

He gave Dee a nod, spun round and pretty much leapt down the dark stairway. I touched the spot on my face where he'd kissed me.

Dee stood, tea-sodden scarf in hand. "What the fuck?"

I shook my head. "No idea."

She dashed over to the window, jerking the curtain aside to peer out. I joined her. Mike stood on the pavement below, scanning the street. After an instant he walked away, fastening his helmet. A moment later the bike gave an earsplitting rumble, then came briefly into sight until Mike turned left, heading back toward the city center. Dee let the curtain drop into place. "He's a dark horse, your gallant soldier, isn't he?"

I crossed over and shut the front door, leaning a shoulder to it to make sure the lock caught. "So is your brother by the looks of it. Did he just drop by or what?"

Her face darkened. "Ach, it was awful, Jen. A couple of teenagers were killed earlier tonight."

I frowned. "I'm sorry. Did you know them?"

"No, they were friends of my wee brother's in Armagh. They were mistaken in the dark for a British Army foot patrol and accidentally got blown up. By the 'RA."

"God, that's terrible." I wondered why Clancy had come to deliver the news if Dee hadn't known them.

She went to the kitchen, drew out the Bushmills whiskey and waggled it at me. "Medicinal purposes?" To my nod she got out shot glasses and brought it all to the coffee table. "Debriefing, Ma'am?" Her pseudo-American accent came straight out of *Dukes of Hazard*.

I grinned. "Why, that would be fine and dandy, little darlin'. Gimme a sec." In the bedroom I peeled off all my clothes and sagged with relief. Glad though I'd been for all the layers at Dunluce and the bike, they now suffocated me and were damp with perspiration.

I thought about her brother's friends who'd been shot by the IRA. I used to wonder why people said 'RA instead of 'IRA'. Dee told me it's because we were already in Ireland so they were the 'Republican Army'.

Shrugging into my pink bathrobe I inspected my reflection in the mirror. My cheeks looked like rosy circles above my tumid lips. A thrill shot through me. I still felt the pressure of Mike's mouth on mine and my chin prickled from his five o'clock shadow.

Dee held out a shot glass as I joined her by the fire. Golden Bushmills glowed in the light from the flames. "I can tell yer date went well, just by looking at you," she said. "So, tell me all about *Michael* on the *cycle*, then."

I snorted. "Ah, a *recital* - of what happened with *Michael*?"

"Touché. Yes. And don't leave anything out."

8

Betrayal

Monday morning it concerned me when Clancy didn't show up for the economics lecture. It was so unlike him. If he hadn't put in an appearance by lunchtime I'd go round to his place to check on him. Then I realized I didn't actually know where he lived. He'd never taken me to the apartment he shared with three other male students, whom according to him were a filthy rabble. But Dee would know his address.

At noon I headed for the canteen. To my relief I found Clancy sitting at a table by the window. Deeply absorbed, he pored over text books and scribbled in a notepad. I bought a bowl of soup and an apple at the counter and approached, clunking my tray down hard. He didn't move a muscle, just stared impassively as I sat opposite.

"How are you?" I challenged. Now that I knew he was all right I felt pissed off. But I added a smile in spite of my sharp tone.

He didn't return it. "I'm okay." He put down his pen. "You?"

"Fine. But then I'm not the one who went storming off on Saturday night. What was all that about?"

He had the temerity to look puzzled. "What was what about?"

I *tsked*. "You and Mike. You've met before, haven't you?"

His hand strayed to one of the text books where his thumb worried at the corner of a page. "What makes you say that?"

"It's pretty obvious, Clance."

He slammed the book shut, startling me. "You need to stick to your own kind, Jen."

I blinked. "You got something against Americans?" I asked, although I knew he didn't mean that.

His lip curled. It actually curled. "We both know better than that. For your sake I advise you to drop all association with the likes of him."

"Or what?"

"Consider this a friendly warning or you'll be considered a collaborator." He glared at me with something akin to hatred. I gaped, completely in shock. "A *traitor*, Jen. Don't see him again." He gathered up his books and without another glance at me, got up and strode out of the canteen.

I fought the impulse to chase after him. Face flushing, I glanced around but no one had witnessed our exchange. My soup grew cold, I couldn't eat now. I toyed with my apple, rolling it on the table while gazing unseeing out of the window. A friendly warning. From people who would consider me a collaborator. No prizes for guessing who - his brother's friends in Ballyben.

⌘

When I got home that night I told Dee what had happened. I'd almost been afraid to.

"Look, he'll come around," she said. "He gets weird ideas at times. Rebel without a cause and all that."

"But he called me a collaborator. A traitor. That sounds like he has more than a cause."

"He feels passionately about a United Ireland, that's all. Give him time."

"But why's he so angry?"

A spark from the fire sputtered onto the hearth. She crouched down to adjust the grate and spat onto her index finger to extinguish the ebbing cinder. "If you don't understand, Jen," she said slowly, "then there's no explaining it to you. Mike McLeod is a soldier in an army of occupation."

A surge of fury rose in me so fast I felt dizzy. I let out the breath I didn't know I held. "*Army of occupation?* Dee, they're here to protect us!"

She spiraled round and met my angry glare head on. "You really believe that, don't you?"

"Well, without them here the INLA or the IR fucking A would kill a hell of a lot more people, that's for sure."

"And then we'd have peace. A United Ireland without the Brits."

My stomach twisted. She meant without Brits *like me*.

"It'd be the end of the Troubles, Jen," she insisted.

"It wouldn't, Dee. I can't believe you don't see that. There'd be a civil war. A bloodbath." My voice shook. The bloodbath that would kill my kind so she and her Fenian compatriots could have her fucking United Ireland. I swallowed and leaned back against the chair. I knew she didn't mean that. She couldn't have. And I didn't mean to think of her as a Fenian. "Look, I'm sorry, Deirdre. You and I should know better than to talk about this crap."

She got up and went to the kitchen to pour us both another shot of Bushmills. "We can't really avoid it." She handed me one. "With you rubbing our faces in it, can we?"

She was right. But I was, too. I wanted to yell in my defense that Mike was an American, not a Brit. But it didn't matter. He fought in the British Army, and almost half the population in Northern Ireland felt so strongly against British rule that they were prepared to go to war over it.

Tears surged. I put the shot down on the coffee table and buried my face in my hands. If dating Mike was going to come between a friendship that had lasted a lifetime, then I knew I'd have to give him up. I felt a hand on my shoulder. Dee handed me a hanky. She was in tears too, and we hugged each other.

"Ach, Jen, I'm sorry. I don't want to spoil things for you. For fuck's sake, I've known ya for twenty-two fuckin' years. I've never seen you go gaga over a guy." She gave a humorless laugh. "I just wish it hadn't had to be a British soldier."

I blew my nose. "So do I. Will Clancy tell on me?"

"I'll talk to him. I'm sure he won't once he thinks about it. Our families have been friends too long. Come on, drink yer Bush."

We smiled ruefully and clinked glasses.

She raised an eyebrow. "Fuck the Queen?"

Somehow it didn't seem funny anymore. "Fuck the Pope." I made sure not to look at the piercing gaze of the Sacred Heart of Jesus on the wall.

⌘

I had to wait three long weeks before the next date with Mike. Most of the time I managed to throw myself into coursework at Queen's to distract myself. The anticipation of the upcoming date helped fill the void that Clancy's absence had created. Used to having him constantly by my side in class, I felt adrift. He hadn't 'come around' as Dee thought he might. To my shock, after our contretemps in the canteen he transferred to the other lecturer. I sought him out and cornered him in an outside alcove by the main hall.

"Still seeing the Brit?" he demanded before I had a chance to speak.

"None of your bloody business, Clancy."

"It is, if you're a collaborator."

"Don't be ridiculous. You know me better than that."

"Obviously I don't know you at all, Jennifer."

The look of disgust on his face made me want to belt him one. "So, you going to tell on me?"

"Not if you've stopped seeing him."

My voice shook. "As I said before, whom I see is none of your business. And you'll tell no one about Mike - I don't think it'd go down too well with your IRA friends if they knew you're *gay*." As soon as the words were out I regretted them.

His face closed up, mouth in a hard line. "Then we have nothing more to say to each other."

I felt ghastly. But he'd betrayed *me*, whether he told on me or not. Fuck him. Bloody bigot.

Dee was busy with rehearsals for *The Shadow of a Gunman*. None of her family could make opening night, and as it fell on the same day Mike had leave, she arranged two front row seats for us. I felt a stab of apprehension in case Clancy might show up, but Dee assured me he was off to Dublin for the weekend. The family would attend en masse the following week, and they were throwing a late supper party afterward in one of the swanky hotels in Belfast. I was invited, but naturally couldn't bring Mike.

On the Friday he was due to arrive I played hooky from Queen's as it was a light day lecture-wise. Every surface and piece of furniture in the apartment gleamed, and I'd finally cleared the floor of clutter. Tired of coats and paraphernalia being dumped willy-nilly by the door, I'd bought a slightly warped-with-age bamboo coat stand at the nearby charity shop.

I put the finishing touches to the apartment by lighting a fire, folding up Dee's cot bed, and putting clean sheets on my bed. Just in case. I felt my face flush. How presumptive of me! But the simple truth was I was tired of waiting for the 'right' man and marriage and all that to come along. If it hadn't happened by now it was never going to. At twenty-two years of age it was high time I joined the ranks of the sexually experienced.

I took my time getting ready, putting on makeup and the dress I intended to wear later to Dee's opening night. A simple rose pink knee-length sheath made from raw silk.

At two o'clock I was ready. He was to arrive any time after two, I wasn't sure how long I'd have to wait. My stomach churned, a mass of nerves. It kept rumbling loudly even though I'd forced myself to eat earlier. I hoped it would shut the hell up when he got here. Roaming from window to fireplace and back, I caught sight of my violin case propped up in the corner of the living room. I'd neglected it of late. Without Clancy to help me at class anymore I had to spend a lot more time studying.

I took it to the sofa and set to, tweaking violin and bow until they were in perfect shape and tune. I tucked the violin between my shoulder and chin, and raised the bow. Closing my eyes I sat still, bow poised above the strings. I loved doing that. Not actually planning what to play, but finding what came to me out of the meditative silence. My fingers found the notes for the traditional Irish tune, *Carrickfergus*. My bow, like a medium, séanced the sorrowful melody from the strings. I sang the lyrics in my head at first, but then the need for song burst from me and I accompanied myself with the violin.

> "'*But the sea is wide and I can't swim over*
> *Neither have I the wings to fly.*
> *If I could find me a handy boatman.*
> *To ferry me over my love and I–'*"

I opened my eyes to find a dark figure standing halfway in the doorway. I screamed, the violin screeching in unison as I raked the bow across the strings.

"It's just me." Mike pushed the door fully open.

"That bloody lock." I put the violin and bow on the floor by the sofa. "You scared the shit out of me."

He closed the door behind him until it clicked and stood uncertainly, a dark blue canvas overnight bag and helmet in hand. Speech escaped me as ever so I got up and went to him, raising up on my tip-toes to kiss him. He tossed the helmet into the nearby armchair, hurled his bag blindly at the nearest corner, and gripped me tightly against him. In a heartbeat we had picked up where we left off three weeks ago in the dark stairway.

I felt him tense. He broke free, looking over my shoulder. "That yours?" he asked.

I looked round and saw the Sacred Heart of Jesus and lamp on the wall.

"Deirdre's. I should put one of the Queen up beside it, shouldn't I? Or of Ian Paisley." He was a prominent Protestant preacher, extremely and loudly anti-Catholic.

Mike smiled but I noticed it didn't quite reach his eyes. I suppose that kind of blatant Catholic thing would give him pause. His reaction made me think of Clancy's warning.

"You remember Clancy from when you were here before?" I asked. Mike nodded, his expression unreadable. "He warned me off seeing you."

"I see." Still no visible reaction. "Did he threaten you?"

"Just a 'friendly warning' not to see you again." I watched his bland expression closely. "You don't seem surprised."

He shrugged. "It's no surprise that the British Army isn't welcome."

"How does Clancy know who you are?"

"I might have seen him about. We see a lot of people." He reached a hand to tuck a wayward strand of my hair behind my ear. Even that light and casual touch sent tingles through me. "Any tea going?" he asked.

"Absolutely." Glad of the excuse to do something I went to the kitchen and switched the kettle on. I warmed the teapot with hot water from the tap, tossed it out and spooned in some Tetley tea leaves. Then I poured boiling water into the teapot.

Mike hovered, his motorcycle jacket still on. I held out my arms. "Let me take that."

He unzipped it and handed it to me. I hung it on the rickety coat stand, hoping its weight wouldn't tip the entire thing over. He settled down on the sofa while I returned to the kitchen, popped the red, white, and blue knitted tea cozy, courtesy of Mum, on the teapot and brought it over to the hearth. Mike studied my every move, making me feel self-conscious and gauche.

Dee and I never bothered with sugar bowls or anything, so I put the milk bottle and bag of sugar on the tray with the mugs, and brought it all over to the coffee table. Mum would be horrified at my lack of social polish. Although she might be more shocked to learn my visitor was the dashing sergeant she'd gotten so giggly over.

By habit I made to sit opposite in the armchair, but diverted and took a seat beside Mike on the sofa. "Two sugars, right?"

He nodded. "Good memory."

I poured the tea and added sugar. "So do you think you might have seen Clancy in Ballyben?"

He brushed at a piece of fluff on the thigh of his blue jeans. "I'd like to forget about work while I'm here, if you don't mind."

I paused with a teaspoonful of sugar in hand. "Clancy is part of your work?"

"I didn't say that!"

I'd never heard him use such a sharp tone before. Except perhaps when he ordered his men to clean up the yard at Mourneview. Face flushing, I stirred the sugar into his tea and handed the mug to him. He put it on the table and snagged my hand, giving it a squeeze.

"Sorry," he said. "Bad week."

His eyes kept straying to the Sacred Heart picture. I hardly noticed it anymore now that I'd gotten used to the eyes following me everywhere.

"Are you looking forward to the play?" I asked in an attempt to distract him.

"Yeah, I haven't seen any live theater here, yet."

"I have to warn you, the play's a bit anti-British."

"I'd expect that from Seán O'Casey. Who's Deirdre playing?"

"Minnie Powell. You know, the brave Fenian heroine helping to murder the British." I cleared my throat. That hadn't been the most tactful thing to say. With his accent it was so easy to forget who he was. I changed the subject again. "Sorry we haven't any biscuits or scones. There's some stale cake left over from Dad's birthday that no one else wanted if you're interested."

Mike put his mug down on the coffee table and brought my knuckles to his lips. "I've everything I need right here."

My heart rate increased. "Ah, you must have been kissing the Blarney Stone."

Plucking the mug out of my hand he placed it beside the other, his eyes glittering in the glow from the fire. "You're the only thing I'm interested in kissing."

He took my face between his hands. I pretty much ignited at the touch of his tongue on mine. We maneuvered sideways so my back reclined against the arm of the sofa. With the length of his torso pressed against me I slid my arms around him, daring to push my hands up under his sweater until I felt bare flesh. As warm and smooth and supple as I knew it'd be. He traced his fingers slowly around the curve of my shoulder and sent shivers through me as he caressed my breast through the material of my dress.

With my spine twisted in an unnatural direction, my muscles cramped, spoiling the mood. I shifted, and Mike rose up on one leg to allow me to move. An almighty crash made us freeze, wide-eyed. The noise seemed to go on forever, then was punctuated by the discordant complaint of a violin. We sat up to survey a total mess of spilled tea, mugs, milk, and sugar. He'd kicked the table over, sending the tray flying. That had hit the violin on the way down, which in turn skittered across the carpet. I lunged over to rescue it. Fortunately unharmed, but the f-holes on its front seemed like raised eyebrows of surprise. I propped it safely against the sofa.

A frantic pounding on the floor followed almost at once. That bloody neighbor! Mike and I collapsed with laughter as we righted the milk bottle and teapot. This was ridiculous, I would never lose my virginity at this rate. Plucking the half-empty bag of sugar from Mike and setting it on the hearth I took him by the hand, pulled him to his feet and boldly led him toward the bedroom.

We were back in each other's arms before we even got there. I felt him fumble for the zipper on the back of my dress and I grabbed the hem of his sweater, yanking it upward. He hauled it over his head, revealing a smoothly toned chest with a little fuzz of dark hair.

He took the shoulders of my dress, drawing it down over my arms. I felt my face flame. Instinctively I crossed my arms over my breasts in their lacy white bra with the pink rosebuds on it. Mike bent his head to kiss me and I allowed gravity to let the dress pool around me on the floor. He shifted his hands down to cup my bottom, squeezing me so hard that his erection pressed against my stomach.

This was actually happening! No going back now.

With his mouth still electrifying mine with kisses, he eased me backwards until I lay on my bed. Yehudi Menuhin gazed thoughtfully from the poster above. I averted my eyes but at least he didn't appear to watch me like Deidre's Sacred Heart of Jesus picture.

Shit, get that image the fuck out of my head!

Mike perched on the bed, bending to undo and remove his boots. With commendable efficiency he took his socks off at the same time. I tried not to smile as he tucked them neatly into his boots. Then he reached into his jeans pocket and drew out a small package, which he placed on my nightstand. A packet of three Durex condoms.

Oh, my God. I almost lost my nerve. Would he be able to tell this was my first time? Maybe I should say something. But then I might spoil the moment.

He unbuttoned his jeans and slipped them to the floor. Underneath he wore what looked like lightweight navy blue shorts rather than the ordinary white Y-fronts I thought all men wore. With a smile he stretched out beside me and took me in his arms. I felt so awkward. I didn't know what to do with my arms - or anything for that matter.

He sensed something amiss and raised himself up on an elbow. "You're okay with this, aren't you?"

By 'this' I suppose he meant us about to make love. I nodded, despising my inexperience and cowardice. He took me at face value - why wouldn't he? Leaning lazily on one arm he slowly traced an index finger down my décolletage, slipping the hand under my bra to caress each breast in turn. Despite me feeling practically numb from nerves the nipples hardened of their own volition. Then his hand slid down my stomach to the top of my white lacy panties. When his fingers breached the elastic I couldn't help but tense. A frown flitted across his face and he withdrew the hand, laying it palm down on my abdomen.

"You haven't done this before," he stated, though he meant it as a question.

I felt so stupid. Unable to lie, I turned my head away and nodded.

"Oh, Jen." His tone sounded somewhere between disbelieving and chiding. "You should have said." He rolled onto his back, taking me with him so I lay with my head on his shoulder.

"But I want to do it," I mumbled, still unable to make eye contact. "I want you."

I felt the muscles in his neck move as he smiled. "We just need to slow down a little." He gathered me tight and kissed the top of my head. "I didn't think you'd still be a virgin at your age."

Stung into defending myself I said, "This is Northern Ireland you're dealing with. Sex is a sin, didn't you know?"

"But you're not a Catholic."

"Doesn't matter. Still a sin."

He let me go and got off the bed, reaching to pull the quilt back. "Get under, it's cold." I obeyed, scurrying under and pulling the quilt up to my chin. "Scoot over." He clambered in, pulling the quilt up over his shoulders and turning so we were face to face. There wasn't a lot of space for two in my narrow single bed.

"I'm sorry, Mike." I felt wretched.

"Are you kidding me?" He put an arm around me and smoothed a hand up and down my back, making me feel like potters' clay under his touch. "I think it's sweet."

Sweet? I didn't want to be sweet.

"It's incredible that you want me to be your first, Jen. I'm honored. Just hope I can live up to your expectations."

I laughed. "I don't think you'll have any trouble doing that."

We started kissing again, but much more slowly and sensually. His lips were so gentle. I felt a pulling sensation between my shoulder blades and realized he'd deftly unhooked my bra using one hand. My breasts spilled free, so pale beside his golden skin.

He rose up on his knees beside me, the covers tenting across his back. Cold air touched me as he reached both hands to peel my panties off. I raised my hips to help and used a foot to slide them to my ankles and kick them away. Mike gazed the length of my naked body. I resisted the desire to cover myself.

"My God, you're beautiful," he murmured.

His words thrilled me. And my God, so did he. His eyes were so dark, the black pupils wide and fathomless. He pulled the cover back over as he lowered himself alongside me. His fingertips grazed down my torso to the top of my thighs.

Then he touched me. I sucked in a breath - everything focused on the gentle pressure of his fingers. He gradually increased the pressure until I couldn't help but writhe against his hand.

God, I never knew it could feel like this.

Mike shifted position and the pressure was replaced by hot breath and the swirl of his tongue. I bounced upright like I'd been shot out of a catapult. Mike lifted his head from where he'd burrowed under the quilt and gave me an inquiring look.

"I've never had that done," I stammered. What if I smelled down there despite my bath? And I hadn't thought to shave - God, what if he suffocated under the heavy quilt?

"Well, it's time you did." He shot me a mischievous grin and retreated back under.

I pushed the quilt down so I wouldn't obsess about whether he had enough oxygen or not. But that was quickly forgotten as waves of intense, indescribable sensation washed through me.

He reduced me to a quivering mass of acute nerve endings and hormonal intoxication by the time he resurfaced. Grinning as he wiped his mouth with the back of his hand, he slid back up beside me, and reached down to pull off his underwear.

Taking my hand, he drew it down to hold him. I marveled at the feel of hard steel with skin as soft as silk. I stole a glance. Looked like he was circumcised if the biology pictures Dee and I had giggled over were anything to go by. He lay back while I started delicately touching him like he had with me. Feeling daring, at the same time I bent my head and ran my tongue around one of his nipples. His skin tasted clean and soapy with his own musky scent mixed in. He groaned deep in his throat - I must be doing it right. Encouraged, I edged my way down his torso, feathering his smooth skin with my lips and tongue. Glad my hair covered my burning face, I brought my mouth close to him and experimentally flicked out my tongue. He drew in a sharp breath.

"Sweet Jesus." He chuckled, pulling away. "Stop." Stretching across me he fumbled on the nightstand.

I watched with a combination of fascination, excitement, and terror as he ripped open the condom package, drew out the transparent rubber and expertly rolled it on.

He slid a knee between my legs and leaned down to kiss me. I tasted my own musk on his tongue, which I found oddly intoxicating. His hand probed me gently, a thumb pressing in tiny circular motions. Already beyond aroused, I strained my pelvis upward and dug my nails into his back.

Hurry up!

Looking steadily into my eyes, he tensed and pushed. I let out a little gasp - it felt like the sting of a rubber band snapping inside me.

Pausing, he rested on one elbow so he could smooth the hair back from my forehead. "All right?"

"Yes," I managed.

He began to move - slowly, achingly slowly. It didn't hurt but I was acutely aware of every incredible nuance as our hips thrust together, growing in intensity. Everything culminated at the same moment - I heard myself cry out and Mike tensed, then collapsed on top of me, letting out a long, hissing sigh.

After a few moments he pulled out of me - an unsettling sensation. In one deft movement he drew the condom off, crumpled it into a ball and dropped it to the floor by the side of the bed.

We nuzzled together in each other's arms. "Awesome, Jen," he murmured.

I didn't have words to describe what I felt. Delight, joy, perhaps liberation. I should have done this years ago.

We must have fallen asleep. The slam of the front door downstairs roused me. Instinctively I knew it was Dee and bolted upright. "Deirdre's back! She'll kill me!"

"Why?"

"She made me promise not to sleep with you on the first date." I pushed him out of bed and leapt up after him.

"This isn't our first–"

"I know, but–"

"Teasing." He had his jeans and sweater on in record time and strode out to the living room, carrying his boots with him.

I scrambled into my dress as best I could, struggling to get the zipper done up. Hauling the quilt over the rumpled bed, I charged into the living room and threw myself beside Mike on the sofa by the fire. He sat nonchalantly, looking as though he'd never left it. Only his bare feet gave him away. There wasn't time to clean up the mess we'd made.

Or the used condom in the bedroom!

The key clicked in the lock and she opened the door.

"Hi, Dee," I greeted her as casually as I could. "How'd your afternoon go?"

She stood in the doorway looking from me and my disarray to the tea things strewn across the floor. Placing a hand on her hip, she looked as disapproving as my own mother would. "Not as well as yours, I think." But a smile threatened at the corner of her mouth. Closing the door she held out a hand to Mike. "Sergeant McLeod, we meet again."

Mike stood and shook her hand. "Hope you're driving more carefully these days."

I watched Dee weigh him up. At least she couldn't say he looked or sounded anything like a British soldier. She set her bag on the kitchen counter, grabbed the dishcloth from the sink and hurled it at me. "Catch!"

I stood like a lemon but Mike shot out a hand and caught it before it hit me in the face. Hunkering down he began retrieving the scattered tea paraphernalia and mopping up. I stowed the violin and bow safely back in their case, and then unobtrusively zipped my dress up completely. Mike took the tray and put it on the counter between the kitchen and living room.

Dee regarded him. "Tell me, Sergeant, what's an American doin' in the British Army?"

He nodded toward her bag, where the script of *The Shadow of a Gunman* poked out. "Jen tells me you have one of the leads in the play. Did it take long to learn your lines?"

Her eyes lit up. "Not too long. The dialog kind of flows naturally and I'd already read the play through several times before the audition."

He smiled his movie-star smile. "I hear you can dance, too."

I listened to them chatter, marveling at how deftly he had won her over and distracted her from her question.

9

They Won't Harm A Girl

Although the Lyric Theatre down by the Lagan River was only about twenty minutes' walk, we ordered a taxi to take the three of us there. While we waited, Dee and I had a hurried exchange when Mike nipped into the bathroom.

"Just tell me you used contraception," she whispered loud enough to carry through the closed bathroom door.

I put a finger to my lips to shush her. "Of course." Although to be perfectly honest it hadn't even occurred to me until Mike produced the packet of condoms.

"He stayin' the night?"

I glanced at his overnight bag in the corner, unzipped and gaping open where he had rummaged for a change of shirt. "Yes."

She sighed. "Well, do me a favor. Move my bed out here before you go to sleep. Don't want to listen to you humping all bloody night."

A huge smile spread across my face. Earlier she'd insisted *he'd* have to sleep out here alone. The thought of an entire lustful night squeezed into my little bed with Mike absolutely thrilled me.

At the theater Dee disappeared backstage to join the cast for a pre-performance warm up while Mike and I settled ourselves in the bar. I decided on the drink de jour, a Southern Comfort and lemonade.

Mike raised an eyebrow. "You sure?"

I wasn't, but wanted to try it. It seemed so American, as though it came from exotic-sounding Virginia like he did. He returned with a glass of golden liquid and a bottle of Newcastle Brown Ale for himself. The Southern Comfort tasted strangely sweet yet sour at the same time. A bit like overripe peaches about to go off.

Mike saw my diffidence and laughed. "Didn't think you'd care for Bourbon."

I loved how he laughed, deep and sexy. I must have gazed at him with unbridled lust, for he sobered and gave me a slow, lazy smile. I felt my cheeks blaze and he leaned over to kiss me on the lips. He was so demonstrative compared to any of the Northern Irish guys I'd been out with. I saw girls glancing appreciatively at him and felt a rush of pride that I was the one with this gorgeous, attentive man.

The auditorium opened up after that and we took our seats in the center of the front row. A small, modern theater that operated with no curtain, our chairs sat less than five feet from the stage, which was only about three feet high. On stage stood a realistic set of a 1920s slum tenancy: fireplace, books, desk, and antique typewriter.

I peered over my shoulder at the rows filling up, glad for Dee that opening night would be packed. Most of the audience had really dressed up for the occasion. Women wore lots of heavy gold jewelry and nice dresses, men in smart suits and ties. The skirt of my pink dress rode up when I sat, exposing more thigh than I felt comfortable with and I kept having to pull it down. Mike teased me by placing a hand above my knee to block me. He wore his blue jeans and a long-sleeved white shirt, open at the collar. He looked gloriously American, carefree and unpretentious.

"I sure wish you'd told me they dress for the theater here," he grumbled. "I feel like a slob."

I raised an eyebrow. "You could have worn your dress uniform."

"Yeah, right."

"At least you'd be the center of attention."

He snorted. "And of a crossfire."

The house lights dimmed and the audience hushed. Mike gently squeezed my expanse of leg and took hold of my hand. My nerves were fraught for Dee, but when she bounced onstage as Minnie looking to borrow a cup of milk from Donal, the main character, she completely blew me away. She was a natural born actress, her flirty performance of Minnie outstanding. Totally believable, at times I found myself forgetting it was she behind the character.

The play however, made me a tad uncomfortable in places. Séan O'Casey pulled no punches, and I sneaked a glance at Mike to see his reaction to some of the anti-British phrases, like *'heartless English tyrant, the Saxon coward an' knave'*. He looked fully absorbed, an elbow on the arm of the seat and his chin resting on his knuckles.

Near the end of the play Minnie saved Donal from being arrested by taking a bag of bombs for him. "*I'll take them to my room,*" said Dee confidently as Minnie. "*Maybe they won't search it; if they do, they won't harm a girl.*" She closed the bag and lifted it, holding it against her chest. Just by her manner and stance you could tell the inner conflict of the character. She was terrified the Auxiliaries would discover the bombs, yet excited to be taking such a risk for Ireland's freedom. Dee walked slowly to the door at the back of the set, commanding the entire theater. The audience was intensely silent, utterly enthralled.

Just before she exited she turned back. "*Goodbye - Donal!*"

Of course they found the bombs and took her away. I'd never sat down and read the play so was startled along with the rest of the audience at the sound of explosions and gunfire offstage. Apparently Minnie was shot through the heart trying to jump from an ambush the IRA had laid in place for the Auxiliaries.

At curtain call tears threatened to spill and my mouth felt all wobbly as

I swallowed back my emotions. I was so proud of Dee. She caught my eye from the stage and I knew her well enough to see she needed reassurance. She had no idea how good she'd been. No idea at all.

I gave her two thumbs up, mouthing '*Amazing.*'

⌘

Mike and I were invited to the opening night cast party afterward. I'd never been to anything like that before and felt a bit intimidated. Dee put me at ease though, fussing over us as though we were the most important people in the world to her. A couple of young men hovered around her, making sure she had plenty of wine and more canapes than she could eat. She practically shimmered with excitement and I noticed every single actor there looked luminescent with energy. They really loved doing this. It wasn't a job to them, they lived for it. More than that in this case, I suspected. They probably felt by bringing O'Casey's words to life that they were doing their bit to help the Irish cause. Again, I felt a frisson of envy. What must it be like to be united in a common desire like that?

"Were the Auxiliaries the Black and Tans?" Mike asked me suddenly. "Why'd that guy in the play have an English accent?"

I dug back in my mind, trying to dredge up what I remembered from Irish history in school. "No, they were a branch of the Royal Irish Constabulary back then. Made up of ex-British Army, I think."

He fell silent and surveyed the room, people-watching. He stayed quiet, only replying if I spoke directly to him. But he kept physical contact by resting an arm around my shoulders.

As soon as we could we slipped away to retrieve our coats from the attended cloakroom. I noticed how Mike scanned the streets as we walked, constantly glancing over his shoulder. We should have taken a taxi back; it never occurred to me that he'd feel vulnerable.

He was so much on edge I began to feel paranoid too. I actually jumped in fright when a black cat scurried out of a driveway across my path. Mike laughed at that, at least. I tried to engage him in conversation as we walked but he answered in monosyllables. I fell silent, listening to the sounds of our feet scuffing on the pavement and the whoosh of the occasional car driving past. Mike kept a vigilant eye on each vehicle, marginally relaxing when it had passed. I vowed I'd never ask him to walk in the streets of Belfast with me ever again.

Back in the apartment he silently took a seat by the fire while I busied myself making a pot of tea. He retrieved the program of *The Shadow of a Gunman* from my purse on the floor and flicked rapidly through the pages. When I brought the tea over I saw he had the program open at Dee's bio. I handed him one of the two mugs.

He promptly set it on the coffee table. "Isn't it unusual to find an Ulster

Protestant who's friends with a Catholic?" he asked bluntly. Looked like this had been on his mind for a while.

"No." I sat beside him. "Most of us don't care what religion each other is." I took a sip of tea. "We just wish the bloody Troubles would disappear and leave us in peace."

He raised an elegant eyebrow. "That's a bit naïve. Your war's not going to be resolved until one side or the other gives in. Or wins."

We both knew the cost if the IRA won. I took my time drinking from my cup. I really, really wasn't in the mood for this conversation. The pro-Irish play had evidently gotten to him and I regretted inviting him. Well, no, I didn't. But I did regret that it had stirred up such an incendiary subject.

He watched my face closely. "Don't you think?" he prompted, a slight edge to his tone.

"Neither side is going to give in," I replied. *Did we really have to do this now?* "'No surrender' and all that. I mean, who's going to give in to a bunch of murdering terrorists?" Familiar ire rose as I thought about it. "I'm certainly not going to."

He cleared his throat and twisted in the seat to face me. "How far would you be willing to go to put an end to terrorism, Jen?"

"How far?" I repeated. *What a stupid question.* "Whatever it takes." I couldn't read the expression in his eyes as he studied me. Shifting in unease I added, "What exactly are you asking, Mike?"

He blinked. "What time will Deirdre be back?"

Again, there he was deflecting my question. "You're good at that, you know."

"At what?"

"Changing the subject."

I thought I'd used a bantering tone but his face changed, like shutters coming down. He placed the program on the coffee table and stood. "Think it's best I leave."

"But I thought you had the weekend?"

He grabbed his helmet from the armchair and jacket from the coat stand. "Sorry." Before I could say another word he was out the door and clattering down the stairs.

I leapt up. The door swung on its hinges. Should I go after him? No, that would be humiliating. At the window I yanked the curtain aside and craned my neck. Mike emerged from the building and hesitated on the sidewalk. He'd reconsidered. He was coming back. But he zipped up his jacket, fastened his helmet and climbed onto the bike. I couldn't believe it. Fists curled, I raised a hand to knock on the window. A sudden burst of rain splattered against the glass and the bike's engine roared to life, drowning me out. Through the blur of the raindrops I futilely watched the red tail light of the bike disappear into the night.

I gaped at the empty street. I'd just thrown away my virginity to someone who obviously didn't give a fuck about me. I should have listened to Dee.

In weary defeat I closed the door, clicking it firmly shut. Ensuring the fire guard was in place on the hearth, I changed into my pajamas and went to the bathroom to wipe off my makeup. My reflection in the mirror above the sink looked chalk-white, and then my face reddened, crumpling unattractively as the tears came. I twisted away, switched off the bathroom light and headed for the bedroom. I'd leave Dee a note that Mike hadn't stayed after all and wait until morning to talk to her. I couldn't face the postmortem discussion right now.

Backtracking to the living room to get a notepad and pen out of my purse, I stopped dead. Mike's overnight bag still lay in the corner, half hidden by the sofa. Anger surged through me and I stooped to grab it. Let's hear how satisfying a thud it made when I threw it out the fucking window onto the pavement. Something heavy clunked inside so I laid it back on the floor and crouched down to investigate. The sweater Mike had worn earlier lay rolled up on top. I lifted it out and couldn't help holding it to my face. His scent immediately transported me to our lovemaking earlier. I bunched it into a ball and hurled it across the room. Next I pulled out a brown leather sponge bag and another packet of three condoms. Presumptive bastard. The heavy thing was tucked into a zippered side pocket. Reaching inside, my fingers closed around the unmistakable shape and weight of a handgun, cold to the touch.

Bloody hell.

It was fastened into a tan leather holster, which I snapped open to let the weapon slide into my hand. A pistol of some kind, black in color with a brown handle. Or butt it'd be called. Some words in French were inscribed on the side, and underneath *'Browning's Patent Depose'*. My hand shook a little so I put the weapon on the floor and stared at it for a while. What was Mike going to do when he realized he'd forgotten this? Stupid fucker. Maybe I wouldn't give it back. Pretend I hadn't found it.

Feeling less shaky I picked it back up and weighed it in my hand. Pointing the barrel away from me, I fiddled until I released the thing that held the ammunition. Inside was a lot of little shiny gold-colored bullets piled like staples on top of each other. They looked vicious despite being so pretty. I wondered how to find out if any of them were actually inside somewhere, ready to be fired. The thought gave me a feeling of vertigo. I pushed at a little lever on the side near the barrel, trying to find the safety catch. On the right-hand side there was a long oval hole in the barrel part. I prodded at it until I worked out the top part of the barrel slid back. I yanked it hard and it pulled back like a - like a metal foreskin, revealing a silver tube underneath. Once again I pushed and flipped at things until pressure from my thumb on a little lever sticking out made it all go back in place. Only then was I satisfied that no deadly bullets lurked within.

Dee would go ape-shit if she saw this. Worse, although hardly likely, what if it somehow got into the hands of one of her brothers? I wrapped the ammo up in one of Mike's socks, clipped the pistol into its holster and replaced everything. Retrieving his sweater from across the room, I stuffed it in on top and zipped up the bag.

Scrawling the note to Dee about Mike not staying, I left it by the kettle and took the bag into the bedroom. Kneeling down I slid it under my bed. I'd find a better hiding place for it in the light of day. My hand touched something cold and slimy, making me yelp. The used condom on the floor. I reluctantly pinched it between finger and thumb and dumped it in the toilet bowl. It wouldn't flush at first, so I had to retrieve it and fill it with water from the tap to weigh it down. Disgusted, I tied off the end and watched it swirl out of sight. I felt a bit like that condom. Used, discarded, and flushed away.

⌘

I slept fitfully, but didn't hear Dee come in. In the morning I woke to find her snoring across the room, the pungent scent of wine heavy in the air. Sneaking out of bed to the kitchen to make tea, I tried to keep quiet so as not to wake her. But the sound of the kettle filling with water must have disturbed her as she appeared almost immediately. She hadn't bothered to remove her makeup from the night before and had a wanton banshee look about her.

I waited until we were settled by the fire with mugs of sweet tea before I told her about Mike storming off. "I don't know what I did, Dee."

She slammed her mug down on the coffee table. "*You* didn't do nothin'. He's the one at fault. Selfish pig." She curled a lip. "What do you expect from a British soldier? I told you they don't give a shite about us. He was only after one thing."

I felt like hell. "And he got it."

"And he got it," she repeated. "Why you couldn't wait, I don't know, Jen. This is probably his *modus operandi*: goes round as many girls as he can, screwing them and buggering off. I told you ya should have waited." She saw my lower lip trembling and sighed. "Well, it's done now. I'm sorry he turned out to be such a slimeball."

"I'll listen to you next time. If there is a next time."

"Course there'll be. I'll set you up with someone from the Lyric."

I made a cross with my fingers as though to ward off evil. "No, please. I'm done. Between Mike being a total prick and Clancy being–" Shit, I almost said 'gay'.

She cocked her head to the side. "What about Clancy?"

"I know he's your brother but he's another moody, unpredictable bastard. Sorry. I'm done with men."

"Sure you are," she teased, infuriating me. "I hope this has taught you a lesson about the Brits. You can't trust them. Any of them."

"*I'm* British, Dee," I reminded her.

"You don't have to be."

I pointedly ignored her and she withdrew to the bathroom. Water sploshed as the bath filled. She really did hate us. The British. I always knew she did, but I never realized she counted me in there. I thought I was exempt, the way I never lumped her in with the IRA Nationalists even if she made it perfectly clear how much she wanted a United Ireland.

Perversely glad to have something other than Mike to obsess about, I listened to Dee hum the Irish melody that had played as *The Shadow of a Gunman* had opened. I found it hard to get my head around the extent of her hatred. *I* didn't care that she considered herself Irish or that she was Catholic. To me it made no difference to who she was. But maybe I was naïve as Mike had accused me of. Maybe it did matter.

Last night while trying to sleep I'd decided to take the bus home to Mourneview today. I'd take the pistol and hide it there. In my bedroom there was a loose piece of skirting board behind which I'd successfully hidden stuff from my parents for years.

Going home to lick my wounds was all I wanted right now. I'd thought through quite a number of things during the long night. It was getting close to the end of March and Easter was just round the corner. Yes, I had improved at Queen's, largely thanks to Clancy. But since he'd fallen out with me, my studies had really suffered. Without his help I saw no point in going on with the pretense that I'd do well enough to graduate.

The taps squeaked as Dee turned the water off, then I heard splashing as she climbed into the bath. Dragging Mike's bag out from under the bed and grabbing my anorak I shrugged it on.

"Bye!" I called through the bathroom door.

"Where ya going?"

I didn't feel like explaining myself so I slammed the door behind me and hurried down the stairs. In the hall I used the payphone to tell Mum I'd be on the 1:45pm bus, arriving at 3:05 in Newcastle.

"Perfect!" she said. If she hadn't been holding the phone she would have clapped her hands. "Just in time for afternoon tea. We'll pick you up and go to that new Percy French café on Main Street. Your Dad's been wanting an excuse to try their desserts."

"Okay."

"What's wrong, Jen?"

My lip did its wobbly thing and tears welled up. She could never know about Mike and the calamitous loss of my virginity. "Well, it's almost

Easter," I blurted. "I'm done with Queen's. I tried but it isn't working."

I heard her intake of breath. "All right, dear. We'll talk about it when you're here."

10
Devastation

Mum and Dad already waited outside the terminus when the bus pulled into Newcastle. I spotted the Jeep parked across the road in the public car park over by the sea front, Mac's black and white head poking out of the passenger side window.

Mum wore her pearls and a navy blue wool coat with shiny buttons, along with her favorite lemon yellow silk scarf draped rakishly over one shoulder. She'd bullied Dad out of his working clothes and into a clean pair of corduroy trousers and sweater. Her hair looked neatly coiffed and she wore a little makeup for a change. Her equivalent of war paint as obviously she expected to go into battle with me about Queen's. Her expression showed worry as she studied my face, and she gathered me into a very warm embrace. Extremely unlike her to show such physical affection. My red and puffy eyes must look worse than I thought. I gave Dad a hug and for once he didn't mention my hair color or length.

"Let's walk," suggested Mum. "It's such a lovely day."

Dad pointed to Mike's bag. "Want to put that in the Jeep?"

"Yes please." It would be a lot safer with Mac to guard it than me hauling it down to the Percy French and back.

We crossed the road and Dad unlocked the door to the Jeep. Mac's tail thumped rhythmically and I stroked his head, tweaking his ears as I slid the bag behind the passenger seat out of sight.

Mum produced four little dog biscuits shaped like bones from her purse and placed them on the seat beside him. Even though I watched Dad relock the Jeep I still pulled on the door handle to check. We left Mac chomping his treats and strolled down Main Street. The Percy French was about a hundred yards along, across from the Royal Arms pub. The café facade was painted forest green, with two huge windows on either side of the glass-paned front door. In summer they could put tables and chairs on the pavement outside, but despite the sun it was way too cold today. Dad pushed open the door and a little brass bell inside dinged.

Brakes squealed and a horn honked loudly, making me jump. Dad held the door open for us and followed us in. When Mum and Dad went out somewhere like this they liked to sit close to a window where they could watch the 'stir' in the street. Today being Saturday the café was pretty full, but luckily a window table freed up as we entered.

Mum gave me a shove toward the table. "Quick, Jen."

I slid across the polished tiled floor and dutifully claimed the table, taking off my coat and hanging it on the back of a chair. Someone with a shock of auburn hair passed the plate glass window. I craned my neck and saw long locks blowing in the wind before disappearing from view. I couldn't tell if it was the leather-coated musician I'd seen in Belfast or not. Hardly likely, but you never know. As Clancy said, Northern Ireland's like a village.

A dark blue Vauxhall Cavalier sat just across the road, no sign of the driver. I frowned. No one should leave their car unattended in the town - a security attempt to avoid car bombs.

Mum and Dad joined me at the table, shrugging out of their coats. Mum kept her bright yellow scarf tied loosely around her neck, almost obscuring the set of pearls. A waiter with black spiky-punk hair arrived to remove the debris left by the table's previous occupants. He presented us with three afternoon tea menus lavishly printed with flowing dark green script on white paper. My parents studied the choices like they held the answer to all of life's questions.

I scanned down the list. Tea and petit fours. Tea and dessert of choice. Tea and finger sandwiches. Tea and scones with jam and clotted cream. *Tea with tea and tea to match.* At the bottom was printed: 'Coffee available up on request', complete with typo making no sense of it at all.

I'd forgotten to eat breakfast or lunch and felt giddy from lack of sleep and food. The waiter brought three teacups and saucers, placing them on the table in front of us. Obviously we needn't bother about the coffee 'up on' request.

"What are ye havin'?" he demanded belligerently.

My mother, not impressed with his manner, adopted a supercilious persona. "I think we'll have tea to start with," she announced in an exaggerated posh tone.

The waiter stared, his expression saying, *'Of course you're bloody having tea, it's a feckin' tea shop.'*

"And after that we'll have dessert," she finished.

My father looked mutinous. He probably wanted his dessert served *with* the tea like anyone else. But when Mum made unilateral decisions like that we knew we'd never win.

The waiter retreated. Mum turned to me, laid her elbows on the table and leaned forward. Straight for the jugular, she demanded, "What's this about you wanting to leave Queen's and it not even Easter?"

Dad assumed a disapproving expression and shook his head. "Your mother and I are very disappointed."

Anger surged through me. I'd come home for comfort, not a guilt trip.

"You can't force me to stay."

The waiter brought a tray with a stainless steel teapot, matching milk jug and sugar bowl, and placed each, one by one, on the table. "Let that soak a while," he instructed as he put down the teapot.

The bell over the door dinged as another group of people left the café.

"No one's talking about forcing you, for God's sake," Mum said. "Any girl would be thrilled to be getting a university education. But not you." She *tsked* impatiently. "For once in your life can't you see something through to the end?"

I felt like marching out. *For once in my life?* I looked to Dad for support, but he fixedly concentrated all his attention on pouring milk into his cup. Then he reached for the sugar bowl, which held several paper sachets of sugar.

"I'm sorry to be harsh, Jennifer." Mum attempted to moderate her tone. "But I can't impress upon you how important a university degree is."

"I know that, but–" I held my tongue as the waiter reappeared with the dessert tray. *If he interrupted one more time!*

He bent down, holding the tray out to us. "Would you's like a sweet?"

We studied the array of glossy cakes and concoctions.

"I'll have a chocolate mousse," Mum told him.

I couldn't care less what I had. I'd probably choke on it anyway. "The same."

We looked expectantly at Dad. He pointed at a yellow-brown mound on one of the plates. "What's that muck?"

"Oh, John," chastised Mum.

"Tiramisu, Sir."

Dad looked affronted. "Is there no bread and butter pudding?"

"I'll ask." The waiter retreated again, tray in hand.

"Must you be so uncouth?" Mum snapped at Dad.

He barked something in reply and I zoned out, staring out of the window. The street thronged with people, all taking advantage of the sunny afternoon. A bunch of excited kids raced past and then crouched down to draw arrows with chalk on the pavement. I used to play that game at primary school. We called it a treasure hunt, but the only treasure we searched for was each other.

The Vauxhall drew my gaze. Still no one in it. That was really stupid, the car would be towed. I wondered if I should tell someone. A resounding thunk jerked my attention back. Dad had drained his teacup and banged the cup onto the saucer. The back of his hand connected with the stainless steel sugar bowl, which went flying. It clunked metallically to the tiled floor and rolled, spilling its sachets.

I'd tuned out Mum and Dad's heated exchange but it looked like Mum had won as usual.

"Ach, Jennifer." She no longer looked angry but concerned. "Will you see sense?"

"I have seen sense," I told her. "I'm quitting and you can't stop me." Sliding my chair back to get up, my foot hit the sugar bowl. I bent double to the floor to retrieve it.

I heard Mum huff in exasperation. "You'll give up your education, young lady, over my dead–"

It happened in an instant, yet seemed like slow motion.

A thundering roar splintered the café windows into a million shards. Burning debris hurtled into the air and a comet of fire lashed through the imploded plate glass, hurtling the table over with the force of a cannon ball.

My ears rang. Distorted screaming sounded from far away. In strangely bright, over-exposed colors I saw Mum and me as we were when I was a child. I giggled and clapped my hands in delight as she lifted me up high to see Blarney Castle on the hill. Green fields and drumlins rolled away as far as the eye could see. An Irish tricolor flag flapped in the summer breeze, the cloth snapping and flagpole rattling.

"*See the flag, Jen?*" said Mum, her voice from a great distance. "*The orange is for the Protestants, the green for the Catholics, and the white for the peace between us.*"

The ringing faded. I rushed back to crackling flames and the sooty fog of billowing smoke. Devastation surrounded me. Someone nearby wailed, hysterical with terror. *Shush,* I tried to say - it'll be okay.

I could only move my head. And one arm. A heavy weight crushed me, making it hard to breathe. Something absurdly bright and out of place drew my eye. A great orange flower, blossoming fast, blotting out daffodil yellow. Blood. Blood soaking Mum's scarf. I tried to reach for it and my hand brushed something gritty by my head.

They were scorched pearls.

"Mum! Dad! Oh, Christ, no."

⌘

I woke up in a hospital ward. It took me a moment to realize it. Inky nighttime seeped through a gap in the window blinds, confusing me. For a moment I thought I was dreaming. Then it all came back in a rush. I took a sobbing breath, pain lancing through my chest.

A nurse appeared by the bedside. She smiled reassuringly and patted the back of my hand before taking my pulse. "You're all right, dear. Very lucky, only bruised ribs. Caused by the table in the café toppling on you, but that's what saved your life."

If I hadn't bent down to pick up the sugar bowl from the floor, my head would have been blown off.

I wish it had.

She told me I'd been heavily sedated for a couple of days to give my ribs a chance to heal. I had snippets of vivid memory, being strapped onto a gurney and of a hurtled, siren-filled journey. I couldn't get the shrieking out of my head, the siren somehow mixed in with the screaming I heard in the bomb debris. And ruined yellow - stained orange with blood.

They say the Downe Hospital is haunted. I'd believe it after this. I woke up during the night to see a dark figure at the foot of my bed, watching me intently. I blinked in alarm, but he'd vanished into the shadows. Then another night I was convinced I saw a supervising hospital matron in an old fashioned starched cap and apron standing just in the doorway. She glared belligerently at each of the ward patients in turn. Scared shitless, I frantically jabbed at the call button before her terrifying gaze fell on me, but she disappeared by the time a nurse came to my bedside.

"It's just the morphine, love. Plays tricks on the mind. Don't fret about it, there's no ghost matron here."

I wasn't so sure.

Neighbors, old school friends, and Reverend Scott came at intervals, bearing baskets of fruit, flowers and get-well cards. I kept saying, 'thank you' over and over, grimacing a smile that hurt my jaw. I just wanted to go home. To Mourneview, to Mum and Dad.

But there was no going back for me.

Not ever.

On the fifth day when I was coming out of the drug-induced fog, a man in a suit, carrying a briefcase drew a chair up close to the side of my bed and introduced himself as my parents' lawyer, Mr. Catchpull. Everything about him seemed designed to make him blend into the environment. Dreggy brown suit and tie, dun hair, briefcase the color of light tobacco. He wore umber horn rimmed glasses, and his nut-brown eyes peered sympathetically at me through telescope-thick lenses.

"The farm is yours," he said in a firm voice, a startling contrast to his looks. "In a case like this it's straightforward."

I shook my head, dizziness swamping me. "Like this?" My voice lacked concreteness, like it belonged to a very lost and frightened child.

"Yes." He cleared his throat. "When there's no doubt as to the cause of death. Sudden, catastrophic death."

I closed my eyes and saw orange swallowing yellow. Why couldn't the bomb have taken me, also? How would I ever get through this alone?

"I need instructions about the farm," he continued.

I kept my eyes squeezed shut. Mourneview and Mum and Dad. Mum and Dad and Mourneview. How could one exist without the other? "Sell it."

"I'll put it on the market. It'll probably take some time to find a buyer, so there's plenty of time should you - change your mind. I do have a buyer for the livestock at a reduced rate for a quick sale. Mr. O'Neill, your neighbor. I can put that sale through, or he offered to wait and take care of them if you like, until you–" He paused. "When you feel better."

I almost laughed. Better? I was never going to feel better. There was no way back from this.

I registered what he'd said. Dee's father in the next farm over was going to take our livestock. I'd never be back, but at least they didn't have to move far from Mourneview. I hoped Sadie the sow would be all right there. She was a cantankerous old sociopath, and less forgiving people than my parents might have no compunction in making bacon of her. "Get rid of everything."

"Certainly. Will you be staying at Mourneview until the sale goes through?"

"No." I couldn't bear to ever go back.

"Will you be returning to Belfast, then?"

I shook my head. *Never.*

"Leave it to me, Miss Hamilton, I'll get you a room in a nice Bed and Breakfast that my sister runs. Just up from the harbor." He coughed. "Shall I make the - arrangements - for your parents? They were most concise in their wishes–"

"Please do," I interrupted. "I'd appreciate it." I couldn't bear to deal with it. Couldn't bear any of this.

Mr. Catchpull took complete charge. There'd be a private burial at Donard Presbyterian Church up in the Mournes, and then as the majority of victims were members, there'd be a community memorial service there on Saturday. What were they going to put in my parents' coffins? A few bits of burnt flesh, along with my mother's charred pearls?

After Mr. Catchpull left I slipped into a merciful doze that released me from the ghastly, untenable present. I was between sleeping and waking when a shadow fell over me, yanking me awake. Dee stood by my bed, preoccupied with making room on my bedside table to set down a vase of flowers.

Oh God, no. The very sight of her made me want to scream. She'd cursed me. She hated the British. People like me and my parents. She supported those who had planted the bomb. People who believed what she believed wanted my kind eradicated. That was the catastrophic price of her United Ireland.

She caught my movement. "Jen!" She leaned over me, arms outstretched to hug me.

I wrenched an arm free from my covers and blocked her. The sharp movement cut across my entire chest. "Don't come near me!"

She halted, her eyes wide. "Oh, Jen, I'm so sorry–" The gold Catholic crucifix necklace she wore slipped from under her sweater and glinted in the sun coming through the window. She'd given me one just like it for my twenty-first birthday.

"Leave. Me. Alone." My ribs burned with every syllable. She just stood there, staring uncomprehendingly. "Go away, Deirdre. Go *away!*" The last word came out as a shriek.

She backed off, a look of horror on her face, and ran from the ward. I sagged back in the bed, so wracked with pain I couldn't even cry.

⌘

After Dee's visit I woke out of my zombie-like state with a shock. What had happened to Mac and the Jeep? And Mike's pistol?

I was no longer attached to a drip, so I pulled back the covers and edged to the side of the bed. It hurt like crazy but I managed to stand. Walking at a gentle pace wasn't hard after that, so I made my way out to the corridor and found a payphone attached to the wall. Mr. Catchpull's office accepted my reverse-charge request.

"Mac's in safe hands, Miss Hamilton, I assure you. Reverend Scott took him in. Both seem to be thriving."

"What about the Jeep?" I held my breath, afraid he'd ask me about the pistol.

"Towed over to our car park behind the office, where it resides in utmost safety. You may pick it up when you're ready."

I had to assume that the bag remained hidden under the passenger seat.

The Downe finally discharged me the day of my parents' funeral. In the watery light of early morning Mr. Catchpull picked me up and drove me to his sister's B&B. She'd prepared a very pretty room, with floral wallpaper and furnishings, which looked out over the harbor. I recognized the suitcase on the bed and lifted the lid to look inside. Mr. Catchpull had had his secretary pack a selection of my clothes and toiletries. She'd included the heavy black family Bible from the half-moon table in the hall at Mourneview. Did she really think I'd find solace in that?

I changed into the black outfit I'd requested from my closet. I'd also asked for Mum's black Sunday-best coat from the hall at Mourneview. As I slipped it on, the flowery scent of her favorite Chanel perfume enveloped me. All that was missing was her silk yellow scarf.

The next couple of hours went by in a daze. Mr. Catchpull took me to Donard Presbyterian. I would rather not have gone through the charade, but Mum and Dad had specified in their will that they wanted a Christian burial in the church they'd been married in. I invited no one, keeping the ceremony simple, with only Mr. Catchpull and me for Reverend Scott to preach to. I don't remember a single word uttered. And I had to go through this all over again at the community memorial service.

Both coffins had a spray of aromatic white lilies on top. I would never be able to tolerate the smell of lilies ever again without remembering this day.

The organ played one of Mum's favorite pieces, the wrenchingly evocative *Largo* from Handel's opera *Xerxes*. I hadn't known anyone was up in the gallery - and the funeral directors bore the coffins out to the graveyard. My parents, what was left of them, were buried deep in the damp, peaty earth. I felt like I watched a movie as they lowered the two sarcophagi made from polished oak into the ground, one on top of the other. None of it felt real to me.

"Ashes to ashes, dust to dust," intoned the Reverend, and then it was mercifully over. He shook my hand and gave me a sympathetic pat on the shoulder. "Mac's welcome with me for as long as you need. It's nice having the old boyo around."

Mr. Catchpull drove me across town to his office so I could retrieve the Jeep. As he handed over the spare keychain from Mourneview he peered at me through his thick lenses, brown eyes filled with concern. "Are you going to be all right?"

I forced my lips into a facsimile of a smile. "Yes, thank you. I just need to be alone."

He pulled a business card and Biro from his pocket and scrawled a number on the back of the card. "Phone me day or night if you need anything. I do wish you'd come and stay with Mrs. Catchpull and me. I don't like leaving you on your own."

"You're very kind. Thank you for everything."

I went out to the car park to unlock the Jeep. While the funeral had left me bereft of emotion, I now had to fight tears, expecting Mac to thrust his head out through the window and smother me with doggie kisses. I'd give anything - *anything* for Mum and Dad to be there too, making all the comments they wanted about my hair and my appearance.

Mike's bag hadn't been disturbed. Patting down the side, I felt the rigid weight of the pistol. Good. I shut the passenger door, went round to the driver's seat and switched on the ignition. I saw Mr. Catchpull at the window and gave him a thumbs up. He returned it and retreated out of sight. I wondered if he knew I didn't have a driver's license.

As the Jeep cranked reluctantly into gear I couldn't help but think that the last human hand to touch the gearstick had been Dad's. I looked across at the passenger seat and remembered with a hollow pain how Mum would sit so prim and proper with her hands clasped together in her lap.

Wrenching myself back to what to do with the weapon, I decided I couldn't bring it to the bed and breakfast. Mourneview was the only other option. Steeling myself I drove up into the mountains, taking the same road where the army helicopter almost collided with us on the brow of the hill. Until now I had purposefully avoided thinking of Mike. Now that I was alone, thoughts of him crowded me. I paused at the top of the hill, foot on the brake, and gazed across the little valley at the farm where I'd spent most of my life. The weathercock shifted a forty-five degree angle as wind from the Mournes breathed on it. I remembered how the helicopter dislodging it had brought Mike McLeod into my life. How strange that just a few months ago my only worry had been about leaving Queen's. What a naïve idiot I'd been, caught up in the first throes of lust, losing all reason. If I hadn't met him, none of this would have happened. The only reason Mum and Dad were in the Percy French was because I took the bus that day. And the sole reason I took the bus in the first place was because Mike had walked out on me the night before. He didn't plant the bomb, but he'd caused this, nonetheless.

From here Mourneview looked exactly the same. How could Dad not be in the yard, shoveling the pigsty or setting up the cows to be milked with faithful Mac at his heels? Or Mum not be in the kitchen or tending to her beloved hens?

I took my foot off the brake and drove the Jeep slowly down the hill to Mourneview. Pulling into the yard, I was struck at the feeling of desolation. No Mac running and yipping to greet me, no smoke pluming from the farmhouse chimney. No squawk of hens, nor belligerent snorting from Sadie-sow.

I parked and switched off the engine, plunging the yard into total silence. Using the house key on the Jeep keychain I brought Mike's bag inside, closing the door behind me. The heating had been switched off and it was as cold inside as out. But the silence. Overwhelming. Mourneview's soul had gone, leaving resounding emptiness.

My footsteps clopped loudly as I climbed the stairs. Irrationally afraid of disturbing anyone, I tip-toed into my bedroom, laying the bag on my bed. Sitting beside it I drew out the Browning. Sliding it from its holster I held its deadly weight in my hand. Experimentally, I aimed it and squinted down the barrel. Then I put it to my head. What if I put the magazine in? Fired a round into my skull?

But I didn't want to disturb Mum and Dad, absurd how that seemed.

I shuddered. I got the uncanny feeling that someone watched me, although it wasn't possible. My bedroom window looked out onto the barren Mournes. I raised the pistol and aimed at a sun-dappled rock halfway up the mountains. I wish I knew the fuckers who'd planted that bomb. I had the means now to get revenge. Or I could just shoot down a few of theirs: tit for tat. I imagined myself bursting into one of the Nationalist bars in Ballyben and pulling the trigger over and over until I was out of bullets.

Dad's weathercock gave a rusty squeak, shifting position as the wind whistled off the mountain. I realized I'd been holding my breath. Easing the air from my lungs I got up and rummaged in the bag for the sock that I'd rolled around the magazine. Removing Mike's sweater I laid it on the bed so I could wrap up both the pistol and ammunition. Hauling the bed aside I tweaked the skirting board loose and grabbed hold of the bundle to shove it in the hiding place. Not able to help myself I brought it to my face and inhaled. Mike's musky scent surrounded me, transporting me to when I'd last smelled it - when Mum and Dad were still alive.

I saw myself crouching on the floor of the room as though my spirit hovered above. Then I imagined looking down at the roof of the farm from the sky. Higher and higher, the farm melded into the shadow of Slieve Donard, then the Mournes themselves merged together. Northern Ireland receded into the island of Ireland, then the British Isles grew smaller and smaller until the earth was merely a blue marble against a black velvet backdrop. That's how much life mattered. A speck, a pinprick, lost amongst the pebbledash of our solar system.

Clasping the bundle of Mike's sweater and pistol to my chest I cried. For the insignificance of human life, for the loss of my parents and everything I loved.

Daylight had faded by the time I could move. I'd cried myself out, curled up in the fetal position on my bed. My chest ached and my throat felt parched and raw. Shivers racked my body from the cold, despite me wearing Mum's warm coat. Moving stiffly like a woman four times my age, I hid the bundle in the wall and slid the skirting board back in place. Looking around my room, I took stock of my life from before. Ballerina music box with open lid, tutu-clad dancer frozen mid step. Pine wardrobe bursting with multicolored clothes spilling out onto the faded old wicker chair by the window. Music stand that leaned like the Tower of Pisa because I'd kicked it over in a teenage temper. All the old posters on the walls: The Bay City Rollers, David Essex, The Osmonds. A bookshelf packed with my old favorites: the *Flambards* trilogy by K.M. Peyton, *Logan's Run* by William F. Nolan, Tolkien's *Lord of the Rings*. All from another, more innocent life.

A life forever gone.

11
Tit for Tat

I don't believe that Donard Presbyterian Church had ever seen so many people. All three sections of pews were crammed with standing room only at the back of the two aisles. Below the pulpit at the front hung a woven tapestry displaying a burning bush on dark blue velvet, the Latin words *Ardens sed virens* scrolled through it. Six framed portrait photos displaying each of the bomb victims sat on the communion table, my parents' picture among them.

Mr. Catchpull had brought me several photos to choose from. Although it was the last thing I wanted to do I forced myself to look through them. I had been torn between their wedding photo from the 50's and the one taken a few years ago at their silver wedding anniversary. I finally chose the latter. They looked so happy and relaxed in it, rather than the formal, serious demeanor of the wedding portrait.

Clothed in the same black outfit I'd worn to the actual funeral, I sat in one of the front pews along with the five other mourning families. At the last minute I'd brought the family Bible, which sat on my lap, its weight oppressive. My knuckles shone white against the worn black leather of the cover. I could barely concentrate on Reverend Scott droning from the pulpit. My neck prickled and my jaw hinges ached from clenching my teeth. I felt like the eyes of the entire congregation were intently focused on the back of my head.

"We must try and forgive those misguided members of the Irish Republican Army," intoned the Reverend, his words finally seeping through to me, "who have accepted responsibility for the deaths of our beloved families, from both the Protestant and the Roman Catholic communities." His voice came in an irritating practiced sing-song cadence, and he dropped his tone at the end of every sentence. "As the Lord said before his death upon the cross, Father forgive them for they know not what they do."

All my attention focused sharply on him. *Forgive* them? Was he out of his fucking mind? I looked around at the other victims' families. Like sheep, all staring up at the pulpit. How could they agree with this?

I surged to my feet, letting the Bible slam to the floor. Reverend Scott paused and I heard a collective murmur run through the church. All eyes were riveted on me. I turned my back on the pulpit and the portrait photos, and stalked down the aisle. My heels clicked loudly on the flagstones but I made no effort to smother the sound.

Twice I'd survived an IRA bombing. Twice I'd watched innocent people reduced to blood and gore. And twice the IRA had not called in a warning. Across Northern Ireland there were hundreds of others losing the people they loved to bombings, hundreds of innocents slain.

Someone in a middle pew jumped to their feet as I passed. "Jennifer!"

I drew up sharply. Dee stood in the center of a group of Catholic neighbors from our community. And Seamus. And Clancy. *IRA sympathizers.* How dare they come here? Bloody murdering - *Fenian* bastards.

I hurried down the aisle, almost faltering again when a figure at the back of the church caught my eye. Mike McLeod, distinctive in his biking leather. How the fuck could he show his face here?

I broke into a run and barreled out to the car park. Hands shaking so hard I could barely function, I fished my keychain out of Mum's coat pocket and unlocked the Jeep. A group of inquisitive people had followed me out of the church. I hurried to get the Jeep started and peeled out as fast as I could. I drove as quickly as the Jeep would allow, sending stones flying until I was on the lane that led to Mourneview.

I unlocked the farmhouse door and went straight upstairs to my bedroom, leaving the doors wide open. Hauling the bed aside I pulled Mike's sweater with the pistol and bullets from its hiding place in the skirting board.

Forgiveness? Not in this lifetime.

Shrugging out of Mum's coat I carefully laid it on my bed. Unwrapping the sweater, I slid the leather strap of the Browning holster over my left shoulder so the weapon rested under my arm. In front of the wardrobe mirror I pulled at the other strap until I worked out how it should go round my right shoulder and buckle securely onto my belt. Sliding the Browning from the holster I lifted the sock from the bed so I could tip the magazine out. My hands steady and sure now, I clicked it into its slot in the handle.

Weapon in hand I returned to the mirror and studied my reflection. The stranger who stared back looked angular and taut, her eyes dark. I slipped the pistol into the holster and left the bedroom. In the hall I put on Dad's ancient Merchant Navy donkey jacket. It seemed appropriate, leaving the good church coat behind and selecting a modern-day warrior's. The red plaid lining of the jacket had faded with wear, the blue wool of the exterior almost black.

I walked out into the yard, not bothering to close the door and climbed back into the Jeep. With screeching tires, I accelerated away from Mourneview. The sun burst through the clouds, sending a cascade of beams over the mountains. I don't think I've ever seen the Mournes with such clarity, perfectly framed against the powder blue sky.

Half a mile up the road, without slowing I took the right turn at a sign reading: BALLYBEN - 7 MILES. I don't remember the drive there but in no time I was approaching the town. It looked pretty, I hadn't been here during daylight before. It had just one main street with rows of pastel-hued original Georgian houses along each side. I passed three pubs within yards of each other, looking closely at the names above.

I spotted what I sought just past a church on the far side of town. Mooney's pub. With the Nationalist tricolor above the door: green and gold with white in the middle - *for the peace between us*, as Mum had told me. I slammed on the brakes and halted the Jeep in the middle of the street. Was I really going through with this?

Fuck, yes.

I only hesitated for a second, then threw open the door and approached the pub. Something thundered in front of me, knocking me back against the Jeep. Mike McLeod had ridden his bike into my path.

Tearing off his helmet, he yelled over the roar of the engine. "Jen, stop!"

I dodged round the bike and reached under the donkey jacket to slide the Browning from its holster. Clicking off the safety I raised it as I reached Mooney's. Mike grabbed me from behind, pulling me away from the door. The bike hit the pavement with a clatter, the engine puttering out.

I struggled. "Let me go!"

People spilled out from Mooney's and nearby buildings, and a crowd rapidly congregated.

Mike hauled me back to the bike. "Jen, come on. We gotta get out of here."

"No!"

In desperation I wrenched free. Raising the pistol again I pulled back the slide. The crowd outside Mooney's parted like sheaves of wheat in the path of a harvester and three men stepped forward, each drawing a firearm.

I didn't hesitate. My enemy now had faces. I aimed and squeezed the trigger. But Mike tackled me hard, spoiling my aim. The shot fired impotently, echoing like a crack of thunder. He chopped the Browning from my grip and it skittered on the road. Shots pinged off the Jeep as the three men fired. Mike dragged me across the tarmac to where the Jeep offered cover and slammed me up against it. He pulled the bike upright.

"Get on!" he shouted.

I looked back. Could I still get to the Browning? Pain ricocheted through me as something hit me in the face. The bike's petrol tank came up off the road to meet me, and I found myself clinging to the tank in front of Mike. He had *punched* me!

The three men took stances and prepared to fire again. Mike gunned the engine and we raced away. The crack of gunfire behind us made me expect to feel a bullet splinter my skull. I clung helplessly to the petrol tank as Mike swerved the bike from side to side, avoiding the salvo until we cleared the High Street. We raced through country lanes toward safety.

"What in the name of God were you thinking?" yelled Mike into my ear.

"They fucking murdered my parents!"

"So you'll let them get you, too?" He slowed the bike to a stop. "Then they win. You want that?"

I sagged, the fight seeping out of me. "I wanted revenge."

"I'll show you how." I twisted my head to look at him. His eyes burned into mine. "The right way."

He glanced over his shoulder at the length of road we'd just traveled. No one pursued. "We gotta ditch this bike. Get on behind."

I obediently slipped from where I had been pinioned between the tank and his thighs, and clambered on. He revved the accelerator on the handlebar and we leapt forward. I grabbed him around the waist and held on tight. For a moment I closed my eyes and tried to remember how it had felt the last time we'd been on this bike together. But it was no use. I couldn't escape, not even for a moment, the stark, brutal reality of the present.

He back-tracked along a labyrinth of lanes at the foot of the Mournes, avoiding Ballyben and Hilltown completely. I idly wondered how he expected to get us all the way back to Newcastle without being stopped by the police for having no helmets.

He took a turn off down a dirt lane that led into a thick covering of trees. The hidden track angled steeply uphill for about a quarter of a mile, then emerged at a derelict stone cottage. It was constructed of the old granite bricks that all the buildings and retaining walls were in the area. A faded red wooden door with planks nailed across it sat squarely in the middle between two boarded-up narrow windows. The roof with its single chimney looked badly in need of repair, with lots of slates missing. We drew up to a lean-to shed round the back in a cobblestoned yard. I climbed off and watched as Mike took a keychain from his jacket pocket and unlocked the shed. He pushed the bike inside and relocked the door. A cottage in the Mournes not ten miles from Ballyben? Nothing surprised me anymore. He moved along the back of the cottage to a weather-beaten door with flecks of green paint on it. Unlocking the padlock securing the latch and then a lock in the door, he shoved it open. Reaching inside he flipped a light switch and gestured that I should precede him. I stepped through, expecting a dirty flagstoned floor and granite brick walls. To my surprise I found myself standing in a modern kitchen complete with all amenities, knotted pine cupboards, and sleek, shiny terracotta tiles on the floor. A little round pine table with two kitchen chairs sat in the corner. I could smell carbolic and noticed a dried-up bar of soap by the stainless steel kitchen sink. Mike put the padlock back in place and clicked it locked. Then he came inside and pushed the door closed. Two sturdy bolts secured it from the inside. He threw these and moved past me to flip a switch on the wall.

I heard a furnace coming on close by and walked through the doorway that led into the main room. It was also modernized, with a pine floor and throw rugs, and an electric bar heater in the original fireplace. *Fiery* bars, Mum had called them to warn me of their danger when I was a child. A plush sofa, loveseat, and armchair were grouped in front of the heater. They had what looked like a Blackwatch tartan covering, with several red velvet cushions arranged neatly over them. A coffee table made from polished pine planks sat in front of the sofa. The walls were smoothly plastered like any modern house and painted a warm shade of ivory. A television set rested on a shelf in the corner, with a wire coat hanger attached as an aerial.

"Tea?" asked Mike.

I nodded and went to explore the rest of the cottage, clicking on lights as I went. A bathroom with a proper shower stall, and two bedrooms. One had two single beds and the other a double. Everything looked clean and comfortable. The sheets on all the beds were fresh and there were plenty of clean towels in the bathroom. All the windows had thick curtains, which were drawn. I pulled them open, one by one, to find that all of them had a heavy black cloth screening them as well as being boarded up on the outside. Some kind of safe house, I guessed.

I shut myself in the bathroom but couldn't lock it as there wasn't one. I ran the hot water tap and waited until warm water replaced the frigid that came out at first. My hands and nails were filthy, like I had been grubbing about in coal. I scrubbed at them with the bar of red carbolic in the soap dish. My face didn't look much better, my jaw already swollen and red where Mike punched me.

I had to grip the edge of the sink hard to stop myself from rushing out and pummeling him with my fists. The water still poured, steaming up the room.

A knock sounded at the door. "You all right, Jen?"

I wanted to scream, *'Fuck the hell off!'* but got myself under control. "Yes."

"Kettle's boiled."

"Okay."

I turned on the cold tap and mixed the water until it was bearable enough to rinse my face. When I came out I found Mike sitting on one of the chairs at the little table in the kitchen. He'd already poured tea into two mugs, which he'd set down on the table alongside a stainless steel sugar bowl that held several sachets of powdered milk and sugar. It looked familiar.

I drew in a sharp breath when I realized why. It was similar to the one Dad had knocked onto the floor in the Percy French. I blinked, remembering how I'd bent down to reach for it, and my mother's words from above the table: *'You'll give up your education, Jennifer, over my dead—'*

I'll never know if she finished the sentence or not.

I tore open two sachets and stirred them into the mug, then turned abruptly, taking my tea into the living room.

"I thought you took milk," Mike observed. I ignored him and settled down on the plush armchair, holding the mug between my frozen palms. He followed me, tea in hand. "Do you want me to take your coat?"

I'd forgotten I still wore it. I shook my head, staring blindly into my tea. He laid his mug on the coffee table and retreated. I heard him open the fridge and ice cubes clattered as he raided the freezer section. He returned, bearing a plastic bag with ice inside.

Hunkering down he tried to hold it to my jaw but I pulled back. "Jen," he said, and waited for me to make eye contact. "I'm sorry about hitting you. You know why I had to do it, don't you?"

I controlled my impulse to throw hot tea in his face. I did understand why but I hated him for it nonetheless. He obviously wasn't going anywhere until I acknowledged him, so I nodded curtly. He straightened, left the ice pack on the coffee table and took his tea back into the kitchen. The wooden chair legs scraped on the tiles as he sat down.

Taking the ice pack I pressed it against my face. I closed my eyes, remaining like that until the ice melted and the bag leaked. I came to with a start as water dribbled down my wrist, soaking the cuff of my sweater underneath.

From the kitchen I heard rattling, and the scent of toast permeated the air. I packed the melting ice bag into my empty mug and took it to the kitchen. Mike had bread under the grill and a couple of eggs bubbled in a pan on the stove. My stomach growled. I hadn't eaten a thing since yesterday.

"Only breakfast fixings in the fridge," he said. "How do you like your eggs?"

"Any way." I couldn't even bring myself to be gracious. Out of curiosity I opened the fridge and found a packet of bacon slices. I held them up, giving Mike an inquisitive look.

He shook his head. "Don't do pork. Sorry."

I was about to retort, *'Yeah, but I do,'* until he added, "I don't fix it, either."

I'd forgotten he was Jewish. With a shrug I tossed the bacon back in the fridge. Eggs would be fine.

Mike put them into little cups, the toast on plates and placed it all on the table. I saw he already had salt and pepper shakers, and butter on a saucer. He'd make someone a wonderful wife one day. I clamped my trembling lips together. Clancy had said that to me once when we'd been friends.

Yeah, friends with someone who applauded IRA atrocities to get their United Ireland.

Mike held out a hand for my mug and gestured that I should sit at the table. He fished out the ice bag, refilled both our mugs and put them on the table as he took the other chair.

I felt numb. I saw myself drinking tea and using a blunt knife to cut the top off my boiled egg, as though I observed through the wrong end of a pair of binoculars. Conversation was impossible from this far away. I buttered my toast, cut it into two pieces and ate it all mechanically, even though my jaw throbbed with every bite. No way to tell what time it was with all the windows boarded up. I glanced at my watch. The glass was broken and the hands had stopped at 4:32. About the time Mike had intercepted me in Ballyben.

My empty eggshell reminded me of a school project where we were supposed to get the egg white and yolk out without breaking the shell so we could paint it up for Easter. Mum had shown me how by inserting a needle into each end. I found it extraordinary, watching the slimy insides dribble out through such an impossibly small hole, after we'd helped it along by sucking–

Feeling Mike's gaze on me I realized I had been sitting staring into my empty eggshell for some time. I stood, the chair legs scraping loudly on the tiles, and took my dishes to the sink. I'd spilled a trickle of yolk that had congealed down one side of the cup. It'd need a good scrub with plenty of good old reliable *Fairy Liquid* dishwashing soap. The television ad jingled through my mind: '*For hands that do dishes that are as soft as your face, use mild green - Fairy Liquid!*'

Mike appeared at my elbow and eased the cup out of my hand. "Perhaps you should get some sleep, Jennifer," he suggested.

That sounded like a great idea. With a nod I moved toward the bedrooms, my limbs leaden. I don't think I've ever felt so bone weary.

"Take either room," said Mike.

I went into the closest one, which had the double bed. Shutting the door, I stood for a moment, forgetting why I'd come in. Oh yes, sleep. I eased out of Dad's donkey jacket, stopping dead when I felt the Browning holster. I'd forgotten it without the pistol's weight to remind me. I put the coat on the chair by the dresser and unclipped the holster. Slipping it off my shoulders, I laid it neatly over the coat. I wondered if I should keep my clothes on and lie on top of the bed. Probably most prudent. But at least I'd take off my heeled boots, they pinched my toes. I sat on the end of the bed to remove them and discovered the bed very warm under my rear. It had an electric blanket, which was switched on full. That decided me. I stripped off all my outer clothing, turned off the light and climbed under the covers wearing only my bra and panties. It was amazing how relaxing it felt, burrowing into that warm cocoon.

I opened my eyes but couldn't see much through the dust and smoke. Pain lanced through me. I couldn't breathe with that weight pressing down on my chest, couldn't move. It was so hot, so unbearably hot. Flames crackled close, flaring yellow and orange. I heard sirens screeching in the distance. Someone screamed nearby. On and on. Oh God, make them stop, I can't bear it. Stop, for God's sake, *stop!*

I heard my name. "Jennifer."

The weight dissipated from my chest. I could breathe, but only in gasping sobs. Arms encircled me and held me close and safe. I opened my eyes for real. It was still dark, but light flooded in a slant across the floor.

"It's all right, Jen," murmured Mike.

My body felt slick, sweat pooling under my arms and between my breasts. He perched on the side of the bed, holding me tight. I tried to push him away. "Don't."

He held fast, bending his head so his lips touched my hair. "You were screaming, Jen. A nightmare. Everything's okay."

"It's not okay," I said through gritted teeth. "It's never going to be okay."

He pulled me onto his lap, bedclothes and all, and rocked me in his arms, ever so slowly. I was too surprised to object.

"I know it feels that way now," he said. "And you'll never be the same again. But it will get better than this, I promise."

"How the fuck would you know?"

I felt him inhale a slow, deep breath, and then exhale. "Because I lost my parents too, thanks to the IRA."

I tried to speak. My mouth opened but nothing came out. Why had he never told me?

"Remember the spate of bombings by OIRA, the Official IRA, in England several years ago?" His tone sounded so distant and unemotional, but a little catch in his voice gave him away. "Mom was in the wrong place at the wrong time when a two hundred and eighty pound bomb went off. My father worked for the Embassy. He got shot by them earlier that year."

Oh my God. He did know how I felt. "I'm sorry," I managed at length, my voice muffled against his chest. And then it hit me. I raised my head. "That's why you're in the British Army!"

In answer he gripped me even tighter, sending pain ricocheting through my ribs. I gasped and he released his hold. "Think you can go back to sleep?" he asked.

I didn't think so. But I nodded. "Yes."

"May I stay?" He sounded like a lost little boy.

I didn't want to be alone in the dark again. I couldn't face a repeat of that nightmare, not tonight. "Okay." I shifted over to make room for him.

He left the door ajar and stretched out beside me on top of the covers. I wondered if he still had his boots on. I could make out his profile in the light coming through the door. He lay on his back, arms under his head. I wanted to reach out, offer him comfort, share in our common loss. But I couldn't. He was responsible for all the bad stuff that had happened to me. I turned away and curled up.

The bed grew too hot and I remembered the electric blanket. Rolling over I peered down my side of the bed but couldn't see the light of a control. I looked over my shoulder toward Mike. "Could you turn off the blanket please?"

I felt him move and heard the click as he complied. "They should have a timer on these things."

"Do they leave it on all the time?"

"No, I switched it on earlier."

Another silence settled between us. I was beginning to fall asleep when he spoke again. "Jennifer?"

I stirred. "Hmm?"

"I'm sorry for the way I acted. At your place in Belfast."

I jerked wide awake.

"I tried to call," he continued. "To apologize. But you were already on your way to Newcastle."

"Because you'd forgotten your gun," I retorted.

"I realized that almost at once. That wasn't why I called."

There were so many things I wanted to ask. To accuse. *If that's so, why didn't you meet the bus in Newcastle?* If he had we wouldn't have gone to the café. *Why did you walk out in the first place?* In the end all I asked was, "Why didn't you come to the hospital?"

"I did, but you were out of it."

I remembered the man in the shadows at the foot of my bed. I thought it had been a dream.

"I was a complete jerk, walking out on you like that," he continued.

"Why did you? Walk out?"

He struggled, searching for the right words. "I had a lot on my mind. I didn't know how to–" He broke off.

I stayed quiet, waiting.

"I can explain better tomorrow," he said finally. "Just know I regret my actions deeply. Please forgive me, Jen."

I bit my lip. I didn't know if I could ever do that. He didn't seem to know what he'd done. "We can talk in the morning."

The bed moved and I stiffened, thinking he might try and spoon or something. I felt him turn toward me but then he rolled onto his side, facing the other way.

I needed to say something. "I'm really sorry about your parents, Mike."

The silence went on so long I thought he wasn't going to answer. Finally he murmured, "Thank you."

I didn't think I'd be able to fall asleep, but must have. The next time I opened my eyes he had gone. I smelled coffee brewing and heard a woodpigeon cooing outside. For a moment I thought I was at Mourneview. Coming fully awake my first instinct was to bury back into the oblivion of sleep.

But I was sticky and grimy after the exertions of yesterday and sweaty from my nightmare. I heard Mike opening cupboards and drawers in the kitchen, so I went into the bathroom to take a shower. He'd already had one, the mirror was steamed up and one of the towels damp. This was obviously a male environment. I could only find Vosene medicated shampoo, and a broken piece of waterlogged carbolic soap. No hair conditioner, I'd never get my tangles combed out.

I kept my mind on the simple routine of getting clean, not thinking about the past, or trying to consider the future. As I dried off I wished I'd brought a change of clothes. I didn't want to wear the underwear that I'd worn all day yesterday. Nor the funeral outfit. I'd like to incinerate that.

A brand new toothbrush had appeared by the sink overnight, along with a plastic tube of toothpaste. I scrubbed the bad taste from my mouth and rinsed.

Mike knocked on the door. "Got coffee."

I wrapped one of the big towels sarong-like around my body and opened the door. Mike, wearing a pair of gray sweats, held out a mug of steaming, aromatic espresso. His hair was still damp, standing up on end.

"There're clean clothes on the bed."

"Thank you."

Offering me a tentative smile he returned to the kitchen, and I took the coffee to the bedroom. A set of gray sweats, still sealed in plastic, along with a packet of three pristine white Y-front briefs awaited me, lying neatly on the bed. Brand new men's briefs were better than nothing even though the waistband reached as far as my ribcage. I couldn't face putting on my bra, not wanting to touch anything from the day before. The sweats turned out to be a little too large, but I rolled up the sleeves and trouser bottoms. Finding a black plastic fine-tooth comb and a short-bristled lint brush on the dresser, I used them to get most of the tangles out of my hair.

The coffee took effect. I began to feel less like the undead. A loud crackling sound came from the kitchen and then the murmur of Mike's voice. A man answered, his voice distorted. I went to investigate. Mike sat at the kitchen table, wearing chunky headphones with a mouthpiece, working at a bulky field radio. 'Clansman' was clearly marked on it. He saw me and immediately terminated the connection.

"Don't mind me." I headed for the coffee pot.

He took off the headphones. "How you feeling?"

I met his gaze. "Better."

He smiled and I managed to return it, even if I couldn't make it quite reach my eyes. "Thank you. For–" I swallowed hard. "Everything."

He got up and gave my elbow a gentle squeeze. "Welcome back." Turning back to the table, he pulled out a chair for me. "Now, let's talk."

12
Wee Tim'rous Beasties

"All I need to know before we proceed," Mike said, "is if you still want to get the people responsible for the Percy French bomb?"

Wasn't that abundantly obvious?

"There's no going back once you take this path." His steady gaze bored into me.

"I'm certain. It's the only thing–"

I didn't have to finish the sentence. He nodded. "I'll take you to a place where you'll be taught how to catch those responsible. Everything will be explained to you there. Okay?"

"What sort of place is it?"

"Training facility."

That's all he'd say. A couple of hours later we stood ready and waiting as a dull brown Ford Escort came up the narrow dirt track to the cottage. Mike ushered me out and locked up the back door as the car tires crunched on the cobblestones.

Mike held the back door of the Ford open for me, then got into the front passenger seat. A very clean-cut man in his twenties, with severely cropped white-blond hair sat at the wheel. His body looked fit and muscular, I'd bet he was a soldier in civvies.

My mind wandered as we drove through the mountain back roads and headed southeast. I wondered about my violin, and the Botanic apartment. What would happen to it all if I didn't go back? Would anyone even notice I'd gone?

We safely bypassed Ballyben and carried on to Newry, one of the oldest towns in Ireland. I wondered if we were going to the British Army base at Bessbrook Mill not far outside Newry, but we headed south to a little town I'd never heard of called Silverbridge. Nationalist tricolor flags hung from lampposts and IRA graffiti embroidered the walls. We passed through and kept heading south. Mike and the driver hadn't exchanged a single word since we'd left the safe house. I felt my eyelids grow heavy, the motion of the car lulling me to sleep. Not far from the border to Eire the driver turned off the main road, which jerked me awake. He took us through a complex combination of lanes deep in the countryside. This far out there were no signposts so I wasn't sure where exactly we were.

On a remote lane shaded by large oak trees, the car pulled up to a pair of pillars with a rusty, padlocked gate between them. High stone walls stretched on either side, enclosing the property. The stucco pillars and walls had once been white but now were brown-gray and moss-covered. The driver got out, leaving the car idling and worked at the padlock on the gate.

"Is this it?" I asked the back of Mike's head.

He nodded. "Yeah."

The gate swung open easily despite its rusted appearance. Mike cracked open the passenger side and got out so he could close and lock the gate after the car had passed through. The track led about a quarter of a mile through a wooded area until it emerged in the grounds of a Georgian mansion. My attention was riveted on a large square of land to the side of the building. Overseen by a drill instructor, a group of soldiers jumped down from the top of a climbing wall and ran toward a huge net. A couple of them had already scaled it and were clambering down the other side.

A man's voice with a Scottish brogue split the air. I heard him clearly inside the car despite the engine and the crunch of gravel under the wheels. Yelling insults at the soldiers, he had his hands firmly planted on his hips and I could see from here that his barrel chest rose and fell with every vehement shout.

A white minivan, army Land Rover, and a couple of nondescript cars sat on the gravel in front of the mansion. Our driver pulled up beside them and parked. Now that we were close I realized that the building had seen better days. Cracks ran through the facade, and peeling woodwork round the windows needed a couple of coats of paint.

Mike got out and opened the back door for me.

"That all, Sir?" asked the driver, getting out as well.

"Thanks, Chalki." I noticed how less American Mike's voice sounded.

Chalki offered Mike an informal salute and headed off round the side of the mansion. He hadn't even looked at me once as far as I knew.

"Come on, ye lazy beastie!" bellowed the drill instructor. One soldier who had fallen behind all the others, dropped from the net and threw himself prone on the ground to crawl under rows of barbed wire. Mike appeared beside me.

"British Army?" I asked.

"Not exactly."

I kept my eyes on the assault course. "Was I always a prospective recruit?"

"No. But then you saved my ass in that Ballyben tavern like a pro. Jennifer, you were in the middle of it all with them applauding your playing. You managed to single-handedly infiltrate somewhere we couldn't."

What an idiot I'd been. I'd been all gaga with the flush of what I thought was first love, and all the time he'd been working at getting me here. The Percy French bomb just expedited matters.

"But I got involved," he continued. "I - didn't want to see you hurt."

I met his gaze. He looked like he believed what he said. But how could

I trust him ever again?

He cleared his throat. "That's why I walked out that night. I didn't want to go through with it."

"Go through with what?" I gestured to the mansion and grounds. "This? Or with you and me?"

"This. I wanted for you and me to continue."

I let that sink in. If that were the case he had a hell of a way of showing it. I felt his eyes on me and recognized concern on his face. Afraid I'd fallen into another fugue. "I'm all right," I assured him. His eyes lingered on my lips. I took a step back. "Let's get this over and done with."

He led the way across the gravel and up four steps to the mansion porch. The large, heavy front door was unlocked. He held it open for me, followed me in and closed it behind us.

A scent of beeswax furniture polish assaulted me from the antique oak wood floor and paneled walls. A threadbare red rug with a curlicue design lay on the floor of the hall and stairs. By the elaborately carved banisters of the sweeping staircase a very old and impressive Longcase grandfather clock ticked loudly, and a vast crystal chandelier dangled in the center of the ceiling.

A mustached man in his fifties, sporting a receding hairline below tufts of sable hair, emerged from one of the rooms that led off the hall. His cobalt eyes had a myriad of lines fanned below them as though he constantly squinted across vast horizons. He wore a tweed jacket over a shirt and tie, with corduroy trousers. His crisp, military bearing told me he'd probably be a lot more comfortable in a uniform.

"Miss Hamilton," he greeted me. His accent sounded gentrified, but local. "Stanley Pierce." He held out a hand and I shook it. His grip felt firm and his palm cool.

"*Colonel* Pierce, that is," added Mike. "Known here as the 'Boss'."

Pierce closed his other hand over mine and held it for a moment. "Welcome to Finley Manor. I'm sorry for your loss." I nodded curtly and he let go. "Come in, please."

He led the way to an office where a large mahogany desk dominated the room. Three burgundy high-backed leather chairs sat around it, two in front and one behind serving as the desk chair. A matching leather sofa that could accommodate about six people sat against the wall, with a large tartan Blackwatch blanket along its back. On the opposite wall an ornate fireplace nestled between two big windows that looked out over the training field. A large bay window at the front of the room had a view of the car park. Maps and mugshots lined the walls, and diagram charts of different kinds of weapons and explosives. A small mahogany table with leather trim stood on the window side of Pierce's desk. On it were two expensive-looking Waterford crystal decanters containing what looked like whiskey and sherry with glasses beside them. Mum would have done her nut. She insisted on buying only the Northern Irish-made Tyrone crystal rather than the stuff made in Southern Ireland. I gritted my teeth, ignoring the thrust of pain in my heart.

Pierce gestured to the sofa so I obediently sat, perching on the edge. "Scotch or sherry?" he asked.

Mum would have done her nut over that, too, always insisting on locally made Bushmills. "Scotch, thank you."

The sharp tang of whiskey permeated the air as he removed the crystal stopper from the decanter. Mike crossed to the window and gazed out while Pierce poured golden liquid into two glasses, handing one to me. "Can't tempt you, Mike?"

"Only if it's Bourbon, Boss."

"Dreadful stuff. You Yanks have no taste."

Obviously a frequent friendly exchange between them. I took a sip from my glass. A very smooth, expensive blend. Nice, but not Bushmills.

Pierce sat in one of the leather chairs by his desk and swiveled it round to face me. "Now, to business. I assume Sergeant McLeod has told you all about us."

I shot Mike a look. "Just that you can train me to go after terrorists."

"That we can. The work is straightforward. We are a small, elite detachment that operates outside of normal channels. We're not soldiers although we incorporate similar training. Our people go into deep cover situations where usual British intelligence can't. It's high risk." He paused, watching my face. I gave a nod to show I understood. "I want there to be no question that you know what you're getting into. If you're caught the government will deny any knowledge of you. Are you clear on that?"

I nodded. "Crystal."

He held my gaze and I was aware of Mike watching from across the room. "And if your cover is blown the IRA will torture you and kill you. Have no illusions about getting out of it alive. Do you understand?"

I swallowed. I didn't give a fuck whether I lived or died. I only wanted to find the bastards who planted the Percy French bomb. "I understand."

"And you still want to go through with it?"

"I do," I said with conviction.

"Well then." Pierce looked from me to Mike and back again, his sky-blue eyes keen. "Begin training in the morning." He raised his glass to me. "Welcome aboard."

Mike took me upstairs to the recruits' accommodations on the third floor. As we passed the second floor he nodded toward the back corridor off to the left. "My room's the third door that way, after the showers."

"I thought you were based at Ballykinlar?"

"Bessbrook, actually."

First I'd heard of it. "Since when?"

"Since always. I have regular business at Ballykinlar, though."

"Do they know about here?"

"Officially, I'm on special assignment. But you're going to have to stop asking questions like that, Jennifer."

Yes, I supposed I would. There was a lot I'd have to stop doing in my new life. And I must never forget why I'd had to make this new life for myself.

On the third floor he led me along the same corridor one flight up, all the way to the room at the end. The entire floor reeked of pine antiseptic cleaning fluid. The room he showed me to had three single beds, two of which had been claimed, judging by the alarm clock and pot of lip balm on one of the side tables, and the packed canvas bag on the bed nearest the door.

"There's only one other female recruit at present," Mike said from the threshold. "That's yours." He pointed at the bed with the bag on it.

I took a step toward it. Warmth flooded me as I recognized a very familiar black shape. They'd brought my violin! I pulled the case from under the canvas bag and embraced it like the lost friend it was.

Mike smiled. "We retrieved some of your stuff from your apartment in Belfast."

"We?" He didn't elaborate. "What did Deirdre have to say about that?"

"She moved out."

"Does she know where I am?"

"No one knows where you are. Not even your lawyer. But tomorrow you need to write to him, not specifying where, but telling him that you'll be away for a few months. We'll give you an address he can contact you at."

"What about the rest of my stuff?"

"The apartment's paid for until the end of June. Everything's secure there for now."

Not that I had anything worth keeping. The violin was the only thing I cared about.

"I'll let you unpack." He pointed at a foot locker at the end of the bed. "You'll find a uniform in there. Get changed."

I was afraid to be left alone. Of the silence. My lip trembled. No, I mustn't cry, not in front of him!

But he noticed and took a step over the threshold. "You going to be all right?"

I wanted to tell him I was scared shitless. That he was the nearest thing I had to a friend now. That I wanted to go back in time to before he and I slept together, so I wouldn't have made that trip to Newcastle. Hell, so that maybe he and I might have had a chance if none of this had happened.

Perhaps we shared the same kinds of thoughts for we moved at the same time and embraced. I clung to him, the feel of his body against mine erupting unexpected desire. I ran my hand down the length of his spine, remembering the smoothness of his skin. He bent his head and his lips claimed mine. I kissed him back with every ounce of life left in me. I had that strange, alluring sensation of falling, but then ice touched my heart, chilling me back to reality. I pulled away, stepping out of his arms.

His eyes were opaque and wide as he met my gaze. "That can't happen again," he said.

I gritted my teeth. "Too right."

"Not while you're here."

"Not anywhere."

The shutters came down over his face again. "When you've changed, come down to the Boss's office."

I turned my back on him and listened to his footsteps on the worn linoleum floor as he headed back down the corridor. Tears welled up and I dashed them away. I felt truly alone now. But that's how it had to be. Mike and I didn't belong together. We never would. The cost of having him in my life had been too much.

I crossed over to the bare casement window. The assault course must be on the other side. Below lay a neglected tennis court with a sagging net, rotting with disuse. Beyond that spread a field with a stream running through, and a dense copse of trees in the distance. I felt a sudden painful wash of homesickness for Mourneview and my life before, then clamped down on it. Finley Manor was my home, now. At least for three months. There was no going back to the life before.

Ever.

Upturning the canvas bag onto my bed, I found an assortment of my clothes. The leopard design cosmetics and sponge bag Dee had given me for Christmas were there too, filled with my makeup and moisturizers. Even my deodorant spray. I opened up the little door on my bedside table and tucked the bags in there. A scratched up oak chest of drawers separated my bed from the one already taken. The three drawers on my side were empty so I dutifully folded my clothes into them. I couldn't help but notice that my roommate had a preponderance toward holey T-shirts, leather belts complete with studs, and tight Sid and Nancy jeans.

In the foot locker I found a pair of black lace-up boots, an assortment of army jackets, pullovers, shirts and trousers, some in camouflage material and others plain. They looked second-hand, with any name tags or identifying patches removed. At the bottom of the trunk were squished two sets of the gray sweats, size small.

I closed the bedroom door and stripped out of my too-big sweats and heeled boots. I wasn't certain exactly what combination of the new garments constituted a uniform. Remembering what Mike had worn the first time we met, I selected the lightweight green denims, long sleeved shirt, and pullover. The camouflage stuff was probably for outdoors. No doubt I'd be told pronto if I had it wrong.

The new boots were just a half size too big, so I wore a pair of my own socks underneath the woolen army ones to make them fit. My roommate had a mirror lying on her foot locker, so I propped it up and peered at myself. I hadn't realized how wild my hair looked. Without conditioner to tame it, it had frizzed up in a messy tangle, like the Worzel Gummidge scarecrow character on ITV. Why did Mike not say anything? It's a wonder Colonel Pierce let me through the door of the Manor at all. I rummaged in my sponge bag, and found the thick-tooth comb and hairbrush I'd kept in the bathroom at Botanic. I kept a couple of elastic hairbands wound around the handle of the brush, so once I combed out the majority of the rats' tails, as my mother would've called them, I pulled my hair back into a neat pony tail. That looked better. Now I looked like I meant business.

⌘

I couldn't see more than a foot in front of me through the sleeting rain. My hair lay plastered to my head and my fingers and nose stung with cold. I inched my way through a morass of mud under curled barbed wire. Every sinew in my body ached, my boobs squashed flat into the mire they called ground.

Heather, my new roommate, crawled past me and began to pull ahead. She looked every bit as miserable as I felt. Not for the first time I wondered why doing exercises like this in any way, shape, or form, helped us train. The kind of work I expected us two girls to do would be in nice, dry places, nowhere near barbed wire fences, swinging ropes, or pelting rain. At least, I sincerely hoped not.

It annoyed me to see the eighteen male recruits way ahead of us, long since having cleared the barbed wire obstacle. I found it vastly irritating that Heather and I could never keep up.

Since the first day it had been that way. I'd have thought that an entire month later that things would have evened out, but it felt like 'us against them' in all aspects of our training. Once the guys realized that neither Heather nor I had any intention of sleeping with any of them, from classroom to firing range and training field to mealtimes, we'd felt very much on the outside of the male camaraderie. Particularly in physical situations like this, where competitive testosterone took them over. They made no secret of the fact they considered that we girls held them back.

"Come on! Move it!" bellowed a Scottish voice. I twisted my neck to look up through the wire. Sergeant Hughes, our drill instructor, glared down me, hands on hips. "You girlies look like fuckin' beached whales!"

And you look like a fucking teapot! I wanted to retort. The recruits called him Tetley behind his back, the brand of tea, because he habitually took on the shape of a teapot when he stood like that. I wisely said nothing and kicked my legs a little harder, trying to push faster through the quagmire.

"Get a bloody move on, girlie! Stop floppin' aboot like a haddock. What d'ye think ye are, a fuckin' mermaid?"

Heather snickered and I forced myself to slosh harder, my elbows and knees on fire.

"*Wee, sleekit, cowrin, tim'rous beastie,*" intoned Tetley. "*O, what a panic's in thy breastie!*" Heather and I exchanged looks. "Robbie Burns, girlies, Robbie Burns. Have ye no heard of him?"

"Yes, Sir!" we answered in unison.

"Then wee tim'rous beasties - *get fuckin' moving!*" he bellowed even more loudly, although I didn't think more volume could be humanly possible. "Shall I throw ye a lifebuoy? Pair of rubber armbands to keep yer pretty arse out o' the mud?"

I wanted to deck him one. For fuck's sake, I was doing my best. Four weeks I'd had to listen to him day and night. Insult after insult. Nag, bloody nag, bloody nag, nag, nag. Come here do this stand to attention girlie shouldn't let people with tits near a weapon and on and on. And I had to take it, because if I wanted to find out who killed my parents I had no other choice.

"See them tits o' yours?" he said in a reasonable tone. "A liability, that's what they are."

I rested on my elbows. "Don't knock them, Sarge, they make pretty good homegrown flotation devices."

A slow toothy smile spread over his face. My heart sank. Why couldn't I just have kept quiet? "Ye can just start all over again from the beginnin', Recruit."

I let my head droop and felt slick, chilly mud touch my burning forehead. Forcing myself to move, I squirmed on, drawing level with Heather.

She elbowed me hard in the ribs. "Why can't you just shut the hell up, Jennifer?"

"And that goes for ye, too, girlie!" Tetley yelled.

"Fuck it," she muttered.

"Shouldn't let people with tits—" The drum of the rain drowned out his voice as he took off toward the other recruits.

"—near a weapon!" we finished for him.

The last spiral of barbed wire was just ahead, and we both made a superhuman effort to clear it. My knees nearly gave out when I hauled myself upright.

"What does he think he has on his chest?" demanded Heather, appearing to have no trouble standing up. "Warts?"

"Beer spigots."

Thank God for laughter. It made things so much easier to bear. Wading through the mire we made our way back to the swinging ropes at the beginning of the course. If it hadn't been for another woman's company this would be completely and utterly unbearable.

I grabbed hold of the rope with both hands and inwardly groaned when across the field I spotted Mike watching from the car park. He only seemed to show up anytime I screwed up. Was it just bad timing or did he take some sadistic delight in watching me fail? Tetley marched over to talk to him.

Dusk threatened and the rain showed no sign of letting up. Heather and I worked diligently with grim determination and managed to get through the field obstacles without flagging. Even though I felt like every muscle might explode. We had different strengths and helped each other wherever we could. I climbed faster than she did so I waited at the top of the net until she'd caught up. Then in unison we swung over the apex and down the other side. Rain had slicked the bars on the climbing frame and our numb hands had trouble keeping hold. My arms burned so badly I was amazed that I managed to 'walk' my way across them all without slipping.

Reaching the barbed wire again, I threw myself prone and began crawling. I got through it by keeping my thoughts focused on a mug filled with hot chocolate dashed with rum, and a McVitie's chocolate-covered digestive biscuit to dunk into it.

"Hot chocolate, drinking chocolate, hot chocolate, drinking chocolate," I muttered over and over, parroting the television advertisement for the brand.

"Oh, yes," agreed Heather. "And a hot shower."

"Dry socks."

"A fag."

I grimaced. Cigarettes were not my idea of comfort.

As we drew close to the end of the wire I realized the guys had gathered to watch. "Come on, girlies!" one of them shouted, mimicking Tetley. Whether they meant encouragement or not, it helped us persevere, and when they cheered en masse as we finished, I couldn't help but smile.

Darkness had fallen by the time we reached the wall, the last of the obstacles. Ten feet high, and slippery in the rain, neither Heather nor I could manage to get purchase. No matter what we did we couldn't get a hand hold. Then I remembered this was supposed to be all about teamwork. I leaned my back against the wall.

"Here!" I called, cupping my hands together in front of me.

She jumped up so I could boost her and she managed to straddle the top. I scrabbled at the wall to pull myself up and she reached down to help. But both of us had soaking wet, numb fingers. We lost our grip and ended up toppling face down in the mud. I found myself wracked with laughter.

Partly hysteria, but mostly because of how ridiculous we must look. Rendered utterly useless, I rolled onto my back and let the rain drum on my face. After a startled moment, Heather joined in, and we giggled helplessly like a couple of teenagers.

The guys surprised us by coming to the rescue. "For fuck's sake," I heard one of them say, "before Tetley comes back or we'll never get shot of here."

They swarmed over. Two of them hoisted us to our feet while the others created a human pyramid in front of the wall for us to climb. Despite being weak with mirth and exertion, we managed to scale both them and the wall. When we clambered over, two more guys scurried round to help us down the other side. A huge cheer went up when our feet finally touched the ground.

Tetley materialized and surveyed us, hands on hips. I knew he couldn't help but have witnessed. The rain thumped into the ground as we waited with baited breath for his reaction. "Get cleaned up!" he bellowed, taking pity on us. "On tha double! Then chow time boys." The corners of his eyes crinkled. "And girlies!"

Another cheer went up and we headed for the back door of the mansion. Heather and I had apparently been accepted at last.

13

A Soldier's Song

"Hamilton and Baird." Tetley halted us, letting the guys get out of earshot. "I have a nice wee treat for ye's two. Some hands-on practical training. Report to the Boss after ye clean up."

Our corridor had two sets of facilities. The larger housed four toilet stalls, four showers and a row of sinks. A smaller room next to Heather's and my room had a single shower, toilet, and sink, allocated for our use only. Even though technically we could use the guys' facilities if we wanted, we had no desire to share with a bunch of dirty males who probably exchanged athlete's foot and other transmittable conditions on a daily basis.

Heather and I took turns showering and I automatically retrieved my violin from our room before we headed downstairs. Heather didn't comment. Anytime the Boss summoned me he also checked up on my repertoire of traditional Irish songs.

At his *"Enter!"* we went into the office. He sat at his desk with Mike opposite, both holding crystal glasses filled with golden liquid. Glancing at the drinks table I saw that a three-quarters full bottle of Jack Daniel's Tennessee bourbon had appeared beside the decanters. The fire was lit, and the pleasant aroma told me peat burned, not coal.

Since coming to Finley, anytime Mike and I came face to face I avoided eye contact, even though every sinew in me was aware of him. Particularly when he sat mere feet away like now. I also never addressed him directly, or even acknowledged him if I could get away with it. He did the same although I often felt his eyes on me when he thought I wasn't looking. I kept my gaze on Pierce as Heather and I stood to attention.

"Relax." He held out a brown letter-sized envelope with a plastic window. As I was closest I stepped forward to take it. "Both of you report to Sergeant Hughes at 1500 hours tomorrow."

I glanced at the front of the envelope and saw the word *Ballykinlar* typed under the plastic window. Without meaning to I looked at Mike. Our gazes locked for a moment and my stomach flipped.

"Questions?" asked Pierce.

"No, Boss."

He waved a hand to indicate we were dismissed and we headed for the door. What, no impromptu violin concerto?

"Hamilton, stay a moment," he added.

Heather opened the door and left, clicking it shut behind her. The Boss gestured to the violin. "As you've brought it, let's hear something." He looked to Mike. "Any requests?"

I felt my face redden. I didn't want to perform in front of Mike, but you didn't argue with a Colonel. Mike shook his head.

"Oh, come on," chided Pierce.

I laid the envelope on the arm of the leather sofa. Raising the violin to my chin I tweaked at the strings, checking the tuning.

Mike's gaze burned into me. "Let her choose something."

Pierce settled back in his chair. "Carry on."

My mind went blank. Every time he said, 'Carry on,' all I thought about was the series of ludicrous British *Carry On* comedy films. Closing my eyes, I drew the bow up and concentrated. What did one play to soldiers upon request?

The bow came down and my fingers picked out the opening bars of *The Soldier's Song*, the Irish National Anthem. An extremely inflammatory tune to play in front of anyone British. I threw myself into the marching beat and peeked from under my lashes to observe how Mike and the Boss were taking it. Pierce's eyebrows had shot up and Mike had busied himself studying the depths of his bourbon. I wanted to laugh out loud. Ending on a crescendo, I swept the bow into the air on the last note as though anticipating applause. None came, of course.

Pierce coughed. "Thank you, Hamilton. Dismissed."

Tucking the bow and violin under my arm I retrieved the envelope from the sofa on my way out. Perhaps he'd think twice about asking me to play again. A guffaw permeated from behind the closed door. Well, at least he had a sense of humor. I turned the envelope over. Sealed, and I didn't dare open it.

I made my way straight to the combination rec room and mess hall, where the stink of boiled cabbage seemed permanently soaked into the walls. I'd missed the lineup for chow but Heather had gotten me a plateful, bless her. I was ravenous after the afternoon's efforts in the mud-soaked training field.

She met me with a glare. "Did you seriously just play *The Soldier's Song?*"

I glanced round the mess and saw the guys shooting me looks that ranged from incredulous to hostile.

"It was a joke," I explained.

Heather shook her head. "Some joke."

Carefully setting the violin and bow on the empty chair next to me, I concentrated on the pile of sausages, mash, and overcooked peas. *The Soldier's Song* made me think of Dee. She'd made sure I'd learned it early on as part of our 'equal opportunity' friendship. It was only fair, since she'd been forced to learn *God Save the Queen*. Sometimes I missed her so much it hurt. The four weeks since the community memorial service had been long enough for me to realize you just can't stop caring for a person, no matter how much you think you want to.

That night in bed I lay awake as usual, unable to get to sleep. Heather was one of those lucky sods who could fall unconscious and be snoring in seconds. As soon as my head hit the pillow, no matter how tired I felt my mind started racing. A common theme was Mike, and after seeing him close up earlier tonight I couldn't get him out of my head.

Most of the time I convinced myself I hated him. Then I'd catch sight of him arriving at the Manor and have a split second impulse to run and greet him, forgetting that I'd made up my mind to cut him from my life. Nights like these were the most difficult. I'd relive that last day with him before he walked out. Before my innocence, in all respects, was lost. Then I'd hate myself when I remembered Mum and Dad.

When I did eventually sleep, more often than not I relived the horror of the Percy French bomb over and over and Heather had to wake me to stop my screaming. A week after getting here, old gruff Tetley, obviously aware of my night terrors, took me aside in the rec room and led me to the table where coffee, teabags and hot water were always available. He held up a glass jar with the word *Horlicks* plastered on a blue label.

"See this, girlie? This is my private stash. Tak a wee bit o' this in hot water to bed every night and ye'll sleep like a bairn." He glared at the other occupants of the room. "Only you, mind."

His unaccustomed considerateness almost made me cry. Other peoples' kindness would be my undoing. "I'll try it Sir, thanks." I hid my emotion under abruptness. Mum had sworn by *Horlicks*, too.

Tetley proceeded to check the jar every morning to see how far the level had gone down. Knowing him, I daren't not drink it in case he decided that extra cleaning duties or something equally nasty would help my insomnia better.

The guys consequently dubbed me '*Horlicks*', pronouncing it *whore-licks*. I pretended to be amused and laughed good-naturedly. With a bit of luck they'd soon get tired of the joke. It took only a week before the teasing petered out. One evening Mike came into the rec room just before lights out. Without looking in my direction he made a big production of mixing himself a mug of *Horlicks* before carrying it up to his room. As he'd never touched the stuff before this was obviously a gesture of support to me. And that put an end to my unfortunate nickname, thank God.

⌘

Next day Heather and I reported to Tetley's office at three o'clock in Admin as ordered. "Ye lucky girlies. Yer not even Paras but yer gonna get jumpin' oot of a plane, and only a month into yer trainin'."

Heather's jaw dropped. "Jumping out of a *what?*"

I braced myself.

"Did I ask ye tae speak?" he bellowed in her face. Vehement spittle sprayed over us.

"Sorry, Sir. But did you say a *plane?*"

"I coulda sed the Starship Enterprise and it still isn't yer place to speak!" he roared.

Come to think of it, his accent did sound a lot like Engineer Montgomery Scott's in *Star Trek*. I fought the desire to laugh. The more I tried not to the more intense the urge became. My breathing grew labored as I struggled for control.

Tetley's ruddy face appeared in front of me. "Wha's the matter wi' ye?" he demanded. "Are ye gonna pass oot?"

I thought I just might if I didn't take a breath soon.

"God, I don't know," he muttered, pulling one of the chairs from against the wall. Shoving it against the back of my knees, it abruptly forced me to sit. "Shouldn't let people with tits near anything."

"Thank you, Sarge." I dug my nails into my palms to try and gain control.

"You sit doon too, Baird," he advised Heather. "Anyone here would give their right arm to do what yer gettin' to do. What a waste." He perched his rump on the desk. "Women's Aid is havin' a sponsored parachute jump for charity. At Ballykinlar, courtesy of the Wild Geese."

I'd heard of the Wild Geese, but wasn't sure whether it was a civilian parachuting team or army.

He coughed. "It's been - *arranged* - for ye two to do it. Great experience and ye'll raise a goodly amount for Women's Aid."

What possible advantage could there be for Heather and me in this? I mean, we'd hardly have to parachute when we were out in the field. *I hoped.* Were we really expected to jump out of an aeroplane with exactly zero training?

I waited for Tetley to give us an opportunity to ask questions, but he didn't. "Yer not to let me doon," he warned. "It's an honor fer ye to be taking part in this." He got up and went round his desk to take a set of keys out of the top drawer. "Now, 'them' at Ballykinlar'll probably put on a bit of a party for ye. Any excuse. Bit of a miserable arse of a place in the back end of beyond."

To our delight he let us loose in a storage shed in the back yard. We raided stacks of cardboard boxes that held all kinds of cast-off clothing and accessories that looked like they'd been meant for a charity shop. I found a gorgeous burgundy dress that I hoped I'd get to keep and unearthed a pair of heeled dark red sandals to match that made my calves look great.

Heather found a black skin-tight sixties style dress with a napkin for a skirt, but Tetley vetoed it much to her disappointment. She settled for a lilac form-fitting dress with a plunging neckline. He let her keep the black satin pumps with pointed toes that she'd fallen in love with. If I'd seen them first I'd have nabbed them for myself.

We had half an hour to pack and report back to him. At the front door he held out the keys to a little blue Mini that had appeared in the car park. Another reminder of Dee. I reached to take them but he snatched his hand back and gave them to Heather.

"Ye don't haf'a license, Hamilton. But here." He placed a second key in my palm. "Ye can take the gate key." He obviously thought he bestowed a worthy booby prize.

We wore our own clothes: jeans and sweatshirts. At Tetley's insistence Heather had toned down her punk look and left the studded belts and holey shirts upstairs.

"Did ye pack your wee dresses for the party?" he demanded.

"Yes, Sir!" we responded enthusiastically.

I couldn't help but feel a sense of excitement. It was the first time I'd felt anything but the numbness of grief. We carried out our overnight bags, both also filched from the storage shed, and stowed them in the trunk of the little car. Tetley accompanied us outside, surveying from the vantage point of the top step.

I caught sight of Mike watching from a window on the second floor. Averting my gaze I concentrated on getting in the car and fastening my seat belt.

"Behave yerselves," advised Tetley as a parting shot. Hands on hips, he waited while we drove down the lane and out of sight. I was willing to bet he stayed there until he couldn't hear the engine anymore.

I got out and unlocked the gate, clicking the padlock back in place after Heather had driven through. Then she turned onto the street and navigated the maze of back roads north. My spirits lifted the further we got away from Finley.

"What are you looking so pleased about?" demanded Heather.

"It's an adventure! Don't tell me you're not happy to get away for a bit."

"To commit suicide? How can I be happy?"

I snorted. "It's just a parachute jump."

"Just a parachute jump? *Just*, she says. Jumping out of a perfectly good aeroplane?"

"Heather, they wouldn't let people do sponsored jumps if it were that risky."

She blinked rapidly while she thought about it. "I suppose so. But still." Her voice trailed off. "Is it really for charity?"

"It must be, they wouldn't make it up. I suppose Mike - Sergeant McLeod arranged for us to do it."

Overtaking a farm vehicle distracted her so she didn't notice my slip. "Why?" she asked. "Exactly what part of our work will involve jumping out of a fucking aeroplane?"

"Beats me, any more than we have to crawl through mud and climb walls." I shrugged. "You never know, I guess."

Once we were on the M-1 it was a straight shot to Hillsborough, and from there I directed us through the back roads via Ballynahinch toward Seaforde. How odd to be on this familiar route again. It had only been a few weeks but it felt like a lifetime ago. As we approached Clough I steeled myself for the first glimpse of the Mournes, but thick cloud obscured them.

Heather took the Blackstaff Road turn-off on the far side of Clough, three miles from Ballykinlar. She reached an arm back and fumbled blindly behind her seat, forcing the Mini to swerve into the opposite lane. I reached round in alarm to retrieve her handbag from the floor and unzipped it before sliding it onto her lap.

"Cheers." She rummaged and deftly withdrew a cigarette from a packet inside. Dumping the bag back behind her she leaned forward to push in the car lighter.

I sighed heavily. "Must you?"

"I must." She waggled the cigarette between her fingers. "Can't deny a dying girl her fag." The lighter popped out and she lit up, inhaling deeply and with smug satisfaction.

Pointedly, I rolled down the window. She'd finished by the time we came to a junction with a sharp right turn, leading to the entrance of Ballykinlar Barracks. My stomach fluttered with nerves as we drew up to the highly-guarded security barrier. Getting the envelope Pierce had given me out of my bag I handed it to Heather.

One of the privates on duty approached the car, casually gripping his SLR. He had a beautiful caramel-colored African complexion, very exotic-looking for Northern Ireland. Heather wound down her window and held out the envelope.

"Jennifer Hamilton and Heather Baird from Women's Aid," she told him.

"Switch off the engine, please," he instructed in a Beatles-type Liverpudlian accent.

While the private ripped open the envelope, another soldier circled the car, holding a long-handled device with a mirror that allowed him to see underneath. Heather fished a cigarette from her bag, clicked at the lighter and inhaled.

The private looked up disapprovingly from the papers. "Extinguish that, please." He waited until she crushed the tip of it into the ashtray in the dashboard. "Open the boot, please."

So polite.

"Let me." I unclipped my seat belt, glad of an excuse to get out of the smoke-addled car. Reaching over to pull the keys from the ignition I got out and unlocked the trunk. One soldier rustled through our bags while another pulled up the cover of the spare tire to inspect underneath.

"Bonnet, please."

I moved to the front and crouched down to fiddle with the catch in the grill to unlatch the hood. I couldn't find it and felt like an idiot fumbling while the soldiers watched. Finally my fingers located it, but it was so stiff I couldn't get it to click open. "I'm not sure how to do this," I called over my shoulder. They stood impassively, neither of them making a move to assist.

At last the catch complied and a *thunk* sounded as the bonnet popped open. I resisted an idiotic urge to see what the soldiers would do if I ducked, expecting an explosion. Hauling up the lid, I safely secured it with its attached little rod. After the engine passed inspection the private tore off the middle pink sheet of a form and returned the rest of it to me. "Report to Admin. It's clearly posted."

He raised the security barrier as I got back into the car, handing over the keys to Heather. She started the engine and drove under the barrier, up the lane toward the base. Two Land Rovers passed us on the way. Soldiers peered out from the open back doors and waved, adding a few wolf-whistles for good measure. One of them popped up out of the top of the vantage point in the first Land Rover and blew us a kiss. I grinned and waved, resisting the impulse to blow one back.

Admin proved easy to find indeed. We parked outside, and a tall blond officer with gray eyes emerged to greet us. My pulse raced. He was the aristocratic English captain whom Dee and I had covered in mud at Christmas. "Welcome!" He wore a ten thousand watt smile as he swept over, shaking each of our hands in turn. I looked him straight in the eye as I handed him the forms but he showed no indication that he remembered me. "Come inside ladies, please." He led the way into the building. "We have a little admin protocol to take care of first." He laughed, indicating the sign on the wall. "Hence *Admin.*"

I smiled dutifully and Heather giggled heartily. Much more than I thought the quip merited. She obviously found him attractive, despite the heavy gold wedding band on his finger. He was pretty dashing, I admitted. But not my type. Which brought Mike's beautiful face sharply to mind. I hadn't put him and 'beautiful' in the same sentence in a while. I thrust him from my mind and concentrated on Stratton. We sat on two green plastic upholstered frame chairs in front of the desk and he took the desk chair, sliding a form in front of each of us. I skimmed it. Standard release forms absolving liability. My heart did a flip-flop. Were we really intending to jump out of a plane? Thrilled yet terrified, I tried not to wonder about the percentages of parachutes failing to open and all that. We both signed and handed back the forms.

"Thank you, Captain," I said. "We're very grateful for this opportunity."

"My pleasure." He studied our signatures, slipped the papers into a file and stood. "Now, let's get you settled in your quarters." He showed us back out to the car park where two squaddies waited. They saluted him smartly. He gave them a half-hearted response, raising his right hand, palm forward. I did a double take. It was reminiscent of Hitler's return salute to the straight-armed *Sieg Heil.* "You have luggage?" he asked and I nodded.

The two soldiers opened the Mini and hauled our bags out. Stratton led the way to one of the many corrugated iron huts laid out in rows on the base. I looked about with interest. I'd spent my entire life just across the bay at Mourneview often wondering what it was like over here. We were billeted in the closest Nissen hut to the Officer's Mess, although it was still a bit of a hike. It turned out that we were to sleep in different rooms.

"I'll send someone to fetch you in an hour for dinner," said Stratton. "Afterward we have a little party planned tonight in your honor. In the Officers' Mess."

As we watched his impressive frame stride away, Heather gave a wolf-whistle under her breath. "He's a bit of all right, isn't he?"

"Yes, but married."

"You worry too much about rules. I don't see her *here,* do you?"

I didn't reply. She was right. I was inclined to see things as black and white, even though I knew a vast area of gray existed in between.

A single narrow cot stood on each side of the two rooms we'd been allocated, with a table, chairs, and two lockers. It looked like both rooms were occupied and we'd be sharing with another person. Communal showers and toilets were next door in a room that had a faint mildewy smell to it. As I got changed into the burgundy dress, the room felt so cold my teeth chattered. I didn't see any electric heaters or anything in the hut. We had it very cushy at Finley, obviously.

14
The Old Webley

Dinner in the Officers' Mess turned out to be a sumptuous affair. Four elaborate silver service courses were served by subalterns wearing crisp, white jackets with bow ties. The red carpeting on the floor felt thickly plush underfoot, and the huge carved wood dining table and leather-seated chairs were heavy and good quality. A beautiful, highly polished black grand piano with silver candelabra sat in the corner by the row of casement windows. Plaques, shields, trophies, portraits of soldiers, battles, and flags adorned every space on the wood-paneled walls.

The twelve officers present looked resplendent in their dress uniforms. About two-thirds wore red short jackets, the rest in navy blue. All wore waistcoats under the jackets, with arrays of miniature dress medals attached to colorful ribbons, and white shirts with black bow ties. I couldn't look at the red jackets without thinking *Redcoats!* Even me, a British Protestant, had a frisson of negative reaction, remembering Ireland's history of the potato famine and the role Redcoat oppression played in the great Irish exodus to America. Dee and Clancy - the entire O'Neill family would blow a fucking gasket if they saw this epitome of everything they hated.

Heather and I had chosen our outfits well. Particularly mine, the burgundy almost matching the Redcoats. Not too dressy, nor too casual. We were the only women there, which we were well used to at Finley. But we didn't know any of these self-assured, confident men and I found it unnerving that they were so difficult to gauge. Every single one of them, including the subalterns, did not let his facial expression give away any clue to his thoughts. I felt ill at ease but reminded myself there was a code of conduct amongst British Army officers. The days of bayonets and pillaging were long gone. I hoped. I would have felt safer if Mike had been around. I'd half expected to see him.

A silent, serious man, who made a point of not looking at either of us sat across the table within earshot. He had to be with Intelligence - he made a good job of not appearing to observe us, but that made him all the more noticeable to me.

Heather and I sat side by side, with Captain Stratton on my left and a very jovial lieutenant on her right. The food was incredible. We started with a lavish prawn cocktail in a halved avocado, then lobster bisque served with fresh warm bread and dollops of real butter, carved into a shell shape. The main course was beef medallions in red wine sauce, with mixed roasted vegetables, and what I thought were mashed potatoes. Until I tried to transfer a forkful to my mouth. Strings of cheese stretched from the fork to the plate and I had to do some rapid and inelegant chewing to get it in my mouth while trying to break the string with my fork.

"*Aligot* potatoes," explained Stratton with a smile. "A French recipe, I believe."

"Lovely," I mumbled, attempting to capture a stray string.

For dessert they had a choice of chocolate mousse or raspberry Pavlova, and different wines were served liberally during each course. A rich Cabernet with the beef, and an extremely sweet white with dessert. Captain Stratton insisted we taste both. He was charm itself, exuding the kind of charisma a stage actor does. When we finished dessert and coffee was being served, he gestured toward the grand piano. "Did I hear that one of you is a musician?"

"She is," confirmed Heather.

"Do play something, please."

Oh, shit. I should have brought my violin. "Pianoforte isn't my strong suit," I told him. Where did 'pianoforte' come from? There was something about talking with an aristocratic Englishman that made one choose those kinds of words. "But I'd be happy to."

"Excellent."

He stood as I got to my feet. All down the table, chairs scraped as everyone else followed suit except Heather. Her jaw dropped and she clutched her napkin, gazing round the table like a trapped rabbit. It was surreal. For all the world I felt like I had wandered into a Jane Austen novel. All I needed was a fan to tap the captain on the arm and exclaim something like, '*Oh, fie, Sir!*'

The men remained standing until I traversed my way around the table. One of the subalterns lifted up the piano lid, revealing a row of perfectly polished ebony and ivory keys. I took a seat on the bench to the sound of rustling as the men all sat back down. I bent my head, hiding a grin behind my hair. What would they do if I stood up again?

Now, what to play? I didn't know that many pieces by heart on the piano. And what would a room full of British military men enjoy? I hid another grin. Not *The Soldier's Song*, that's for sure. Raising my hands I let my fingers caress the keys, allowing them to find their way like they would on the violin. They settled in the key of D Major, and I began bouncing out the opening notes to Franz Schubert's *Marche Militaire*. It was a lighthearted and fun piece to play with lots of 'fiddly bits' so I could show off. The piano was in perfect tune, and I took joy in playing such a beautiful instrument. But I'd have done so much better if I'd had my violin instead. In future I was just going to have to haul it along wherever I went. Bringing the piece to its resounding finale I lifted my hands from the keyboard. Polite applause followed and I rose to my feet.

Before any of the men could scramble up, I halted them with my hand. "Please, stay seated," I ordered with a smile, again feeling that I should be using a flirtatious fan and have a floor-length Regency gown rustle modestly as I walked back to the table.

The subalterns unobtrusively served port, and a large silver box holding cigars materialized on the table along with the coffee. Several of the men lit up and soon the room filled with a not disagreeable, heady tobacco aroma. I wondered if this were Heather's and my cue to 'withdraw', à la Regency times. I accepted a glass of port, even though my head was getting foggy with all the wine I'd had at dinner. I wasn't sure how much I'd had, actually. My glass was never allowed to get empty, and the subalterns were so deft I didn't notice them refilling it.

The lieutenant beside Heather obviously felt the effects of the wine, too. His voice had grown loud, cheeks and nose ruddy. "Are you comfortable enough in your billet?" he asked Heather in a cultured English accent.

"As comfortable as one can be in a tin shack," she quipped.

Wrong answer, I thought, cringing. Heather was pretty naïve, despite being a punk rocker.

"I'm sure we could find you somewhere much more suitable—" His sentence ended in a suggestive upbeat.

"We're fine, thank you," I interjected firmly. "We've already unpacked."

Looking nonplussed he took a large draught from his glass of port. I caught a couple of the officers exchanging amused looks.

"Bloody cold, this God-forsaken place," he expostulated to no one in particular. "Drive a man to drink." He leaned closer to Heather, resting his elbow on her shoulder. "We had a man go native, you know." Apparently he thought he was speaking in an undertone. I became very aware of the ultra-stillness of the intelligence officer, and felt certain that Captain Stratton had tensed although his demeanor gave nothing away.

"Really?" asked Heather, glancing round at me.

"Oh, yes, quite." His words slurred. Captain Stratton cleared his throat significantly. "We had to give him the old Webley, you know," continued the lieutenant.

She shook her head. "What's that?"

He gave her a knowing look. "He could turn himself in, or—" He held two fingers, barrel-shaped, to the side of his head.

"Kill himself?"

"Indeed."

"And did he?" I demanded.

"He had to." He basked in our shock.

Captain Stratton placed his napkin neatly on the table and stood. "Let's retire to the lounge." He fixed his gaze on the lieutenant. By the steel in his gun-metal gray eyes I wouldn't be that officer for anything.

All the men rose and the captain moved round behind my chair, placing his hands on the back. "Shall we?" He pulled the chair out for me and I got up, almost staggering. The port proved a very bad idea on top of the wine. He led the way out of the dining room and indicated along the hall on the left. "The powder room is just down there."

"Thank you." I could splash cold water on my face and neck - maybe it would help sober me up a little.

The bathroom had two stalls, and was decorated as abundantly as the rooms outside. Over the door hung a picture frame which displayed a huge pair of ancient army women's olive green knickers. The handwriting indicated it was dedicated to some lady or other, but I couldn't make out to whom.

I made sure no one was in the stalls. "Jesus, I'm half cut already," I told Heather.

She snorted. "Me too. Great, isn't it?"

"I don't know. Tetley told us not to let him down, and we will if we get so shit-faced we can't stand up."

She sighed, heading into one of the stalls. "Fuck, you're right. Better slow down, I suppose."

"Operation 'go-slow'," I quipped, turning on the cold water tap. I ran it over both of my wrists and then dabbed some between my breasts and the back of my neck.

The Ladies' room smelled stale, as though it wasn't used too often. I thought I could detect a faint trace of a sweet perfume like Avon's *Timeless*.

When we left, Heather paused to look up at the framed knickers. "Just be glad we don't have to wear those."

I didn't tell her they weren't so different from the gym knickers I had to wear at grammar school.

Captain Stratton awaited in the hall and showed us into the lounge bar. It had an open, parquet area in the center of the room for dancing, beside which a man played records - obscure jazzy waltzes, mostly. Stratton claimed me as his partner immediately, leading me onto the dance floor. He stayed at a civilized medium pace. It was all very proper, but I couldn't help but feel conspicuous, just the two of us dancing while everyone else watched.

I felt less of a spectacle when another officer claimed Heather, but still - just the four of us? Surreal. Most of the waltzes I'd never heard before and would not voluntarily want to hear again. If this hadn't been officially arranged via Finley, I would have become increasingly nervous about being one of only two females present.

Whirling around the dance floor with Stratton turned out to be quite fun. Like Mike he had well-toned abs and strong arms. I gave myself a mental slap around the head. Any more to drink and I might end up doing something really stupid.

Stirring myself, I asked, "How come the Army is hosting the sponsored jump?"

"Oh, we provide a lot of community service," Stratton answered, with his movie star smile. "It never gets publicized. People don't like to acknowledge us in case they become terrorist targets. But we do it all the same."

"What other community service do you do?"

"Cleaning rivers, repairing and painting houses that have been burned out."

I'd had no idea. "You should tell more people about this sort of thing. They might view you with less hostility." *Oops*, that hadn't come out right. I felt my face flush.

His smile didn't waver. "We rely on people like you and Heather to do that for us."

The waltz came to an end and it looked like things were wrapping up for the evening. I glanced at my watch. Amazingly, it was almost eleven o'clock. The night had gone by fast.

"How did your Operation 'go-shlow' go?" Heather asked me, when we'd been safely delivered back to our tin hut.

"Not so well."

"Yeah, mine was a bust, but I have a strong constit-tution."

The hut was absolutely bloody freezing. Heather staggered off to her room, and I opened the door to mine. In the light flooding in I glimpsed a shape tucked up in the far bed. Female, I assumed. I abandoned trying to remove my makeup and just scrambled into my pajamas. The sheets felt frigid and the mattress unyielding when I slid into bed. Stretching out, my head bumped against something solid under the pillow. A glass jar. I couldn't make out what was in it, so crawled back out of bed to open the door a crack so I could see.

Horlicks. I held a jar of *Horlicks.* Only one person here could have known about the *Horlicks* at Finley. Mike.

⌘

"You're late!" snapped a male voice.

Huh? I peered over the top of the covers, blinking in the sudden nasty wash of fluorescent light. I'd only just fallen asleep!

Whoever owned the voice retreated, leaving the door ajar. My unknown roommate still lay comatose across the hut, despite the light. I curled up into a ball and pulled the cover over my head, only to have it yanked away. Heather stood over me, the door yawning behind her.

"Hurry up, we're late!" she hissed.

"It's still night." I squinted at the little alarm clock by my bed. Seven AM? I didn't remember going to sleep.

"What the hell are you doing with that?" She pointed to the *Horlicks* jar by my pillow.

"Long story." I scrambled out of bed.

"It doesn't work that way, you know."

"Ha, ha."

I grabbed my stuff and we retreated to the bathroom to do the best we could with our appearances, as fast as we could. I scrubbed my teeth and wiped away any obvious makeup smudges with a dampened tissue, and tore a brush through my hair. I sneaked a little touch up to the mascara, and as long as no one got too close, I'd get away with not bathing. I sprayed my deodorant liberally over most of my body before I got dressed in the jeans and sweatshirt I'd worn yesterday.

A very young squaddie waited outside the hut, chain smoking and wan face creased with anxiety. Cigarette butts piled in a semicircle at his feet. He hustled us as unobtrusively as he could to the canteen, where on a long table two massive plates of bacon, eggs, sausages, and baked beans awaited us, along with a pot of tea. The smell and the layer of grease over the plate almost made me hurl. Heather tucked in with gusto, but all I could manage was a cup of tea and some bread soaked in baked bean tomato sauce.

The swinging doors banged open and in strode Captain Stratton, looking august in combat jacket and green denims. He wore a maroon colored beret with a silver wing shape badge.

"Training began ten minutes ago!" he announced, not quite hiding his impatience. Turning on his heel he marched out again.

We abandoned breakfast and charged after him, passing a couple of helicopters on the way to a whitewashed building by a runway. Stratton pushed open the door and waited for us to follow.

"Take a seat in there," he ordered, pointing to another set of doors. They led into a lecture-type room with tiered seating, which looked like it doubled up as a cinema. About fifteen soldiers were already assembled on the back couple of rows. The inebriated lieutenant from dinner last night waited by a projector halfway down in the center. His jovial mood had dissipated. We felt his baleful glare as we scurried over to sit down in the front row.

I gave him an apologetic smile. "Sorry."

His silence spoke volumes. A snicker ran through the privates, and he turned his antagonistic glare on them. Then the lights went down and a film began, a documentary on military parachuting. As the opening credits scrolled across the screen, one of the soldiers let out a resounding fart worthy of a gale force rating. Did guys ever grow up?

The film wasn't exactly riveting, but it certainly got my attention when we were treated to a particularly graphic scene. Something went wrong in a jump and a soldier's arm was completely torn off when he hit one of the engines.

"Did you get that?" demanded the lieutenant, and ran it over again just in case we hadn't.

Then he ordered us outside to a hangar. Heather and I trailed behind him, followed by the rest of the soldiers. By their whispered snickering, I knew they were studying our butts.

In the hangar two ramps had been set up on either side of a square-shaped pile of sandbags. Mats padded the ground in the center of the pile and rows of harnesses and helmets lay out on a counter to the back of the hangar. The lieutenant joined the waiting Stratton and a sergeant came in through a back door behind the counter and handed out harnesses to the soldiers. Stratton glanced at us and spoke to the lieutenant, who came over.

"Do you have jackets?" he demanded.

We'd been in such a rush we hadn't thought to bring them. I shook my head. "Sorry." I seemed to be saying that a lot.

"Wait." He left the hangar by a side door and returned with two camouflage smocks, which were in a lot better condition than the jackets we had at Finley. I wondered if we'd get to keep them. We slipped them on, zipped them up and buttoned the flaps. Then Stratton came over, took one of the harnesses and held it out for Heather to step into while the lieutenant did the same for me. They were not unfriendly, just impersonal in their professional mode. I wondered how they managed to compartmentalize themselves so efficiently. No doubt another thing taught in military training along with the shuttered-down expression.

I had to brace myself so as not to topple over when the lieutenant pulled the straps over my chest and clipped them securely together. He very deftly managed not to touch my breasts in the process. Then he checked the back straps and hunkered down to tighten the straps round my legs. Next came the helmet, which was surprisingly heavy. He secured that for me, too. I felt very strange all trussed up. My terror-filled excitement mounted. I hadn't seen a plane outside. Were we jumping from a helicopter instead?

The soldiers formed in two lines on either side of the sandbags, at the bottom of each ramp. Stratton pulled one of the soldiers out of line. "Show them how to land," he ordered.

Blushing to the roots, the young lad valiantly rose to the occasion. "When you land," he mumbled in a Cockney accent, "keep yer knees bent." As Stratton watched he demonstrated, his hands on his harness just above his chest at the shoulders, and jumped in place. The others in line laughed but he ignored them. "Then roll to the side like this." He performed the jump again and in one smooth movement let himself fall over onto the side.

Stratton nodded. "Good. You join this line," he said to me, "and you over there."

Heather crossed to the line at the far ramp and I fell in behind the soldier who'd given the demonstration. Stratton joined the lieutenant at the front of the sandbags, where both officers could be clearly seen from either ramp. He dropped dramatically to one knee and pointed to the first soldier in line opposite. "Go!"

The soldier at once obeyed, racing up the ramp. He jumped and landed on the mat, rolling onto his side and leaping right back up. Stratton nodded and he ran through the openings in the sand bags to the back of the line. As soon as he cleared the mats, Stratton pointed to the soldier at the front of my line. "Go!"

Very soon Heather and I faced each other on top of the ramps. I hoped I wouldn't make a fool of myself in front of everyone. Stratton pointed at me. "Go!"

I dashed up the ramp. Leaping off, I landed exactly as I'd been shown. But I hadn't expected the helmet to be so heavy - my head thumped hard on the mat. Pain resounded through my skull, but pride made me pretend it hadn't happened and I scrambled quickly to my feet. "Again!" he called. Damn it, he'd seen. Everyone waited, watching my every move as I charged back around and returned to the front of the line. "Go!"

This time I remembered to brace myself and compensate my balance, so I wasn't top heavy upon landing. Stratton nodded me on, to my relief. Heather performed the jump perfectly first time. Bitch.

I ended up having to repeat the jump seven times. I felt a bit dizzy, but I'd drop dead before I let on. At last Stratton shouted something in a decisive tone and the soldiers filed toward the counter at the back.

The lieutenant intercepted Heather and me. "You two! This way."

Stratton waited outside in an open-backed Land Rover. We drove the length of the runway to where a group of soldiers were congregated. There was no one else. As this was a sponsored jump I'd expected some kind of audience.

"Is anyone coming to watch us?" I whispered to Dee.

Stratton overheard. "No public," he replied tersely. "Security."

Heather and I exchanged glances. How can we do a sponsored jump without witnesses?

Stratton oversaw the soldiers as they worked with a myriad of ropes, tying them to a tow bar at the back of the Land Rover. They unfurled a huge brown swathe of cloth and pulled it all the way out so it lay on the ground. A parachute.

It dawned on me that we were not going to be leaping from a perfectly good aeroplane after all. I smiled at Heather. Tetley must have been winding us up. Trust him, I'll bet he had a great laugh at our expense. I felt relieved, but a little disappointed too.

My turn first. They attached the parachute to my harness, and secured it to the rope attached to the Land Rover. A couple of soldiers moved to each side of the parachute and pulled it taut off the ground.

"Ready?" asked Stratton.

My heart pounded. "Yes."

He got into the back of the Land Rover, and they started off down the runway. Stratton kept his attention fully on the rope the whole time. It snapped tight and I felt a surge. My feet skittered as I got pulled forward. The soldiers had stretched the parachute wide open, and air caught. It flapped loudly and I was off, soaring upward. I opened my mouth to scream but burst into surprised and excited laughter instead. The ground receded quickly under my feet. Captain Stratton in the Land Rover grew smaller and smaller as I rose higher. My fingers cramped and I realized I was gripping the harness so tightly I'd cut off my circulation. I looked at the billowing mushroom above. It wasn't attached to anything, so whether I held on for dear life or not made no damn difference. I undug my nails from the leather straps and made myself relax. I couldn't stop smiling. I had never expected this feeling of freedom, of joy, of being removed from the world and all its troubles. It was the first slant of happiness I'd known since the Percy French. The Mournes looked as though they'd been polished in the sunlight that dappled their peaks. Sea merged with sky, azure and clear as a summer day, reaching away as far as the eye could see. I recognized a black and yellow striped tower in the far distance: St. John's Lighthouse at Killough. Far below the ground spread like a patchwork quilt of green fields. No bombs and guns or Troubles up here. For this moment in time I had perspective. I was completely divorced from everything bad. The only sound was the gentle flap of the parachute silk in the wind. A sense of complete and utter peace encompassed me. For just this moment in time, nothing else mattered. When things got dark in the future, which I knew they inevitably would, I'd remember being up here where I had escaped it all.

The ground grew near again and my spirits diminished with every inch I descended. I watched the field below my feet get larger until the soles of my gutties had no choice but to meet the damp grass. I did Captain Stratton proud, remembering to bend my knees, then topple over on my side. A couple of soldiers stood ready and rushed to capture my parachute as soon as I was down. "That was fantastic!" I said, unable to suppress my excitement. They must have been warned not to talk to me, because they didn't even acknowledge me as they gathered the ropes and rolled up the parachute.

Then it was Heather's turn. She shrieked as the wind bore her upward. I waited on the ground, envious as she sailed high above. The soldiers stood nearby, saying nothing to me or each other. I wandered away, giving them the opportunity to break out some cigarettes and light up. I noticed they didn't let me get very far away. Heather came down at more of an angle than I had, practically performing impromptu splits when she landed. I rushed over with the soldiers, but she wasn't hurt. They expertly seized her parachute before it dragged her, and I helped her to her feet.

"Wasn't that incredible?" I asked.

She looked at me like I had lost my mind and removed a squashed pack from her pocket. With shaking hands, she pulled out a squashed cigarette and attempted to light it.

"Never again," she said fervently. "I'd rather shoot myself."

15
Tarnation

By the time Heather and I left Ballykinlar it was nearly three o'clock in the afternoon. Captain Stratton saw us off, after taking back our borrowed DPM smocks.

"Well done. Good job." He shook our hands in turn.

"I can't wait to do it again," I said, making him chuckle. "And I want to try the real thing, too."

"You never know. We'll make a Para out of you, yet."

I knew he was joking, they didn't let women in the Parachute Regiment.

We hadn't had any lunch, so stopped at *The Plough Inn* in Hillsborough on the way through. A welcome little normality in civvie-land for an hour or so. How lovely to sit on a comfortably padded seat at a table in the bar, close to an open fire. I felt conspicuous, as though we somehow broadcast who we were and where we'd just come from. But the highly guarded Hillsborough Castle just up the hill with Her Majesty's Northern Ireland Secretary in residence, I don't suppose we were in particularly dangerous surroundings.

I couldn't seem to warm up, so I ordered a hot port. Heather opted for a pint of cider, and then we perused the bar food menu. After not eating a proper breakfast, missing lunch, and having such a physically active day, I was ravenous. I remembered with a pang how Mum and Dad would study menus like they held the answer to all of life's problems. It used to annoy me so much but I'd give anything if - I wrenched away from that train of thought. No amount of regretful memory was ever going to bring them back.

The menu listed chicken and chips in a basket, cheeseburger and chips in a basket, or fish and chips in a basket.

"Do you think they have anything in a basket?" I asked. "Or with chips?"

Heather gave me a pitying look before she realized I was joking. She didn't know me well enough. Dee and I would have jested back and forth, probably teasing the waiting staff as well. I felt such guilt at how I'd treated her. She hadn't planted the bomb; I was so in the wrong to take out my anger on her. I wished I could call and apologize, but there was no going back. I'd taken a path she could never follow.

Our drinks arrived. Very soon the port warmed me enough so I could take off my coat. The fact that I hadn't bathed for two days was pretty apparent. To me, anyway. Thank God for the hot showers at Finley, that's the first thing I'd do when we got back.

The waitress came to take our food order. I went for the chicken. "Does it come with chips?" I inquired, hiding a grin.

"Yes."

"In a basket?"

She pursed her lips. "Everything comes in a basket." She rolled her eyes and headed toward the kitchen.

Heather shook her head. "Why do you let people think you're stupid like that?"

Is that what I did? Perhaps there was no room for my kind of humor in this new life I'd chosen. I'd have to bear that in mind next time I felt tempted to open my mouth in jest.

Back at Finley Manor, Heather parked the Mini and we retrieved our bags from the boot, locked the car up and took the keys into Admin. I was about to point out the 'Admin' sign to Heather and quip, '*Let's take care of a little admin protocol,*' à la Captain Stratton. But I felt stung at her comment about me appearing stupid so kept quiet.

Tetley wasn't there so we left the keys with Chalki - his - what? He'd never been formally introduced. He wore combat gear like us with no distinguishing patches or insignia and functioned as Tetley's aide. Maybe that's what he was.

Heather checked the grandfather clock in the hall. "Just in time for chow."

I was still full from my chicken Maryland and chips, plus the two bags of Tayto Cheese and Onion crisps I'd scarfed in the bar while waiting. "I'm going to take a shower."

"Want me to save you anything?"

"Maybe a mug of *Horlicks* when you come up?"

She headed down the corridor toward the rec room, leaving me to haul our bags all the way up to the third floor. I dumped them on our foot lockers and went straight into the bathroom. I turned the shower tap on immediately as it usually took a while for hot water to get up to the third floor, unless the boys were running their showers. Sitting on the little wood bench outside the plastic curtain, I untied my muddy gutties, then undressed completely.

I dangled my hand in the shower under the running water. Ice cold. Shit. Fiddling with the settings didn't get it any warmer. I wanted to burst into tears. Not a very soldierly thing to do, not that I felt like one. Even less so after spending time with some real ones at Ballykinlar. I'd never be that controlled, that regimented. I don't think I'd want to be.

Fuck it.

Switching off the shower, I snapped one of the bath towels off the rack and wrapped it around myself. I grabbed my bottles of shampoo and conditioner and bar of *Cusson's Imperial Leather* soap, shoving them into my leopard sponge bag. The guys' shower should be deserted at chow time, so I padded down the corridor and pulled the cord that switched on the light in there. At least Tetley made them keep it spotlessly clean, although a couple of tins of *Mycota* anti-fungal foot powder sat out by the sinks, reminding me of why I had avoided using these showers before. I chose the furthest stall in the corner and turned on the water. I waited, but still ice cold.

Bloody fucking hell.

It still hadn't warmed up after three whole minutes. It wasn't going to. Thwarted and depressed, I switched off the light and headed back to my room, passing a door on the right across the hall from our bathroom. It led to a dark, creaky set of stairs that the servants used in the old days of the Manor. They were out of bounds but Heather and I sometimes sneaked down them when we were running late.

I sat on my bed, pondering my options. No point in going down to Admin, Chalki had left. Even if I tracked old Tetley down, he'd probably yell at me that cold water built character or something. I glanced up at the door across the corridor. What if I sneaked down to find out if the showers on the instructors' floor had hot running water? At this time they'd all be in their Mess, having dinner. If I were quick I might get away with it. Colonel Pierce had his own bathroom in his quarters across from the Mess, so there was no danger of running into him.

Shit, what had I to lose? I got up and retrieved my sponge bag. What's the worst they could do if I got caught anyway? Make me clean the damn bathroom? As if I hadn't already done that fifty times already over the past few weeks.

I felt my way down the pitch-black servants' stairs to the lower floor, treading carefully on the bare boards so as not to make any noise. Edging open the door to the corridor, I peered out. The doors were all closed, but I didn't see any light showing underneath the door opposite, or from Mike's room just down from it. I didn't think he was here tonight, as the souped-up brown Ford Escort he usually drove wasn't in the car park. As for the showers, there was only one way to find out. I crept out and scuttled past Mike's door, slipping inside the bathrooms and pulling the light switch cord. *Please let there be hot water*, I prayed, going behind the curtain on the nearest shower cubicle. Yes! I was rewarded almost immediately with a powerful stream of warmth. Not like the pitiful trickle we had upstairs. Obviously the phraseology was true: rank has its privileges. Hanging my towel over the top of the curtain rail I quickly lathered up with my soap. I poured a glob of shampoo into my palm and scrubbed hard, then rinsed. Using my fingers to comb conditioner through my hair, I rinsed it off right away. Didn't have time to let it sit.

What a relief to get all that dirt off. I squeezed as much excess out of my hair as I could and grabbed my towel. I'd better dry off, otherwise I'd leave a tell-tale trail down the corridor. Rubbing vigorously, I wrapped the damp towel round myself and pulled back the shower curtain. The mirrors over the sinks had steamed up but I didn't dare take the time to cover my tracks. Dumping my stuff back in the sponge bag, I clicked off the light cord and pulled the door open a fraction to see if the coast was clear. I felt incredibly pleased with myself, and looked forward to an early night after a mug of Tetley's obligatory *Horlicks*.

As I approached the door to the stairway, the door opposite clicked open a crack and light flooded the corridor. My heart nearly stopped. I flattened myself against the wall. The door swung fully open and I heard the light switch being turned off as a footstep sounded on the threshold. I slid along the wall, trying to get back to the bathroom. My hand fell on a doorknob. Twisting it, the door opened and I lunged inside Mike's room. With my ear against the door I listened to the officer head down the corridor, and then a momentary swell of male voices as he opened the door to the Mess. A shiver ran through me. I'd freeze to death waiting in this drafty room and damp towel. But Mike would have dry towels in here. Reluctant to switch on the light and maybe alert someone to my presence, I edged my way across to his bed. All the instructors had proper bedsteads, sink, and carpets on the floors. I felt my way round the bed to the sink, where the towels hung on a rail beside it. I let my towel drop to the floor and wrapped a clean one around me, then briskly used a second one to towel-dry my hair. There'd be time in the early morning to slip the towels into the laundry room and replace them before Mike showed up again. I could stroll back in here in the light of day for cleaning duties with clean linen without raising any eyebrows.

It felt surreal to be in his room like this, a hot-water fugitive skulking in the dark. I thought of him sleeping in this bed, with me just upstairs. This is where he ran to when he left me, that night in Belfast. To my confusion I felt an urge to climb into his bed, bury my face in his pillow and cry. I shook myself, annoyed.

Gathering up all the towels I found my way back round the bed. As I approached the door, it thumped open without warning. The silhouette of a man stood framed against the dim light of the corridor. I froze, caught red-handed. He reached a wrist inside the door frame and snapped on the light. My stomach flipped. Mike. He stepped inside, quickly pulling the door shut. He must have just arrived - he still wore his Barracks uniform.

"What in tarnation are you doing in here?"

What the hell was a tarnation? "The showers upstairs weren't working–" I broke off, seeing how he looked at me, eyes hooded and lips parted. Shivers coursed through me, and not from the cold. The last and only time he'd looked at me that way, it had been just before we'd made love. Why was I still so attracted to him, after all that had happened?

"You have to leave, Jen."

I bit my lip and nodded. He opened the door a fraction and checked the corridor as I retrieved my sponge bag from the floor. He stood back and beckoned me. I felt the heat from his body as I passed, every nerve ending tingling at his proximity. He took a sharp breath and stepped close behind me, reaching over my shoulder to push the door shut before I could go through.

I held my breath as he laid a tentative hand on my shoulder. I tried to garner the strength to pull away but couldn't. Desire to be close to him won. I let my head drop back against his shoulder and he leaned down to gently kiss my neck. Goosebumps rose all over my body.

Voices and laughter sounded in the corridor. I froze and Mike snapped off the wall light. We waited until they'd receded then he slid a hand round my torso to cup my breast. Something like electricity shot through me. I arched my back against him. The sponge bag fell from my grasp as he dragged the towel away, my body tingling as his hands squeezed and kneaded my breasts. His strength scared me a little, he'd been so gentle the first time. But then I understood it wasn't *fear* I felt. His assertive masculinity had aroused something primeval in me. I felt his desire thicken at the small of my back, and I took his hand, guiding it over my abdomen and down to the slippery cleft between my legs. His breath caught and he pressed his fingers hard against me. The aftershock sensation I'd experienced from the first time we'd made love hit me now like a monsoon.

He lifted me off my feet and in two steps had crossed the room to bend me over the bed. His belt jangled as he unclipped it, his hands working to unbutton his trousers. Silk-covered steel bobbed against my thigh and he pushed a knee between my legs. He slid inside me so suddenly that I yelped. Encircling my waist with his hands he began to pump hard. I met each thrust with equal force. Oh, God - I was going to climax already. My fingers curled into the bed cover, gripping ferociously to stop myself from crying out. A palm clasped over my mouth, ripping me back to reality. I bucked in surprise and let go the bed cover, scrabbling at his hand.

"Mmmph!" I mumbled urgently through his fingers.

He froze, yanking his hand away at once. "Sorry, I'm sorry." His breath came in gasps. "You were making too much noise."

So much for me preventing myself from crying out. "It's okay."

He flipped me onto my back, and in the dim light filtering under the door I saw his teeth gleam in a smile. Bending his head he kissed me with a hunger that ignited me almost as much as the intense fucking had. He pushed inside me again and we moved together with such force it bordered on violence. In the throes of climax I managed to bite into the back of my own hand, smothering my cry. He shuddered to orgasm just after me, collapsing on top and burying his face against my neck. I lay quivering, feeling his breath on my skin, startling in its warm contrast to the icy room.

Now I knew the answer to whether he had fought the same demons of desire as me.

We navigated ourselves so we lay full length on the bed, heads on the single pillow. He wrapped his arms around me and I closed my eyes, completely content in the moment.

"Told you you should have left," he murmured.

It felt like a dash of frigid water in my face. "I did try, Mike." Hurt filed my voice to a rough edge.

The bed jiggled as he rose onto one elbow, looking down at me. "That's not what I meant, Jen. I'm glad it happened. I've missed you."

I'd missed him too. But I couldn't stop all the original feelings of resentment flooding back. I wouldn't be at Finley if not for him. I pushed my way out of his arms and sat up, swinging my legs over the side of the bed. "I'd better go."

"Suppose."

I wished he'd said that he wanted me to stay, despite my conflicting emotions. But chow time was almost over. The rooms and corridors would not be deserted for much longer. I shivered and got to my feet. Now that the heat of passion had dissipated, the night air felt icy on my bare skin. Bending to retrieve my towel from the floor, my fingers brushed a sticky patch on my upper thigh.

Mike snapped on the bedside light and caught me dabbing at the patch. "You are on birth control, aren't you?" he asked.

It was semen. I hadn't experienced this with the condom. I looked at him, wide-eyed. "No."

"Crap." He sat up. "I thought they'd have put you on it by now."

"Who would have? Why?"

"In the field. You don't want - periods - messing up your emotions."

I blinked rapidly. "But I'm not in the field, yet."

"You will be soon enough. These things take a few weeks to - take, don't they?"

I felt like crying. "I don't know. How would I?"

He got up and buttoned his fly. "It'll be okay, Jen. You won't get pregnant from one time." I hoped he was right. He noticed my shivering. "You're freezing." Going to his wardrobe he pulled out a navy blue terrycloth robe. "Put this on."

He had such a tender expression on his face. God, he looked so sexy in the subdued lighting, his pupils enlarged and lips puffy and full from kissing. But I had made a huge mistake coming here tonight. I'd never be able to get past the Percy French bombing, no matter how much I wanted to. He held the robe open so I could slip into it. Taking my face between his hands he gave me a lingering kiss. I responded, despite my reservations. Why did he have such a hold over me? Handing me my towel and sponge bag, he cracked open the door to peer into the corridor. Then he escorted me over to the servants' stairs where I slipped upstairs before anyone came back from dinner.

Reeling from the enormity of what I'd just done I climbed into my bed, keeping Mike's robe on. Ostensibly for warmth, but I liked the feeling that he was still with me.

16

Boom, We're All Dead

In class the next morning my thoughts kept returning to the encounter with Mike. It didn't help that I throbbed a bit from our rough coupling. I couldn't say I regretted it, because it seemed to have quelled my demons within. And last night was the first good night's sleep I'd had in weeks. But I didn't yet know the ramifications of what I'd done. Mike was already proving to be a distraction if this morning was anything to go by. And fraternization, particularly between one of the instructors and a recruit, was strictly forbidden. If it came to light I expect I'd be the one thrown out on my arse, not him.

"Are you with us, Hamilton?" inquired Colonel Pierce, appearing in front of my desk. He wore his Barracks dress uniform, which he always did on the days he taught.

"Yes, Boss." I surreptitiously drew my sleeve over the back of my hand. I'd bitten myself harder than I thought and teeth marks showed clearly, angry and red.

With an effort I wrenched my errant mind back to the present. Hands clasped behind his back the Boss strolled toward a blackboard where a detailed diagram of an improvised plastic explosive device was chalked. A large oblong table with a home-made bomb mock-up on it sat under the blackboard, facing three rows of ancient school desks, each complete with attached bench, ink pot, and graffiti scored deeply into the pitted wood.

This apparently used to be Finley Manor's ballroom. The parquet floor reminded me of the Officer's Mess at Ballykinlar, and like there each of the long casement windows had wooden internal shutters. Usually the Boss kept them fastened but they were wide open today, letting in a little bit of warmth with the sun.

He whirled back and pointed at me. "Right, Hamilton. You're up."

Damn it. I stood and headed over to the table, taking a seat on the plastic chair facing the blackboard.

"The rest of you gather round," he ordered.

I heard a flurry of rustling behind me and then the warm press of my classmates' bodies as they grouped round. No pressure here.

"Let's see you defuse it, Hamilton. Without blowing us all to kingdom come."

The bomb consisted of a quart-sized aluminum beer keg, which contained a liquid, supposed to be diesel. Around the outside, black electrical tape secured a blasting cap of a halved black powder shotgun shell, also wrapped tightly in electrical tape. Wires ran from it to a car battery, and one thin wire acted as the filament needed to ignite the blasting cap. It looked pretty basic and straightforward, but this device had several more wires than needed for a simple completion of a circuit.

If only I'd been paying attention!

I desperately tried to recall what the Boss had been saying. Five components - activator switch, fuse initiator, explosive charge, a battery power source, and the 'body', the metal keg. It didn't have any fragmentation-generating objects, no ball bearings or nails. It was called a command wired device, as the trigger appeared to be trip wires, and not timed.

Right. I was clear on what it was. Now, how to disarm it. All I needed to do in theory was stop the blasting cap from going off. A simple matter if there weren't so many fucking wires. There might be a hidden tilt switch, which if cut would interrupt the flow of current and activate the detonator.

"The pressure's on," intoned the Boss, doing a good job of stressing me out even more. "Imagine there's a timer. It shows you how many seconds you've left before it explodes and it's ticking down. The bomb's hard to access, tucked beneath a sink in a public restroom. Or maybe in the boot of a car–"

A vision of the blue Vauxhall Cavalier outside the Royal Arms in Newcastle intruded. The terrible, awful aftermath - the blood, the smoke, red bleeding to orange. My palms grew clammy, sweat prickling the hairline at the back of my neck. If only I'd reacted when I looked out of the window of the Percy French and saw the unattended car. Why hadn't I realized immediately that it was a bomb?

"–in other words," he continued, "in a place where a controlled explosion cushioned by sandbags is impossible. There's no time to evacuate the public and you're the only one standing between them and their God." He came to a standstill directly behind me. "What do you do?"

Itchy sweat beaded my brow and a trickle oozed down in front of my right ear. I furtively wiped at it. Only one power source from the battery - the most effective way to disarm the bomb might be to disconnect the wires from the battery. But if there were more than one power source, that wouldn't work.

"Carry on, Hamilton."

I almost laughed. *Carry On Sergeant!* One of the silly exchanges between characters in the movie came to mind: Captain Potts asking, "Your rank?" and a soldier replying, "Well, that's a matter of opinion." I guess it had been funny in its day.

Grabbing the little wire cutters lying on the desk I reached decisively toward the battery wires. But then my hand betrayed me by trembling. I flexed my fingers, trying to steady them - and my nerves. Here goes. I hovered over one of the wires, then hesitated. What if I was wrong?

"Hesitation means indecision," snapped the Boss. "Indecision means death. For everyone."

I gnawed on my lower lip. *Fuck it.* The blasting cap wires. I swiftly clipped one of them in half.

"Boom, we're all dead, Recruit. Try again."

I went cold all over. Furious with myself I returned to the original choice of the battery wire and smartly snipped it.

"Good."

Queasy, I sagged over, my elbows on the desk. The rest of the class let out a collective sigh of relief. I'd forgotten they were there.

The Boss laid a hand on my shoulder. "But there are no second chances with a real bomb. You should have gone with your first choice, Hamilton. Don't second-guess yourself, your instinct is spot on." Returning to the blackboard he wiped off the chalk in huge decisive swipes. "That's it for today. Dismissed."

As the others gathered their stuff, chattering and laughing together, I rushed across the hall to the unisex toilets. I made it just in time before throwing up. Vomiting always makes me cry, so I huddled miserably on the freezing tiles, drained and exhausted. A thought struck me. Shit, I couldn't get pregnant immediately, could I? I had no idea if it was possible to have morning sickness at once or not. What an idiot! Oh, Jesus.

"What's all this?" demanded Tetley from outside the stall.

I shouldn't have been surprised. He didn't miss much, his office being next door. Pulling the handle to flush I unlocked the cubicle door. He stood with his customary hands on hips.

"I'm all right, Sir."

"Anything - amiss?"

That could cover a multitude of sins. Bet he was wondering the same thing as I was. "No, Sergeant."

"Can't gae pukin' up on the job, girlie."

"I won't."

He studied me intently. "Aye."

It had been the memory of the Percy French that had triggered me, pregnant or not. I'd have to get hold of myself and my emotions otherwise I'd wash out of this training altogether. "It won't happen again, Tetl-Sarge."

He ignored my slip. "Report to the Boss, Recruit."

"Now?" I asked, forgetting myself.

"No, not now. After ye've had a wee cup o' tea and a sticky bun." His volume increased exponentially. "Of *course* now!"

"Sorry, Sir."

He sighed heavily. While he stood impatiently by, I splashed cold water over my face and rinsed out my mouth.

"Move it, Hamilton, we haven't all bloody day."

I hurried after him to the Boss's office where he rapped the door sharply.

"Enter," called Pierce. He sat at his desk, poring over an open file. Tetley gestured for me to precede him, and he followed, shutting the door and staying by it. The Boss looked up, his gaze impersonal. "Have a seat, Hamilton."

As I dropped into one of the chairs in front of his desk, I glimpsed the Polaroid photo that Tetley had snapped of me on my first day clipped inside the file.

He closed it over, blotting out my mug shot. "I'll get straight to the point. Frankly, we're having serious doubts about you, I don't think you're cut out for this."

I blinked. "Why not?"

"You're showing signs of acute stress. Not to mention your consistent problem with authority."

What problem with authority? I hadn't done anything out of the ordinary that I could think of. Except sneaking into the showers last night. Had Mike told on me? Did he also happen to mention that he ravaged me in his room afterward? I stared straight ahead at a knot in the wood paneling just to the left of Pierce's head.

He waved a hand. "Speak freely, please."

I cleared my throat. "I don't know what to say, Boss. I want to be here. I'm doing the best I can." Oh, what the fuck. I didn't need to be here putting up with all this bullshit. I could find terrorists on my own if I wanted to. I felt a *qué sera, sera* sort of feeling descend and gave a Gallic shrug. "I guess if my efforts are not good enough there's nothing I can do about it." I looked him in the eye. "But regardless of whether I rout out who killed my parents as part of this detachment or by myself - I will find out who did it. And act accordingly."

He sat back in the chair and tapped his fingertips on the leather armrest. Determined not to let him unnerve me I watched the neat half-moons on his manicured nails moving in sequence like piano keys. Tetley was unnaturally still by the door, also waiting. I avoided looking in his direction.

The Boss finally gave Tetley a curt nod, and immediately Tetley opened the door and slipped outside. The Boss reopened the file on his desk and pulled out a piece of paper, which he held out to me. "Take this to Admin. Then report to the assault course."

It was a requisition for contraceptive pills. All the emotions I'd been so successful in quashing rose to the surface again. I felt like a whore being sent out onto the streets by her pimp. *Fuck the Boss*, I thought, getting to my feet and heading for the door. Hmmm, he was probably right about my authority problem.

I took the paper straight over to Admin as directed. Tetley made me sign it and then stuck it on a spike on his desk that already had a clutch of papers impaled on it. "Be back here tomorra to pick it up first thing."

If I didn't know any better I'd think he was blushing. "Thank you. Is there one for Recruit Baird?"

He wagged his ballpoint pen at me. "Now, ye know I canna tell you that."

"Sorry, Sarge." I left and stomped toward the back door. What delightful things did the assault course hold for me today? To be honest, I welcomed the prospect of some hard physical exercise. The way I felt, the only remedy would be the equivalent of several rounds in a ring against a heavyweight.

Shoving open the back door I stepped into the courtyard. A sharp crack on the back on my head sent pain scorching through my skull. I almost passed out and my knees buckled. Rough hands forced something over my head - a hood. Everything went dark and I couldn't get a breath. Then I was dragged over the uneven cobblestones.

Through my shock I realized that this had to be a counter-interrogation training exercise. We'd been told early on that when they thought we were ready, an enactment of being taken captive would happen. I thought there might have been some warning, though. Whoever had hit me wasn't fucking around. That had been hard enough to cause a concussion.

I made myself focus. The most important thing we'd been told to hang onto was how to survive the capture. You made a decision and went with it, and if you had the option to shoot your way out of it, you did. But I didn't have that option.

A door creaked open and I was bodily thrown into a building. I fell onto hard cement, jarring my shoulder. One of the back sheds, maybe? But the sound echoed. Bigger, maybe a garage.

It's an exercise. It'll be over in no time. Go along with it. Don't be scared. Above all, don't panic.

It was hard not to. The door slammed shut and boot steps slowly approached across the cement floor. Automatically I shrank away, my breathing ragged under the hood. Someone big, male, and substantial snatched hold of the back of my collar and yanked me to my feet. He pushed me onto a wooden chair, which scraped a few inches along the floor when I landed.

He grabbed the back of the chair and twisted it so I faced away from him. "What a fuckin' amateur," said a voice in a gruff Belfast accent. Under the bottom of the hood I saw that I faced into a corner. "Didn't see that comin', did you, stupid cunt?"

Okay, I recognized the initial part of an interrogation process. He wanted to make me feel disappointed in myself that I'd been captured so easily. That I'd failed.

I kept quiet. I recalled the simple rule of thumb of interrogation: if I said nothing they'd have nothing to expand their interrogation on. Hell, I didn't even have a rank or serial number to rattle off.

He pulled the hood off. I gasped for breath and turned my head, trying to get my bearings. He gripped my chin with pliers-strong fingers, forcing me to look away. But in that glimpse I saw he wore a ski mask. He let go and cuffed the back of my head where I'd already been clubbed. Pain blinded me. He bent close, his breath warm on my earlobe. "Why don't you save us all a lot of time and yourself unnecessary pain - and simply tell me your name."

You already know my name! I clamped my lips shut, heart hammering hard in my chest. He straightened, and I tensed, waiting for another blow. I counted to ten before he moved, his boots scraping on the floor.

"All right, if that's the way you want it." He dragged the hood back over my head.

My instinct was to fight, but I managed to stay still. He forced the chair round to face him, almost toppling me out of it. I flinched when he snatched hold of my left wrist, racking my arm straight out in front of me. "I hear you're a dab hand at the fiddle, that right?"

I swallowed hard. An implied threat to harm my hands. He'd zeroed right in on something vitally important to me. To any musician.

He twisted my wrist. "Teeth marks?" I'd forgotten about the bite on the back of my hand and heat flooded my face. "Like it rough, do you?"

I yelped. Pain ricocheted up my arm as he forced my hand into a hairpin position, fingertips unnaturally close to the inside of my wrist. I gritted my teeth and stayed still, trying not to imagine broken bones, my fingers misaligned and unable to pick out notes on the violin.

"That's the girl," soothed my torturer as though talking to a pet dog. "So, make it easy on yourself. Just tell me your name, that's all. Nothing much, is it? You're not telling us anything we don't already know."

Then why are you fucking asking me, you prick? The pain made my eyes water and my nose run. My breathing grew labored, snuffling through the congestion.

"And then I'll take the hood off," he continued. "You can blow your nose and have a nice cup of tea." His tone sounded so sane and reasonable. *Cup of tea, my arse.* And the whole time he exerted pressure on my wrist, increasing it until that was all my mind focused on.

"So, what's it to be?" he asked, in that mild, calm voice. I bit down hard on my lip. "Not going to play?" He let my wrist go and with a cupped hand, clapped me hard over my ear. I cried out, hunching over, trying to protect my wrist and my head at the same time.

"Maybe you need a bit more time to think about it." He grabbed hold of the lapels of my combat jacket. I felt like a sack of potatoes as he hauled me to my feet. He kicked the chair aside, which toppled with a clatter, and flung me face first into a wall. I slid down to huddle on the ground, the shock numbing me for a second. But then such agony shot through me I was afraid he'd broken my nose.

He hauled me back on my feet and put me facing the wall. Yanking my arms over my head, he pressed my palms flat on the wall surface, then kicked at my feet so I was forced to take a wider stance, about a foot back from the wall.

"Stay there," he ordered. "Don't move an inch."

He backed off and I took the opportunity to gasp a couple of breaths through my mouth. His boot steps crunched on the concrete floor, then the door creaked open. He apparently went out, letting it bang closed, and a lock clicked firmly into place.

"She needs a bit of time to consider her options," I heard him say, voice muffled. "If she still doesn't feel like talking, maybe a good old-fashioned fucking will help change her mind." Another man's voice sounded in a lewd chuckle.

Oh dear God. Again, another threat as part of the process - the psychological torture phase. Bastard. He wouldn't dare follow through.

But he *had* just injured my wrist. I tested it, flexing it away from the wall. It hurt like fuck but moved easily enough. Not broken or sprained then, thank God.

Shit, he'd told me not to move. I placed my palm back against the wall. Concrete like the floor it felt damp and chilly under my palms. I listened hard but couldn't hear a thing. Even though we were right in Finley's back yard, no Tetley yelled from the training field, no pots or pans clattered in the kitchen, nothing. Wait, there was something. I strained to hear and recognized the dull metallic thud of water dripping into a sink somewhere in the room. My mouth felt so dry, my tongue seemed swollen enough to choke me.

A pang shot down my spine. I must only have been standing there for a few minutes but already my back and shoulders throbbed. My lungs felt too tight and every time I tried to take a breath the hood flapped into my mouth. The cloth was dry and rough and I couldn't spit it out or get enough saliva together to swallow properly. The pain in my head was indescribable. Bending my neck I let my head droop forward and eased it from side to side, attempting to stretch out the discomfort.

Just count one minute, for fuck's sake. If he hadn't returned after I'd reached sixty, I'd ease my arms down just a little. I went slowly through the numbers, but once I reached sixty I was still too afraid to move. He had to be watching.

Okay, I'd count to a hundred this time. Then I'd decide whether to risk moving. What the fuck was I supposed to do, just stand here and meekly do what I was told? Shouldn't I at least try and escape? Wait, no. I was supposed to survive. But wouldn't that include attempting to escape? Holy shit, I wish I had fucking paid attention when the Boss had talked about this. If I got out of this unscathed, I vowed I'd never lose concentration in class again.

But it wasn't real, I mustn't forget that. This would soon be over and I'd be having a hot chocolate in the rec room with Heather afterward and laugh about it all. Not to mention I could pull this hood from my head anytime I wanted and tell that fuckhead captor to go fuck himself. Then I could walk out that fucking door and out of Finley Manor forever. To hell with this.

So, I'd count to a hundred.

At seventy-five my shoulders cramped so badly, I felt it all the way down my back and legs, and the soles of my feet hurt like crazy, all pins and needles. Fuck, I'd lost count. I started again, concentrating hard.

God, a hundred counts was not even two minutes but I felt like I'd been standing here for hours. I don't know how much more I could take.

I extended it to two hundred, then tried for a thousand. By seven hundred my lungs felt lit on fire, I was certain I'd pass out. I was never going to make it. The Boss had been right, I wasn't cut out for this.

But Mike must have thought I was or he wouldn't have recruited me. He had seen something in me at that *céildh* in Ballyben. How had he become so inextricably entwined with this whole thing? Because of him I went home the day the Percy French bomb killed my parents. Because of that I wanted to do a tit-for-tat killing, and because of that he brought me here. All because of Mike.

I was so confused. How can you hate someone yet at the same time want them in your life? He was always in my thoughts, no matter how hard I tried to exorcise him. I wondered if sleeping with someone, letting them actually physically enter your body made them part of you forevermore.

My thoughts triangulated on the wild, untethered sex last night. I never imagined it could be so - urgent, angry - *thrilling*.

I came to with a jolt, realizing I'd effectively taken my mind off what was happening here. I felt significantly more calm and in control. Mike had his uses, that was for sure.

But how long had it been?

I listened carefully and still could only hear my own breathing, sounding hollow in the concrete room. I eased my weight from one foot to the other and flexed my toes. The pins and needles began to subside but sharp pain took their place. My entire body racked with agony. I tried to move my left arm but it had overextended so much it cramped and I couldn't shift it. I concentrated and with an effort got it lowered, then my right arm. I sagged against the wall and took a profound breath of relief.

The hood ripped from my head. Pain seared through me as some of my hair was torn out by the roots. "I told you not to move an inch!" The voice snarled from right behind me.

That bastard *left!* I heard him lock the door! How the hell had he been there all along?

He slammed my arms back up into place, pain wracking me anew. I was done, tested beyond my mental and physical limits. In addition my bladder felt heavy, warning me I couldn't hold out for much longer without the bathroom.

What if - maybe I could just - I mean, what if I just told him what he wanted? It was only my name. Then he might let me use the toilet. Let me sit down.

I felt a rush of fury. No, he wasn't going to win. I fucking well *could* hold out longer. If I pissed myself, so what? Maybe I'd piss on him.

His footsteps sounded on the concrete. I heard the tap squeak as he turned it and water pulsed into the enamel sink. Then the sound altered. I risked a glance over my shoulder. He held a towel under the stream. I turned my face to the wall again as the tap squeaked off and he wrung out the towel. "You must be thirsty," he said.

Shut the fuck up.

"What's your name, that's all I want to know. Tell me that and I'll let you have some water."

Jennifer. At the mention of water, my name was all I could think about. Just say *Jennifer,* and I could relieve myself, and then drink down a gallon of cool water, let it slide down my ragged throat. *Jennifer.* I let out a groan.

"Sounds good, doesn't it?" His voice sounded silky.

Prick, cunt, curse you to hell. I hope you roast forever for this.

He grabbed me by the hair. Pulling my head back he thrust the sodden towel in my face. "Or I could have my colleague hold you down while you get all the water you want."

Terror raced through me anew, my heart rate accelerating. He'd force the towel over my face and pour water on it, choking my breathing passages and making me feel like I was drowning. It would go on and on - as long as I stayed conscious. They'd revive me as soon as I passed out and it would start all over again.

My muscles betrayed me, I shook with fear.

He sensed victory and let go of my hair. "All right, you can drop your arms and turn round."

I did so. Behind him I saw a heavy wooden table with restraints attached. My vision went hazy as I also glimpsed a set of headphones resting on it – thank God I'd been spared sound torture. So far.

"Now, tell me your name."

My lips and tongue kept trying to form the word, *Jennifer.* Think of another word, for Christ's sake. *Mike.* Of course! *Mike, Mike, Mike, Mike, Mike, Mike.* The man gave a sudden sharp laugh. My heart pounded. Had I spoken aloud?

"Take off your jacket."

"What?"

"Do as you're told, bitch."

Part of my addled brain acknowledged that this was the beginning of the humiliation part of the exercise. My hand trembled violently as I raised it to the top of the zip on my jacket. If I were a guy, once he was deprived of his garments, he'd receive a barrage of insults about his genitalia. They'd try to undermine who and what he was by stripping away his dignity as well as his clothing.

But I was a woman.

I had to do something to bring this to an end, *now*. One way or the other.

I didn't move fast enough for his liking. He grabbed hold of my zip and forced it all the way down. He almost brought me to my knees as he used both hands to pull the jacket back off my shoulders and tug it down my arms. Even though I wore a T-shirt underneath, I instinctively crossed my arms over my breasts.

There was a window to my left, I glimpsed peeling white paint around squares of dirty paned glass.

"Just tell me your fucking name, and this will stop right here and now," he told me. "Come on, why put yourself through this? It could be over in seconds."

I twisted away and back again as though having an internal struggle, while surreptitiously taking in as much of the room as I could. The wooden chair lay close by on its side on the floor. My captor stood between me and the door, but I noticed the wood in the window frames was rotted and warped. Bushes were visible outside so that confirmed we were on the ground floor, and it was still daylight.

Focusing, I concentrated on every single muscle in my body. I allowed my knees to flex and bend, ever so slightly.

"Go ahead," he cajoled. "You can end this with one word. Just say it."

I finally allowed myself to speak. "All right." My voiced sounded fractured. Defeated.

He leaned close. I could sense his elation. "So, tell me."

Adrenaline canceled out the pain. I moved fast, whipping myself forward and cracking my forehead as hard as I could into his face. It nearly knocked me unconscious. I staggered, tears blinding me. I hadn't expected it to hurt me as much as him. He made a *duuuhhhnnn* sound and brought his palms up to cover his nose. Fighting dizziness I got orientated, lurched round and grabbed hold of the chair. Bringing everything I could to bear, I raised it high above my head and smashed it over him. "Fuck you, you bastard!" I screamed.

His legs gave as the chair splintered into pieces across his back and shoulders. "Hold it, hold it!" he shouted.

I snatched up one of the legs. Grabbing my jacket from the ground I wrapped it round my right forearm and pummeled the chair leg against the window. The rotted wood gave way easily and I shattered the glass from the frame. The chair leg hurtled from my grasp and my arms were pinioned from behind. I jerked my knee up and kicked back as hard as I could. I felt his knee snap straight. He gasped but didn't let go.

The door thudded open. "Stand doon, Hamilton!" bellowed Tetley. "It's over. Stand doon, I sed!" For a moment I thought someone was pretending to be him, I'd forgotten it was an exercise. But it was him, standing in the door frame in his teapot stance. Hacking for breath, I sagged with relief.

My interrogator released my arms and I lurched round to face him. He stood with his arms folded, his smile looking sinister under the ski mask. I couldn't meet his eyes.

"Remind me never to piss you off," he said with a good-natured laugh.

"Bastard," I breathed.

"Aye," said Tetley. "We're paid to be bastards."

Now that the danger was over I felt too weak to stand up straight. I was shivery and over-hot. Damp too. To my shame I think I must have peed myself even though my bladder felt painfully full.

"Yer to say nothin' to the others aboot what happened here, y'understand?" continued Tetley. I nodded and he stooped to retrieve my bunched up jacket from the floor. He flapped it out and placed it over my shoulders. "Yer bleedin', girlie." He shot a quizzical look at the interrogator, who shook his head. "Go tae Medical and get checked. Ye held out well, Hamilton, but the next time won't be sae easy."

I couldn't bring myself to look at either of them as I stumbled to the door. *Easy?* It took everything I had and more just to get through that.

17

Entropy

I stumbled across the courtyard, turning briefly to see where I'd been held. An innocuous-looking building annexed to the old stables. It didn't look like anything more than a disused storage shed from here. Hoping not to meet anyone on the way I headed into the Manor and to the ground floor toilets. I quickly discovered what had concerned Tetley. I hadn't wet myself, my period had started and had leaked through, causing a bloom of scarlet to stain the back of my trousers. In the past I'd have been crippled with mortification, but I didn't give a rat's ass now. Cleaning up as best I could I used a wad of toilet paper to tide me over until I could get a tampon.

Medical was further along the corridor from the kitchen. I'd only visited it once for a mandatory physical when I first arrived. Dr. Harding, a balding, bespectacled man in his early sixties, awaited. He got up from his desk, pushing his wire-framed glasses up his nose.

"Have a seat. Let's take a look." His accent was upper crust Tatler English.

I laid my jacket on a chair by the door and climbed onto his examination table. He picked up an instrument from a tray and shone a light into each of my eyes. "Hmm-hmm." Then he studiously checked my neck, shoulders, and arms. I winced when he touched my wrist.

"Remove your boots and socks." He pressed all around my ankles and feet, then told me to stand up. "Touch your toes." His fingers walked the length of my spine, then he tapped me on the shoulder, indicating I could straighten up. "You'll live. I assume this is menstrual blood?"

I nodded. "Got taken by surprise."

"You certainly did." He chuckled. "Right, sit back down. We'll just bind up that wrist for a couple of days and you'll be as right as rain." He pulled open a metal cupboard and produced a crepe bandage, sticky on one side. Without bathing the skin, I assume because I hadn't any lacerations, he wound it around my wrist.

"I'll be able to play the violin okay?" I asked.

He patted my knee. "Certainly. Just refrain for two to three days. Come back after that and I'll take another look."

The big blue and chrome Metamec clock on the wall behind him caught my eye. Six o'clock? That couldn't be right. Glancing at the doctor's wristwatch confirmed it. That meant I'd only been in the exercise for four hours. It had felt like *twenty*-four.

A pill bottle rattled as Harding unscrewed the cap and tipped several white tablets into his palm. Taking a paper cup from beside the sink, he dropped the pills into it and handed the cup to me. "Take two now. Two at bedtime, and then just one at mealtimes as needed."

"Thank you."

"Good show. Carry on." He waved a dismissive hand and sat back down at his desk. I suspected he had been a career army doctor. Probably in the same regiment as the Boss. They were cut from the same cloth.

I flattened the cup, rolled it in half and slipped it into a leg pocket in my trousers. Sliding off the examination table, I collected my jacket and boots with the socks inside and padded barefoot out to the corridor. Not wanting to run into anyone, I slipped through the door into the servants' stairs. Halfway up the first flight I found I couldn't go any further and sat heavily.

I'd come through. I hadn't let myself down.

Now that I was alone the tears came. Putting my head in my hands I let myself cry, using the jacket wadded up to stifle any sound. I don't know how long I huddled there, but a footstep on the stairs above startled me. I leapt up, my boots clattering as I knocked them over.

"Only me." Mike's voice.

He materialized out of the gloom and pulled me into an embrace. I clung to him, grateful to have someone to hold onto at that moment. Settling us into a sitting position on the stairs he held me tightly while my shoulders shuddered with silent sobs.

"This is good, Jen," he murmured into my hair. "Getting it all out. You need to. You can't keep it bottled up."

I used my jacket to wipe my nose, glad of the cover of darkness in the stairwell.

He cleared his throat. "Hughes said you were bleeding?"

"Oh. We needn't worry that I'm pregnant. My period came." I wondered in a macabre way what my would-be rapist's reaction to all that blood would have been.

"You kept your head all through the exercise. That's way more than we'd expect at this stage." He stroked my cheek with his knuckles. "I hate to see you like this, Jen. You can still pull out - you haven't signed your life away yet."

I felt so miserable, so demoralized, that I was tempted to.

"God, Jen - I wish I'd never gotten you involved. If I hadn't walked out on you that night you wouldn't be here in the first place."

I went still. There it was. He'd voiced what I'd been thinking all along. A great weight in my heart lifted. By doing so, by admitting tenuous responsibility, he'd helped me take the first step toward being able to forgive him. To acknowledge it I hugged him as tightly as I could. He understood, squeezing me so hard I gasped. He bent his head and we kissed, very gently.

"Much as I want to, I can't stay, Jen. Want me to walk you upstairs?"

I didn't think I could move. "No, you go on. I want to be alone for a bit."

He planted a quick kiss on my forehead and got up. Light slanted briefly into the stairwell as he opened the door and slipped out into the corridor.

Feeling around I located my boots. I was beginning to feel most troglodyte-like, lurking here in the dark. Pulling out the socks I hauled them over my cold feet. Taking my snot-soaked jacket I flapped it like Tetley did earlier and slipped it on, hoping it didn't look too disgusting. As I lifted a boot to slip my foot into, I heard the back door slam.

"Aye," came Tetley's distinctive Scottish burr from the corridor. "All that fuckin' blood I thought ye'd half killed her. Time of month. Who'd have thought?" Chuckling together they headed down the corridor, their footsteps stomping on the lino.

Abandoning the boot I slid on my backside down the stairs and put the ear he hadn't half-deafened to the door. Cracking it open, I crept out and followed. They were laughing heartily, not paying attention. I'm *so* glad they found their work so very entertaining. Hurting people for a living must be really rewarding. The more I thought about how much the interrogator seemed to enjoy it, the angrier I got. Coldly so. The get-even kind.

I tucked myself underneath the stairs beside Admin. Hearing my name, I listened hard but couldn't make out anything else they said. I had to know what they were saying about me!

I'd cleaned this place often enough so I knew a few things about the layout. In the wall that separated the toilets from Admin, I remembered seeing a metal Victorian grill in the wall. Some kind of heating vent, but it hadn't been used in years. Glad I'd left my heavy boots back in the servants' staircase, I hurried into the toilets and hunkered down in front of the grill. It dislodged easily and I laid it carefully on the floor. The space in the wall was just about big enough for someone my size to squirm into. Ignoring the thought of spiders and other ghastly things possibly lurking in there, I got prone and wriggled inside. Light shone in dusty fragments through a similar grill that opened out into Admin. I slid along until I could peer through it and saw the back of Tetley's chair and desk. The two men were further in the room, out of my line of sight.

"Next time concentrate more on the humiliation aspect," I heard Tetley say. "Watch."

There was the whine of a tape rewinding and a series of clicks. They'd recorded the whole thing?

"That's when she escalated to the escape attempt."

I heard my own voice scream, "Fuck you, you bastard!" scuffling, then splintering wood.

"This shows promise," concluded my interrogator, and the tape clicked off. He didn't sound like he was from Belfast at all now, but I couldn't identify the accent. Who the fuck was he?

"Aye, it does that." Tetley laughed. "I take back what I sed aboot lettin' people wi' tits near weapons. Sae, who's next?"

Papers rustled. "Murphy."

"Goot, he's regular army, that one. Let's grab him when he's tucked up in his bed like a bairn."

The rest of their words were muffled but I picked up, "Servants' stairs," and "Zero-four-hundred hours."

Cupboards clicked opened and shut as they wrapped up. Then Tetley came round his desk and slid open a drawer. He slipped a green file into it, took out a set of keys, relocked the drawer and returned to the other side of his desk out of sight. In seconds they'd left and locked up. I heard the front door slam and a car started out in the car park. So much for my great espionage attempt.

If I'd felt tired before, now I was completely drained. Scurrying back to the servants' stairwell, I retrieved my boots and climbed up to my room on the third floor. Looking in Heather's mirror I scarcely recognized myself. My hair had come loose from its ponytail, and stray greasy locks hung round my face. Happily, apart from a little dried blood around my nostrils, my nose didn't look permanently damaged. No doubt by morning I'd look distinctly raccoon-like when the bruising around my eyes darkened.

I felt shattered. My head throbbed, my ear ached, my shoulders and back hurt, and my wrist was killing me. I remembered I was supposed to take two of those pills the doctor gave me. I retrieved the folded up cup from my trousers and went to the bathroom to wash a couple of tablets down with water from the sink. They looked like the same kind of painkillers I'd been discharged with for my bruised ribs from the Percy French bombing.

I stopped dead. I'd just thought of the Percy French and for the first time didn't feel a rush of nausea. The training was working! I felt a sense of empowerment. I'd survived this exercise, I would survive more.

Turning on the shower I pondered if I should put a plastic bag or something over the bandage. It seemed too overwhelming a decision to come to. I peeled off my grubby clothes and sat on the wooden bench to think about it. My arms and legs looked like I'd been in a car accident, covered in a mass of red marks. No doubt they'd make fine bruises tomorrow too.

Lucky me, being the first in my class to be 'taken'. I wondered how the rest would do. I wished I could warn Heather but I mustn't. It wouldn't be fair to her, and Tetley and my unknown tormentor would probably kill me.

Warm water came through the shower head relatively quickly and I gratefully stepped under its flow. After all my pondering I forgot about the bandage, so it got soaked by default. When massaging shampoo into my hair I discovered a painful lump on the back of my head. Did they really need to be so vehemently realistic? What use would any of us be out there if we got brain damaged in here?

I stayed in the shower as long as I could, letting the heat and steam work their magic. By the time I came out I felt dozy, so sat back on the bench to dry myself. Pity about the bandage, all sodden and heavy. I picked at the end where Dr. Harding had stuck it down. The glue hadn't fared well in the steam and it peeled away easily. I decided to just unwrap the entire thing. I'd be careful with my wrist tonight and go to Medical in the morning to get it replaced. It didn't hurt very much now, anyway.

One-handedly I towel dried my hair and combed out the tangles. It all took so much effort. I realized I'd swallowed those heavy duty painkillers on an empty stomach, a rather stupid thing to do. I put on Mike's terrycloth robe, remembering the comfort of his arms around me.

Leaning my chest on the edge of the sink, which if I'd thought about it, didn't seem possible, I managed to squeeze toothpaste on my brush and scrub at my teeth. My face ached and I ran my tongue around feeling indentations where I'd clenched and bitten into the insides of my cheeks. I could barely stay awake, so I kicked my dirty clothes into a pile in the corner and switched off the light. I did a kind of bottom-of-the-swimming-pool amble to the bedroom. Not bothering to turn on the light I climbed into bed, keeping Mike's robe on. In moments I was out for the count.

⌘

Moonlight filtering through the window gradually eased me awake. It illuminated the dials on Heather's bedside alarm clock and I craned my neck to see the time. Three-fifteen in the morning. I'd slept for almost eight wonderful hours, without any nightmares. Or any dreams at all.

I burrowed down and tried to go back to sleep, but my stomach and wrist had other ideas. I hadn't eaten since lunchtime yesterday and the painkillers had worn off to the point I couldn't ignore the throbbing. Sitting up, the rest of my body sharply recalled what it had been put through the day before. Then I also remembered that Tetley and the mystery man had discussed abducting Murphy in about forty-five minutes. I'm glad I woke up when I did. If I wanted to discover who interrogated me, this might be my only chance. On a mission, I got out of bed and quietly opened up the drawers on my side of the dresser. Not that Heather was easily woken.

I put on a pair of black slacks and sweater, and my soft-soled gutties. First stop would be either to raid the kitchen or to get a bandage from Medical, depending on whether both were locked up or not. On the ground floor of the servants' stairwell I cracked the door to check the coast was clear, although I'd be very surprised if anyone were around at this hour. Except for those up to no good, like Tetley and his psycho friend.

The corridor was almost as dark as the stairwell. I tried Medical first. Locked. The kitchen door opened and I slipped inside, quietly shutting the door behind me. The pantry and huge commercial refrigerating unit sat on this side of the kitchen against the wall. The cook put a padlock on it at night and locked the pantry up, using a big ward key. Possibly the original from when the Manor had been built last century.

This wasn't the first time I'd raided the kitchen for food out of hours, and I had discovered a trick to the fridge. The chain was a little on the long side, so someone who wasn't a large man - me - could reach their arm inside and grab whatever was nearest. I clicked open the handle of the humming behemoth and stretched my uninjured right arm through the gap. My fumbling fingers found a stiff brick-like shape in foil, most likely butter. Then a raw chicken or something, which felt disgustingly like a person's dead, bony hand. I strained all the way up to my armpit, and an oblong package rustled under my fingers. Cold cuts. Perfect. I withdrew it and unwrapped the white butcher's paper. Peeling off a slice I popped it into my mouth. Tongue. Well, beggars can't be choosers. I ate four slices, probably all I could get away with without alerting anyone to the theft. Rewrapping the meat I slid it back into the fridge. That should tide me over until breakfast at seven o'clock.

Now, where to hide out? It must be close to twenty minutes or so before Murphy's abduction was scheduled. Tetley and company would go to Admin first, where they'd switch on the light. If I lurked here in the gloom I'd see nothing, and I'd be willing to bet they'd don ski masks before they headed upstairs, anyway.

I left the lights off in the ground floor toilets as I found my way to the grill in the dark. It felt like a set in a horror film, the only sound an intermittent drip from one of the sinks, followed by a loud, ominous plop. I set the grill upright at a right angle, leaning against the adjacent wall of a toilet stall. Slithering into the vent, I hooked a foot into one of the ornate metal curlicues in the grill and pulled it back against the aperture. The vent was too narrow to bend back to get it exactly in place, but it would be close enough should any early risers venture in.

The grill on the Admin side gave no resistance. I wriggled out, making sure to replace it properly. Like the Boss's office across the hall, Admin looked out from a three-paned bay window onto the gravel car park at the front of the Manor. Of three ancient red velvet curtains, the center and right sides were always drawn, but the one closest to the front door was tied off to the side with a threadbare piece of gold cording.

I needed to get in place right away before anyone showed up. External carriage lights on either side of the front door lit my way past Tetley's desk to the window. The right-hand side window curved toward the outer pane of glass while the curtain hung straight, so it left a space big enough for me to hide comfortably. I lay on my side, curving my back into the rounded wall, with my head under the window. If I remained standing, even between the panes, I could be seen from the car park. Hidden down here I had a clear view of Tetley's desk and the row of locked cupboards against the wall.

I settled down, checking multiple times that the curtain concealed all trace of me. The bare floorboards were chilly and my hip bone already complained on the hard surface. Now that I was actually in place I felt completely daft. This bordered on obsessive-compulsive or a hint of psychosis, I recognized that. But I had to know the identity of the interrogator. I just had to.

I heard the approach of wheels on the gravel outside. Headlights flashed briefly on the wall and then the vehicle came to a stop. The car door clunked open and shut again. Footsteps crunched on the gravel and a few seconds later the Manor front door clicked unlocked.

"Morning, Sarge," came the interrogator's voice, muffled in the hall outside.

"G'mornin'," rumbled Tetley. He inserted a key in the lock, and the Admin door opened. Florescent lights blinked on. Even though I couldn't see from here, I knew Tetley used a foot to slide the brass doorstop of a galloping horse in place to prop the door open.

The two men came to stand in front of the cupboards, Tetley blocking my view. *Move! Bloody move!* A flurry of unlocking and opening cupboards ensued. Tetley drew out a policeman's truncheon and slipped it into his belt.

For the love of God. That must have been what he hit me with yesterday. Bastard, sneaking up behind me after I'd left his office. He lifted what looked like a black dishcloth and shook it out. A hood. A second item dropped from it to the floor. He stooped to retrieve it and tugged it over his head. A ski mask. I craned my neck, peering past him at the mystery man. An open cupboard door continued to block his identity as he took out a series of items. He slipped them one by one into the varied leg pockets of his trousers. A roll of thick cloth-like tape, a couple of small rope coils, and something metal that I couldn't make out. He also inserted a truncheon into his belt, then pulled something from the top of the cupboard and swung the door shut. In one smooth movement he drew a ski mask over his head. I only glimpsed his face for a second, but saw enough to make me want to cry out in betrayal.

It was Mike. *Mike* had hit me, twisted my limbs, humiliated me - threatened me with rape? I stuffed my knuckles into my mouth to stop myself from either screaming or bursting into sobs, I wasn't sure what. *My Mike* - a psycho monster at heart. I heard the unmistakable clicking of an ammo magazine being inserted into a pistol and Tetley reappeared in my line of sight. He held the weapon out butt first toward Mike, who took it and slid it into a holster on the outside of his right thigh. *Holy God.* It was apparent how much he'd gone easy on me.

"Don't ferget these, Sir." Tetley held out a cigarette packet.

Mike tucked it into one of his breast pockets. I knew he didn't smoke so they were to inflict burns on Murphy. Oh, Jesus God. "Ready?" he asked.

"Aye. Let's git him."

Their footsteps sounded much heavier now as they walked with purpose across Admin and out the door. One of them flipped the light switch, plunging me into darkness again. Although they closed the door behind them, I noticed they didn't lock it. I expected that Tetley would return as soon as they'd hijacked Murphy and taken him to the interrogation room.

Listening to their steps clumping off down the corridor, I rolled to a sitting position. I was in total shock. Of all the people in the world I never expected Mike to be my interrogator. His Belfast accent was laudable.

Feeling like I'd been assaulted all over again, I crawled out from behind the curtains and crept to the door. Returning to the toilets I put the grill properly back in place, then stole up the main stairs past the officers' level to the third floor. A couple of steps from the top the sound of scuffling halted me. Ducking down behind the banister, I watched Mike and Tetley drag the hooded Murphy out of his room and over to the servants' staircase. He wore only his Y-fronts. Cringing, I put a hand to the sore lump on my head, remembering how they'd dragged me across the courtyard. I padded after them, veering left to return to Heather's and my bedroom.

Her clock showed ten minutes past four. What the heck was I going to do with myself for the next two-and-a-half hours? My bed looked so very inviting. Heading into the bathroom I fetched my discarded clothes from last night, and brought them into the bedroom. Rummaging in the trousers I found the flattened paper cup with the painkillers inside. I washed one down with water and peeled off my clothes. I was about to slip Mike's robe back on, but dropped it as though it were contaminated and got into my flannel pajamas instead. Sliding into bed I lay thinking about Mike, trying to put the man I thought I knew, and interrogator-Mike into the same person. How could I have got it all so incredibly wrong?

18
Banshee

One by one, over the next five days the others were taken. They knew something was up the morning after my exercise. You could see the questions in everyone's eyes as each disappeared. I recognized the glassy-eyed shock on the faces of those who returned, not to mention the tell-tale bruises. But none of them could have been as in much shock as me. The exercise was bad enough, but to have found out it had been Mike who conducted it was a thousand times worse. Betrayal didn't even begin to describe how I felt. How I might react when I came face to face with him again, I simply couldn't guess. I dreaded it and moved through the next few days in a kind of horrified fugue.

At classes Tetley, Chalki, and the Boss made allowances, thinking my state was a result of the counter-intelligence exercise. All of us tried to pretend nothing was going on. I assumed optimistically that if Mike or Tetley hadn't killed the ones who didn't return, they must have failed the exercise and had to leave Finley. Poor old Murphy didn't make it. Etched into my memory was my last sight of him being dragged away - his bare feet hanging helplessly, toes curled and pointing inward.

By the fifth day my black eyes and bruises had diminished to an ugly shade of green. I had begun taking the contraceptive pills three days ago, so my period had already gone. Tetley handed me a six-month supply, and even though the leaflet inside the boxes said to take the placebo sugar pills every three weeks, he instructed me to toss them and move on immediately to the next box. I wondered what kind of effect it might have long term, not allowing my body to menstruate. But it wouldn't be forever and it certainly would be nice not to go through painful cramps.

They grabbed Heather almost a week after me. I worried about her all through the day. Now that my wrist was so much better, after dinner I distracted myself by practicing the violin up in our room. How long would she last? I'd only stuck four hours before I took matters into my own hands. I knew as one of the first females in training, I'd taken them by surprise. They wouldn't allow that to happen again.

To my relief she finally showed up shortly after eight thirty. She'd lasted almost eleven hours. "How did it go?" I asked, although I could see how by the state of her.

She sank onto her bed, resting her elbows on her knees. She probably felt like I had - shock, disbelief, anger, self-pity, and a serious doubt as to whether she'd made the right decision in coming to Finley at all. Her hunched body language was defensive so I didn't immediately rush to comfort her. I left the violin and bow on my bed and perched beside her, giving plenty of space between us as I gave her shoulder a gentle rub. After a moment she tilted toward me and I put an arm round her. She laid her head against my chest, tears streaming down her face. I felt awkward, unused to this level of intimacy except for those few occasions with Mike.

"It's good to let it all out, Heather," I told her, parroting what he had said to me. "You can't keep it bottled up."

She was made of stronger stuff than me. She wept for a short while, but not nearly as much as I had. Her shudders gradually subsided and she sniffled, straightening up and reaching for a piece of the toilet roll in lieu of tissues that we kept on the dresser.

"Did the doc give you any pills?" I asked. She shook her head, so I went into the bathroom to rinse out and fill the glass we kept our toothbrushes in. Reaching into the shower I let the water run and took the glass into the bedroom. Retrieving the stash of painkillers from my bedside table, I dropped two into her palm. "They'll really help," I told her. "And then get in the shower, water should be hot by now." I reminded myself of my mother as I bustled about, opening Heather's clothes drawers and finding her a clean set of pajamas. She tossed back the pills but remained sitting, glass in hand. I recognized one of the signs of shock. Hunkering down I swiftly unlaced her mud-caked boots, yanking them wide enough to get her feet out. When she still didn't move I took hold of the backs of her heels in turn and pulled off the boots.

"Come on." I took the glass out of her hand and placed it on the bedside table. Then I clasped a hand under her elbow and helped her stand. "Are you hungry?" She shook her head. I walked beside her, easing her toward the door and into the bathroom, where I handed her the pajamas. "When you come out I'll have a hot chocolate waiting for you, okay?"

She managed a smile. "Thanks, Jennifer. You're a mate."

It was disconcerting to see the stalwart Heather so subdued. But then - at least *her* lover hadn't turned out to be the fucker who tortured her.

I slipped down the servants' staircase and headed to the rec room.

Cigarette smoke filled the air, mixed with a dirty-feet aroma to complement the ever-present stench of cabbage. No wonder I only came in here when I absolutely had to.

The mammoth hot water urn was empty. None of the guys would ever think to refill it. The little electric kettle had enough in it, so I clicked it on. Leaning against the table while the kettle heated up, I surveyed the room. A couple of the boys played a game of snooker on the single table and another three lounged on the furniture in front of the television in the corner. By the cacophony of cheering from the set, a rugby or football match played. One guy sat by himself, reading. Another four played poker at a table.

I could tell who had gone through the counter-interrogation and who hadn't, besides the obvious physical marks. All the guys who were yet to go worked hard at pretending they hadn't noticed the state of the others. Two of the three watching the match chit-chatted away and shouted periodically at the screen, while the third sat quietly. The two at the billiards table loudly cracked a series of suggestive jokes, trying to outdo each other. The card-playing quartet was notably silent other than necessary game play comments. I knew of five who had already dropped out or been washed out. Those were frightening statistics. How many of us would vanish after the next round? God, would I be able to get through it again? I seriously doubted it.

I lifted two mugs and used a teaspoon to lever open the tin of chocolate powder. Dumping some into one mug, I put some *Horlicks* into the other. I'd grown to quite like it. Who knows, maybe it had helped with my sleep. The nightmare appeared less frequently. I filled both mugs before the kettle had completely boiled and took them out to the corridor. Not wanting to navigate the servants' stairs blind with my hands full of hot liquid, I took the long route up the main staircase. Our shower was still running. Good. Heather would feel a million times better after a long steam in there.

The bedroom door had closed over so I pushed it ajar with my foot. Pitch black. I didn't remember switching off the light. Dread shot through me and I froze on the threshold. Mike and Tetley wouldn't be hiding in here, ready to abduct me for another exercise, would they? I backed out, still gripping the mugs. My heart thumped as I slowly eased to one knee and placed one of the mugs down by my feet. Straightening, I slipped my wrist inside the door frame, fumbling for the light switch. I flipped it on but nothing happened. After snapping it up and down a few times I chastised myself for my paranoia - the bulb had merely burned out. I headed over to switch on the little reading lamp on the chest of drawers between the beds. Three steps in, the door clicked shut, cutting out the dim corridor light. Turning round, I felt, rather than saw, something coming at me. Acting on instinct I jerked the mug, flinging hot liquid.

"Christ!" uttered a man's voice in a northern English accent.

I hurled the mug and ducked, throwing myself to the side. The mug hit him with a thud and clunked to the floor, giving me his approximate location. I frantically felt around for something to use as a weapon. My hand fell on one of Heather's boots. I grabbed it and lunged, wielding it like a club. The steel toecap connected with something hard. His head, I hoped, and I kept bashing. He went down with a thump. I felt the air displace violently as he waved his arms, trying to snatch the boot from me.

"Jesus Christ!" His voice shook, sounding suspiciously like he was laughing. "I give up! I yield, whatever - just stop the fuck hitting me!"

"Stay down!" I commanded, backing up and feeling for the chest of drawers. Keeping the boot out in front of me, I located the lamp and clicked it on, blinking rapidly in the sudden light. At my feet huddled a large, muscular guy in ski mask and combat jacket, armed to the hilt with a huge revolver in an underarm holster. He shuddered so hard with laughter he'd been rendered helpless. Peeling off the ski mask he revealed a shaved head and little goatee beard. I gauged his age to be late twenties, early thirties. I failed to see anything funny about this at all. "You want to explain yourself?" I demanded.

He rolled to a sitting position, using the ski mask to wipe tears of mirth from his eyes. "Wrong room, obviously. Sorry."

"Who are you?"

"Never mind who he is." Chalki stood in the doorway, ski mask pushed up over his forehead. "Other end of the corridor I said, you twat. Front of the Manor." He pulled the mask completely off. "Have to abort now, fucking idiot." He melted into the darkness of the corridor.

The English guy looked down at the mess on his smock. "Did a fucking elephant just come over me, or what?"

I snorted, then found myself in just as helpless a state as he'd been in. The boot fell from my grasp and I held my sides, sinking onto Heather's bed. "*Horlicks*," I managed.

"Pardon me?"

"The drink."

He dissolved once more and we snickered and snorted in unison, struggling to keep our hysteria quiet. Finally he recovered and held out a hand. "Adams, at your service."

I shook it. "Hamilton."

"Well, bugger me! The Wild Banshee woman."

"What?"

"She who smashes chairs and beats guys over the head."

I blinked. "Who called me that?"

"His nibs, Chalki."

"Oh. Did Mi-Sergeant McLeod tell him about it, then?"

He chuckled. "Learned it first hand, love. Got a bump on his 'ead the size of an ostrich egg to prove it."

Wait - had I got it wrong again? "*Chalki* interrogated me?"

"Oops. You probably weren't supposed to know."

A joyful smile of relief spread across my face. I grabbed both his hands and squeezed them. "I won't let on you told me. Thank you, Adams - thank you so much." He looked taken aback and I quickly withdrew. I was no doubt giving him totally wrong signals. "I thought it was someone else," I explained.

He grinned. "Between you and me, that nut job needed a good bashing." He nodded toward the abandoned violin and bow on my bed. "I just count myself lucky you didn't shove that stick up me arse." He was being gracious - only his sense of humor had given me the advantage. He could snap my neck with one hand.

"Just gave you the boot," I teased, holding up my erstwhile weapon.

He chuckled and got to his feet. "Well, Miss Banshee, I'd better go get reamed out good and proper by 'is nibs." He nodded toward the empty third bed. "Lightbulb's on that nightstand over there. Sleep tight." He stepped into the corridor and disappeared.

By the time I crossed over to the door to close it he had completely vanished. I twirled a circle in the middle of the room like Julie Andrews's character in *The Sound of Music*. Mike hadn't tortured me! Thank God. Then I sobered, immediately feeling terrible for having thought he was capable of it in the first place. But he *was*. I'd seen him prepare for Murphy's interrogation.

I noticed the shower had stopped running. Moments later the bathroom door opened and the light cord clicked off. Heather shuffled into the bedroom, wearing her pajamas.

"Feeling any better?" I asked. No need to mention anything about our visitor.

"Yeah." She had a glazed look about her, the painkillers had obviously taken effect.

I pulled back the covers on her bed. "Get in." She meekly obeyed. I realized her hot chocolate was still out in the corridor. Miraculously it had survived, so I placed it on her bedside table, put the violin and bow safely away, and went next door to take a quick shower. By the time I'd finished she'd fallen asleep, her drink untouched. I put on a clean pair of the general issue gray sweats, and settled down on my bed to read. Pushing the lamp closer to my side, I also stole her lukewarm chocolate. I might as well, seeing as the *Horlicks* had become a cropper. Elephant ejaculation! I smothered a laugh.

I'd been saving this book, filched from the rec room, for when I had time to read it. *Shogun* by James Clavell. I quickly lost myself to the adventures of Dutch Captain Blackthorne, shipwrecked on the alien and ancient shores of feudal Japan. It was set seventy years after England broke with the Papal Court at Rome and became Protestant. Had this mistrust between Catholics and Protestants always been there? Was it just the nature of humanity to hate what it didn't understand? We were still at it many hundreds of years later, and I saw no bloody end to it.

A light tap sounded at the door, making me jump. I glanced at Heather's clock. Nine-twenty. Sliding off the bed I opened the door to find Mike, leaning an arm against the door frame. I smiled in delight.

"You alone?" he mouthed.

I cracked the door open enough for him to see Heather, fast asleep. "She had her interrogation today."

"Your shiners are going down nicely."

I self-consciously put a hand to my face. I'd forgotten about them.

"Report to the Boss's office in five," he said. "What you're wearing's fine."

I closed the door and sat on the edge of the bed to slip on my gutties. I was so glad that I'd found out about Chalki before seeing Mike again. My reaction could have ranged from giving him a solid slap across the face to shoving him head first down the servants' stairs.

What could the Boss want with me at this time? A recital, most likely. I grabbed the violin and made my way along the corridor toward the main stairs. Some of the lads had come up to their rooms. Music played and showers ran. The door to Jackson's room lay open, no light on. Had Chalki and Adams grabbed the poor sod after all? I wondered if he'd be back, or if he and his belongings would disappear. I descended to the ground floor and knocked on Colonel Pierce's office door.

"Come in," called Mike.

The office was almost in darkness, just the green-glassed banker's lamp on the desk casting an intimate glow. Mike stood in front of the burning fire. He had a bashful smile on his face. "Anyone see you come down?"

"Don't think so."

"Lock it."

So, not an official summons. I couldn't help a grin as I twisted the key as ordered. Mike had pulled the leather sofa away from the wall and dragged it in front of the fire. All the interior wooden window shutters were firmly latched, guaranteeing total privacy. "Where's the Boss?"

"Not here," came the enigmatic reply.

"So, what can I do for you, Sergeant?" I asked playfully.

"Put down that violin for a start and come over here."

I laid it on the desk as I passed. Mike's eyes looked so dark and serious. I paused a few feet away from him, sensing he wanted to kiss me - and more. Was I ready for that? A questioning look crossed his face. I blinked and propelled myself forward into his arms. To hell with being ready. I needed him.

He bent his head and we kissed, his lips gentle. He gestured to the sofa. "Have a seat." Turning to the drinks table he held up the bottle of Bourbon. "Drink?"

"You know I only take Bushmills," I joked as I eased out of my shoes and curled my legs under me on the sofa.

"How about thirty-year-old Scotch?"

"Suppose I could force myself. Won't the Boss miss it, though?"

He smiled and poured me a large glassful from one of the crystal decanters. Then he got himself some Bourbon and brought both glasses over.

"To what do I owe the honor of all this?" I inquired as he settled on the sofa beside me.

"Do we need an excuse to spend time together?" A concerned expression flitted over his face. "This all right with you?"

I knew he meant the Percy French and my parents. "It's fine, Mike. We're moving on, right?"

He held out an arm and I slid over, cuddling up next to him. We clinked glasses. "Her Majesty?" he suggested.

"Her Majesty." As with every toast made, I immediately thought of Dee. The crackling fire also reminded me of the Botanic apartment, and all the booze shared in front of it.

I pulled myself back to the here and now - the warmth of the fire, the taste of expensive, smooth Scotch on my tongue, and the feel of Mike's body close beside me. A brief slice of heaven.

He laughed suddenly. I turned my head and gave him a quizzical look. He met my gaze, his eyes warm and so full of expression and kissed the top of my head. "Wild Banshee woman."

"Oh, that." I laughed too.

"Adams regaled us with your encounter, earlier. Think he's got quite a crush."

"Us?" I hope he didn't mean the rest of my classmates.

"Our guys. Trainers."

"Torturers, you mean."

He chuckled and we settled back into a companionable silence. I got the feeling he had something serious on his mind. But then, when didn't he? I knew better than to inquire. If it were work-related he wouldn't tell me, anyway.

It grew hot and uncomfortable sitting so close to the fire. Mike didn't appear to be affected even though he wore his full Temperate Barracks gear, pullover and all. "Are you not boiled in that sweater?" I asked, breaking the silence.

"A bit. But I'm too done in to move."

So tiredness had prevented a repeat of the instant ravaging from last time. I'd been kind of hoping we'd do that again. I adopted a teasing tone. "Poor baby, let me help you." I set my Scotch on the floor and took hold of the bottom of his sweater. He grinned and handed me his glass. I placed it beside mine and turned my attention to pulling the sweater off over his head. He obediently raised his arms to help and I tossed the garment over my shoulder.

"And my feet hurt too much to take off my boots," he said in a pained tone.

I raised an eyebrow. "Really?" Sliding to the floor I knelt in front of the fire and slowly unlaced his boots, gently easing them off. Then his wool socks, one by one. I wondered how he'd react if I took the toe of his sock between my teeth and wrenched it off, but on second thoughts, the sock *had* been on his foot all day. His toes looked skinned and red, with a couple of angry blisters. I lifted both his feet and placed them on my lap so I could massage them. With a groan he collapsed his head on the back of the sofa and closed his eyes. By the state of him, he had trudged many exhausting, hard miles. I worked hard until I felt his tendons relax. "It's so *hot* in here, isn't it?" I murmured.

He opened his eyes and I made a big production of slowly gathering up my gray sweatshirt and peeling it off over my head. A huge smile lit his face when my breasts sprang unrestrained by a bra. He bent forward, took hold of me by the forearms and hauled me up onto my knees. He slipped a hand round to squeeze my bottom. "What else don't you have on under there?"

I giggled. "I'll never tell."

He gave me a playful smack on the rump. "Back to interrogation with you, young lady." He grabbed my sweatpants waistband. Using one hand to hoist me upwards onto his lap, he used the other hand to yank my sweatpants down. "Dirty girl! No panties."

I pretended to resist, squirming and wriggling, laughing the whole time. He drew the sweatpants over my ankles and tossed them to the floor. Wrapping his arms round me he pulled me into a kiss. I straddled his lap, resting my hands on his shoulders for balance. I liked the contrast of my naked skin against the course cloth of his shirt and trousers. He moved a teasing hand to my nipples, making me gasp. With deliberate slowness I unzipped his Nordie shirt at the neck so I could push it up over his chest. Slipping out my tongue to tease him, I licked and kissed each of his nipples in turn. He responded by gripping a handful of my hair, tightening his grip as I worked my way down his abdomen until I had to slip backwards off his lap. Kissing all the way down his stomach, I fumbled to unbuckle his belt. He placed a hand on mine, stilling me and I looked up in surprise. "Jennifer, we need to talk."

Oh, God. I knew he had something on his mind.

He gently pulled me up to sit beside him, and hauled his shirt back down. Absentmindedly he ran the fingers of one hand over the yellowing bruises on my thigh. "We're going to have to send you in earlier than we thought. Something's come up."

I experienced a sudden rush of adrenaline. My mind reeled, trying to shift from lovemaking to work talk.

"The IRA might be planning something big," he continued, "on an international scale. We need eyes on the ground to find out what substantiation there is to this."

I found my voice. "Why me?"

He gave a slight frown. "The circles we need to infiltrate involve the traditional music scene. It can't come as a surprise we want you involved?"

It wasn't. I just didn't expect it to be so soon. "Am I ready, Mike?"

"For this, yes."

"What'll I be doing?"

"Just what you did that night I saw you in Ballyben. Nothing complicated."

I didn't know how to react, it was all happening so quickly. But then it all had. *This* was what I'd been working toward since the Percy French bomb. I should be overjoyed.

Dark eyes glittering in the glow from the fire, Mike reached a hand to caress my face. "You won't be going anywhere until those bruises fade, at least."

That wouldn't be long. I realized with a weight of sadness that this would be the last time he and I would be alone together like this at Finley.

"There's something I want you to have, Jen." He reached into a trouser pocket and drew out a folded brown paper envelope. Opening it he produced a silver ring, which he held between finger and thumb. It looked vintage with a beautiful myriad of flowers and leaves engraved on the outside. "This was my Mom's. And her Mom's before her."

I blinked. Did he just carry his mother's heirloom ring about with him wherever he went? He took hold of my right hand and slipped the band onto my ring finger. Okay, a ring given in friendship - that I could accept.

He held my hand in both of his and looked into my eyes. "The engraving on the inner band reads: *'All I refuse and thee I chuse.'* I want you to read that, Jen, while we're apart, and know that I'm with you - in spirit."

A lump formed in my throat. Tears threatened and I swallowed hard. "Mike, I—"

He rescued me by kissing me firmly on the lips. I checked my tears as I hungrily kissed him back, fearing it might be the very last time we ever would.

19
Archangel

Heather lay so still I almost held a mirror to her face to make sure she was breathing. She gave a little snore, which reassured me and I climbed into my bed. The room felt freezing after the warmth of the fire in the Boss's office, so I kept my sweats on. Reaching to switch off the reading lamp, Mike's silver ring caught my eye. I drew it off to look at the inscription inside. *'All I refuse & thee I chuse'* in classical, flowing script. I loved the olde-worlde spelling of *choose*. Thoughtfully, I put it back on my finger. *'All I refuse'* wasn't quite true, though. We'd both chosen fighting terrorism over each other.

In the morning I woke to the sound of Heather humming as she made her bed. Only one of her eyes had bruised, giving her the appearance of a jaunty pirate.

"I'm starving," she announced, seeing me awake.

"You look chipper," I mumbled.

"Right as rain."

Her clock showed seven o'clock. I sat bolt upright. Mike hadn't told me when I'd be briefed, but I'd better be up and ready. Having had a shower the night before, I passed on one this morning to save time, just giving my face a quick rinse in the bathroom sink. Mike's ring glinted in the light and I twirled it on my finger, finding the feel of it reassuring.

Ripping a comb through my hair I went back into the bedroom to get dressed in my clean combats.

Heather had made up my bed. "Thank you," I said gratefully and sat on it to fight with my bootlaces.

"Least I could do, Jen. Thanks for taking care of me last night." She held up a mug, the one I'd thrown at Adams the night before. "Did this spill? There's dried muck all over the floor."

I hid a smile. "Afraid so, sorry. I'll clean it up later."

We hurried down the servants' stairs and into the rec room. Breakfast was lumpy porridge followed by tea and toast with marmalade. I caught sight of Jackson at the end of one of the tables. Adams and Chalki had taken him after all, by the looks of his ravaged face, but he'd made it through. Glancing around at the others I think only four still had to go through it now. At least I wouldn't be here to suffer through the next exercise. There was, at least, one benefit to leaving early.

I was on rota this morning for target practice. After breakfast I went to Admin to sign out a Browning and found Chalki at Tetley's desk. I had trouble meeting his eyes, but made myself do it. Then I couldn't look away, my gaze burning into his. I wanted to demand how he could live with himself torturing people like he did.

He paused, pen poised above the form he'd been filling in for me to sign, and stared right back. I realized belatedly that throwing down the gauntlet in a battle of wills with a professional torturer hadn't been the wisest move. Seconds crept by, feeling like minutes. Chalki's face remained expressionless but his blue eyes darkened as his pupils dilated. My eyes felt grainy and I was in danger of blinking. How the heck could I back out of this gracefully?

Not breaking eye contact he made an 'x' beside where he wanted me to sign. Shoving it under my nose he held up his pen. "I have all day, Hamilton."

Boot steps approached from the corridor, getting closer until they abruptly stopped inside Admin. Keeping his gaze fixed on me Chalki put down the pen and took out a keyring from the desk drawer. The newcomer approached to take them and a hand smacked me hard on the backside, nearly catapulting me over the desk. Livid, I spun round, fists clenched.

Adams disarmed me with a boyish grin. "Morning, Miss Banshee."

I found myself spluttering. "What the hell do you think you're doing? You can't do that!"

"Just did, love."

He and Chalki guffawed while I continued to splutter in disbelief and anger. Adams jangled the keyring and went back out to the corridor. I turned back and Chalki and I locked eyes again.

He raised a blond eyebrow. "Want to go for round two?"

Asshole. I huffed and grabbed the pen from the desk, scribbling my signature. He got up and unlocked one of the cupboards, handing me a Browning along with an ammo clip. To my annoyance I was so furious my hands shook as I tried to insert it.

Chalki took the weapon and did it for me, then handed it all back with a holster. "It wasn't personal, Hamilton."

I nodded. "I know that." Didn't make it any easier to swallow, though.

He cocked his head. "Get out of here. Before you realize I just gave you a loaded pistol and you can shoot me."

A genuine smile broke through my resentment. "There's a thought."

He gave a rare grin and I headed down the corridor toward the back. We might have made our peace but I'd never trust Chalki, not on my life.

I pushed the back door open, and like I had every time since I'd been jumped by Tetley and Chalki, I paused and checked that no one hid there. Except this time someone did.

"Adams?"

"Just wanted a word. Better a slap on the rear than a pistol to the head, if you get my meaning."

I frowned. "Not really."

"Just stay on the right side of Chalki, okay? He's not someone you want to piss off."

"Well, thank you - I think." My bum still smarted. "Did you have to slap me so bloody hard?"

He laughed and clapped me on the back, unbalancing me. "See you around, Banshee."

I recovered and continued toward the barn. Off to the right the assault course was shrouded in morning mist, making the obstacles appear like great Nordic trolls ready to attack. As I entered the field behind Finley, I heard shots from the barn ahead and quickened my pace. Tetley was overseeing the target practice and pointed me toward a vacant slot at the far end of the barn. I grabbed a pair of noise-canceling earphones that hung on a nail on the wall and slipped them on. A paper target with a charging soldier circa World War II awaited me. I drew out the Browning and took aim.

The summons came twenty minutes later. To get my attention, Tetley lifted the earphones an inch from my head and let them snap back. Flinching, I immediately clicked the safety back on the pistol and holstered it before turning round.

"The Boss's office," he ordered. "On the double."

"Should I return this first?"

"Give it here, girlie. "

"Thank you, Sarge." I removed the holster and handed everything over.

The mist had cleared. As I made my way across the field I noticed that clusters of sun-golden daffodils had erupted along the hedgerow. Spring was just about here, I realized.

The Boss's door lay open when I got there. He wasn't at his desk so I knocked. "Come!" he called.

He and Mike stood in front of a series of mugshots pinned up on the wall over by the fireplace. I clamped down on my instinctive rush of emotion at seeing Mike, and entered the room. "Close the door, Hamilton," ordered Pierce.

I did so. As I passed the sofa to join them I felt my face flush, remembering what transpired on it only a few hours ago. What would the Boss have to say about that, if he knew?

He leaned an arm along the fireplace mantelpiece. "I believe Sergeant McLeod has told you why you're here."

Mike was in professional mode, his bland expression giving nothing away.

"He has, Boss," I confirmed. Adrenaline shot through me, a mixture of terror and elation.

He tapped one of the mugshots with his finger. "Getting close to this man is your objective. Name of Séan Maguire."

I blinked at the image of the flame-haired guy. "I know him."

Both Mike and Pierce directed their full attention on me.

"How?" demanded Mike.

"Well, not know him exactly, but I've seen him about in Belfast. And I think his band played at that *céildh* in Ballyben after us, but I'm not certain."

Colonel Pierce raised a quizzical eyebrow.

"The event that brought Hamilton to our attention in the first place, Boss," Mike explained.

"Ah yes." He frowned. "Does Maguire know who you are?"

I wondered that myself. If he had been there that night, he must have seen me playing the fiddle on stage when Seamus had introduced me as 'Fionnuir', but that didn't necessarily mean he knew my real identity. I shared this, adding, "I very highly doubt that Seamus would have told him. He made a point of hiding I was a Protestant, even changing my name."

Pierce nodded, stroking his chin.

"I agree," said Mike. "When we raided the place and picked up the two suspects at the *céildh*, there was no sign of Maguire or his associates. If they were there they high-tailed it back to Belfast at the first sight of us."

I watched Mike and the Boss exchange long looks. Was telepathy as well as unreadable facial expressions taught in British Army training?

"It's a risk," Pierce said. He turned to study Maguire's image. "But we don't have any other options."

"We can pull her out at once if it turns out she's compromised," answered Mike, "but we'll only know that after we send her in."

"Agreed."

Part of me wanted to object to them talking about me as though I wasn't there. Another part wanted to yell at them to hurry up and tell me more about what they wanted me to do. Yet another part, the self-preservation, longed to run away and bury my head somewhere dark and safe.

There were several more photos, taken from a distance, of three other young men. I studied them, memorizing their faces. "Kieran Lynch, Liam Doherty, and Declan Feeney," said Mike. "The other band members. Maguire took out an ad in the *Irish News* for a fiddle player, yesterday. Apparently the last one blew off his fingers when he triggered a home-made booby trap. As he was building it."

I stifled a laugh, my gallows humor bubbling to the surface. Ignoring the Boss's startled expression I studied a fifth photograph on the wall of an older man wearing an expensively-cut jacket.

"Brian Sutherland," said Pierce. "He's kept a low profile but recent increased activity has brought him to our attention. He's been spotted at various meetings among senior Nationalists and Republicans in both the West Belfast and Dublin areas." He moved to his desk and sat. "Please," he gestured that Mike and I take the two chairs in front of his desk. "There is believed to be a hard core of about forty middle-ranking members of the IRA who make operational decisions in Belfast. Most are known to us, but not all. We suspect Sutherland might be one of them. One of our field operatives got wind of something significant in the works, and Sutherland has begun traveling regularly to the States."

"Boston, specifically," interjected Mike.

"Indeed. At first we thought he was responsible for an increased number of arms being smuggled into the Province, but that's not the case. Instead he's concentrated his attention on developing a presence in the traditional music scene. This is a very new development, and completely foreign to his usual activities." The Boss leaned his elbows on the desk, his fingers forming an upside-down 'v' under his chin. "The suddenness of it is suspicious. That, along with the American visits and increased arms smuggling, indicates some new plan of attack may be in the offing." He looked at Mike, who took over.

For once I wasn't distracted when he locked eyes with me. "Your role is straightforward," he said. "We've suppressed the publication of Maguire's advert until Friday, and taken down the hand-written notices he'd put up locally." He lifted a manila envelope from Pierce's desk and drew out an A-4 sized piece of paper. I saw *Wanted!* Printed in large letters at the top, *Fiddle player with Flair* underneath, and details in smaller print. At the bottom someone had snipped tear-off rows into the edge of the paper with the same address, date and time written on each. Mike tore one off and handed it to me. The date was for Friday morning at ten o'clock. "Audition for the band," he continued. "We've helped the odds significantly and with your musical skill you'll be a shoo-in. The challenge is getting access to Sutherland. Maguire's your ticket." He leaned forward intently. "Remember, a fact-finding mission. Perform with the band, scout out whatever Nationalist pubs and clubs you have access to and learn anything of interest. Do *not* do anything that'll risk blowing your cover. You won't be armed. You don't have the resources or training to embark on a deep cover mission. Understood?"

I felt like I'd fallen into a James Bond film. "A fact-finding mission," I repeated, to let him know I got it. "Don't do anything to risk my cover being blown. Yes."

"And if you think you're in danger of discovery, get the hell out at once. Understand?"

"Yes, got it." Christ, this was for real. I needn't expect 007 to come rescue me if it all went pear-shaped.

Mike pulled a little dark blue booklet out of the manila envelope and handed it to me. A Northern Irish driver's license under the name *Fionnuir Moylan*, but with my photo. According to the details Fionnuir was born in the town of Coleraine in County Antrim. And with a name like that was naturally a staunch Roman Catholic. Growing up with Dee as my friend had given me the edge on that. I already knew the subtle differences in colloquialism and speech to make myself sound like I was born Catholic. And I was familiar with their mass and communion thanks to all those times I'd sneaked in with Dee, both of us too young to know I'd committed an unpardonable sin against their church. I also knew how to make confession if I ever needed to, although I hadn't actually done it.

I'd come out of this younger than I went in, if it didn't kill me. Fionnuir's date of birth was different, a few months younger than me. And a Leo, not a Scorpio. "But I haven't passed my driving test," was all I could think of to say.

"You have now." Mike took the license and piece of paper back from me and slid them into the envelope.

"Sergeant Hughes will go over all this with you," said the Boss. "You'll have a chance to ask questions then. That will be all for now, Hamilton."

I got to my feet and Mike surfaced briefly from under his professional mode to give me a very discreet, slow wink. I started for the door but the Boss stopped me in my tracks. "Oh, Hamilton?" He reached down and produced my violin case from under his desk. "You, ah, appear to have left this in my office." He held it out to me.

I took it, my face flaming. I managed to avoid looking at Mike. How stupid! I'd completely forgotten it last night and hadn't had time today to miss it. Not an auspicious beginning to my first assignment.

"I had her drop it off earlier," said Mike smoothly. "In case we needed to go over the repertoire with you."

How effortlessly he lied!

"Ah," rumbled Pierce. "Not necessary." He waved a hand at me and I retreated.

I started down the corridor for the back door, but Tetley's voice halted me.

"Hamilton!" he roared in his delicate fashion. I dutifully diverted into Admin to find him at his desk. "Sign out yer weapon." He produced the form that I'd signed earlier. A stickler to the last, was Tetley.

⌘

On Wednesday morning, two days before the audition, as usual Heather and I went down together to the rec room. Rarely did any of us miss a meal, especially breakfast. Today we were treated to a glorious full Ulster Fry, with potato bread, beans, sausages, the works.

I'd been given strict instructions not to discuss my assignment with anyone, which was hard. All week I knew I'd be leaving any day, and would have no chance to say goodbye to anyone. I wasn't sure how I felt. Why did my emotions have to be so divided all the time? I was impatient to get out in the field, yet at the same time reluctant.

Tetley ran me to ground in the corridor outside the rec room after breakfast. "Gae upstairs and pack, girlie." He zipped up his combat jacket. "Chalki'll tak ye to Belfast directly." He patted at the pocket. Drawing out a brand new jar of *Horlicks* from an interior hiding place he handed it to me. "Don't ferget this."

I felt an impulse to give him a hug but resisted. He'd probably have a heart attack. I think I'd miss him, he'd been kind to me in his own gruff way. "Thank you, Sarge. For everything."

He cleared his throat. "Yer clear on yer orders?"

"Yes, Sir."

"So what are they?"

"Audition for Séan Maguire's band and gather as much intel as I can about Brian Sutherland's activities."

"And?"

"If it looks like I'm compromised, get out immediately."

"And?"

"Don't get personally involved."

He nodded, satisfied. "Take care of yerself, girlie."

The back door slammed as he headed out to the assault course, and I went to my room to pack. All my civilian stuff, that is. The military kit had to all be returned.

I left Heather a parting gift, an unopened packet of McVitie's Chocolate Digestive biscuits I'd kept hidden in my bedside table. I left them balanced on her alarm clock where she'd see them as soon as she came into the room.

Retrieving Dad's ancient donkey jacket from my closet, I slipped it on and took my bag and violin case down to Admin. A good many weeks had passed since I'd arrived here wearing this coat. I was a different person altogether from the sobbing, wretched mess I'd been back then. Physically, too. My muscles had become wonderfully defined and I'd never been in such good physical shape.

Chalki took one look at the donkey jacket and shook his head. "Oh, no. Too military. Got to go."

"It was my Dad's," I said mutinously.

He raised an eyebrow. "Really, Hamilton?"

I subsided. "It's all I have of him."

"I'll keep it safe for you here, how'll that do?"

I shrugged it off and handed it over. He unlocked one of the cupboards along the wall, took out a clothes hanger, and carefully hung the jacket inside. "Do you own another coat?"

I tried to remember what had been left in my closet in the Botanic apartment. There might be an anorak, but I wasn't certain. My beautiful leather jacket had been ruined in the Percy French bomb. "I don't know."

Chalki opened up a drawer in Tetley's desk and withdrew a set of keys, dropping them into my palm. "Five minutes in the storage shed."

I raced down the corridor, out the back door, and fumbled at the padlock on the shed. When Heather and I had raided this for our Ballykinlar gear, I'd spotted a really nice black quilted coat with a hood. I threw myself at the boxes inside, trying to remember where I'd seen it. I emerged triumphant, and hauled it on to make sure it fitted. It did, as long as I didn't put on any weight. Hearing a chuckle I looked up to see Chalki leaning on the door frame. I didn't like him blocking the doorway. I don't suppose I'd ever be able to get past him being my interrogator-slash-torturer.

He consulted his large wristwatch. "One more minute."

Feeling like I'd won a lottery, I dug further. I found a pair of black leather ankle-length boots, with nicely comfortable half-inch heels. Catching sight of something very soft and shiny I hauled it out, holding it up. A full-length negligée in sheer ivory satin, edged with chocolate-colored lace.

"It's yours," he said. "Time's up."

Clutching my prizes I waited while he locked up the shed, then followed him back through the Manor. Retrieving my bag and violin from Admin I followed him out the front door, where a nondescript dark blue Ford Cortina awaited. He opened the boot and I hurried to unzip the bag and stuff the new clothes inside. Slinging my bag in the boot, he got behind the wheel and started the engine.

I began to lower myself into the passenger seat. "*Hey, Jen!*" someone called. I paused, looking over my shoulder. Heather and the lads had gathered on the other side of the wire fence in the assault course, waving madly. Tetley stood off to the side, hands on hips. With a lump in my throat I waved back before settling into the car and slamming the door shut.

Chalki backed out of the parking space and began to roll down the gravel path. As I watched, the lads all turned their backs, bent over and dropped their trousers. I let out a surprised yelp and burst out laughing at the sight of so many wiggling white buttocks. That was my final image of Finley: a row of bare bums and Heather waving with both arms.

20

Mirror, Mirror

The last time I'd seen the trees on Botanic Avenue they'd been stripped winter-bare. Now they'd begun to sprout budding leaves. It's hard to describe my mixed feelings as the car drew up to the curb outside my old apartment. It was so sharply familiar you'd think I'd never been away. Had the people in the other apartments even noticed my absence? Probably not. Students came and went at all hours on this street, it would be hard to tell if anyone was up in the attic apartment or not. Except maybe the third floor neighbor who was allergic to noise.

Chalki switched off the engine and opened the car door.

"No need for you to come up, thanks," I said hastily. I'd avoided talking to him for the entire drive here.

"Have to. Orders."

Well, I suppose it wouldn't hurt to have company at first. Maybe keep the ghosts at bay for a little while. He got my bag out of the boot and we made our way through the front door and into the hall. I hit the timed light switch and headed for the stairs past the payphone on the wall. I couldn't help but remember the last time I'd used that phone. To call Mum and Dad to tell them I was on my way on the bus before the Percy French bomb.

I shoved those thoughts aside. Concentrating on the here and now, I mounted the stairs, moving quickly so I could beat the timed switch before it extinguished. God forbid I'd be stuck in the dark with Chalki. On the top landing I waited while he unlocked the apartment door. Waving a hand palm down, he indicated I should stay back while he checked inside. I rolled my eyes. Honestly, what did he think would be lurking there?

After a few moments he beckoned and I stepped into the living room. Memories swamped me. I didn't remember the apartment being so small and claustrophobic, and judging by the stale mustiness it hadn't been aired since I left. I placed the violin on the sofa and looked around. Dee's Sacred Heart of Jesus picture still watched from the wall. The bulb had gone out on the little red lamp, though. I must remember to pick up a battery next time I was out. Wonder why she left it?

The door clicked shut and Chalki dropped a keyring into my palm. Three little shamrocks painted green, white, and gold. He slipped a hand into the breast pocket of his leather jacket and drew out the driver's license with my new identity.

"Here you go." Rummaging further he pulled out a folded envelope. "And this from Sergeant McLeod."

I glanced at the silver poesy ring on my finger before unfolding the envelope. Inside was a Catholic prayer card and pewter medal.

"St. Michael, patron saint of paratroopers," said Chalki.

There was a note, too. *'Saint Michael the archangel will protect you from evil. Sorry I couldn't see you off. Love, your archangel xoxo'*

I smiled. Archangel was what I was supposed to say when checking in.

"I'll take that." Chalki plucked the paper from me.

I almost snatched it back. But nothing that could incriminate me could remain. "Will you put it with Dad's donkey jacket please?"

He gave me a steady look and slid it into his breast pocket. I wondered how much he knew about Mike and me. The kettle caught my eye in its customary place by the stove. Instead of Mum's red, white and blue cozy, it now sported one with a riot of shamrocks and harps on it. I moved toward the kitchen. "Want a cup of tea, Chalki?"

"No ta, got to get back. But, hey–" He curved a finger through one of the belt loops on the back of my jeans, pulling me up short. "Want to model that negligée before I go?"

I wrenched out of reach. "Are you fucking kidding me?"

He held his hands up as though warding off an evil spirit. "Sorry, bad joke."

Fucker. Taking advantage because we were alone and away from Finley. 'Chancing his arm' as they'd say in Belfast. I moved so the kitchen counter was between us and laid the St. Michael card on top of it.

He switched gears. "You got the phone number memorized?"

I recited it.

"Remember, use a public phone box in the street to call, not the one downstairs. When you checking in?"

"Friday at three, after the audition."

"What's the word?"

"Archangel."

"And your codename?"

I really wish they'd picked something else. "Banshee."

"Right, that's it, then." He moved to the door. "Best of luck."

He closed the door firmly behind him. I let the tension flood out of me and went to the window, watching until he emerged onto the pavement. The Cortina started up and bore him away. He was someone I wouldn't miss, that was for sure.

I turned from the window. Alone. Really alone for the first time in weeks. What was I to do with myself until the day after tomorrow? There were too many echoes of the past in this place. Launching into busy-mode to avoid the silence I began with getting some heat into the frozen apartment. The scuttle held plenty of coal and a pile of newspapers lay on the hearth along with a large box of *Swan Vesta* matches. As I twisted the pages into shapes that would kindle easily, I noticed they were all the *Irish News*. Once the flames were crackling lovely and high, I investigated the apartment to see what other changes like the tea cozy had occurred. My *Ulster '71* keepsake mug with its Red Hand of Ulster coat of arms, celebrating the country's fiftieth anniversary, had gone from the kitchen. The china piggy bank still squatted in place and I rattled it. Heavy and full. Nice. I snagged a couple of coins and shoved them into the hot water meter for a bath later.

A new toilet roll had been threaded onto the holder, and four spare rolls sat atop the cistern. The old camp bed that Dee had slept on had gone and the Yehudi Menuhin poster above my bed had been replaced by a carved wood crucifix. Holy shit. I opened the top drawer in my dresser, where I'd kept my student ID, bills, bus passes and the like. All had been cleared out. So had my photos, both framed and loose, of Mum and Dad, or me with Dee or school friends, and even of Mac. On top of the dresser sat my old jewelry box from Mourneview. I lifted the lid and wound the key. Tchaikovsky's *Swan Lake* played tinnily while the tutued ballerina whirled around. A thousand memories flooded back. Not all sad. Lovely ones as well, like the Christmas when I'd been given this box - but good memories were still painful when you'd lost everything. My jewelry was all there, including the gold crucifix necklace that Dee had given me. I fingered it, remembering how I'd only worn it once or twice around her to let her think I liked it. My old watch was in there, too. It worked fine but the leather strap was scratched up. I wound it, set it to the right time, and fixed it on my wrist. Underneath the box I discovered four envelopes. Each contained a back-dated renter's agreement and payment book, a cluster of Belfast library tickets, a bus pass, and a National Insurance card, all in Fionnuir's name. Wow, what attention to detail. I'd kept some emergency cash in my bedside table. Investigating, the amount had significantly increased, with a pile of crisp five and ten pound notes. They'd thought of absolutely everything.

The silence became noticeable and oppressive, so I went back out to the living room to find a record to play. My LP collection had been replaced with only traditional Irish and folk records. That was a bit of overkill, I thought. Surely Fionnuir would like pop and rock music like anyone my age. That made me check the bookshelf underneath, where I'd kept all my text books. In their place was a row of Mills and Boon romance novels that looked like they'd been bought in bulk at the charity shop. I scanned some of the titles: *Devil's Mount, Kilted Stranger, Satan Took a Bride*. Dear God. I wish I'd brought *Shogun* with me.

But I had library tickets. I'd head over there later and get Fionnuir some better reading material. I probably needed to do some grocery shopping, too. Opening up the fridge I found that wasn't the case. It was stocked with a bottle of milk, half-a-dozen eggs, loaf of bread, cheese, and some cold cuts. Not tongue, I hoped, but didn't check. At the bottom of the fridge I found a six-pack of Newcastle Brown Ale. Ah, they'd missed one vital thing! Fionnuir would have Harp or something local, not an English import.

The food cupboard had also been stocked. A box of teabags, bag of sugar, tins of soup, beans, and a jar of Marmite. Remembering Tetley's *Horlicks*, I retrieved it from my bag and placed it in the cupboard beside the teabags. A sound from downstairs intruded and I looked expectantly at the door. God, I kept expecting Dee to walk in at any moment. Or Clancy.

I needed some air. Raiding the emergency cash and collecting the library tickets, I headed outside. The library was just down the road. Maybe I should try out being Fionnuir. This'd be a great opportunity to experiment.

"Have ya got *Shogun?*" I asked the librarian, affecting a regional accent from Coleraine direction.

Not batting an eyelid she directed me to the correct bookshelf. In the Off License I picked up a six-pack of Harp, then stopped into the Chemist. Although thanks to the pill I wouldn't be having periods, I thought I'd better at least have a few tampons around. People probably wouldn't pay that kind of attention to detail but I wanted to cover every eventuality. Whilst in there, a shelf displaying all colors of hair dye caught my eye. I paused. Fionnuir, the *Fiddle Player with Flair*, wouldn't have mousey brown hair like mine. She'd be more flamboyant - how about a redhead?

I couldn't see anything other than blonde, black, or brown until I noticed a sachet of henna underneath. The instructions looked straightforward: mix with boiled, distilled water into a paste, coat the hair with it, put on the plastic cap included in the box and leave it on for about three hours, and rinse it out with lukewarm water. Hey presto! Instant Celt. Well, a three hour Celt anyway.

I dropped it into my basket. Then for good measure I added a sachet containing a mud face mask and a dark copper shade of nail polish. All part of my transformation. The mingled scents from the perfume display drew me over. I had been using Avon's *Sweet Honesty* for years, never thinking to change it. An innocent, girly scent. Fionnuir would need something fresh and more vibrant. I tried a few of the sample sprays, and when I spritzed Revlon's *Charlie* onto my wrist I knew I'd found her signature perfume. Light and citrusy, with both floral and musk undertones. Perfect.

Back in the apartment I unloaded my purchases onto the coffee table in front of the fire. I was getting to know Fionnuir, while she was finding her own identity. For dinner I made myself comfort food of beans on toast and had a tin of Newcastle Brown Ale, making a start on destroying the evidence. Afterward, I tried out the patch test on my skin that the henna company recommended. If I didn't break out in a rash, I'd spend tomorrow beautifying myself and mentally preparing for the audition the next day.

⌘

Friday morning came quickly. With my violin case in hand, I took a bus into Belfast and waited at a stop across from the City Hall to catch another to take me up the Falls Road. I wore my navy blue flared jeans with the new ankle boots, along with a black sequined tube top of Dee's that had been inadvertently mixed up with my clothes. I'd slipped on a black cashmere cardigan for warmth, but would take it off as soon as I arrived at the audition. Cashmere hardly went along with my new rocker image.

I double-checked that the collar of my new coat hid the gold crucifix hanging round my neck. I'd considered leaving Mike's poesy ring behind but in the end couldn't bear to take it off. Only I knew its significance, and as he'd said when he gave it to me: *he'd be with me in spirit if not in body.* I also tucked the St. Michael's medal he'd sent with Chalki into my purse.

As buses pulled up to bear people other places, I kept catching sight of my reflection in the windows. I couldn't believe how dramatically different I looked. The henna turned out to be amazing. It drew out the warm tones in my brown strands, adding a rich, textured head of lovely auburn hair. I'd taken the transformation one step further and carefully cut a feathered fringe across my forehead, which sat just above my eyebrows. The rest was superficial. I'd painted all my nails with the dark copper polish and experimented with the makeup set that I'd been given for Christmas. Coal-black eyeliner and mascara made my eyes look striking and much larger than usual. Somehow having taken such care with my appearance had given me a sheen of confidence I hadn't experienced before. I hid a self-satisfied grin as I noticed men glancing appreciatively at me as they passed.

All I had to contend with now were my nerves. My stomach was in knots and my hands felt like blocks of ice. The Falls bus drew up to the stop and I took a deep breath as I climbed on board. I couldn't believe I was heading into notorious west Belfast, where no Brit in their right mind would tread.

But not Fionnuir. She'd be perfectly comfortable there.

I took a seat downstairs at the back of the bus, keeping a wary eye on everyone who climbed on and off. I avoided making eye contact, but they all looked as normal as anyone I'd seen on buses anywhere. I mean, really. What did I expect, cloven hooves and horns?

We quickly left Belfast city center behind. As the bus inched further up the Falls, the Nationalists' tricolor flag flew more and more prominently. As my stop drew near I grew sweaty and hot, yet my hands remained numbingly cold. With watery knees I stood and made my way to the front to let the driver know I wanted to get off.

"Thanks," I said as he let me out.

He grunted in reply and closed the doors after me. I fingered the gold chain around my neck and pulled the crucifix out over my coat to make it clearly visible. I swallowed hard and surveyed the street, getting my bearings. This was it. Two days ago I was a recruit-in-training. Today I was on the job.

My heart thumped as the bus pulled away from the stop, revealing an inverted burning car blocking the other side of the road. A group of teenage boys danced around the flaming pyre and one of them hurled a tin of hairspray into the flames. I tensed, waiting for the explosion, which still made me jump. The boys spotted me and cackled with delight. Evil wee pricks. They'd do that over the in the Loyalist areas, too.

In case they had any ideas about coming over to torment me further, I quickened my step to my destination, the Emerald Bar. Protective wire gratings covered the windows and a metal shutter guarded the double doors. Above them an etching showing the year 1901 faded into the stone. The doors themselves looked pitted and scarred, the brass knobs worn dull.

I looked down at Mike's ring, steeled myself and pulled open one of the doors. The scent of beer and sawdust assailed me as I stepped into a narrow hall. The doors behind me clicked shut, plunging me into gloom. Through the glass panels of a set of swinging doors I glimpsed a sawdust-sprinkled cement floor, and an elaborately framed portrait of the Pope prominently displayed on the wall. Stools balanced upside-down on round tables throughout the bar.

In the corner on a raised dais knelt two guys working with wiring, while a third shifted an amp over. The stage had a drum kit already set up beside a spinet piano, which had an accordion resting on top of it. Microphones on stands stood ready. As one of the guys turned round to plug in a lead I recognized Kieran Lynch, the weaselly guy I'd seen with Maguire in Belfast. Overseeing them all was a fourth man. His shock of flaming red hair told me exactly who he was.

Now or never. I reached up to unzip my coat and unbuttoned my cardigan so my cleavage was visible. Maybe that'd distract them from seeing how nervous I was. The three men on the dais looked over as I pushed my way through the squeaky doors, gave me a cursory glance then ignored me. Maguire didn't turn, but the vigilant tension in his body told me he was well aware of someone behind him. Up close his hair looked like the color of newly fallen autumn leaves, burnt sienna. A thousand subtle hues of amber and red gold were highlighted in the filtered sunlight dappling through the grated windows.

I cleared my throat. "Hi, I'm Fionnuir Moylan. Fer the audition."

"No girls," snapped Kieran.

Declan Feeney, whom I also recognized from the photos at Finley, smiled apologetically. "Sorry, love. He's right, 'dis is a man's band." His accent sounded strongly County Cork in Southern Ireland. Or the Free State, as they'd call it on the Falls Road.

I produced the torn-off piece of paper from my pocket. "It doesn't say that on the ad."

Maguire turned around slowly to face me, the sun through the windows lighting up his glorious hair. Up close he looked even more striking, with a deep cleft chin and unusual light amber-colored eyes that made me think of a lion. Exactly how a real Celt should look - the Red Warrior come to life. A smile played around his lips and I realized I was staring. To my consternation I found myself rendered as speechless as with Mike when I first met him.

He rubbed a hand over his carefully cultured golden five o'clock shadow. "Sorry 'bout the ad, but Dec's right." His voice was sheer Belfast, stilted vowels. "This's no job fer a girl. We play in a few rough places, so we do."

His harsh accent broke the spell and I found my voice. "I don't care. All I want to do is play."

His full lips quirked, humor lighting his eyes. "Y'any good?"

I brought all my female attributes to bear. I gave the Gallic shrug I was so fond of, pressing my breasts together and emphasizing my cleavage as my shoulders rose and fell. Then I switched on a hundred-thousand megawatt smile, worthy of Captain Stratton. "Why don't ya give me a try?"

Kieran puffed himself up. "No feckin' girls allowed." He gave a loud sniff.

Liam Doherty, who was well-built with a broad, kind face laughed. "Wise up, Kier. Don't take the fuckin' head staggers." His accent sounded like he came from somewhere like Ballymena up in the north. I'd have to be careful, as Fionnuir was supposed to be from up there, too.

"At least let me play one song as I've come all this way," I pleaded. "I'll buy you's all a pint if you let me."

Maguire smiled indulgently. "Okay then. But put yer money away, darlin'."

I shrugged out of my coat and cardigan before he could change his mind, and bent down to lay the violin case on the floor so I could unclip it. Tweaking the violin into tune I ran a couple of scales as slickly as I could, hoping to impress.

"All right, fellas," ordered Maguire, and the guys jumped onto the dais. "How 'bout some introductions. This is Liam." He gestured to the guy with the Ballymena accent, who gave me a nod as he strapped on a set of uilleann pipes. "Declan." He bowed. "And Kieran." The weasel scowled. He clasped a double-ended drumstick tipper and big bodhrán in his hands, its skin painted a Celtic dragon in green and blue. I forced a smile. He wore a perpetually disapproving expression on his face like the embodiment of

Dylan Thomas' *Thou shalt not on the wall* quote from *Under Milk Wood.*

"And I'm Séan." He leapt onto the dais to take possession of a distinctive blue Fender guitar. Slinging the strap over his shoulder he held out a hand tipped with nicotine-jaundiced fingers. "C'mon." I took it and stepped up beside him. His palm felt warm, his grip strong. "Yer freezin'!" he exclaimed.

"I'm nervous."

"Sure, it's only us." He plucked the violin and bow from me and laid them on one of the amps. Then he grabbed hold of both my hands, huffed his warm breath onto them and rubbed them vigorously. I gave an embarrassed laugh, but as Maguire forced the ice from my fingers, I felt the rest of me begin to thaw, too. "That's better, darlin'." He handed me back the violin and bow, and when I held them ready he nodded to the waiting lads. *"The Men Behind the Wire."*

Ha! Thanks to my experience with Seamus' band in Ballyben I now knew this one well. As Maguire strummed the opening chords Declan pressed a button on the accordion and Kieran began a steady beat on the bodhrán. Without being prompted I joined in, improvising rifts to complement the others' playing. Maguire exchanged glances with the others, then broke into song. He had a great voice, melodic and deep, without a single trace of a Belfast accent. He made even this song sound tuneful.

> "*'Through the little streets of Belfast*
> *In the dark of early morn*
> *British soldiers came marauding*
> *Wrecking little homes with scorn—'*"

He gave me a nod. "Now you."

I put everything I had into it, as though I meant every word.

> "*'Heedless of the crying children*
> *Dragging fathers from their beds—'*"

We did the last three verses in unison with Maguire singing harmony. When he raised a hand to make a wind-up gesture we slowed and brought the song to an end. I'd put so much into making a good first impression that I was out of breath. I blew a strand of hair back off my face, having tossed it around so much it was a mess.

Maguire gazed steadily at me, his amber eyes giving nothing away. The others stared at him in silence. As the moment drew out I felt a tendril of apprehension.

"Let's do somethin' else," he said. "Somethin' slow. D'ye know Carly Simon's *Nobody Does It Better?*"

"What's the point?" snapped Kieran, his voice high with outrage. "She can't join anyway." He sniffed again. Did he have a cold or was that a nervous habit?

"Do ya fuckin' see anyone else linin' up to audition?" demanded

Maguire. "Let's see how she does. She'd give us a bit o'class, so she would."

Liam swapped the uilleann pipes for a bass guitar and leered at me. "Get her in a short skirt maybe she'd get in more paying customers."

I shot him an arch look. "Maybe I should just wear a corset'n stockings and offer blowjobs instead of playing at all."

Maguire chuckled. "Jesus, darlin', don't take the hump." He winked, reminding me sharply of Mike.

Startled, I realized I hadn't thought of him at all since I'd come into the Emerald. I'd practically forgotten why I was there to begin with. Not a very promising start.

"Let's hear ya, then," ordered Maguire. "Just singin', like."

Declan laid the accordion on top of the piano and sat. He picked out the beginning notes of the song while Kieran scrambled to get behind the drum set at the back of the dais.

"Nobody does it better, makes me feel sad for the rest—'"

I tried to make my voice as sexy and smoky as I could. When I got to the words: *'The spy who loved me, is keeping all my secrets safe tonight,'* my throat went dry, making my voice shrill off key. The *spy*? Paranoia gripped me, but I recovered and sang through to the end. The last words I aimed at Maguire with an impish grin, hoping to ingratiate myself. *"'Baby, baby, darlin', you're the best—'"*

He shot me a lazy, sexy smile, which completely disarmed me. I was probably being totally naïve but he certainly didn't behave like I thought a suspected terrorist would. Declan finished with the closing refrain on the piano and like before, Maguire regarded me in silence while the others watched him closely.

"Well?" I demanded.

He smiled and slid his guitar off, leaning it upright against the amp. He took my arm, guiding me off the dais. "What ya drinking, Fionnuir?"

That had to be a good sign. "Harp."

He trotted toward the bar. "Bottled, okay?"

"Yeah, thanks."

He vaulted over the counter. I put my bow and violin back in their case and clicked the latches shut.

Liam jumped off the dais to join me. "That was pretty good, so it was. I liked yer improvisation in *Men Behind the Wire*."

I felt a rush of pride. "Interesting song for an audition."

Maguire popped up from behind the bar. "Thought I'd see how ya handled it," he called.

I put my hands on my hips, realizing belatedly that I probably looked like Tetley. "And?"

A series of bottle caps being clicked open sounded. He lifted the flap in the counter to come out, clutching a variety of beer bottles. He handed them out, one at a time. He drank Harp, too.

"We'll give it a go, Fionnuir. *Slàinte*."

Pleasure and relief flooded me. I couldn't wait to make my check in call! "*Slàinte*," I replied. We all clinked bottles, Kieran reluctantly.

"Start tomorra suit ya?"

"As soon as you like!"

He laughed. "Well, can ye stay fer an hour or so now and run through some stuff?"

"Gladly."

We played through a list of traditional songs in preparation for tomorrow night. Maguire only had us play each song long enough to confirm I knew it so we got through them quite quickly. "We only do traditional stuff in the Emerald," he told me. "But we play in all kinds of places where we'd use modern songs. Weddin's and birthday parties and the like."

In the background a stout, middle-aged man with a shaved head went round the bar placing the stools on the floor and wiping down the tables. He switched on the lights, immediately making the Emerald look more cozy and inviting. At eleven a few men began to trickle in, and nursed pints as they watched us rehearse.

I wondered if Maguire found it odd that no one else showed up to audition.

Just before one o'clock, he gave me a pat on the shoulder. "Okay, we're done. Thanks, darlin'." I climbed off the dais. "Oh, Fionnuir? We all wear black when performin'. Yer top's all right, but do you have high heels and a skirt? A short, sexy one, like?"

"I can find one."

He nodded, satisfied. I packed up my violin and pulled my cardigan and coat back on. Realizing they were staying I hesitated at the door. Kieran beat out a rhythm, and Maguire joined in on the guitar. A *Horslips* song. They'd introduced a fusion of rock and Celtic music.

> "'*My love is colder than black marble by the sea*
> *I am the flash of silver in the sun*
> *When you see me coming you had better*
> *Run, run, run from Dearg Doom—*'"

Wow, he looked and sounded incredible, with great stage presence. He was like an avenging angel up there, with *Dearg Doom* as his theme tune. It meant the Red Destroyer.

21
Red Destroyer

Once back in the city center, I had about an hour to kill before my check in call at three. I dawdled in a couple of shops, checking out the new boutique in Robinson & Cleaver's across from the city hall to see what they had in the way of black miniskirts. I found a wonderful satin pleated one that looked like part of an X-rated schoolgirl's uniform, but it cost a whopping great £8.99, which was a lot more than I wanted to spend. I wandered around their shoe department looking for heels but everything looked staid and sensible, for nice, mild-mannered middle-aged ladies.

Then I remembered those fuck-me black suede boots with the four-inch heels that Dee had tried on just before the British Home Stores bomb. That seemed like eons ago now. I hadn't been back to Corn Market since so I steeled myself. McManus was still there, but displaying summer glossy, bright-colored sandals and pumps instead of winter boots. I could see from here that the British Home Stores had done well with the rebuild, the front completely revamped with bigger windows. More glass to shatter in the next bomb.

Inside McManus I spotted the boots in the far corner. Only a couple of the fuck-me pairs were left in black. Sending a prayer to the boot-gods, I lifted them down to check the sizes. Six-and-a-half. I bent and swiftly untied the boot on my right foot so I could try on the four-inch heels. Yes, it fitted fine.

I baulked at the price, £7.99, but had to have them. Then I headed out of Corn Market, along to the back of the City Hall and on up the Dublin Road toward Shaftesbury Square. I wished that Dee could see the new, dramatic me with red hair, makeup, and the proud owner of the fuck-me boots she'd so coveted. I fingered my crucifix necklace, feeling dreadful guilt for the way I'd treated her.

Where was she now, I wondered. I could easily find out if she'd stuck with the acting, but then what would I do? I couldn't very well seek her out, march up to her and say, '*Oh hi, Dee. Congratulate me, I found myself a job. Working for the Brits gathering intel, don't you know.*' Yeah, that would go down as well as a business of ferrets in a rabbit hole.

I found a cherry-red phone kiosk at the foot of University Avenue, just where the Lisburn Road branched off. It sat on the traffic side of the pavement, so the chances of anyone being able to overhear were very slim. My watch showed three o'clock exactly. Nerves flooding me, I lifted the receiver and dialed the number engraved into my brain. Shoving in my coin at the sound of the pips, I said, "Banshee," to the silence on the line. I felt ridiculous. What if I'd dialed a wrong number?

Mike answered, "Archangel." I couldn't help how my heart lifted to hear his voice. "How'd it go?" he asked.

"Meet the new member of the Falls Road Fuckin' Five."

I could hear his chair creak as he leaned forward. All sound was amplified in those big rooms in Finley. Assuming that's where he was. I suppose he could have been at Ballykinlar or Bessbrook for all I knew.

"That's not the band's name?" He sounded incredulous.

"Of course not. It's called Curadh." I pronounced it *cure-add*. "Means 'warrior' in Irish."

"Good job. When do you start?"

"Tomorrow night." I told him about the all-black outfit I had to put together.

He chuckled. "All you need is a ski mask to look authentic: *Terrorists-R-Us*."

"Very funny." I was about to tell him about the incredible boots I'd just spent a fortune on, but he spoke first.

"You need to look for somewhere to live over there."

I cleared my throat, taken aback. I hadn't expected that. "Do I really need to?"

"You gotta do whatever it takes."

I paused to take that in. "Okay, I'll ask around."

"Cool, check in on Sunday at three. I'll be waiting to hear about the gig."

With a click the dial tone sounded in my ear. He'd hung up already? I thought we were going to have a personal chat when the business stuff was out of the way, I'd been looking forward to it. Glumly, I went into the charity shop on Botanic and managed to find a fake leather black skirt for the princely sum of seventy-five pence, which cheered me up a bit. Back at the apartment I dug out a pair of black tights and tried the skirt and boots on with the glittery tube top I wore. The skirt fitted okay. Maybe a little tight but it would do until I got something better. I dug out a wide leather belt with a gilt buckle, which cinched in my waist and hid the tightness of the skirt's waistband. The boots maketh the costume, though. And they were surprisingly sturdy and comfortable, despite the lethal-looking heels.

I felt strangely empty and let down, now that the audition was over. I hadn't realized how solitary I'd feel in this endeavor. I'd imagined coming back at the end of the day to some kind of safe house, and maybe compare notes with other people on the job, have a drink, and help each other get through it all. A bit like at Finley. I wish they'd warned me.

⌘

Heading up the Falls Road after dark the next evening I felt a lot more nervous than I had the day before, if it were possible. At least the burned out car across from the bus stop had been cleared up and fortunately the gang of youths was nowhere to be seen. The double doors to the Emerald lay wide open and a cacophony of laughter and conversation spilled from within. Intimidated, I hesitated. I could practically hear my mother's voice. *'For God's sake, catch yourself on, Jennifer. You don't belong in there.'*

'But I'm doing it for you and Dad.'

I knew what her reply would be. *'Let it rest, dear.'*

But I couldn't. Any more than she could if I'd died in that bomb instead of she and Dad. I pushed my way through the swinging doors and stepped into a wall of rank cigarette smoke. The place was packed. Clusters of men from age eighteen up stood around, drinking and talking. At my appearance, the wives and girlfriends who sat in clumps together at the tables all turned to stare. Ignoring them I wove my way to the dais. The rest of the band was already there, dressed in their black stage outfits. With relief I joined them, slipping off my coat and cardigan, and piling my stuff behind the dais. When I turned back I caught the guys giving my legs the once over. Maguire greeted me with a big smile. I noticed a couple of his teeth were a little crooked, and although white, they looked dull compared to Mike's perfect movie star smile. But he kept them clean, which is more than could be said for a lot of other Northern Irish men I knew.

"Nervous?" he asked.

He had no idea how much. "A bit."

He reached a hand to feel my fingers. "Not as bad as yesterday, like."

I laughed. "No."

He let his gaze drop to my expanse of thigh below the hem of my skirt. "Ya don't need to be nervous at all. Dressed like that, you could screech like a banshee and no one'd notice."

My throat went dry. There's no way he could possibly know the significance of the word, *Banshee*. I'd have to stop looking for hidden meanings in everything. I forced a smile. "Wait till you see these." I produced the fuck-me four-inch black suede boots.

He whistled sharply in appreciation, drawing attention. "Holy Mother of God!"

I raised an eyebrow, ignoring the sudden sea of faces turned our way. "She's got nothing to do with it," I said archly and bent to unlace my boots.

A bottle of Harp materialized in front of me. Perks of the job, apparently, as I saw the others had drinks lined up, too. Declan slung on his accordion and the others picked up their instruments. I got my violin and bow from the case and clambered up with them, moving carefully in my new heels. That would be a great first impression if I tripped arse over tit before I'd even started.

We took a few moments to warm up and looked expectantly at Maguire. "*Raglan Road*," he announced. With a guitar strum he broke into song:

> "'*On Raglan Road of an autumn day,*
> *I saw her first and knew—*'"

We came in a few beats later, Liam on a tin whistle instead of his uilleann pipes. I played around him, letting him lead. At the end the bar patrons applauded loudly and I flushed with pleasure.

Maguire gave me a nod. "*Virginia Reel*."

Oh crap, talk about throwing me in at the deep end. I took a breath and jumped right in. The others followed, and I took delight in seeing the tapping feet and nodding heads around the bar. Kieran's bodhrán beat was steady and strong, making sure I kept time.

We performed another song, then an instrumental before taking a break. All four of the guys lit up cigarettes immediately, adding to the swirling fug. Five girls flocked over from one of the tables. They separated like single celled organisms becoming multicellular, two attaching themselves to Liam and Declan respectively, the other three converging on Maguire. I retreated to the rear of the dais and perched on the edge. To my amusement the girls hung adoringly on his every word, jostling each other for his attention. He held himself aloof, not favoring one girl over the others. No one approached Kieran, I noticed.

My body was soaked in a sheen of sweat and my feet throbbed in the new boots. I thought about taking them off to give my toes a break, but it might be harder to put them back on afterward. I drained my Harp and considered going up to the bar for another when I noticed a good-looking young man with curly brown hair and beard observing me. He caught me looking and came over, a pint of Guinness in each hand.

"Here." He offered me one.

I hesitated, but then took it with a smile. I wasn't that fond of stout, but I was hot and thirsty. "Thanks."

"*Slàinte*. Welcome to the Emerald."

"*Slàinte*, yerself." The Guinness was very welcome. I wiped a finger delicately along my mouth, making sure I hadn't given myself a foam mustache.

"What d'they call ya?"

"Fionnuir. What's your name?"

Maguire appeared behind him and tapped him on the shoulder. "Make yerself scarce," he ordered. The guy's face fell and he melted into the crowd. "Do me a favor, Fionnuir. Don't talk to any of these jokers, okay?"

I swallowed my natural instinct to challenge him. I didn't like anyone telling me who I could talk to or not, but I *was* here to observe Maguire, and he was my boss, so to speak. "Okay, if ya don't want me to. But why not?"

"I'd just rather ya didn't, like."

I wondered why. Kieran materialized from the crowd with two bottles of Harp. Maguire took one and plucked the pint of Guinness from my hand, depositing a Harp in its place. He really was high-handed. Kieran took charge of the Guinness and wandered back toward the bar while Maguire settled on the dais beside me. The girls who'd been fawning over him looked on with barely concealed hostility.

"Ya feel up to singin' a solo?" he asked.

My heart skipped a beat. "If ya think I'm ready."

"Only one way t'find out. You said you knew *Only Our Rivers Run Free?*"

I did, thanks to Dee. She'd said it was one of the best Irish songs written in the sixties. What would she say if she saw me here? It was due to her I could move freely amongst these people in the first place.

Yeah, these people whose bomb destroyed my life.

After the break Maguire told the others I was about to make my singing debut. I clutched my violin and bow for moral support, even though I wouldn't be playing in the song. Maguire strummed us in, and I took a deep breath.

> "'When apples still grow in November*
> *When Blossoms still bloom from each tree*
> *When leaves are still green in December*
> *It's then that our land will be free—'"*

The enthusiastic applause afterward thrilled me. They'd liked it, really liked it. They'd liked *me*. My spirits soared like they had with Seamus' band on Boxing Day. Something in this music called to me, perhaps touching some ancient genetic memory. I had Irish blood mixed in with my British, no doubt about it. And I felt proud.

We finished just before closing time at eleven, ending up with *'The Soldier's Song'* sung passionately by Maguire. The entire bar patronage stood militantly erect throughout it. I imagined Colonel Pierce's reaction to this display of staunch Irish patriotism, remembering how he laughed after I played the anthem for he and Mike. He wouldn't laugh now.

We put away our instruments and cleared up as the bar emptied, then with relief I changed out of the fuck-me boots. Declan and Liam bid a couple of the amoeba-girls goodnight, kissing and boldly fondling them in front of everyone before they left. I didn't know if they were permanent features yet or not. The three groupies who'd been hanging around Maguire had somehow multiplied into five. Their bleached blonde hair and over-plucked, drawn-in eyebrows made them look terrifyingly clone-like. They hung back at one of the tables, watching and waiting for him to ask them to stay, I suppose. They'd apparently decided to cope with my presence by pretending I didn't exist.

The middle-aged skinhead man from yesterday held the door open. "Come on, girls. Let's be having you's." They ignored him. Impatiently he called, "Hey, Séan!"

Maguire glanced at his fan club, who all turned pleading, doe-like eyes on him. "Scram," he told them. Deflated, they gathered their coats and handbags, and filed out. As they left, they finally acknowledged me by shooting me murderous glares. The skinhead threw the bolts in the doors after them and then cleared the tables. He went round hauling stools back on tables and sweeping the floor while another man with a full white beard hummed as he washed glasses in a sink behind the bar.

Maguire produced a metal cash box and sat at one of the tables. We gathered round, sitting in adjacent chairs to watch avidly as he counted out five equal portions of cash. "Not a bad haul," he announced.

Declan winked at me. "Having the bit o' skirt helped, so."

I pretended offense. "And the violin playing had nothin' to do with it, of course."

Maguire handed a wad of notes to each of us.

"Fuck me!" exclaimed Kieran. "Twenty quid."

I looked at my cache, scarcely believing it. That was more than I'd ever made in a week. Maybe I could afford that sexy black satin skirt in Robinson & Cleaver's, after all. I went over to my bag by the dais to tuck the money safely inside one of the fuck-me boots.

Liam beamed. "I think the skirt's here to stay, if this is anything to go by."

I rolled my eyes. "It's so nice to be appreciated."

"Want to see how much I appreciate ya, darlin'?" Declan danced around me doing a caveman imitation, fists pummeling his chest.

A thundering roar crunched the air, forcing a shock of vibration underfoot. Lights flickered, and bottles and glasses rattled loudly behind the bar. A bomb. *A fucking bomb!* I felt like the oxygen had been sucked from my lungs.

Declan turned back to the table. "Dat was close."

Everything slid into a sort of monochromatic haze. Oh God, I mustn't pass out. I tried to take slow breaths but my lungs refused to comply. I turned away, leaning on the dais and pretending to tie the laces on my boots to hide my distress. Sirens shrieked in the distance, sounding like screaming. I could smell the cordite and burning flesh as though I were there. I remembered Mum's pearls, charred black cinders–

Oh, Christ, why couldn't I get a breath? I abandoned my laces. I couldn't even see them, and if I stayed bent over like that I'd topple head first onto the floor. Maguire must have realized something was wrong. He appeared at my side, slipping a hand under my elbow to help me sit.

"Hey, darlin', you're okay. It was miles away."

The others exchanged uneasy glances. This was so unprofessional. Tetley would blow his top if he knew how I'd reacted. Maguire nodded to the guys who moved to a discreet distance over by the bar. I tensed as he perched beside me and threw an arm around my shoulders. Mortified, I fought to regain control.

"I'm fine."

"You're not. Shush, now. Did you lose someone in a bombing?"

I nodded. I was in danger of leaning against him and crying unrestrainedly against his chest, so I made a supreme effort to break away. My nose ran and I had nothing to wipe it with, so I surreptitiously brushed at it with the back of my hand. Maguire gallantly pulled out a spotless white Irish linen handkerchief from an inner pocket in his long coat and handed it to me. I wondered who'd laundered that so immaculately for him. Dabbing at my face and under my eyes, I hoped my mascara hadn't smudged too badly. "I don't usually do the damsel in distress thing."

He patted my knee. "Yer all right."

A figure detached itself from the shadows close by, making me jump. A trim man in his mid-forties approached. His dark hair had a smattering of silver through it, and a heavy gold signet ring glinted on his right hand.

"Hallo there, Miss Moylan. You did wonders for these jokers up there on stage."

Maguire got to his feet and gave a deferential smile. "Fionnuir, this is Brian Sutherland."

My stomach lurched and I stilled, focusing all my attention on the newcomer. This was the man I'd been sent here to find out about.

"Call me Brian," he said jovially, in a cultured and soft-spoken voice. He looked like he did all right for himself, judging by his expensively tailored jacket and hand-made leather shoes. "Take a hike, lads," he told the others, who immediately headed for the door. "Not you, Séan." He held out a hand to me. "Come and sit down, my dear."

I followed him back to the table Maguire had just vacated. He held out a chair for me, and then sat opposite. All the time I felt keenly aware of his intense basilisk focus. Even if I hadn't already been briefed on him, he would scare me anyway. He was fastidiously polite but I got the feeling that his impeccable manners carried an undercurrent of menace.

His manicured fingers sought his breast pocket and he drew out a large cigar. Maguire promptly stepped forward and snapped on his lighter. Brian puffed, taking a couple of deep pulls from the cigar. Then he relaxed back in the chair, crossing one elegantly trousered leg over the other. He exhaled, the smoke curling upward between us.

"Who did you lose in the bombing?" he inquired.

My thoughts raced. Fionnuir's story hadn't included this. If I told him it had been her parents it would be a simple matter for him to research and find out it wasn't true. "M'best friend," I answered. "From school."

"Which school?"

"Saint Joseph's." No hesitation there, it'd all been covered. "In Coleraine."

He puffed out a perfect smoke ring that hovered between us. I kept my mouth firmly shut, refusing to be intimidated into filling the silence by saying more than I needed. The smoke ring lost its shape and dissipated.

"I'm not aware of any bombing in Coleraine," he said mildly.

"We were shoppin' in Derry," I lied. A good Catholic 'tell' saying 'Derry' instead of the Royalist 'Londonderry'.

"Ah." He seemed to accept this. Ash had collected at the end of the cigar. He stretched his arm toward the table and Maguire unobtrusively slipped an ashtray within his reach. "So, what brings you to Belfast?"

I shrugged. "The music scene. This band." My tone implied that that should have been obvious.

He raised an eyebrow. "I thought Coleraine, with the University there, was a hot spot for up-and-coming musicians."

I shook my head. "If yer a drunk student, maybe. But not if yer serious about it."

"Where else have you lived?"

His questions were so random that no amount of drilling could have anticipated all of them. "A few weeks in Scotland." The best lie is one based on truth. Mum and I had taken a trip over there a few years ago to visit a childhood friend of hers.

"What did you do there?"

"Auditioned fer the Royal Scottish Academy of Dramatic Art." Also true. A teenage daydream of mine. I gave a rueful smile. "Didn't get in."

"Not a good actress, then?"

A tendril of apprehension unfurled. Was he accusing me of acting now? I needed to bring this inquisition to an end. I bristled. "I can't see how it's any of your business."

"Fionnuir." Maguire's tone held a warning.

Brian waved him aside. "Everything that happens around here is my business, my dear." He ground out the unfinished cigar and left it in the ashtray. "How serious are you about a career in a band?"

I met his gaze. "Deadly serious."

He smiled approvingly and got to his feet. "We'll talk again, Miss Moylan." Strolling back into the shadows of the bar, he paused and turned. "Get this young lady safely home, Séan." Then he stepped behind the counter and out through a door in back.

The tension rushed out of me as soon as the door clicked shut after him. I hadn't realized how taut my nerves had been stretched. I resisted the urge to sag over the table, fold my arms and lay my head down. Maguire produced my coat from behind the dais and held it out for me to put on. The skinhead came out from the back room to let us out. I retrieved my bag and violin case and we emerged into the night. I felt like I had been literally put through a wringer.

We paused to let an elderly woman with pronouncedly bowed legs pass by, carrying a plastic shopping bag. I did a double-take. It seemed extremely late for someone her age to be out in the streets.

"Mrs. Ford," Maguire told me. He tapped his finger against his head to indicate she was a bit 'touched'. "Her son Colin is buried in the cemetery down the road. She visits him at all hours, poor dear."

I watched her stumble off, wondering if rickets was the cause of her leg deformity.

"You done well there with Brian, Fionnuir," said Maguire, bringing my attention back to him.

I felt giddy with relief and rolled my eyes. "That was like the bloody Spanish Inquisition."

He threw back his head and laughed. It wasn't deep and sexy like Mike's, but it was warm and infectious. Striking a pose, he shrilled, "*No one expects the Spanish Inquisition!*" in a ludicrous high-pitched English accent, perfectly mimicking the Monty Python upper class twit voice. "That's the one good thing to come out of fuckin' England, isn't it?"

Well, I could think of several more things. Like David Bowie, for instance. Or Shakespeare. Copying the silly accent, I retorted, "*Look, matey, I know a dead parrot when I see one, and I'm looking at one right now!*"

He came back with, "*No, no, he's not dead, he's - he's restin!*"

A great thundering from the street cut us off. Two British Army Land Rovers crawled by, soldiers crouched in the open back doors. I glanced over sharply, but of course knew that Mike wouldn't be amongst them. I was glad for Maguire's company when I recognized the youths I'd seen yesterday with the burning car, loitering across the street. As the Land Rovers approached, they scrabbled on the pavement for stones and rubble to throw, and chased after them, yelling not-so-original variations of "Fuckin' Brits out!" and "Go home, ye bastards!"

An empty beer bottle shattered on the pavement close by, sending shards of glass flying. Mrs. Ford shrieked, dropped her shopping bag and put a hand to her head. The Land Rovers drove round a corner out of sight and the youths returned to their hangout spot, laughing and jeering.

I rushed over to Mrs. Ford. "Are you all right?"

"Think so, love," she whispered, voice quavering.

"Let me see." I gently eased her hand away to see a bloody gouge at her hairline above her temple. God, if it wasn't sad enough that she'd lost her son, she couldn't even visit his grave without getting hurt. The only thing I had to hand was Maguire's handkerchief that I'd blown my nose into. I used a clean corner of it to gently dab at the cut. Like all head wounds it bled a lot but wasn't deep, so I applied gentle pressure.

Maguire stalked across the road toward the group of youths. His long coat flew behind him like Dracula's cloak. My jaw dropped as he snatched hold of one of the boys by the lapels and slammed him against a wall.

"Watch the fuck what you're doin'!" he roared into his face.

The youth looked terrified and the others hung back. "S-Sorry, Séan," I heard the boy stammer. "Didn' know it was you."

Maguire glared for a tense moment, then let him go and stepped back. The stunned lad slid down the wall, scrambled to his feet and hot-footed it over to his friends. They took off, running as though a horde of demons chased them. Maguire watched them go then crossed back to us. "You all right, missus?"

"Aye, thanks Séan, love," she said with a coy smile.

I lifted the handkerchief away to look. Stopped bleeding, thank goodness. I gave Maguire a nod and he bent down and retrieved the shopping bag from the pavement. The handles were tied together so nothing had spilled.

"I'll take you home, dear," he told her, then turned to me. "How you gettin' back?"

I indicated the bus stop across the street. I just hoped the boys wouldn't return while I waited there.

He scowled. "No fuckin' way." He looked over at a black taxi idling at the curb. Thrusting the shopping bag into my hand he sprinted over to lean in the open passenger side window to talk to the driver. Moments later, he pulled the back door of the taxi open with a flourish. "Yer carriage awaits, madam. Courtesy of the Emerald."

Mrs. Ford grinned toothlessly at me. "Séan'll always look after ye," she said with pride.

I handed the shopping bag to her and went over to the taxi. Maguire mimicked a footman, holding out a hand for me to take.

"*Mo bhanríon,*" he murmured, bringing my knuckles to his lips. "Just call me yer knight in shining armor."

I withdrew my hand, feeling my face flush. I wondered what *mo bhanríon* meant. Maguire was so very charming but I must concentrate on why I was here in the first place. Remembering Mike's urge for me to move to this area, I said, "I can't take taxis every night. D'ye know of any apartments going around here?"

"I'll keep m'eyes open for ya, darlin'."

I climbed into the back and Maguire slammed the taxi door shut. The driver pulled away from the curb and did a U-turn. As we headed into Belfast, I saw Maguire solicitously take Mrs. Ford's arm and walk her down the street. He bent his head close to her so he could hear what she was saying.

"Where ya headed?" inquired the driver.

I didn't want to reveal exactly where I lived. I'd have him drop me a couple of streets away. "Yeah, thanks. Camden Street off the Lisburn Road." I settled back, watching the empty Falls Road pass by. My thoughts kept returning to my interview with Sutherland. The man gave me the creeps, and set off every instinctive alarm I had.

"Busy night?" asked the driver, startling me.

"Aye, it was great, thanks. Busy for you, too?"

"Just steady, y'know."

At this time of night it was a quick run into Belfast and up the Lisburn Road. He slowed at Camden Street, and turned left onto it. "What number?"

Shit, I didn't know the street well enough. "Just here'll do." He braked and slowed to a standstill. "Do I owe ya anything?" I asked.

"Nah, all taken care of."

I didn't know if I should offer him a tip, but he didn't seem to expect it. I thanked him profusely and stepped out onto the street. He remained by the curb with the engine idling. I realized he was going to wait until he saw me go inside. Bloody hell. I should have thought this through better. I crossed the street behind the taxi and saw that the nearest house had bushes along its front wall and by the steps to the door. I paused before heading onto the little patio area at the bottom of the house steps. I gave the driver a wave and stepped out of sight behind the bushes. Then I ducked down and crouched under their cover. I waited, holding my breath. After a few seconds, to my relief I heard the gears clunking and off he went. Returning to the street, I made my way back to the safety of my apartment.

22

Love Will Keep Us Together

Bloody fly. Buzzing round my head.

I swatted in irritation, then came fully awake. What had invaded my dreams was not a fly but the ringing of the downstairs phone. All the way up here in the attic it sounded like a low buzz instead of a bell.

Launching out of bed I made it to the top of the landing just as it stopped. I'd hoped it might be Mike calling. In case whoever it was rang back, I left the door ajar to listen and shrugged into Mike's navy blue robe. A fusty smell assaulted me. I hadn't washed it since he gave it to me and it was definitely due a good laundering. I just hated to wash his scent away, no matter how strong the pong. I put the kettle on to boil and headed for the bathroom when the phone rang again. I charged downstairs in record time.

"Hallo?" I mumbled, making my accent ambiguous.

"Fionnuir?"

Not Mike. Every fiber in my being tensed. "Yeah?"

"Séan. From Curadh. I didn't wake you, did I?"

"No, not at all." I quickly recovered.

"Ya got home okay, then?"

"Aye, thanks again for the taxi."

"My pleasure, darlin'. Anytime. Hey, we got a gig Tuesday night at Saint Malachy's youth club. Alfred Street near the City Hall. Ya know it?"

I had passed it a few times, but never taken much notice. "What time?"

"Seven o'clock. It's a Christian thing, like. Wear black but not yer miniskirt or them boots, okay?"

"Got it. What're we playin'?"

"Just traditional stuff, nothin' hard. Okay?"

"Okay, see ya then."

We said goodbye and I returned upstairs. My spirits soared at the thought of playing again so soon. A Catholic youth club probably wasn't exactly what Mike and Colonel Pierce had had in mind when asking me to gather intel, but it was better than nothing. And might lead to more.

At two forty-five I walked down Botanic Avenue and round to the public phone box I'd called from before, at the bottom of University Avenue. I couldn't wait to talk to Mike. This time I'd tell him I expected to chat for a bit longer than before. I just needed some reassurance.

"Banshee," I said after I'd pushed in my coin.

"Archangel," answered Chalki.

Disappointment swamped me. "Where's the other archangel?"

He ignored me. "How'd the gig go?"

I filled him in, leaving out the part where the bomb had upset me.

"Great," he said when I told him I'd already met Brian Sutherland. I heard him scribbling notes as I talked.

"We have another gig on Tuesday at St. Malachy's youth club."

"Good. Check in Wednesday, usual time."

Panic rose. I couldn't wait till then to talk to Mike. "Wait, Chalk–" Shit, I wasn't supposed to use names. "Can you get a message to - the other archangel?"

He didn't mention my lapse. "Okay."

"Please ask him to call me on the downstairs phone. Today, if possible. Do you need the number?"

"No. Bye."

⌘

The phone rang within the hour. "What's wrong?" demanded Mike.

Relief spread through me. "Nothing. I just needed to talk to you. It's been a *week*." I listened to static on the line for a moment or two.

"But you're okay?"

"Yes. You got my report?"

"Sorry, I gotta go. When you call Wednesday, I'll give you a time and place for us to meet."

But I wanted to talk *now*. "Mike, wait!"

He left me with the buzz of the dial tone. My mood plummeted. He'd sounded so cold and impersonal. Maybe he was angry that I'd asked him to call. But what was wrong with that? We were in a relationship, weren't we?

Self-doubt flooded me. I fingered his poesy ring as I climbed the stairs. Maybe I'd just assumed we were because he'd given this to me. If only he wasn't so bloody closed up and emotionally unavailable! One straightforward conversation would take care of all these questions. But we only talked on his terms, his timing. I felt justified in being resentful.

The feeling continued through the next couple of days and into the youth club gig, which went well. It was an easy couple of hours, more of a paid rehearsal session, really - and I earned another welcome £10.

When I made the check in call the next day, Chalki answered again. My resentment rode on a tidal wave to downright anger. Was Mike avoiding me?

"Message for you," said Chalki, when I'd finished telling him about the youth club. "Inside the Palm House, Botanic Gardens, ten o'clock tomorrow morning, okay?"

"Okay."

I hung up and made my way home. All this cloak and dagger stuff seemed so unnecessary to me. Why on earth couldn't Mike just come to the apartment, for goodness' sakes? He'd already been there, and who would ever put it together we were colleagues of a sort, now? It almost felt like he was toying with me. If he didn't want to continue our relationship, why didn't he just say so? I could deal with that better than wondering what the fuck was wrong with him.

⌘

At just a minute or two before ten I strolled into the Gardens and approached the Palm House. It looked impressive gleaming in the morning sunshine. I remembered reading somewhere that the architect was the same one who designed the Lanyon Building in Queen's University. It looked very Victorian, a curvilinear cast iron glasshouse with sweeping white-painted ornate frames holding the spread of glass panes. An elegant high dome rose in the center, with two wings stretching out on either side. One held the tropical display, and the other contained plants from cooler climes.

Twisting the brass doorknob, I pushed the door open. Tropical heat engulfed me and a little bell dinged over the door, which slammed me right back to the Percy French. Mum and Dad, disappointed in me - the heat and roaring blaze - the unending, terrible screaming, the yellow bleeding to orange.

I took a deep breath, stepped inside and gently shut the door behind me. A circular mini tropical forest lay before me, with a curving iron grill walkway around the outside of it. I circled it, looking for Mike. If he deigned to show up, that is. At this time on a weekday morning, it looked like I had the place to myself. Sweating already in the damp heat, I shrugged my quilted coat off. I completed the circle and checked my watch. He was late. Unless he was in one of the wings.

I crossed over to the door that led into the left-hand side, and peered through the glass. I didn't catch any movement, but with the abundant plant and shrub display, I mightn't be able to. Opening the door, I went in. A banana tree immediately caught my eye. Or rather, the bunch of emaciated, green bananas sprouting from the top did. I ambled toward the back of the long display row, to where the wall was covered in leafy, climbing plants.

Mike loomed out of the shadows. I expected him to do something like that so managed to curb my reaction. He wore jeans and black leather jacket, and the intense expression on his face made him look like a brooding hero from an action film. My heart skipped a beat, despite my being angry with him.

He smiled. "Hi, Red."

I blinked. Of course, he hadn't seen my hennaed hair. "You noticed!"

"Hard to miss. Suits you."

"Thank you." I wanted to put my arms around him, but he seemed distant.

"Jennifer, we need to talk."

I laughed. "Well, obviously. That's why I asked you to phone!"

"You can't just demand I call you on a whim. And you were expressly told not to use the phone in your building."

I bristled. "You told me to ring you anytime! And how else would you return my call if not on that phone?"

"We covered this." His voice was like ice. "You leave a day and time, and the number of the call box, and be there, waiting for our call at the appointed time." I'd never seen him so angry before. "And I told you to phone me in an *emergency*, Jennifer. I don't see any crises here that warrant my hasty appearance."

My fury bubbled to the surface. "Oh, you don't? How about telling me why you haven't bothered to contact me since I left Finley?"

He looked both aggravated yet concerned at the same time. "You're on the job, Jen."

"That doesn't mean we can't talk, does it?" I knew I sounded childish and petulant.

"It means exactly that!" I watched a muscle in his right cheek pulse as he got his temper under control. He took me by the arm and settled us both on a stone ledge that ran along the back wall. "Look, it's obvious we sent you in before you were ready. It isn't fair. You don't have the training - or maturity to carry this off."

"*Maturity?*"

He backtracked. "Wrong choice of word. Experience."

I stayed calm. "Okay, I'll grant you that. But I'm doing just fine, Mike. Didn't you see my report?"

"Yes, you've done great."

"Well, then!"

"But I don't think you can handle going in any deeper."

I felt something akin to panic. "You can't pull me out now, Mike! At least wait till I get more information on Sutherland. And Maguire."

He took my hand. "Look, I'm worried sick about you. We - I expected too much from you too soon. You don't know how to cope with the isolation, for example. Or we wouldn't be having this discussion."

I wanted to slap him, but that would do the opposite to convincing him I was capable. "True, I did find it really difficult being on my own so suddenly after constant company at Finley. But now that I'm in Curadh, that's changed. I'm having a fantastic time playing in the band." I gave a little laugh. "It's like a dream come true - if you ignore why I'm in it in the first place."

He looked steadily into my eyes and gave my hand a squeeze. "All right. But I need you to be honest with me, Jen. If you want out at any time, tell me."

"I will, I promise."

He let go. "What are your personal impressions of Sutherland?"

"One scary bastard. He's definitely the big cheese there. Maguire and the others are really deferential to him."

"What of Maguire? I take it he wasn't at the *céildh* in Ballyben?"

"He didn't seem to recognize me, and he never brought the *céildh* up."

He nodded. "Cool."

"I think you're on the wrong track with him, Mike. He actually seems like a really nice person."

"Nice?" he repeated with annoying incredulity.

"He helps old ladies get home safely, for God's sake."

Mike gave a cynical bark of laughter. "What's that fable about a wolf in sheep's clothing?"

I sighed. "Not everyone has an agenda, Mike. He seems a genuine enough guy."

Something flickered in his eyes. "Don't forget why you're there, Jen."

When I didn't reply, he asked, "All right?" with an edge to his voice.

'All right' did I understand, or did I feel all right? "Yes."

He got to his feet. "We'll talk again soon."

I looked up, surprised. "You're leaving already?"

"I have to."

"You're not coming back to the apartment?" I asked before I could stop myself.

"Can't, Jen, I'm sorry." He reached down and pulled me into his arms.

It felt like a pity hug, a consolation prize. I fought angry tears and remained rigid, my arms at my sides.

I wanted to shout *'After you came all this way, you're just going to turn around and leave?'* but forced myself to stay silent. A nasty suspicion wormed its way into my head. Me being 'on the job' seemed like an excuse. If he really liked me he'd find a reason for us to see each other. It was evident he'd lost interest in me, if he'd ever really had it. Could it have all been about recruitment, after all? Had any of it meant anything to him? I couldn't bring myself to return his embrace. After a moment he let me go.

"You'd better go if you're going." I kept my tone mild. Feeling his questioning gaze I avoided meeting his eyes.

"Check in on Sunday, usual time, Jennifer."

"Right."

"Wait a few minutes to go until after I leave. Hey - take care of yourself."

"You too."

I listened to his footsteps crunch on the cement floor, and the door creaked as he opened it. It clicked shut and I heard his steps clang over the iron grill walkway.

⌘

Two nights later, Curadh had an engagement party gig. I found myself squished beside three hulking lads in an ancient Commer van as we fought rush hour traffic heading out of Belfast on the M-1. Maguire was the only one of us who was comfortable. He slouched on the front bench seat with the driver, his Fender safely beside him. The rest of us had to cram onto the narrow bench seat in back, and behind us amps, crates of electrical stuff and instruments were packed to the roof. I kept my violin cradled on my lap, not wanting it to get crushed. The worst of it was that everyone except me smoked. The van was as putrid as an old London pea soup fog. I reached over to roll down the window beside me about half an inch, so I could breathe.

Our taciturn driver was called Paddy, and had the look of a professional nightclub bouncer - shiny bald head, tattoos and muscles. He apparently worked regularly as a driver for Brian Sutherland, and doubled up from time to time as roadie.

He took the exit marked 'Lurgan' and in a hundred or so yards turned into the driveway of a red brick, modern building called 'The Country Club'. With that name I had been expecting a posh, swanky spa-type establishment. Someone had attempted to make it look stylish by having a glass case in the lobby displaying an Yves St. Laurent shirt and silk tie. In front of that was an easel holding a cardboard poster with 'Curadh' pasted on it. A frisson of excitement swept through me when I saw it. My first real gig outside of the traditional scene!

"Thank Christ yer with us now, Fionnuir," said Liam, blowing cigarette smoke out of the side of his mouth, as we began dragging our stuff from the van to set up. "I'd have had to sing the fuckin' duet with Séan. People'd think we were gay."

The bride-to-be had requested *Love Will Keep Us Together* by The Captain and Tenille.

"What did you do before I joined?" I asked.

Kieran sniffed. "Told her to go fuck herself."

I sighed. "About singing love songs for this kind of thing, I mean."

"We'd'a sung love songs all right," said Maguire. "Just not duets and the like, you know? But we wouldn't have got as nice a gig as this. Brian got us booked now you've brought a bit o'class." He smacked a loud kiss on the top of my head, and ruffled my hair like I was his wee sister.

I laughed and batted him away. "So, Brian is our manager, then?"

"Aye, sort of. The girl who's gettin' married, her Da's a friend of his, like. Owns some kind of electrical store or somethin' here in Lurgan."

When I had a chance I popped out to the Ladies' room and made a note of the names on the display: engagement of Frances Devlin and Derek Murphy, hosted by Richard Devlin. At the sight of the groom-to-be's name I flashed back to poor Murphy at Finley Manor - his pale, helpless bare feet dragging on the floorboards as he was hauled away to the interrogation exercise in his Y-fronts.

That brought Mike sharply to mind, and I'd been doing a very good job since the Palm House of not thinking about him. Returning to the dance hall, I helped to finish setting up, and then we tuned our instruments. Guests began to filter in, and a rotund, red-faced man in a spangled waistcoat approached Maguire. He turned out to be Mr. Devlin. What he wanted was for the guests to be assembled first, drinks in hand, so that the engaged couple could make a red carpet entrance.

We started off with Maguire singing *Feels Like the First Time* by Foreigner. This was the kind of song his mellow voice and guitar were best suited to, but my violin seemed as out of place to me as the bodhrán would have been. After that we did 10cc's *The Things We Do For Love,* which at least had a part for the violin.

At ten minutes into the party Devlin signaled to Maguire. Time for the duet. I moved over to the mic stand and we launched into the song, singing in harmony. The newly engaged couple made their entrance like film stars. The groom was decked out in a suit and tie, and the bride wore a clinging red glittery dress. Arm in arm they promenaded across the floor to great cheers and applause.

All their friends and relatives crowded round to congratulate them. As I watched I felt a stab of envy. The girl didn't look any older than me. Why couldn't I have had a normal relationship like theirs? To the nice farmer my parents had wanted me to marry? Why did I have to choose an emotionally unavailable career soldier to fall in love with?

Maguire gave me a subtle nudge with his elbow. I'd zoned out. Turning toward him I focused my full attention on singing.

"'*Stop, I'll be thinking of you*
Look in my heart and let
love keep us together—'"

Our heads were close together on either side of the microphone. His gaze met mine and he blinked both eyes at me in a slow, sexy way. I felt my face flush. Disconcerted, I looked away.

⌘

The next night we were back at the Emerald Bar for a traditional Saturday *céildh*. I had to admit that by far I preferred playing this sort of thing to the vapid love songs at the engagement party. Mum and Dad would roll over in their graves. But this had real heart and soul - something that stirred the very depths of your being.

About an hour into the evening, with a jolt I remembered why I was there. How could I have forgotten, even for a moment? I scanned the bar, looking for Sutherland. Close to the end of the second set he came in, much like a celebrity. Lots of hand-shaking and back-clapping ensued as he made his way to one of the tables near the bar.

It had been vacant all evening, now I knew why. He pretty much held court there, Paddy and another man of similar intimidating build close at hand. I observed a steady stream of people come and sit across the table, engaging in intense conversation. Mostly men.

What kind of business was he conducting? During the break I asked Maguire, trying not to be too over-curious.

"Ach, he helps out the community," he answered noncommittally.

"Like a politician or something?"

"Somethin' like that."

"Hey, maybe he'd know of somewhere to live around here, then."

"Why don't ya ask him?"

Sutherland was currently deep in discussion with an anxiously animated, gray-haired man. Not the kind of conversation you interrupted. "When he's free. Don't want to bother him right now." But I would as soon as I could. I think I'd be glad to get out of my apartment. It simply held too many memories. Memories I'd rather not have thrown in my face all the time. For example, every time I got into my bed I couldn't help but remember when Mike had been there with me.

Thinking of him again.

Stop. It.

The gray-haired man got up from the table, and as no one took his place I seized the moment and approached. Sutherland smiled expansively, managing to convey warmth and trust, just like a politician. If there had been any babies present, no doubt he'd be kissing them.

"Miss Moylan! What may I do for you?" His voice oozed as smooth as honey.

I wouldn't trust him as far as I could throw him. "May I have a quick word, please?"

"Of course." He gestured that I sit opposite. "You're looking for an apartment in this area, am I correct?"

Nothing escaped him, obviously. I forced a smile. "Séan said ya might be able to help."

"Be happy to, my dear. Leave it with me."

"Thank you, Mr. Sutherland."

He gave a magnanimous wave. "Brian, please."

So dismissed, I returned to Maguire on the dais. "You already told him!" I chastised.

He grinned, offering me one of his slow, sexy blinks. It was hard not to be affected by it, I could feel my cheeks growing pink. His posse of groupies, examining his every move from a table nearby, would no doubt have seen and hate me even more.

"He'll sort ya out just fine, Fen."

My heart thumped. For a moment I thought he'd said 'Jen'. I guess Fen was a logical abbreviation of Fionnuir.

⌘

Check in time came around quickly at three o'clock the next day. I steeled myself so I'd be on guard should Mike answer, but I got Chalki again. I never thought I'd be relieved to talk to him instead of Mike. He noted the names of the Lurgan people, and I told him about Sutherland's steady stream of clientele the night before.

"Okay," he said. "Check in on Wednesday, usual time."

"Right."

"All well with you?" he asked.

I paused. "Yes, no problems." Mike had presumably given him the heads up that he thought I couldn't hack it.

"If you say so. Talk to you Wednesday."

23
No Illusions

On Sunday evening Maguire phoned, his voice vibrating with excitement. "Rehearsal on Wednesday, Fen! We've a big gig on Thursday." His enthusiasm was infectious.

"Where?"

"Brian hasn't toul' us yet, but it's somewhere over yer side of town."

"Another friend of his getting married?"

He chuckled. "Not this time."

I wondered what he meant by 'my side of town'. Not too close, I hoped, although it was unlikely anyone would recognize me with my new look.

"So, ya'll be at practice?" asked Maguire.

"Yeah, what time?"

"High noon."

"Okay, pardner, see you then."

⌘

The reason for the rehearsal became apparent as soon as I walked through the door of the Emerald. A *Horslips* song blasted from the speakers. I'd overheard Maguire saying that he wanted to cover a few of their songs, particularly now that we were getting more gigs in better parts of town.

"I want t'do this one first," he announced, scratching the stylus across the LP so it played *The Snow That Melts the Soonest*. It opened with the piano, joined by guitar, then a violin solo. "Think ye can play that, Fen?" he demanded, snatching up the stylus.

I nodded. "Got the sheet music?"

He swung round and rummaged in his guitar case, pulling out a battered sheet of paper, which he thrust into my hands. He'd penned the notes by hand on blank manuscript paper, his handwriting elaborate, with sweeping pen strokes through all the quaver variations. "Well, can ya?"

God, he was impatient. "Yeah, I can." I laid it across the top of one of the amps and dug out my violin and bow. Maguire's impatience was palpable and I could feel all eyes on me as I tuned up. The notes weren't that complex but I would need to take time to practice a few times before I could play with confidence. Declan sat at the piano. The notes cascaded easily from under his deft fingers, and Maguire had the guitar down pat.

Shit, I messed it up in the first stanza, throwing them off.

"Again," said Maguire.

Concentrating, I listened so carefully to Declan's playing that I managed to miss my cue. They halted once more. "I'm sorry, Séan."

He barely kept his patience. "Come on, Fionnuir, focus. This should be second nature to ya."

A third time in I congratulated myself on not screwing up, but Maguire stopped us again. "Darlin', yer going sharp there, instead of flat."

My face blazed with embarrassment and frustration. "Bet ya regret hiring me now."

He smiled, mollified. "Keep tryin'. You'll get it."

The fifth time I screwed up Kieran threw his tipper down. It bounced off the dais and clattered onto the dance floor. "Fuckin' hell!" He sniffed vehemently. "It's a standard Celtic beat, ya stupid bitch."

Maguire cleared his throat. "That's enough, Kier."

Kieran thrust an angry face close to mine. "Are you Irish at all, ya thick cunt?"

Maguire tore the guitar and strap over his head, dropping it by one of the amps. I jumped out of the way as he launched at Kieran, decking him hard in the face. Kieran flew backward and Declan leapt to his feet to steady the drum kit as Kieran careened into it. The bodhrán thumped to the floor and rolled to the edge of the dais.

I was frozen in place. *Oh, my God! Oh, my bloody God!*

Maguire stood over Kieran, fists clenched. "You'll apologize to Fionnuir or you're out of the band."

I opened my mouth to speak but nothing came out. No one had ever gone to bat for me before - but to actually have someone punch a guy out for swearing at me? I didn't know how I felt about me-Tarzan, you-Jane.

White-faced, Kieran picked himself up, holding a hand to his bleeding nose. "Sorry," he mumbled at me, then tried to sniff. He cringed.

"It's okay, Kieran." I was anxious to placate him. "Sorry I keep screwing up."

"You've nothin' to be sorry for," said Maguire. He hauled the amp back upright as Declan sat back down at the piano. I jumped, startled, when Maguire laid an arm across my shoulders. "You okay, darlin'?"

I nodded. He gave me a squeeze and picked up his guitar. Kieran snatched the bodhrán from the floor and scrambled off the dais to retrieve his tipper. As he climbed back up he shot me a look of sheer hatred. My stomach lurched. I glanced at Maguire but he was busy sliding the guitar strap back over his head. I pretended I hadn't seen Kieran and concentrated on tweaking at the violin strings to tune them.

⌘

The rehearsal ran way past three o'clock. The late afternoon regulars began trickling in from four-thirty on, and Maguire with evident reluctance told us we could go. "Look, come out tomorra afternoon at - say four o'clock to go over some more stuff," he said. "We'll head to the gig straight from here."

I hurried out ahead of the others. The Falls was already chock-a-block with rush hour traffic. I spotted a phone box just down the road from the Emerald. Should I make my check in call from there? I decided against it. Too much foot traffic for me to feel safe. Crossing the road I waited for the bus. It was late and then edged its way slowly through the traffic into downtown Belfast. I alighted onto the pavement in time to see the Botanic Avenue bus pull up to the stop. I tore over and scrambled on board just before the driver shut the doors. It was pretty full, so I climbed the stairs and found a seat right at the front. It was always a little disconcerting, sitting right up at the upper windscreen like that. I had the feeling that if the driver braked suddenly I'd go hurtling through the glass onto the road below. I'd get off at Shaftesbury Square and make my call from the usual phone box. A loud laugh made me jump. I blinked in confusion. We had passed the Square and were already halfway up Botanic Avenue. I must have dozed off, lulled by the warmth and the motion. *Bugger.*

I got off at my usual stop and backtracked to a closer phone box on Botanic. This time Mike answered. I truly hadn't expected him to, and was taken unawares. "You're doing okay?" he asked after I'd told him that Sutherland had been finding and arranging better gigs.

"Doing great," I replied curtly. It hurt to hear his voice. He was so familiar, yet so aloof. But I was tired of playing by his rules. Fuck him. I was no longer available for him to string along. I listened to the line crackle as we both waited for the other to speak.

"Is that everything?" he asked.

"Yes."

"Check in tomorrow. Friday."

"Why so soon?"

"Report on the new gig."

"Right." I hung up before he had a chance to. It felt liberating.

⌘

Paddy picked us and our equipment up in the van from the Emerald at seven-thirty. The rehearsal had gone a hell of a lot better than yesterday, and we had *The Snow That Melts the Soonest* as good as it was going to get.

Kieran had evidently decided not to acknowledge my presence, other than to shoot me hostile glances when he thought I couldn't see. He sat up beside Paddy and Maguire, and I sat right behind between Liam and

Declan. Maguire still wouldn't tell us where the gig was, and we were so wound up with curiosity and excitement we were like a bunch of primary school kids on an outing.

"So, why the big secret, Séan?" demanded Declan.

Maguire tapped the side of his nose. "Wait'n see."

Declan grabbed him from behind in a headlock. They mock struggled, squashing Liam and me against the window.

"Quit it!" I laughed, protecting my violin case in my arms. I couldn't wait to see where we ended up. Maguire was so tightly wired about it, I had visions of us playing in the Ulster Hall or the Grand Opera House. He produced an engraved silver flask and passed it round. The pungent liquid inside nearly burned the tongue off me. I almost spat it out but grimaced and swallowed hard.

"What *is* that?"

He laughed. "Good mountain *poitín*, that. Can't get any better."

I made a mental note not to try that again. I wouldn't be surprised if blisters lacerated my tongue. Paddy drove the van toward Belfast city center. I held my breath but we didn't head to the Ulster Hall. Instead he took us through College Square into Great Victoria Street past the Europa Hotel. My mind raced as we passed familiar landmarks. There were pubs around there, but none that I could think would have a traditional band play.

As we approached Shaftesbury Square I found myself biting my lip so hard I tasted blood. We passed the Botanic Avenue turn off and headed up University Avenue toward Queen's. I looked dispassionately at the lovely Lanyon Building as we passed, feeling nothing. It was like I had never studied here - like my life before the Percy French bomb had belonged to a different person entirely.

My heart thumped as Paddy slowed the van and did a U-turn. He pulled up outside the Students' Union bar opposite the Lanyon Building and parked.

Oh, Jesus Christ.

I never thought in a million years that we'd be playing here. But I remembered seeing traditional music nights advertised around campus, so I shouldn't have been surprised.

Paddy and the others clambered out of the van and set to, dragging out the instruments and equipment. I sat frozen. I was compromised - we were bound to meet someone who knew me from before. Maguire leaned in the passenger side door, giving me a quizzical look. He held out a hand and I slid over, letting him help me out. He gave my fingers a squeeze. Probably because he felt how violently I shook. Hopefully he'd think I was just nervous about playing here. Shit, if only he knew.

"Listen to me, darlin'," he said quietly, pointing to my crucifix, which had slipped out onto the collar of my coat. "Better take that off - it's traditional night but ye never know, like."

I nodded, shoving it out of sight.

Liam beamed at us. "This is fuckin' fantastic."

All four of the lads grinned ear to ear. A group of young men came out of the Union and approached. They were the welcoming committee, and helped carry our stuff inside and up the stairs to the bar. To my relief I didn't recognize any of them. I slipped into the Ladies' room to take off my necklace, and leaned on one of the sinks, trying to get hold of myself. My reflection in the wall mirror reassured me. I really did look totally different to how I had when I was a student here. The red hair and fringe across my eyebrows changed me enough that unless someone knew me really well I'd be fine. I hadn't made any close friends at Queen's - unless you counted Clancy, which I didn't. Some friend he turned out to be.

I remembered the briefings at Finley. If I thought I'd been compromised in any way, I'd to get out at once. But I wasn't entirely sure I'd been compromised. I hadn't come across anyone I recognized. And it didn't seem likely anyone would recognize the mousy little introvert I'd been.

Decision made to stay put, I got my makeup bag out of my purse and outlined my eyes in bold black liner, contouring them à la Cleopatra. If that didn't throw anyone off, I don't know what would. I made my way to the dance area in the bar and joined the others setting up the stage. It looked like we were going to have a nice big audience - the bar was already filled with the babble of well-lubricated people intent on having a good time.

They parted like sheep before a border collie as Paddy strode through with an amp in his arms. I felt a pang as I thought of my collie Mac. Was he happy in his new home with Reverend Scott?

Paddy deposited the amp on one side of the stage. "See you's at twelve, then," he said before heading back out.

At nine o'clock Maguire started us off with the fast-paced *Rocky Road to Dublin* - always a good one to get things going. Gratifyingly, almost at once the floor filled with couples and groups jigging right in front of the stage. Over their bobbing heads I made out the smoky bar where people thronged shoulder to shoulder, vying to buy drinks from the harried bartenders. I relaxed. So far I hadn't seen a single person I recognized.

Maguire looked so exciting in his long leather coat and flaming hair, making a big show of working at the guitar slung across his hips. A group of girls gathered in front of the stage, gawping lustily at him. A sliver of pride flared in me. With Maguire's talent and charisma spearheading us, Curadh had a very good chance of making a success of this. The rock-Celtic-slant on the traditional stuff worked very well indeed.

After we soared through four more songs my trepidation at being recognized completely evaporated. I began mimicking Maguire in his showmanship, tossing my hair and using my whole body to play and weave in time to the music. To my surprise very soon I began to garner my own group of male admirers.

Then I became aware of someone standing very still in direct contrast to the surging dancers. Only the discipline of so many years holding a bow prevented me from dropping it in shock. Clancy O'Neill stood regarding me, a pint of beer clutched in his white-knuckled fist. There was no doubt he knew who I was. When he saw I'd clocked him, his lips curved into a smirk. Turning his back he ploughed through the dancers, disappearing from my view into the bar.

The song felt endless. In autopilot my fingers picked out the notes while slicing the bow across the strings. Maguire shot me a frown and I forced myself to concentrate.

I thought I couldn't hold it together any longer but finally the set came to an end. I laid the violin and bow on one of the amps, for once not carefully placing them in their case, and plunged off the stage. I tunneled my way through the wall of people to the bar, but found no sign of Clancy. I tried the hall, stairs, and then risked a peek into the men's toilets.

Nothing.

I fought my way back to the stage to stand on tiptoe and look over people's heads. Should have done that to start with - I wasn't thinking straight.

Then it felt like someone punched me in the solar plexus. Clancy and Maguire leaned on the bar, heads close together.

I had to run. Now.

Grabbing the violin and bow, I thrust them into the case and snapped it closed.

Kieran blocked my route off stage. "Where're you goin'?"

Declan and Liam jumped up, bottles of beer in each hand. Declan held out a Harp. "Here." Automatically, I took it.

"Where's the boy wonder?" asked Liam. I looked blankly at him. "Our glorious leader," he added. My gaze darted to the bar, and he turned. "Hey, Séan!" he yelled at top volume.

I saw the fiery gleam of Maguire's hair as he looked round at us. He clapped Clancy on the back in a comradely way and beelined for the stage. Immediately, he fell afoul of the clutch of groupies, who clustered excitedly around him. With his back to me I couldn't see his expression.

Clancy caught my eye and smiled widely, raising his empty glass. Then he turned and picked his way through the crowd toward the exit. I thrust past Kieran, jumped off the stage and shoved my way after Clancy. Catching up, I grabbed him by the arm, swinging him round.

"What did you tell Maguire?" I glanced over my shoulder. Maguire was distracted with the groupies and people loitering on the dance floor hid me from the other lads' view.

"Nothing."

"You didn't tell him who I was?"

"I don't know who you are, now."

My fists clenched. "Clancy, for fuck's sake!"

"All right, all right. No, I told him nothin' except I'd seen you about. But he has no idea that we know each other from home, or Queen's. Or that you're a Prod."

I took a breath. He seemed sincere, thank God. "So, what the fuck was that all about, raising your glass at me and whispering with Maguire at the bar?"

"You're paranoid, that's what. What the fuck are you of all people doing here in a *traditional* band, anyway?" He shook his head. "Wait, never mind, it's none of my business. Glad to see you didn't kill yourself, like everyone thought you had." With a curl of the lip, he stalked away.

I flashed cold all over, yet sweat prickled uncomfortably at the back of my neck, pooling between my breasts and armpits. I was about to vomit. Clapping a hand over my mouth I fought my way out to the hall to the Ladies' toilets. The stalls were occupied and two girls blocked the sinks, leaning close to the mirror to reapply their makeup. I shoved past, retching, but only dry heaves, fortunately.

"Do you mind?" demanded one of the girls with a disgusted sneer. Both of them looked outraged as though I did it on purpose.

Ignoring them I splashed cold water over my face and wrists. My heart raced and I could feel a vein pulsing in my neck. What should I do - run for it? Or believe Clancy when he said he hadn't compromised me?

The door banged open, making everyone jump. I looked up and to my shock watched Maguire's reflection in the mirror as he strode in. The two girls at the sinks beside me gaped, lipstick and mascara wand frozen mid air.

"All of you's get out," he ordered, his tone giving no room for negotiation. Like panicked hens with a fox in their roost, all the girls gathered their bags and scurried to obey. I gripped the sink, unable to take my eyes off his reflection. Every sinew in me prepared for fight or flight. But he looked worried, not angry.

"Fen, are ya'll right?" His voice was soft.

Maybe Clancy had been telling the truth. Maguire would not act like this if he suspected I was not who I said I was.

I swallowed hard. "Séan, I'm really sorry. I just got so nervous."

"Ya were doin' great, darlin' Why nervous halfway into the gig?" His amber eyes held my gaze.

I had trouble maintaining eye contact. "I - haven't eaten much today." My words came out in a rush. "On top of the beer it just wasn't a good idea. I fucked up, sorry."

He stepped close behind me. I tensed but he merely gathered my hair in his hands to lift it away from my damp neck. Pulling it to the side he gently draped it over my shoulder. "Yer okay, darlin'. Take as long as ye need."

He flashed me a smile and left me alone in the bathroom. I sagged over the sink, feeling like all my energy had just spiraled down the drain. Cold water gulped straight from the faucet revived me a little.

I dried my hands and pulled open the door. Both Maguire and Declan blocked the stairs, lounging on either side, smoking. Declan gallantly held out an arm for me to take. On the other side Maguire offered his arm, so I had no choice but to be escorted to the stage. I felt safe between them. Everything was going to be okay.

"Did you puke up?" inquired Declan.

"No."

"Betcha there were carrots. There're always carrots in puke even when you haven't eaten any."

He was trying to be funny but I wasn't in the mood. "I didn't throw up, Dec."

"But if you had, there'd have been carrots."

"Would you ever shut the fuck up about yer fuckin' carrots," said Maguire.

I joined in their laughter, giddy with relief.

Back on the stage Maguire slipped on his guitar and struck a pose at the microphone. Checking over his shoulder that we were ready, he dramatically raised an arm up high and held it until he was sure all eyes were on him. The lights on the dance floor dimmed, and he strummed the opening of our next song. I blanked on which one and squinted at the list on the floor by his feet. The *Ballintore Jig*. Thank God, only backup for me, no violin solos.

I performed like a wooden marionette. The notes were all correct, but I'd been so unnerved by Clancy that I couldn't put any verve into my playing. Near the end of the jig, Paddy arrived. He waited just inside the doors to watch, then leaned against the wall with his arms folded. His presence earlier than expected spooked me all over again.

When we broke after the next set I made my way out to the toilets, saying hi to Paddy as I passed. Outside the Ladies' room door I stooped, ostensibly to tie one of the laces on my boots, but really looking to see if he was observing me.

He was, solidly on guard where he could monitor the bar, hall, stairs, and the door to the Ladies' toilets. I wouldn't have a chance if I tried to run down the stairs. But he'd been affable enough, I reassured myself. Clancy was right; I was paranoid and I didn't need to be. I'd be so glad when this night was over. My head pounded. I felt as tightly coiled as the old carriage clock at Mourneview I'd broken when I'd wound it up so far it got stuck, never able to unwind.

The students had grown louder the more they drank, and their dancing more uninhibited. The gaggle of inebriated Maguire groupies in front of the stage had multiplied, and they acted like hyenas over marked prey. Their shrieks kept increasing in volume as they tried to outdo each other in attracting his attention. I just tried to block it all out and get through the rest of the evening.

At last we wrapped up just after midnight. That had been the longest three hours of my life. Once the bar stopped serving drinks the students filtered out, and the place had emptied by the time we packed up. The boys' spirits were high. As far as they were concerned the night had been a rousing success. All I wanted to do was to go home, have a hot bath and sleep for twenty-four hours.

We had the packing routine down pat, and with Paddy's help in no time at all were ready to head out. The lads rapidly sucked on the tail end of their cigarettes, stamped them out and clambered into the van. I hesitated on the pavement. The Botanic apartment was minutes away, and I was reluctant to let them see where I lived. Paddy slammed the back van doors shut and came round.

He raised his chin at me. "Get in."

I plastered on a smile and shook my head. "I'll just walk from here. Sure, I'm only five minutes away."

Paddy's fist gripped my elbow like a vise. "Can't let you do that. Mister Sutherland's orders."

I barely managed to hang onto the violin case as he bodily swung me up onto the front bench seat beside Declan. The sliding door slammed closed, the warmth of the van enveloping me. Stunned, I watched Paddy get into the driver's seat and pull the van away from the curb. I twisted to look over my shoulder at Maguire. He was busy lighting up yet another cigarette.

The van turned down the street that ran along the side of the Students' Union to the Lisburn Road. Camden Street ran parallel to it, where I'd had the taxi driver drop me before. "Here'll do, Paddy - I'm on the next street." My heart lurched when he ignored me, turning onto the Lisburn Road and gathering speed as we headed into Belfast. Fear thrust through me. "You're going the wrong way, Paddy."

"We'll loop back, okay?" he grunted.

I looked at the others. No one met my gaze. *See no evil, hear no evil, speak no evil.* Oh, Clancy, you fucking murderer - you've signed my death warrant. I considered yanking open the sliding door and hurling myself out, James Bond style. But even if I managed not to land in oncoming traffic or break my neck, all Paddy had to do was stop the van and drag me back in again. Adrenaline consumed me.

Fight or flight. But I was too fucking late.

Declan's bomber jacket rustled as he reached into his inside pocket and pulled out a pewter flask with a Celtic cross engraved on it. Unscrewing it he took a swig. "Dat was the best fuckin' gig yet." He held out the flask to me. I smelled the acrid tang of *poitín* and shook my head. Twisting round he handed it to Kieran, who took a drink and offered it to Maguire. I glanced at him over my shoulder but he diligently avoided eye contact. How well he had hidden the fact that Clancy had touted on me. I had been completely taken in by them both.

The van pulled up to the Emerald. A dark figure emerged from the doorway, fiery sparks spiraling as a cigarette butt flicked away. I recognized the other bouncer guy Brian Sutherland always had with him. He pulled open the sliding door.

"'Bout ye, Seamus," Paddy greeted him.

Seamus made a thumbing motion. "All right boys - out." Declan clambered past me and they all burst out onto the pavement. I made a move to follow, but Seamus blocked me. "Not you."

Real panic set in as he heaved his bulk onto the seat beside me, sandwiching me between he and Paddy. I made a move to escape over the back of the seat but he easily stopped me, his sausage fingers encircling my upper arm. He pulled his jacket back, revealing the butt of a firearm poking out from the waistband of his trousers. "I said, not you."

Colonel Pierce's words came back to me: '*If your cover is blown the IRA will torture you and kill you. Have no illusions about getting out of it alive.*'

Maguire started to close the sliding door. "Séan, wait!" I entreated. He met my gaze at last, his amber eyes opaque, then slammed the door shut. He slapped the roof of the van twice and Paddy hit the accelerator.

A mocking, "Nighty-night, Fionnuir!" catcalled from outside. Craning my neck to peer past the equipment and out of the back windows, I saw Kieran waving from the curb, a gleeful smile on his face. Maguire, Declan, and Liam stood like statues behind him, watching us drive off.

24
Good Dog

Paddy turned the van down a side street and drove through a sequence of roads threading into an industrial area. I kept straining in futility to think of ways to escape. We slowed to a stop outside a darkened red brick warehouse. I looked around in panic - nowhere to run, the entire area appeared derelict. Seamus raised a hand to pull something from the inside of his jacket.

A hood.

The exercise at Finley Manor rushed back - black suffocating cloth blinding me. I cringed away, whimpers rising in my throat. No, I couldn't go through that again! But he easily jammed it over my head, plunging me into darkness. Flailing, I tried to wrench it off, but he snatched hold of my arms and dragged me from the van. With bruising hands he and Paddy hauled me over the pavement until my feet skimmed a threshold. I struggled to balance and felt unyielding cement floor under the soles of my feet. A heavy door slammed, making me flinch. The sound echoed. A dungeon. A place of torture and execution.

Oh God. Mike, where are you?

But no rescue was imminent. No one from Finley knew where I was.

My feet skittered on the floor as Paddy and Seamus propelled me forward, their footsteps crunching on cement flooring. Seamus wheezed unhealthily with every intake of breath as they hauled me up a flight of stairs. My knee twinged sharply as I stumbled.

"Come on," muttered Seamus, jerking me back up.

They hustled me through a doorway, across a length of floor and thrust me onto a hard wooden chair. Pain stabbed my shoulders as one of them yanked my arms behind me, then I felt rope burning my wrists as they were tied together. The knots looped through the slats on the back of the chair, imprisoning me.

'The IRA will torture you and kill you,' came Colonel Pierce's voice again in my head.

Blind panic consumed me. My breaths came in ragged sobs and I pulled so hard on the ropes that I almost dislocated my arms. The hood knocked askew, and what I saw on the concrete at my feet paralyzed me. A huge stain of blood.

Fucking Christ!

I breathed in sharply, gagging as I inhaled cloth. Hawking, I jerked my head from side to side, spitting the fabric out of my mouth. The hood was snatched off my head. Thank God. But bright light seared my eyes. A desk lamp pointed right at me, just like in a B-movie. Heart racing, I squinted past it, and recognized Brian Sutherland by the cut of his tailored jacket. He sat behind a dark green metal desk, leaning on his elbows. Every atom in me stilled, my senses razor sharp as though I were prey under the deadly gaze of a predator. Which I was.

I attempted to force bravado. "What the hell do you think you're doing?" My voice betrayed me, shrilling with fear.

Sutherland smiled - a coiled serpent about to strike. "Straight and to the point. I like that in a female." He settled back in the chair, elegantly crossing his legs. "I'm sure you've had time to work it out. Tell me about Michael McLeod."

I felt the blood drain from my face. Of course Clancy had told them about Mike. I was already dead.

"Not a particularly prudent choice to have intimate relations with, my dear," continued Sutherland, his tone afternoon-tea polite.

I realized I'd been straining against the ropes when something gave. I could move one of my wrists! Paddy and Seamus stood near the door off to the side where they couldn't see the back of the chair. Trying to conceal my movement my fingers found a knot and I scrabbled at it.

"Talk to me, my dear. What's a talented, intelligent girl like you doing with a British soldier?"

"I didn't know he was in the army when I met him!" I blurted. "He's American!"

Sutherland chuckled, succeeding in making it sound sinister. "Clancy O'Neill is the only person who seems to actually know anything about you."

My forearms and wrists sizzled with pins and needles but I kept working at the rope.

"He thinks your name is Jennifer, not Fionnuir," he continued.

I faltered at the sound of my real name on his lips. "That's Gaelic for Jennifer," I managed.

Sutherland slipped a hand into his inner jacket pocket and drew out a packet of slim cigars. I watched as he studiously removed one, tapped it against the back of his hand, and produced a lighter from another pocket. "Seamus?"

Seamus came over and stepped in front of me, his eyes slits of charcoal. I shrank back. Stale sweat stank from his armpits as he grabbed hold of my cotton T-shirt and ripped it. The material parting like gossamer, I gasped as cold air flooded my exposed torso.

"No!" In panic I stamped both feet on the ground and tried to push the chair back from him.

"The bra, too." Sutherland blew out a couple of smoke rings. His mouth opened and closed like a deadly Tiger Fish, a glimmer of teeth visible. "Wires hide in the strangest places these days."

For a second I thought he meant bra underwires. But he suspected I was jarked. Seamus slid a brass and wood hilt from his belt and clicked the blade open.

A sob escaped my lips. "Please, Brian. Don't do this. I'm not a fucking spy, I'm not!"

Cold steel touched my skin. Seamus made a sharp movement and my breasts sprang free. Frigid air immediately hardened my nipples, making them stand out prominently. My face blazed, shamed.

"Have a cigar, lad," said Sutherland.

Seamus took one from the proffered packet and bent close to Sutherland, who clicked open his lighter.

Oh, Jesus. God help me.

"Boss," murmured Paddy. His feet scraped on the concrete floor.

"If you haven't the stomach for this, get out," snapped Sutherland. Paddy retreated, slamming the door behind him.

Seamus strolled toward me, sucking hard on his cigar. A feral smile spread across his face and he blew a long trail into my eyes. My nails gouged the flesh on the inside of my wrists as I dug at the ropes. He took another draft of the cigar and stretched his arm out, slowly bringing the lit end close to my face.

Oh, God, Jesus, no!

Heat pinpointed my cheekbone. Clenching my jaw, I strained my head back so far that pain tore down the length of my neck and arms.

"Tell me about the Yank, Jennifer," Sutherland requested in that deceptive mild tone.

I screwed my eyes tightly shut. Words babbled through my mind. *Get this psycho away from me don't hurt me please please please.* Seamus grabbed hold of my chin, forcing me to look at him. His pupils were dilated and very black.

"Let's say I accept you didn't know he was army when you met him," said Sutherland. "But when did you find out he was a Brit?"

God, I was going to lose control of my bladder. "When Clancy told me!" I flinched as ash dropped off the cigar onto my breasts.

"But you didn't stop seeing him once you knew."

"I did! I did stop seeing him! Honestly."

"We both know that's not so, my dear."

"Just once," I stammered. "But that's all, I swear it."

In my peripheral vision I saw Sutherland give a nod. To my shock Seamus grabbed my left breast in one hand and savagely groped it. "No!" I screamed. He pinched the nipple so hard I thought he'd tear it off. Then he shoved the burning cigar right into my breast. I froze in disbelief, and for a second didn't feel anything. Then agonizing pain lanced through me - like nothing I'd experienced before.

A shriek ripped from me and I tore violently against the ropes at my back. Seamus took a drag from the cigar and then hovered it close to my right breast. Sobs wracked me, tears flooding my face.

"Next time tell the truth first off," ordered Sutherland. "Why did you continue seeing McLeod?"

I gulped, unable to form words. Seamus groped at my uninjured breast, viciously pinching and squeezing. "Please Brian, please. Get him off me. I'll tell you everything." At a nod from Sutherland, Seamus immediately let go. "I - liked Mike. I didn't believe he was a Brit. I mean, I didn't want to believe it - that he'd lied to me."

"How long's he been in Northern Ireland?"

"I don't know. I don't know anything about him! He wouldn't tell me anything!" I saw Seamus' hand twitch and terror flooded me anew. "He was just a date - please, don't hurt me anymore." I hated the begging whine in my voice, but I'd do anything not to have that cigar thrust into my flesh again.

"Such beautiful breasts." His voice rang with convincing regret. "Such a waste to have to ruin them both."

I wrenched at my bonds with such force they finally gave, almost catapulting me from the chair. Acting on sheer instinct I tore my arms free and surged to my feet. Surprise was my only advantage. Using the momentum I slammed a fist into the bridge of Seamus' broad boxer's nose. The cigar flew from his grasp and he staggered back, both hands clapped to his face. I followed through with the hardest kick to the groin I could manage but he recovered in time to block me.

Winded, I found myself flat on my back, my arms pinioned. He pressed his bulk onto me, painfully crushing my spine against the cement floor. I couldn't shift him no matter what. Blind panic set in as he shoved a knee between my legs and brutally forced them apart. To my sickening disgust I felt his rigid penis against me.

Oh, Jesus, God.

He released one of my arms and shoved a hand under my skirt, ripping at my tights and panties. I grabbed his only tuft of hair, tearing with all my might. He pressed a forearm against my throat, exerting pressure. I couldn't breathe. I couldn't swallow. My head felt like it was going to explode as my vision dimmed.

I was strangling. *Get off me - get the fuck off me!*

My flailing hand hit something solid at his side. Snatching the revolver from his waistband, I shoved the barrel into his face as I clicked the hammer. The pressure on my throat released immediately.

"Get. Off. Me," I rasped. "You fucking fat piece of shit." My voice sounded like I'd smoked heavily for a lifetime. I kept the revolver trained on him, sitting up as he eased backwards off me. I stumbled to my feet, trying to control my shaking by gripping the weapon tightly with both hands.

Sutherland calmly ground out his spent cigar in the ashtray, basilisk gaze fixed on me. My heart thumped. I fully expected him to pull a gun from under the desk and put an end to this. With Paddy on the other side of the door I couldn't shoot my way out anyway. No matter what I did I was dead.

Unless—

Keeping Seamus at a safe distance I approached Sutherland carefully and deliberately. Placing the revolver in front of him on the desk, I stood back and yanked the edges of my torn T-shirt together to cover my breasts. "I'd expect this crap from the Brits. Not from my own people."

A smile played at his lips. Taking out another cigar, he lit it and got to his feet. Grabbing a navy blue parka from the back of his chair, he came round the desk and held out the coat. "Cover yourself up, my dear."

The rough fabric chafed against my burn. I gritted my teeth and zipped it up. Sutherland put an avuncular arm across my shoulders and I forced myself not to shrink away. He turned me to face Seamus, whose face was livid. He managed to look murderous yet humiliated at the same time.

I clenched my jaw, fury replacing fear. "This wasn't necessary, Brian."

Taking my hand, he patted it with the other, cigar resting between two of his fingers. The smell of it made me want to vomit. "Regrettable, my dear, but entirely necessary, I assure you."

Torturing me was necessary? Attempted rape was necessary?

I caught Seamus smirking. Snatching the cigar from Brian's hand I reached the fat fucker in two steps and shoved the lit end into his face. The flesh made a sizzling sound I hadn't heard when he'd burned me. Roaring he twisted away, staggering back. I was surprised how much satisfaction I got from his pain and hurled the cigar after him. "I hope you understand how necessary *that* was."

"Fuckin' cunt." He lunged but Brian snapped his fingers. Seamus halted at once, slinking back, rage twisting his doughy features.

Not able to resist, I sneered. "There's a good dog."

Sutherland chuckled. "I'll have Paddy take you home, young lady."

"No. I'll get myself home." I wanted to get as far away as possible from these thugs. I'd call the number. Mike would pull me out of here. I'd never have to face anything like this ever again.

Sutherland shook his head. "Couldn't hear of it, my dear. Not to worry, you'll be safe with Paddy. And we'll talk later - Fionnuir."

My Gaelic name.

He'd fallen for my story - accepted it. I had proven Colonel Pierce wrong. I *had* survived.

⌘

I held onto my composure all the way back to my apartment. But once I closed the door behind me, making sure it was shut fast and locked, my legs gave under me. On the floor I buried my face in my hands and cried in the dark. I'd made it. I was safe.

But how could Clancy have done this to me? He must have known what would happen once he'd touted. Scrambling to my feet, I just made it to the bathroom in time. Kneeling over the toilet I heaved until I thought I'd never stop. But I did eventually, shivering with cold or maybe shock, my entire body stiff and sore. I'd go downstairs right now and phone the check in number. What did it matter where I called from - I was finished here now. Hanging onto the edge of the sink I hauled myself to my feet and jerked the cord to switch on the light. My reflection in the mirror over the sink shocked me. Raccoon-black eyes from tear-smudged mascara. Dark daubs lined my chin and cheek, which turned out to be ashy fingermarks.

Oh God. Seamus holding me down, his erection grinding against me - it all came back. I fumbled to turn on the hot water faucet in the bath and put in the plug. If I hadn't stopped him with his own revolver, would Sutherland have sat there and watched while Seamus raped me on the hard cement floor?

I grabbed the zip on the parka and wrenched it down. Get anything that had touched Sutherland away from me. I was scared to look at my wounded breast as I eased the coat off. The burn was as bad as it felt. A bulbous blister throbbed angrily next to my livid and swollen nipple. Bruises flowered all over me. My skin looked like the hide of a dappled horse.

The warm water finally got through the ancient pipes and steam rose from the bath. I grabbed the bottle of Dettol fluid from behind the toilet and poured about half of it into the tub. My eyes stung from the antiseptic and tears splashed, mixing with the water. God, all the disinfectant in the world wouldn't be enough to wash me clean of Seamus.

A heavy thudding jarred me upright. Someone pummeled at the apartment door. "Fionnuir!" came a man's voice. "Open up!"

I yanked the parka back over my shoulders, wincing as I pulled it across my chest. The pounding grew more frantic as I stumbled out of the bathroom and across the dark living room.

"Fen!" I recognized Maguire's voice. "I know you're in there!"

I was afraid to open the door. "Leave me alone!"

"Not until I know yer all right. Please darlin', open up."

I hesitated and he pounded the door again. My hands shook as I unlocked it and pulled it open a crack. Maguire's face looked pallid and strained, eyes dark and wide.

"Let me in, please, Fen."

Hesitantly, I stood back. He paused in the unlit room, his long leather coat making a soft creaking sound as he turned round and closed the door. I bent to switch on the table lamp by the sofa and the parka slipped open. His gaze dropped to my exposed breasts until I hastily pulled the coat back over me and crossed my arms.

"Oh, holy fuck, Fionnuir." He reached a hand toward my face and I stepped back. "Ah, darlin', I'd never hurt ya." He licked his thumb, and like my mother used to do when I was a child and had chocolate smears on my face, Maguire gently brushed at the finger smudges. I felt my lower lip tremble. "Jesus, I'm so sorry, darlin'. I can't believe he'd hurt a girl."

"Well, he's IRA, isn't he?" I blurted, cutting myself off before I added, *'What do you expect from a fucking terrorist?'*

Maguire's wary expression made me backtrack. "I mean, I understand. He had to find out for sure who I was, didn't he?"

I watched him take in the room, his gaze resting on Dee's Sacred Heart of Jesus picture and lamp. He turned back to me, eyes soft. I found myself folded gently into his arms and the aroma of leather engulfed me. I closed my eyes, resting my head against his chest - it felt good to be held. My throat tightened and ached as I soaked his shirt with tears. He bent his head to rest his cheek on the top of my head, and held me even tighter. I felt safe in those strong arms. A strange feeling, considering who he was.

"What is that fuckin' stench?" he asked.

The bath! I broke away and hurried to the steamy bathroom, turning off the tap. Maguire followed. He grimaced at the sting of antiseptic, holding a forearm to his nose and mouth. Spotting the bottle of Dettol by the bath he dropped his arm, a look of horror dawning on his face.

"Fen, did they—" I saw him struggle to find the right word.

"No." I couldn't bring myself to say how close it had come, though.

He thrust off his coat, rolled up a sleeve and plunged an arm into the hot water to yank out the plug. He grabbed the bathroom sponge and forcibly encouraged the astringent water down the drain. All I could do was stand and watch, arms crossed over my chest. I couldn't stop trembling, my teeth practically chattering.

Maguire closed the bathroom door, keeping in whatever steamy heat the hot water had emitted. The bathwater drained with a gurgle and he stooped to turn on the hot water tap and insert the plug. He held his fingers under the flow until he was apparently satisfied the water was hot enough, and then let cold water mix as the bath filled.

To my surprise he took me by the shoulders and sat me on the edge of the bath. Crouching in front of me he began unlacing my boots.

"I can do this, Séan. I'm okay." I tried to shift away but my limbs felt leaden.

He gave me a 'yeah, right' look and eased the boots off, then stood, reaching for the parka. I kept my arms crossed over my chest. "Come on, darlin'," he insisted. "Let's be havin' that."

He shouldn't be doing this. I should tell him to leave. Instead I let him aid me out of it, and then he systematically helped me unpeel the ragged T-shirt and bra. At this point I was beyond modesty. He eased me to my feet and expertly unbuttoned my skirt, letting it pool around my ankles. I saw him take in the fact that my tights and panties had been practically ripped off. Shame flooded me even though I recognized it to be totally inappropriate. He supported me as I climbed into the warm bathwater, and then located my loofah and bar of *Cusson's* behind the taps and placed them in my hands. "I'll go make up the fire, okay?" He swept out, leaving the door open a crack, and a few moments later I could hear the coal scuttle rattling on the hearth.

I sank back, but ricocheted off the side of the tub when the water stung my burn. Huddling with my arms wrapped around myself, my throat ached as I swallowed my sobs, not wanting Maguire to hear me. I was lucky. Very, very lucky. Tetley said he'd never heard of anyone once fingered as a tout by the IRA, walking away alive. I had to pull myself together. If he could see me sniveling away in this bath, he'd scream blue bloody murder. I imagined him standing by the bath, hands on hips, face like an apoplectic-blueberry. '*What d'ye think you're doing, floppin' aboot in there, girlie? Get the fuck oot of there at once, ye look like a beached whale!*' I knew he'd be mortified to see me naked and for some reason found the thought hysterical. My sobs turned to laughter, which I stifled in case Maguire heard. He'd think I'd completely lost my mind.

Maybe I had.

But things weren't so bad. I had survived. I hadn't been raped, and one burn was nothing, considering what could have happened. And Sutherland had called me 'Fionnuir' in a way that made me feel I'd passed a test. With flying colors.

I gently sponged all around the blister then soaped and scrubbed the rest of my body. The self-inflicted scratches on my wrists from undoing the ropes were scarlet, and my fall on the stone steps had taken a gouge out of my knee. I methodically cleaned them all, biting my lip and ignoring the pain. With some effort I hauled myself out of the bath and towel-dried my hair and body. Exhaustion covered me like a heavy blanket - all I wanted to do was sleep. I tried to wrap a towel around me but cloth against the cigar burn felt like shards of glass. I dug out some bandage plasters in the bathroom cabinet and affixed a large one over the burn, making sure to tent it so it didn't press on the blister. Mum would have sliced off a piece of potato to soothe the wound but of course I had none in the kitchen.

I still had a few of the heavy-duty painkillers the doctor at Finley Manor had given me after my interrogation exercise. Seemed fitting that I take a couple now. Washing them down with water from the tap I emerged from the bathroom to discover Maguire dragging my mattress, complete with bedding across the floor. He let it flop in front of the crackling fire and I stole into the bedroom to find some pajamas. Back in the living room I paused, perplexed. Séan had switched off the lamp. He was staying the night?

He folded back the covers and patted the mattress. "You get in here where it's warm, darlin'. I'll take the sofa, I'm not leavin' ya tonight."

I glanced at his six-foot frame to the tiny two-seater sofa but said nothing. Easing under the covers I turned onto my side, huddling between the ice cold sheets.

Séan hunched onto the sofa, pulling his leather coat over himself as a blanket. He looked painfully uncomfortable with his knees drawn up tight against his chest. And pretty ridiculous. "Ach, Séan." I indicated the mattress behind me. "You can sleep here. On top."

He chuckled. "I like bein' on top."

I couldn't help but smile. He slipped off the sofa and lay at my back in a spooning position without touching me. Leather rustled and creaked as he tried to cover himself with his coat.

"There are some spare blankets in the bedroom closet–" I began. This was daft. "Oh, just get under with me."

He didn't need telling twice. Hauling off his Doc Martens he clambered under, fully clothed. His body felt like a furnace at my back, and the bed quickly warmed. Already half-asleep, I nestled against him, happy he was there.

25

A Brave One

The next morning I awoke to find Séan standing motionless by the window. He held an unlit cigarette between his fingers and thumb, his face tight and serious as he stared at something outside. I guessed he wasn't actually looking at anything in particular, just staring off into space. He was inhumanly still.

Some sixth sense made him turn his head and he smiled when he met my gaze. "How ya feelin'?"

I considered for a moment. "Surprisingly not too bad at all."

"Great." He jammed the cigarette between his lips but made no move to light it, thank God. "Listen, I gotta go, darlin'."

I glanced at the little clock on the mantelpiece. Nine o'clock. The thought of being left alone made me uneasy but I needed to make that check in call. "Thanks for taking care of me last night, Séan."

"Darlin', it was my pleasure." He retrieved his leather coat from the sofa and put it on. "I can come back later?"

I spoke before I thought. "I'd like that." Shit, would I really?

He unlocked the door and opened it. "Lock this behind me Fen, okay?"

I obediently hauled myself from under the bed covers and got to my feet. Pain stabbed through my breast as the cigar burn reminded me it was there. And then the physical ravages of the night before made themselves apparent. I was so stiff and sore I could barely move. I hobbled to the door, feeling four times my age. I couldn't imagine I looked anywhere close to attractive, shuffling along in my flannel jammies. All I needed were hair curlers and thick night cream slapped on my face.

He paused on the landing. "Take it easy today. You like fish and chips?"

I nodded, having trouble putting the two together.

"I'll pick us up some for tea." He descended into the darkness of the stairway.

No one used that timed light switch except me, it seemed. I pulled the door closed and locked it. Fish and chips for tea, not dinner. That meant I could expect him from about five o'clock on. Plenty of time for me to make the check in call beforehand. Though in the light of day I wasn't so sure I still wanted be pulled out of here. My position in Sutherland's eyes had become more secure because of what had happened. I should press the advantage - if I could keep my nerve.

I went into the bathroom to check on the burn. Carefully I peeled the bloodied and damp plaster off and bathed the area again. The blister had leaked some pus and shrunk a little, but still looked horrific, an ugly bulging dome. Affixing another plaster, I took the last two painkillers and headed back to bed. My head felt heavy and foggy. I would be delighted to take it easy today, although I didn't need Maguire's permission to do so.

⌘

I started awake and rolled over to look at the clock. A quarter to four? How could I have slept all this time? Bloody painkillers. I jumped into a pair of jeans and got dressed. I needed to decide what I was going to say. Would they take the decision out of my hands, whether I should be pulled out of here or not?

A rap on the door made me jump. Séan back already? How did he keep getting into the building without ringing the doorbell? "It's me!" he called, confirming it.

Fuck. The check in call would have to wait again.

I opened the door to the tangy scent of yeasty battered cod and chips smothered with vinegar wafting in. My stomach rumbled - I hadn't realized I was ravenous until I smelled the food.

"Thought maybe we could run over a couple'a things." He dumped the paper bag containing our tea into my arms. Pulling a folded up wad of manuscript paper from a coat pocket he smoothed it out on the kitchen counter. I took the bag to the kitchen and got out two plates.

"Do we have a gig this weekend?" I asked.

"Well, no."

His inflection made me look up sharply. "What do you mean?"

"Brian found someone ta fill in fer us. Under the circumstances, you know?"

I flushed. "I could have played. There's nothing wrong with my arms."

"Aye, but ye have ta hold the fiddle over yer–" He gestured toward my left breast.

True. I hadn't thought of that. I gave a wry smile. "Hey, if Brian'd been on the ball, he'd have had Seamus burn the other one instead."

Séan gave me a startled look, then laughed. "Yer a brave one, darlin'."

His praise warmed me. I unwrapped the food and laid the two pieces of fish on the plates, divvying up the chips between us. Séan made himself at home. He took off his leather coat and hung it on the coat stand, then relit the fire without being asked to. As I brought the plates over to the coffee table he opened up the fridge to retrieve the bottle of Heinz tomato ketchup and two tins of Harp. We shoved the mattress aside and sat on the sofa and chair with the plates on the coffee table in between.

It was as though we'd lived here together for years. I couldn't help but remember the times Dee and I had shared our meals like this. And Clancy. And Mike, too. That afternoon when he'd accidentally kicked the table over.

I became aware of Séan studying me. He grinned. "Penny for yer thoughts?"

Oh yeah, he'd like those. That you work for a murdering terrorist bastard whom I am going to help bring down. And that I'm thinking of my British soldier ex-lover, and how anxious I feel that I haven't been able to check in today as scheduled with the people out to get Brian and everything he stands for. *Ha!*

"I'm annoyed about you having to cancel the gig. When and where was it supposed to be?"

"Tonight, at a club in the Ardoyne. We can go watch if ya like. Ya up to it?"

My stomach lurched. "Will Brian be there?" I asked, my voice small.

"Nah. He don't go to things like that. Just the Emerald, like."

I swallowed. "Okay, then." Maybe while we were out I'd get a chance to slip away to do my check in on a public phone.

"How 'bout a film first - early show?" He pronounced it 'fill-im'.

I hadn't been to the pictures in months. "What's playing?"

"*Superman.*"

"With Christopher Reeve?"

"Aye."

That sounded like a great distraction to me. Take me out of my thoughts for a while. After we'd finished eating I went into the bathroom to get ready, not letting on that I hadn't actually washed today, yet. I noticed my roots looking a bit dark. Better get more henna as soon as I could.

Hair and make-up done, I changed clothes, making sure to wear a long-sleeved top to cover my scratched-up wrists. I searched my closet and found an ivory-colored silk scarf of Mum's that I'd borrowed years ago and never returned. Twisting it into a thick band I tied it around my neck to cover the bruises.

The movie started out being excruciatingly boring with a seemingly endless narration. I didn't mind because I let my mind wander, sorting out my thoughts. Eventually once Superman got to Earth the film picked up and I began to get immersed in the story.

The theater was almost full and it seemed like everyone except me smoked. I smelled a cigar from a couple of rows back and had to look over my shoulder to make sure it wasn't Sutherland or Seamus. I don't think I'd ever be able to smell a cigar without thinking of my interrogation.

I squinted at my watch. My check in call was five hours overdue.

The lights came up at intermission, and a girl decked out with a massive tray on straps around her shoulders walked down the aisle to the front.

"Fancy an ice cream?" asked Séan, and without waiting leapt to his feet.

He brought back two cornets wrapped in foil and unpeeled mine before handing it to me. How considerate he was. I found it hard not to compare him with Mike. Right now, Séan was leaps and bounds ahead in so many ways. What would he be like to make love with? *Oh, goodness.* Flushing, I concentrated on my ice cream. I was whimsically tempted to put the cornet over my sore and itchy burn to cool it down. I resisted.

"D'you like it?" asked Séan.

I stared blankly, then realized he meant the film. "Yeah, it's great. Can't beat a man in tights."

He roared with laughter, and pulled me to him, crooking his arm round my neck and ruffling my hair. "You're somethin', Fen, you really are."

Embarrassed, I disengaged myself and stood. "Heading to the Ladies'."

"All right, darlin'."

I did need to go but not urgently. Finding a phone was more important. But I couldn't locate one in the lobby. On the way in I'd spotted a red phone box across the road on a side street - Howard Street, I think. I debated whether I'd time to run over before the film restarted, and decided not. Just as well. As I headed back to the auditorium I met Séan coming out. He had an empty packet of cigarettes in his hand and held them up by way of explanation. I waited while he put money in the automated cigarette vendor in the lobby and selected a new pack. The lights dimmed as we re-entered. Séan grabbed my hand, leading me to our seats.

He laid his arm along the back of my chair and rested his fingertips on my shoulder. I didn't pull away. Didn't want to. He made me feel secure and for once I didn't feel like I needed to be looking over my shoulder all the time. How different it all would have been if Mike hadn't withdrawn from me after I left Finley. If only he'd held me all night in his arms after the IRA interrogation instead of Séan. I felt a pain in my chest that had nothing to do with the cigar burn. I think I'd loved him. Maybe still did. Which was bloody stupid. What good did it do me to love someone who obviously didn't love me?

I shifted my arm and let my fingers touch Séan's. He'd been there for me when I needed someone the most. He laced his fingers in between mine and I leaned against him. I'd never gone to a film with Mike - never done anything normal like sitting cuddled up like a 'courting couple'. This felt nice.

We got out at around eight-thirty and walked down the street to where we could catch a black taxi up the Crumlin Road to the Ardoyne. Séan and the driver chatted at first, then Séan settled back beside me. We rode in silence. He wasn't much of a small-talker, and I was too new to pretending to be someone else to engage in idle chitchat. I didn't dare risk letting my guard down.

Tricolors flew aplenty the closer we got to the Ardoyne area. They still made me uneasy. But not as much as they had. The taxi dropped us outside a prefab, squat building. A Republican club. Fear shot through me - a knee jerk reaction to such a diehard IRA place. I heard a reel playing as Séan pushed open the door. A couple of grim-faced men stood inside and nodded to him, letting us pass. They filled me with dread - both of them resembled Seamus, tattooed, heavyset, and balding.

Inside was a hall and bar with a stage, where our replacement band played. The stage was festooned with Irish tricolor curtains and a huge flag attached to the back wall of the stage. My heart thumped faster. I couldn't believe that I was in the veritable armpit of the enemy.

A few couples danced in front of the stage, the rest grouped around tables. The band was ultra-traditional: five older men playing fiddle, uilleann pipes, bouzouki, accordion, and bodhrán. The latter looked as big as a Lambeg drum, which was what Dad's cohorts in the Loyal Orange Order would march to. There was something about those drums that got the blood pumping - almost a genetic memory of a call to arms.

Fuck, good old Protestant Lambeg drums were the last thing I should be thinking about in a place like this.

Everyone seemed to know Séan. As we navigated through the hall, lots of men nodded or came over to shake his hand and exchange a few words. Women smiled widely at him, then slid inquiring glances my way. Séan gave me a gentle push toward a free table. "Grab that, Fen." He headed up to the bar.

I nabbed the table and sat, self-consciously watching the band. Séan's bossiness did rub me the wrong way. Even army-trained Mike had not issued me orders. At least, not when we were socializing. I bit my lip. I had to stop comparing them.

He returned with two bottles of Harp, and proceeded to hold court like Sutherland as people trickled over to greet him. He introduced me to every one of them, and I attempted a phonetic system in my head to remember as many names as I could.

Oddly, it began to feel less like the armpit of the enemy and more like being in the welcoming presence of friends. *They* were no longer a faceless enemy, I realized. They had become individuals to me, who followed lives not very different from 'my' side. I slotted this away for future perusal.

Séan nudged me. "Want ta dance?"

Fuck, I was no good at the waltzes and such that they danced in places like this. Dee had tried to teach me but I just couldn't seem to master the steps. My dour Orange Prod blood, she'd joked.

"Ach, I'd better not, thanks. Still not up to snuff."

He nodded and gave my hand a squeeze. The band took a break and came straight over to our table, effusive with thanks. I gleaned that Maguire had recommended them to Sutherland when it was decided that Curadh wouldn't be playing.

One of them slapped Séan on the back. "Come on, lad, give us a tune!"

"Ach, no. Ya don't need me crampin' your style."

"Ah, come on, mucker!"

Séan gave me an inquiring look. "Go on," I said. Although I felt nervous about being left alone, he was obviously dying to get up there. He borrowed a bouzouki and ploughed right into *The Irish Rover*. I gazed around the hall, trying to recognize anyone on the list at Finley. Another Harp arrived but I couldn't stomach any more. In fact, now I really needed the loo, having not gone during the film. The toilets were over by the door, I'd noted them when we came in. Gathering my nerve, I got up and meandered around the tables, exchanging smiles and 'hellos' as I went.

A payphone hung on the wall across from the toilets. I thought about it for a second, but it would be dicing with death to try and make my check in call from there.

I stopped in consternation in front of the two toilet doors. They were in Gaelic! One read *Mná* and the other *Fir*. Which was which? Jesus, if I hesitated any longer someone would clock that I didn't belong here.

Thank God. The *Mná* door opened and a middle-aged woman came out. Her face looked clownish with way too much makeup plastered on.

In the Ladies' I listened with amusement to the two women in the stalls on either side of me.

"See my Brendan?" said one. "I can't stand the stink of his socks."

"Aye, I know," replied her friend. "I make Andy take his off at the door before I'll let him in the house." They both cackled. "There's a bucket there where he throws them in and then I chuck them in the wash."

They sounded just like how Mum and Mrs. O'Neill used to when they'd had a few drinks taken.

Back at the table I watched Séan perform two more pieces with the band, very much in his element, and then he rejoined me. He looked closely at me. "You all right, darlin'?"

Despite sleeping all day I felt pretty ropey again. It must have shown.

He held out a hand. "Let's go. All right, Jimmy?" he called to a rotund little man with salt and pepper hair, who tapped his forehead and waddled toward the door. "He's runnin' us back to yer place," he said by way of explanation as he led me after Jimmy.

Wait, he was coming back with me? Why? I stopped dead, making him turn round. "You don't need to see me home, Séan. I'll be all right, thank you."

He leaned down and kissed me lightly on the lips. I blushed, feeling many eyes on us. "I don't think ya should be alone, darlin'. Look, don't worry, nothin's going to happen. It'll just be like last night, okay?"

⌘

I slept fitfully with Séan at my back and his arm around me. I was afraid I'd have the Percy French nightmare and give myself away in my sleep. I fretted that I hadn't made the check in call. I was now twelve hours overdue. What would happen if I delayed much longer?

When I did sleep, I dreamed of Mike. We were at Dunluce. I kept glimpsing him as he disappeared around the pillars and rocks in the castle ruin but I could never catch up with him. I woke with a start, thinking I'd called his name aloud.

Séan wasn't in the bed, and I heard thumping noises from the bedroom. I slipped from under the covers and got up. My muscles still complained but thankfully not as much as the day before. Crossing quietly to the bedroom I peered through the doorway. My suitcase lay open on the divan with Séan dropping some of my clothes into it.

"What on earth are you doing?" I demanded.

He spun and grabbed me, whirling me around. "I have a surprise for ya, darlin'!"

I pulled away, laughing. "What is it?"

He tapped the side of his nose. "Wouldn't be a surprise if I tol' ya, would it?"

He'd been frighteningly thorough in his packing. Even the Bible and rosary beads from my nightstand were included. He obviously had no compunction about going through other people's personal stuff.

"We'll add yer makeup and things after ye've got ready." He looked very pleased with himself.

I grabbed Mike's robe from the back of the door and folded it into the case. Catching a sour whiff I remembered I still hadn't taken it to the Laundromat. "We going on a trip?" I fished.

Séan tapped the side of his nose again. "Wait'n see. Now, get a move on - get dressed, darlin'."

On my way to the bathroom I filled the kettle and put it on to boil. Washing quickly I put another plaster on the burn. It had begun to acquire a crater-like appearance and the blister looked less fierce. I threw on a bit of mascara and blusher, and tucked my toiletries and makeup into their respective leopard design bags.

Was I wise, letting Séan take me off on a mystery trip? No one would know where I'd gone.

We had some tea and toast, then locked up the apartment and headed down the stairs. As I opened up the front door the payphone shrilled, startling me. Séan paused, my case in hand and nodded at the phone.

"You gettin' that?"

I shook my head. "Sure, you're the only one who calls me."

He chuckled and we stepped outside, pulling the door behind us. It wasn't until it clicked shut that it occurred to me that someone from Finley might be calling to look for me.

26
One o' His

A black taxi idled outside, the driver smoking and reading a newspaper. *The Irish News*. He drove us into Belfast and I waited with anticipation to see what route he took out of the city. Séan grinned as we headed up the Falls Road. I wondered if I should be worried.

I smiled disarmingly. "Give me a clue, Séan. Where we headed?"

"You'll know in five minutes."

I bit my lip as we took a turning into a little red-brick terrace called Ivie Street, with rows of two-up two-down houses on either side. The driver dropped us off and tipped his hat to Séan as he drove away.

"Who lives here?" I asked.

Séan produced a key and unlocked the door to number eight where the woodwork had been freshly painted green. "Welcome home, darlin'."

I gaped. He'd found a place already? He shoved the door open with his shoulder and before I knew what he was about, swept me off my feet. "Hey!" I pretended to object, laughing. Somehow managing to balance both me and the suitcase, he carried me over the threshold. "Put me down! The neighbors'll think we're married."

He dropped the case, kicked the door closed and let me slide down to my feet. "Sure, what's wrong with that?" The suitcase had burst open when it landed - a mass of lace and satin lay strewn on the floor. I realized he'd avoided packing anything cotton and functional. Looking abashed he helped me stuff the clothes back as best we could.

The little house was already fully furnished. A three-piece ivory leather suite sat in the living room around a fireplace, with a television in the corner beside it. A TV of my own! Nestling in the corner stood a small dining table and upright chairs by a door that opened to a kitchen, and narrow stairs led to the upper floor.

"There's no phone, yet," said Séan, "but you're on the list to get one put in. Couple of weeks."

I couldn't use it to check in, anyway.

"Let me give ya the grand tour." He pushed the door to the kitchen ajar so I could see inside. It had an electric stove, fridge, and joy of joys - a washing machine! No more pounding clothes in the bath and wringing them out until my fingers numbed. Grabbing the suitcase he led the way upstairs into the one bedroom on the right. It looked out over the street and had heavy net curtains preventing nosy neighbors from seeing in. I loved the bed, a double with a very feminine little canopy over it. Every room had central heating radiators. What a luxury after waking up to frost on the inside of the windows in the Botanic Avenue apartment! But how much would all this cost?

Séan placed the case on the bed. "What d'ye think?"

"It's amazing, but how much is the rent?"

"Don't worry yer head about that."

"Why not?"

"Brian's taken care of it all."

I stiffened. "He's a good person to know as long as you're on his side, isn't he?"

His gaze shifted. "Wait till ya see the bathroom."

I crossed the tiny hall to look. The exterior wall had been extended, doubling the original size, and had a large glass stall big enough for two people, with multiple shower heads. I pulled open the door to check it out. "I cannot *wait* to use this."

Séan leaned on the door frame. "Why wait?"

The laugh died in my throat as I realized he was serious. I met his burning gaze and my stomach did flip flops as I ploughed through a fight or flight response.

He bent his head and gently kissed me. I should step back, run away as fast as I could. But hormones took over and all my doubts crashed by the wayside. I clung to him, relishing the feel of his body against mine. He broke away and in one swift movement divested himself of his sweater. I followed suit, pulling mine over my head and dropping it to the floor. The rest of our clothes quickly joined the pile. As I let my bra fall, I glanced at my injured breast in the wall mirror. The plaster had become unstuck so I flipped it off all the way. The burn still looked awful.

Séan's furnace of a body enveloped me from behind, one hand sliding up my torso to cup my other breast. I flashed back to when Mike had done that during our forbidden liaison in his room at Finley. Turning quickly to face Séan I shook the image from my mind.

He gave me a quizzical look. "Y'okay?"

I felt my face flush. Fucking hell, I had to get Mike out of my head. "Yes, course I am."

He reached into the shower stall and turned on the water, which ran hot immediately. I peeked as he turned back. Not circumcised. Good, totally unlike–

I forced myself not to finish the thought.

Séan maneuvered us under the cascading shower heads, letting the flow of water rinse the sweat from our bodies. His skin felt smooth and soft - a light ginger down of hair on his chest and arms. He bent his head to kiss me, and at the touch of his tongue excitement coursed through me. I slid a hand round the back of his neck and hungrily returned the kiss. Oh God, I could barely contain myself. I pressed against him, wanting him more than I'd wanted anything in a long, long time.

He put his hands on my waist and lifted me so I perched on a tiled ledge that ran the length of the shower stall. My breaths coming in gasps, I wrapped my legs high around his waist and dug my nails into his shoulders as we moved urgently together.

⌘

It was close to four o'clock when we trekked back downstairs, after drying off and dressing. Séan put his clothes back on, but I extracted the satin dressing gown from my case to change into. Now that the passion had been sated I felt really awkward. And incredibly stupid. This was probably the most moronic thing I could possibly have done.

Don't get personally involved.

But I had done exactly that. How was I supposed to act now with Séan? I opted for nonchalant as though what we just did hadn't been a big deal for me. I was shriveling inside, hoping no one at Finley would ever find out. Especially Mike. The thought made me feel sick.

Séan went straight to the kitchen and opened the fridge. Empty. He slammed it shut and grabbed his coat. "Let me get a Chinese takeaway to celebrate your new place. There's a chinky just up the road."

"Okay."

The door slammed behind him and I wandered around the house, wondering what I should do. At the very least I'd better make my check in call and tell them where I was. I'd spotted a phone box close by on the Falls, maybe I could slip out later. Heading back to the bedroom I unpacked, throwing the underwear in a couple of drawers in the dresser and stowing my toiletries and make up in the bathroom. I'd have to iron anything else before hanging it in the wardrobe, so I left the rest in the suitcase and shoved it up against the wall.

Mike's silver ring caught my eye, and I took it off to look at the inscription. Sadness swept through me. *All I refuse & thee I chuse.*

Not anymore.

Carefully placing it on the nightstand I went down to the kitchen. Locating a couple of mismatched wineglasses, I set them on the counter along with plates and serving spoons. Moving across the living room I gazed out the window at the row of matching red brick houses opposite, and an old gray Morris Minor parked just down the curb. Everything looked so gloomy, all dark and oppressive. I jerked the curtains over the window and clicked on one of the table lamps. An electric fire sat snugly in the fireplace, so I plugged it in and switched on the fake flames. Exploring, I found a packet of utility candles on a shelf in the cupboard under the stairs. No matches, though, but I turned on the electric stove and held a piece of paper to the filament until it ignited, then lit the wicks. Holding the flame on each candle to the bases, I dripped wax onto a couple of saucers so I could secure the candles in place. Setting them on either end of the mantelpiece I sat on the leather sofa to admire my handiwork. It made the room look quite cozy and romantic. I hesitated. Did I want to be romantic with Séan?

Too late if not. I heard the key in the lock and got up to meet him. He looked admiringly around the room as he handed over the bag containing the takeaway. "This looks grand, darlin'." Reaching into his coat pockets, he produced two bottles of sweet German wine and waggled them at me.

With a grin I took the bag into the kitchen. He followed, opening and closing drawers until he unearthed a wine opener. Removing the foil containers from the bag I unpeeled the cardboard lids. An aroma of chow mein, sweet and sour chicken, and fried rice permeated the air. I grabbed one of the serving spoons.

"How hungry are you?" I asked.

"Just bung it all on there, like."

He made a movement and the wine cork popped with a bang. A memory of Mike popping the champagne cork at Dunluce invaded me. Swallowing a pang I divvied up the food and carried both plates to the living room. So used to sitting on the floor at Botanic, I lowered myself down, cross-legged. Séan paused by the little table and chairs then joined me, setting the glasses on the hearth so he could pour the wine.

I nodded to his leather coat. "Are you keeping that on?"

He chuckled and shrugged it off, laying it on the sofa behind him before sliding one of the wineglasses along the hearth closer to me. We got ourselves sorted and dug in. I looked up in surprise - Séan slurped every time he shoveled food into his mouth. It was a bit off-putting.

"Wish we had some music," I said.

He put his plate down and got up. "Think I saw a radio in the kitchen."

He returned with a transistor so ancient that all the metallic patina had been worn away. It crackled when he switched it on, and then he fiddled until it tuned to Radio Luxemburg. "Anything else ya need, Madam?"

Just everything you know about Brian Sutherland, thank you. I shook my head. "Got everything, thanks."

I was more hungry than I realized, and managed to polish off everything on my plate. The wine went down very nicely with it, and before I knew it I was in a mellow fog after three glasses.

Séan reached over to his coat. "Forgot somethin'." He produced two beige colored curly things and held them out on the palm of his hand. "Fortune cookies. The owner said he brought them back from San Francisco. Pick one."

I chose the one furthest away. Séan snapped his apart and I followed suit. Inside I found a tiny slip of white paper on which was printed: *You have many hidden talents.* I bit back a laugh. Wasn't that the truth.

Séan looked at his and smiled widely. *"Love is yours for the taking."* He cocked an eyebrow at me. "That so?"

I flushed. Love had nothing to do with this. Lifting my glass to take another sip I realized it was empty. The bottle lay on its side on the floor alongside the detritus of our dinner. I held the glass up close to my eye and peered into it like a telescope. "There's something wrong with this glass."

"What's that?"

"It leaks."

He laughed and went to fetch the second bottle, uncorking it and filling both our glasses. Settling back he reached over to his coat and pulled out a cigarette pack and lighter from the pocket. "Wait, this calls for something special." He dropped the cigarettes and rummaged in the pocket once more. Producing a packet of slim cigars he lit up with gusto. The smell immediately made me feel ill.

"Do you have to?"

Surprise crossed his face, then he put two and two together. Extinguishing the cigar on the hearth he shifted over beside me and gathered me into his arms.

"Look Fen, I'm sorry Brian had you hurt, but ya got to try and forget it. He's a good man, you know."

"So you keep saying."

"Without him Curadh wouldn't have got off the ground."

I remembered Colonel Pierce saying that Sutherland's interest in a traditional band was a recent development. "Is he a promoter or something?"

Séan laughed. "Nah."

"So, why's he helping the band?"

"'Cause he knows we're the next Horslips, that's why."

That wasn't an answer. "But did you ask him to help, or did he offer?"

"We got talkin' in the Emerald one night. He likes business opportunities and offered. I'd be stupid to say no. He got us the van and all, like. Had to take taxis and Kieran's ratty car before. And now you're on board he's findin' us much better gigs."

He checked his watch and reached over to switch on the television. Music blared, the theme to *Starsky and Hutch*, an American cop show. I stretched down to click off the radio. "Ya don't mind, do ya?" he asked.

Too bad if I did. "'Course not." It was a rerun of an episode I'd already seen but as Séan watched, it gave me a break from being Fionnuir for a bit and sort through my thoughts. And it was nice, just sitting with him like this. Mike and I had never watched television together.

There I went, thinking of him again. Why in the name of God did I feel so horrible inside - like I'd cheated on him?

As the credits rolled Séan patted my knee and got up. "I got to go, darlin'."

I'd be able to make my check in call at last.

He grabbed his coat and slipped it on. "You going to be all right on your own, Fen?"

"Yes, particularly now I've got a telly to watch. Thank you."

"You can thank Brian when you see him."

Yes, mustn't forget about him. "I will." I walked Séan to the door.

He took my hands in his, looking very grave. "This is important, all right? Don't be going out nowhere after I leave. Promise me, like."

I frowned. "Why not?"

"I haven't had time to tell people about you yet. Ye'll be all right after then." He gave me a bear hug and released me. "Promise me ye'll stay in, darlin'."

"All right, if it's that important." What he wouldn't know wouldn't hurt him.

I opened the door and he stepped outside. Turning round, he took my face in his hands and gave me a long, passionate kiss. I responded, easily aroused, my body molding against his.

"Fen, yer a she-devil," he murmured, his lips against mine. I giggled, and without breaking the kiss, we began maneuvering back into the house. A horn honked, startling us both. A shiny black Ford Capri drew up to the curb, Kieran at the wheel. Nothing ratty about that car. "Go inside," ordered Séan, gesturing to my state of undress.

I pulled the door over as he ran round to the passenger side of the car. Leaning through the door crack I waved gaily at Kieran, who predictably scowled before accelerating away.

I'd give it a few minutes and then head out to that phone box, regardless of what I'd promised Séan. The street was dark and deserted. If

I were careful, no one would see me. I left the television on as background noise and cleared up before heading upstairs to change back into my clothes. With the light off I peered out through the net curtains. In the time it had taken me to tidy up, a trio of men had congregated down on the corner. They each clasped a tin of beer and looked like they were there for the duration. I went downstairs and unlocked the back door in the kitchen. It opened into a yard, scarcely bigger than a coffin, with another door that led out to the alley behind the row of houses. I unlatched it and eased it open.

"Can I help ya, missus?" snapped a male voice, making me just about jump out of my skin. Five teenage guys sat in a row on a battered old couch against the wall. One of them drank from a large brown bottle of Strongbow cider.

"Just moved in," I said quickly. "Checking to see what was out here."

"Well, ye've seen it."

I retreated, making sure to securely bolt the door. No exit that way, the alley must be the little gang's hideout. Checking out the front window again I saw the group on the corner had lit a fire in an old metal barrel. I was well and truly stuck. Admitting defeat I slumped in the chair by the electric fire. Barring climbing out a window and clambering across the rooftops, there simply was no way out to that phone box tonight. The call would just have to wait. The local headlines came on television. Not wanting to hear any bad news tonight I got up and turned off the set. Might as well catch up on some sleep. Switching off the fire and lights I dragged myself up the creaky stairs to the bathroom. I cleaned my teeth, shed my clothes again and climbed into bed naked. It was so lovely and warm in the house I didn't need any jammies. Even if Séan had remembered to pack them.

⌘

I lurched awake some time later. Something heavy banged repeatedly on the front door below and I sat bolt upright, heart hammering. A splintering thump ricocheted through the house as the front door apparently burst open. Before I could move, heavy footsteps thundered up the stairs. In the light from the streetlamp outside I watched what looked like an entire squadron of British Army soldiers burst into the bedroom. I crouched in the bed, knees drawn up and the covers gripped under my chin. The overhead light snapped on, washing the room with light and half-blinding me. Three soldiers took positions in a semicircle around my bed, rifles pointed at me. A fourth with two corporal's stripes on his arm oversaw from the open door.

"What the fuck's going on?" I demanded, too shocked to be afraid.

"Shut up, paddy," he snapped. "Secure, Sir!" he shouted over his shoulder, and Mike McLeod in uniform stepped through the open doorway.

My stomach flip-flopped, confusion flooding me.

"We've reason to believe you're sheltering a known IRA fugitive," he announced and gestured to the men. The corporal left with two of them, one staying behind. Resting his SLR up against the wall by Mike he systematically hauled out each of the drawers in the dresser, turned over my bedside table, and tore all the hangers out of the empty wardrobe.

"Is this necessary?" I inquired icily.

Mike ignored me. The soldier kicked over my suitcase, rummaged through it and then left with his rifle. From the bathroom came the sound of plastic and glass bottles thunking into the sink. Below I heard the living room being torn apart, furniture thudding as it got turned over. Then from the kitchen came the crash of cupboards and drawers being ransacked. The bathroom passed muster and the soldier's steps clattered down the stairs. Mike locked gazes with me. I glared back, disbelieving and furious.

"How'd you know where I was?"

"You don't think we have this area under observation?"

They'd been watching the entire time? "If you wanted to see me, Mike, all you had to do was call."

"I tried."

I remembered the phone ringing in the downstairs hall at Botanic when Séan and I left. Outside, voices rose in anger as the neighbors screeched abuse at the soldiers. Then came a terrible din of metal rubbish bin lids clanging on the ground. I threw back the covers and jumped out of bed, belatedly remembering that I was naked. I turned away from Mike and bent quickly to grab my T-shirt from the floor. But he never missed anything. His impersonal military bearing dissipated and he became my Mike again.

"Jesus, you're hurt!"

I struggled to find the armholes in the T-shirt. "It's not as bad as it looks."

He took me by the shoulders and turned me round so he could inspect me. He didn't seem to notice that I was completely naked, but I was acutely aware of it. Of him, in spite of the circumstances.

"That's a cigar burn, for chrissakes. What happened?"

I hauled the T-shirt over my head, covering my torso. "Clancy O'Neill recognized me at the Students' Union gig. He told Séan about you, and then Brian Sutherland wanted to know all about you."

"He tortured you?"

I retrieved my jeans from the floor and stepped into them. "One of his henchmen tried to, yes."

"What did you tell them?"

"Nothing. All he got out of me is that you're an American."

His dark eyes glittered. "Which motherfucker did this to you? Seamus or Paddy? I'll haul the cunt in."

I'd never heard him use such language before. "Seamus, but you can't. He'd know I told."

"It won't be linked to either of us, don't worry." His gaze lingered on my ringless right hand for a moment. I realized the poesy ring had gone flying across the room during the soldier's marauding search. Mike's eyes hardened. "Christ, Jen. This has gone far enough. I'm taking you out of here - now."

Panic rose in me. "No, not yet. I'm only just making headway with Séan."

His face tightened. "Yeah, I saw that."

He couldn't have seen Séan and me together, could he? I flushed as I remembered the lustful kiss in the doorway before Kieran showed up.

"You didn't report in," he continued. "You weren't at the apartment. We had to check up on you."

"How do you expect me to do my job with you looking over my bloody shoulder?"

"Making a whore out yourself with the enemy is not part of your job."

I had trouble taking a breath and my voice shook. "You're the one who told me to do whatever it takes, Mike. And I haven't found out if he's the enemy yet, or not."

He scoffed. "Is there any doubt?"

"Plenty!"

"That's it. I'm pulling you out before you get yourself killed. You were ordered not to get personally involved."

"I'm not personally involved!"

"Could have fooled me. And with a goddamn terrorist."

I suddenly understood. "This isn't about the job, is it? Mike, you're jealous!"

He blanched. "What?"

"And Séan isn't a terrorist. So what if he feels passionately about the Brits leaving Northern Ireland? I think I'm beginning to understand why."

His shutters came down, freezing me out. "So, that's how you survived the interrogation. You've gone native."

If he'd punched me in the face it couldn't have hurt any more. "You bastard. I did nothing of the kind - I *protected* you!"

The sound of booted feet ascended the stairs and Mike took a step back. "Nothing, Sarge," the corporal reported.

Mike nodded. Turning his back on me he strode from the bedroom, the corporal following. I just stood there in shock, listening as he ordered his men to withdraw. At least he'd let me stay. But I felt sick to the stomach. Accusing me of changing sides to get out of the interrogation? How little he thought of me. My eyes filled with tears and I angrily dashed them away.

Engines revved and cheers went up from outside. Going to the window

I watched the neighbors, dressed in various sleepwear, crow in triumph as the Land Rovers disappeared down the street.

A female voice shouted from downstairs. "Are ye all right, dear?"

I went to the top of the stairs to find a woman wearing a baby-blue fleecy dressing gown standing in the living room. She looked like a cartoon caricature of a housewife, with big curlers in her hair and huge fluffy slippers on her feet. I couldn't tell her age. Fifties maybe.

"Are ye all right?" she repeated.

I started down the stairs. "Aye, thanks."

"What'd they want?"

"Accused me of hiding one of the 'RA."

I stopped dead when I saw the state of the living room. It looked like a tornado had swept through. Even the electric fire had been pulled out of the fireplace and dumped on its side on the carpet.

"Don't worry, dear. It always looks worse than it is. We'll help ye put it to rights."

A second woman with a net over her hair pushed in through the splintered door. Leaning close to speak in what she must have thought was an undertone, she said, "Just phoned Mr. Sutherland. She's one o' his."

One of his what - floozies? He'd said something respectable though, as the curlered woman's attitude transformed from guardedly concerned to maternal protectiveness.

"Ach, dear." She descended on me, putting an arm round my shoulders. "Let's get that kettle on."

Her name was Eileen, the other Agnes. When they discovered I had no tea, milk, sugar, or any provisions they spirited in a few things from their kitchens. They fussed round, treating me for shock. I *was* in shock. But not for the reasons they thought.

Several men came in, and under Agnes' guidance they righted the furniture, put the fire back in the fireplace, and returned all the drawers back to where they belonged. They clumped up the stairs and I listened as they righted my nightstand and shifted everything back in place. While we women watched over our cups of sweet tea, the men finished up by hammering a couple of planks onto the door to cover the hole where it had been kicked in. One of them fiddled around with the lock until he made certain it worked properly.

"All right, love?" he said to me in parting.

I was overwhelmed by their kindness.

"We should go, too," said Eileen. "It's four in the bloody morning!"

She and Agnes got up from the couch and I took their empty cups. "I don't know how to thank you–" I began.

"Not at all." Agnes took my hand and gave it a little squeeze. "The least we can do for Commander Sutherland."

I forced myself not to react. Following them to the door I waved as they trouped into their respective houses. *Commander* Sutherland? A ranking officer in the IRA. At last now I had something definitive to report on my check in call.

Switching off the lights I headed upstairs. Systematically I searched the bedroom until I found Mike's ring caught in the groove between the carpet and skirting board by the wardrobe. I dropped it into the nightstand drawer. Next time I saw him I'd return it. Bastard. I wish I could have flung it in his face. I lay in the darkness growing more angry, the whole raid burgeoning over and over in my head. He hadn't needed to burst in, guns blazing. And then to insult me! Call me a turncoat, questioning the fact that I'd come through an IRA interrogation intact. But a thought kept creeping in, no matter how many times I tried to banish it. Would his reaction have been as furious if he didn't still have feelings for me?

27

Dreamcatcher

After snatching a couple of hours sleep, I woke as dawn crept over the rooftops and chimneys of the houses opposite. I lay for a moment in a sleepy fog until the events of the night rushed back and stung me wide awake. I dragged myself out of bed at once. At this time of the morning, people would be out heading to work. I could just mingle naturally with them on the way to the phone box and not draw any attention. If there was a newsagent's close by I'd drop in there for some milk or something to cover my tracks. As Mike had been here I probably didn't need to check in, but that wasn't why I wanted to make the call.

I threw on the clothes I'd worn the night before, made sure I had some coins in my pocket, and slipped out the front door. Strolling to the corner I walked to the end of the street and onto the Falls. The phone box was where I thought I remembered seeing it, only a few yards down and across the road. A few people were about on foot, but no one took any notice of me. The stench of stale urine assailed me when I pulled open the phone box door. All public phones in Northern Ireland seemed to smell like that. On the shelf inside sat half a Mars candy bar with the butt of a cigarette stuck into it. Charming.

Dialing, I waited for the pips to beep and pushed in a ten pence piece. "This is Banshee."

"Archangel." Chalki's voice.

I scanned the street through the windows, ensuring no one was close enough to overhear. "I've confirmed Brian Sutherland is an IRA commander. I believe the official Lower Falls battalion leader. When I know more, I'll call." My voice quavered as I tried to stay in control. "Until then you need to keep Serg - the other archangel the hell away from me! He's going to fuck everything up."

"Why, what happened?" Chalki sounded genuinely concerned.

"Look, I don't want to see him anywhere around here again, okay?" I slammed down the receiver, belatedly realizing I hadn't waited to find out when to check in again. I shoved my way out of the rancid box and gulped in the fresh morning air.

Oh, well. Now I would call at my convenience, not theirs.

⌘

I took a shower and got into my satin dressing gown while I ran a load of laundry through. Curling up on the sofa I delved into the unchallenging content of *Woman's Own* magazine I'd picked up at the local shop along with the milk and some bits and pieces. I just wanted to give my brain a rest from going over and over the happenings of the night before.

A knock came to the door just after eleven. I opened it to find Séan on the doorstep, clutching a paper bag. "Sticky buns," he announced.

I grinned and stood back to let him in. "How can I resist?"

"You get raided?" He indicated the boarded up door as he followed me inside.

"Yes, would you believe. Accused me of hiding one of the IRA here."

"Welcome to the neighborhood, darlin'."

We went into the kitchen where he perched on one of the counters as I boiled the kettle and made tea. He looked like he'd been up all night - long hair unkempt and five o'clock shadow thicker than usual. "You and Kieran have a good night?" I asked.

He offered me a lopsided grin and dug in the pockets of his leather coat. "Got you a wee present, darlin'." Drawing out a little velvet pouch he held it out.

His hands were caked in dried mud, fingernails black. "Did you have to dig up buried treasure to find it?"

He laughed. "Just open it, *mo ghrá*."

I tipped the pouch over and a pair of gold hoop earrings slid onto my palm. They were heavy and good quality with 18 carat gold hallmark stamps. "Wow, these're gorgeous, Séan, but they must have cost a fortune."

"Never mind about that, Fen. You're worth it."

I slid my arms around his neck and planted a kiss on his lips. "Thank you. Sticky buns *and* jewelry? You certainly know the way to a girl's heart."

I emptied the cakes onto a plate and we took them and the tea into the living room. As we sat on the sofa, I reached across to switch on the radio. Luxembourg was crackly, so I spun the dial to the local Downtown station.

Make Me Smile by Cockney Rebel was playing. I slipped on the earrings one at a time without having to look in a mirror.

Séan nodded approvingly as I modeled them. "There's more," he said. "I've brilliant news."

I swung round sideways to face him, pulling up my legs and crossing them on the sofa. "Do tell."

"Brian's got us a crapload of bookings all over Northern Ireland. We'll be touring like a real band, like."

"We are a real band."

He laughed. "Aye, but you know what I mean."

"That *is* brilliant. But did you not play other places before?"

"Nah. Strictly Belfast - until now."

"So, why tour now? Did Brian say?"

His face darkened. "What's with all the questions, darlin'?"

He really didn't like being asked stuff. I shrugged. "Just curious."

"If I tell ya, you can't tell the others. Not yet."

My ears practically pricked up like a dog's. "I won't, cross my heart." *And hope not to die.*

"All right. He wants us to get ready for a special gig outside Northern Ireland in the summer. Touring'll be good practice."

What did Sutherland have in mind? Were we to be a cover for something nefarious? "A special gig, where?"

Séan tapped the side of his nose. "Never you mind, darlin'. If it works out it'll be the best thing ever happened to us. You'll see."

"Come on, Séan, give me a clue!"

"As soon as Brian gives the go ahead I'll tell ya, okay?"

I'd have to content myself with that for now. But this was the first sign that Sutherland was planning something more than just promoting a band, I was certain. "Where are we headed first on the tour?"

"Queen's Court in Bangor!"

Nothing at all there to warrant Sutherland's interest that I could think of. A sweet little seaside town about fourteen miles away on the Ards Peninsula. I matched Séan's delighted smile. "I can't wait!"

The song ended and the local news came on. "*Last night a Protestant man was beaten to death in East Belfast. He owned a jewelry shop on the Cregagh Road and was a father of three. He was not known to be involved in any sectarian activities—*"

Séan reached over and snapped off the radio. "Don't want to hear that shite."

I blinked. "Maybe I do."

"Ach, darlin'." Scooting closer to me, he grabbed my ankles and yanked. I slid unceremoniously onto my back and exploded in laughter as he started tickling me. I was helpless to resist when he pulled my legs wide and stretched over me, kissing his way up my torso.

"There's much better things we could be doing," he murmured, capturing my lips with his, effectively silencing my giggles.

⌘

Later that day I popped over to Eileen's house to thank her for helping me after the army raid. I bought a gift tin of McVitie's Victoria biscuits in the corner shop and took them with me. Apart from genuinely wanting to thank her, I also thought it might be worth a try to get some more information about Sutherland.

Her face lit up when she opened her door and I presented her with the biscuit tin. "Ach, come in, love! I just put the kettle on." Without her curlers she looked younger, maybe late forties. She wore a nylon house dress with a tiny little flower print, and her ever-present fluffy slippers.

I found myself bundled onto a chair at the kitchen table and plied with enough tea, scones, and cake to feed a platoon.

"Was that Séan Maguire I saw leaving your house, earlier?" Her eyes twinkled.

"Yes. Do you know him?"

"Ach, everyone knows Séan, love. The white-headed boy."

I'd heard my mother use that expression - it meant a favorite.

"He's so kind, is Séan," she continued. "He grew up round here, you know."

"No, I didn't know."

"Aye, his mammy had the house just round the corner. Then they moved to one of the bigger houses in Andersonstown." She squinted into my cup. "More tea?"

"Yes, please." She filled my cup from the oversized brown porcelain teapot on the stove. I wanted to ask if Séan still lived with his mother, and cast about for a way to phrase it. Eileen'd probably think I should already know that. "He doesn't spend a lot of time there, though," I fished.

"Naturally not. Not since the shootin', God rest her soul."

Startled, I admitted, "I don't know anything about that."

"I'm not surprised, love. The wee lad never talks about it."

"What happened?"

"'Twas awful for him. He was about ten at the time. Bloody army was searching the houses and his mammy was creatin', like we all did, you know. Telling off the soldiers to have a titter of wit and bugger off and bother someone else. Wee Séan tried to get between her and them and no one knows what happened. There was a lot of shouting and pushing and some neighbor men barged in the back door to try and protect them. Two of the soldiers upped rifles and shot at them, but Séan's mammy got in the way. She bled to death right there in front of him."

I didn't have to feign shock. No wonder he was so protective of that little old lady in the street when she'd been hit by the bottle.

"He'd been the apple of his mammy's eye. She'd never been able to have the childer, and when he came along she said it was a bloody miracle. So, wee Séan was left in his daddy's care. A feckless, drunken sod if ever there was one." She gave a hollow, self-deprecating laugh. "Ach, listen to me. Séan wouldn't like to hear nothing said against his daddy, all the same. Don't you be telling him I said nothin'.'"

"Of course not," I assured her. "But he was okay, was he? Growing up after that, I mean."

"Aye, well - he was never the same. Who would be? Doesn't think kindly of the security forces, that's for sure."

"I can understand that." Eileen got up and refreshed the teapot. "So, when did Commander Sutherland start helping him out?" I asked.

"He's always been there for wee Séan. Like a daddy he is to him - better than his own."

I tried not to act surprised. "Oh, I thought they hadn't known each other that long." That's certainly the impression Séan had given me. "Didn't the commander just start helping out the band?"

"Aye, that's so. But he's been looking out for Séan since the shooting. That's all I know."

I could see she felt uncomfortable about saying so much. I didn't want her to realize I'd been fishing for information, so I changed the subject by pointing to a round hoop with netting in the center pinned on the wall. Soft feathers and bright beads decorated the netting, and hung in long strips below the hoop.

"That's pretty. What is it?"

"Funny you should notice that. Commander Sutherland brought me that back from Americay a few weeks ago. It's an Indian dreamcatcher. I toul him I liked them cowboys and Indians, and the *Dukes of Hazard*, like." She chuckled. "He says he couldn't find Boss Hoggs so brung that instead."

"He's good to - us, isn't he?" I almost said, 'his people'. I remembered Colonel Pierce telling me Sutherland had been in America. Presumably to rustle up shipments of armaments and explosives for the IRA, courtesy of NORAID. Sadly misguided, donating to a charity that buys the means to murder. Their money didn't go to help widows and orphans, it helped to create them.

Eileen's voice dropped as though Sutherland listened outside the window. "To tell you the truth I don't like it at all. Gives me the willies, so it does. Maybe I don't want my dreams caught."

I got up to take a closer look. It made me think of wild plains, buffalo, and tepees. I touched a finger to one of the beige and white feathers. I wondered if it was from an eagle.

"I'd give it to you, dear, but the commander might be offended."

I hastily withdrew my hand. "Oh, you're kind, thank you, but I wouldn't dream of taking it." A miniature brass cockerel weathervane on the windowsill caught my eye. It made me think of Dad's weathercock at Mourneview - when this all began. "I love that," I remarked.

She immediately plucked it from the sill and put it in my hand. "Then it's yours. A housewarming present, like."

"Oh, I didn't mean that!" I should have kept my mouth shut.

"No, no - I insist. It's just gathering dust there."

There wasn't a hint of dust anywhere in her kitchen but there was no way to refuse without offending her. "Well, thank you. Very much."

I took it back with me to the house and put it in honor of place on the mantelpiece. The visit had given me a lot to think on, beyond the information I'd gleaned about Séan and Sutherland. Keeping up a different persona in an intimate, friendly encounter like this had been really hard. I'd found it comfortingly familiar to sit at a kitchen table with the scent of fresh baking in the air. It made me feel part of a community, not unlike the farming one I'd been brought up in around Mourneview.

⌘

The Bangor gig was followed by a traditional night in the Emerald. We had another over at the Ardoyne Republican Club midweek, and then on Saturday were booked to play in the Town 'n' Country in Banbridge, a town roughly twenty-five miles southeast of Belfast.

I dreaded going to the Emerald. Sutherland and Seamus would be there. I hadn't seen either of them since the interrogation, although Sutherland had arranged a moving company to pack up and move the rest of my things from Botanic.

He appeared shortly after we'd begun playing. Revulsion swept through me and I kept my eyes well above the crowd, making sure to avoid eye contact. Thank God Seamus didn't accompany him - a different man came in with Paddy. Did Mike make good on his word and haul the fucker in? I truly hoped so. Hoped he was being beaten and sleep-deprived, rotting in a cell in Castlereagh. I also hoped Sutherland wouldn't put two and two together if Seamus had been arrested, but Mike had promised me it wouldn't be linked to me.

Yet Mike had broken promises before.

Sutherland took his customary table, proceeding to receive the usual stream of visitors. I didn't have time to worry too much about him. Séan had decided on fiddle-heavy pieces tonight so I was kept busy and distracted. At the break I stayed put at the dais while the others went up to the bar. I sat down, pretending that the bow needed attention, keeping my head bent while I tweaked and resined.

Séan returned promptly with a bottle of Harp. "Brian'd like to speak to ya, Fen."

Bile rose in my throat. "I can't!"

"Sure ya can." He took hold of my arm to pull me up.

I resisted, spilling beer over us both. "No!" Everything in me wanted to run as fast as I could out the door and never come back.

"Come on, darlin', just get it over and done with."

Sutherland appeared at Séan's elbow. "Fionnuir, *a chara*." He took hold of my right hand. I managed not to wrench away as he held it between both of his. "How are you, dear child?"

"Well," I lied.

"Fully recovered, I trust?"

"Yeah." The burn and abrasions may be healing but I didn't think I'd ever get past having someone deliberately harming me.

He patted my hand, and I was able to withdraw it. "Glad to hear it. How is the house working out for you?"

That at least I could be honest about. "It's great - thank you very much. I really appreciate it."

"Least I could do, my dear."

I silently agreed. The blood-money house made up for a lot.

He smiled. "Keep up the good work, both of you. Band sounds top notch." Patting Séan on the back he returned to his table.

Séan folded me into a hug. "That wasn't so bad, now, was it?"

"Suppose not." At least I was in Sutherland's good graces now. Hopefully it would open doors to important information that would help bring the bastard down.

"Did you notice anything?" asked Séan, lighting up a cigarette.

"Like what?"

"Seamus."

"Well, he isn't here, thank Christ."

"Exactly. Turns out he was runnin' a racket on the side, selling drugs, like."

My eyes widened. Was that true or had he been framed? "He was arrested?"

"Arrested?" Séan burst out laughing. "Fuck, no. They deal their own justice around here. Let's just say he won't be torturing nobody for a very long time. Got broken ribs, fractured leg, smashed fingers, and a good kneecapping to boot. Someone had a whale of a good time with him."

A lot more severe than what he'd done to me but I couldn't raise any sympathy for him. Fuck, could the army or Special Branch have been that vicious? "Who did it?"

"Jesus, darlin', you're really not from round here, are you?"

My heart started hammering again. I couldn't let my guard down for a second. "You know I'm new to Belfast."

"Aye, well - the 'RA of course. No crime tolerated here. Nothing that takes away from the Cause, like."

Again I understood just how lucky I'd been to walk away alive.

⌘

After the gig, the boys drove to Ivie Street to drop Séan and me off. The van idled at the curb with the sliding door open after we'd clambered out. I looked inquiringly at Séan.

"See you tomorrow, darlin'," he said.

"Oh, okay. Where you headed at this time?"

A frisson of impatience crossed his face. "Ach, Kieran and me - we've business in town."

"At almost one in the morning?"

His jaw tensed. "Don't be like that, Fen."

I checked myself. "I'm not being like anything, I'm just surprised." I tiptoed to kiss him on the cheek. "Night, then. Be safe."

He captured me in his arms and kissed me properly. It lasted long enough to make the guys begin jeering and catcalling. He chortled and leapt back into the van. It moved off after I'd unlocked the house door and gone inside.

A break from Séan's intense personality would be very welcome. I needed to think and regroup and I'd have a chance to be alone and relax as Jennifer again for a bit. Placing the violin case on the arm of the sofa I reached to switch on one of the lamps.

A shadow separated itself from the chair near the fireplace and the silhouette of a man loomed. I gasped and jumped back, fumbling for the door. The lamp clicked on and I stopped dead at the sight of Clancy.

"Jen, it's me. I'm not here to hurt you." He kept his distance, his expression wary.

"What the fuck do you want?" I sputtered. "You've got some nerve showing up here. How'd you get in, anyway?"

"I need to talk to you, Jennifer."

"It's *Fionnuir*," I hissed. "And we've nothing to talk about. You lost the right to talk to me ever again after what you did."

"Please." He looked genuinely stricken. "I'm sorry, I didn't know Brian would hurt ya."

"Are you completely fucking stupid? Of course he'd hurt me after you told him about Sergeant McLeod!"

"I only told him I'd seen you out with him the once and that I'd warned you off."

"But why? Why say anything, Clancy?"

"I remember what a diehard Brit you were at Queen's. I couldn't believe my eyes when I saw you in Séan Maguire's band. I made a joke about him being forward-thinking with a non-sectarian band, and when he didn't believe I knew you, I brought up McLeod. I didn't mean any harm and once I'd opened my mouth it was too late."

How plausible. "But you let me think at the gig that you hadn't said anything."

"I'm a fuck up, I know. I was messing with you - I really didn't think you were in any danger."

I took that in. I suppose it's possible he was genuine. "I didn't know you knew Séan."

"I've been following Curadh since the band formed last year. You know he's been looking for a roadie when Paddy can't do it? I went there to ask about the job."

I scoffed. "Give me a break. A university boy as a roadie for an unknown Celtic band?"

"A university girl and classically-trained concert violinist as a fiddler for said band?" he countered. "What's the difference?"

I could argue the difference but that wasn't the point. "Semantics."

He shuffled his feet. "Well, it's too late, anyway. I'm starting at your next gig."

"Quit."

"Yeah, right. Look - did you tell Séan anything about me?"

Ah, here's what this really was about. Had I ousted his homosexuality. "Not a thing, Clancy." Weariness dulled my voice. "Not even when they did this." I wrenched my T-shirt up to display the burn on my breast.

"Jesus." He averted his gaze. "Séan did that?"

I let the shirt drop. "No, of course not. Do you think I'd still be around him if he did? Sutherland had that fuckhead Seamus do it."

"I'm so sorry, Jen."

"Fen or Fionnuir. Don't forget it. Now listen, Séan hates gays. All the band does. They'd do worse than this to you if they knew about you."

"No one'll know if you don't tell them."

"Have you told anyone else you saw me? Dee or your brothers?"

"No, I swear."

I decided to trust him. "Okay then. Keep my secret and I'll keep yours."

"Deal." He smiled tentatively. "Any tea going?"

I snorted. "Don't push it." But I went into the kitchen and put the kettle on to boil.

He followed, leaning up against the counter with his arms folded. "So, what are you doing in the band?"

I shot him an incredulous look. "What?"

"It's a valid question."

"I'd have thought it was bloody obvious what I'm doing in the band. Making a new life for myself as a professional musician."

"But you're a Protestant."

"What's that got to do with it?"

"Oh, come on, you're being dense on purpose. Your family was murdered by a 'RA Nationalist bomb. But look at you! You're wearing a Catholic crucifix, for fuck's sake. No one can live here in the Falls without supporting the Cause for a United Ireland. Don't you understand? No one can live in the Falls and *not* be involved with the IRA!"

My fists clenched. I needed to get him out of here before I lost my temper. "Clancy, it's about music, that's all. There are no Protestant traditional bands that I know of, so it was this or nothing. Get it? There's no question of me supporting any cause. I'm happy here. I belong here in a way I never did before. I have a job I love, this house - and Séan." I stopped, confused. Truth rang from my words.

"You *love* Séan?"

His look of horror made me laugh. "I didn't mean that, but we're practically living together. What are you so upset about, anyway? You were the one who told me to stick to one of my own instead of a Brit."

"Aye, but I meant a Prod."

"For God's sake, Clancy. You're the worst bigot I've ever met."

He looked so pale I thought he might pass out. "It's not that, J-Fen." He drew me into the living room where he sat us both down on the sofa. "Look, I'm taking a terrible chance here - but maybe our friendship at Queen's meant something to you. The truth is, I'm an undercover British operative, trying to infiltrate Séan's scene. You being here is compromising me."

My jaw dropped and I stared. If that were true wouldn't Finley know about it? "Show me your ID."

"It'd be suicide to carry it. You know that - being undercover yourself."

Terror cut through me. I leapt to my feet. "I'm nothing of the kind, you stupid piece of shit. And neither are you."

He stood too. "Think about it. How come I knew who Mike McLeod was in the first place?"

I shook my head. "I don't know. But it's not because you're a fucking British agent." I went for the door to open it but he grabbed at me. I instinctively seized his arm, preparing to put him into a half-Nelson. I stopped short, shoving him away instead. A civilian like me wouldn't know how to do that unless she'd been professionally trained.

He held up his hands in surrender, backing toward the door. "Don't worry, I'm not going to tell anyone."

"Too right you're not. You've lost your fucking mind, Clancy. If you say one word to anyone about these insane fantasies I'll tell Séan and everyone that you're as gay as a bloody maypole. And that'd be your death warrant. Got it?"

He nodded, his face grim. "We're at stalemate, then."

A whistle pierced the air as the kettle boiled but I made no move to go into the kitchen. "It'd better stay that way, Clancy. I'd hate to see you with every bone in your body smashed to a pulp."

"Jesus, Mary and Joseph, what's happened to you? Your parents would be ashamed if they knew what you've become."

My fist smashed into his face before I could stop myself. He reeled back, blood spurting from his nose. "Get the fuck out," I hissed.

"I'm going." He unlatched the door and opened it. "See you on the road, Fen."

I slammed it after him. My breath came in gasps and sobs as I strode to the kitchen. Snatching the whistling kettle off the stove I dug out my bottle of whiskey. Jameson. I didn't dare buy Bushmills in case Séan questioned why I hadn't stayed 'loyal' to Jameson. So stupid. Dispensing with the niceties I unscrewed the top and took several deep swallows straight from the bottle. I drank too fast and ended up half-choking. My skinned knuckles stung as alcohol dribbled over them.

That bloody sick fuck. Bringing my parents into it. But he was right. They'd be ashamed to see me *happy* in the midst of IRA territory like this. I'd been deluding myself. Did I think that when I'd finished passing on information to the British about Brian Sutherland that I would continue playing in Curadh? That I'd ever be able to walk freely in Northern Ireland again after touting on the IRA? I was a fucking idiot. Patting icy water on my neck and wrists, I tried to calm down. At least I could thank Clancy for making the situation abundantly clear to me, reminding me I wasn't here to play happy families with Séan. I found some change and made my way out to the phone box on the Falls. I didn't care if anyone saw me. I'd say I felt nervous on my own and was trying to contact Séan. To cover my story I'd call Liam or Declan to ask them about Séan's whereabouts.

Dialing the check in number first, I pushed my coin in when the beeps sounded. "It's Banshee."

"Archangel." Expecting Chalki I was taken aback to hear Mike's voice. "You all right?"

To my fury I wanted to burst into childish tears. "No, I'm not." I forced myself to stay calm. "I need to know if Clancy O'Neill works for us." Rotating my neck I kept vigilance on the street outside.

"Did he tell you he did?"

There wasn't time for his usual evasions. "Just answer me."

He paused. "Not that I know of. Brought him in a couple of times when he was covering for his brothers and he sang like a canary."

"What does that mean?"

"Told us everything he knew to get out of trouble, but he wasn't recruitment material. What's going on?"

"That's all I need."

"Do you want him brought in?" he asked.

I gripped the receiver tightly. "Absolutely not. I'll deal with it. I don't want you anywhere near here."

"Listen to me. You need to abort. You're done."

"I'm not. Nowhere near. And no, before you accuse me again, I haven't gone native."

He breathed in sharply. "But you've done what was asked of you. A fact-finding mission, remember?"

"I haven't all the facts, yet."

"Come on, I could have you removed forcibly."

I scoffed. "Right, you try that. But you'll have to come through Brian Sutherland and the entire Lower Falls 'RA Battalion to do so. Don't think you want to do that, do you?" I waited but he didn't answer. "And you're putting me in danger by keeping me on this phone. Next time I want to talk to someone else who isn't personally involved. Leave me alone. Let me do my job!" I hung up. Feeling dizzy I leaned forward and pressed my hot forehead against one of the cold panes of glass. What a mess. I gathered myself and slammed out of the phone box. Only when I'd reached the corner of Ivie Street did I remember I hadn't covered myself by making a call to Liam or Declan.

⌘

Our next gig was in the Millbrook Lodge in Ballynahinch the next Saturday. I faced the same kind of angst about playing in there as I had at the Students' Union. It was close enough to Newcastle that someone I knew might be there. When Clancy showed up my stress level doubled. Why hadn't I let Mike take him into custody? But if I had, suspicion would undoubtedly have fallen on me for reporting him. For all I knew, Clancy's story might have been some kind of sick test by Sutherland to see if my loyalties were sound.

Séan introduced Clancy to the others, who was all hail-fellow-well-met, joking and fitting in with the lads as though he'd always been their roadie. Then Séan introduced him to me as though we'd never met.

"Great to meet you," Clancy said with a guarded smile.

I looked him in the eye. Wish there was some way I could dissuade him from this. Still, what was that saying - keep your friends close and your enemies closer? "Welcome aboard."

During the break while Séan was at the bar I took Clancy aside. "How's the undercover work, these days?"

He flushed. "Shut up."

"Checked in and told them we've made contact, yet? What they say?"

"Shut the fuck up. Forget I ever told you that."

"So, you made the whole thing up?"

"I should never have brought it up."

"Why did you?"

"Look, you need to stay away from Séan Maguire. He's dangerous."

"You pose more of a danger to me than him."

"You don't understand what he's like."

I frowned. "How long have you known him, Clancy?"

"Long enough."

I saw Séan lift the pints of beer from the counter and make tracks toward us. "Why do you think he's dangerous?" I asked.

"Isn't it bloody obvious?"

"This something the The Det told you?"

He blanched. "What?"

"14 Intelligence Company, I believe it's called. Isn't that who you work for?"

Séan arrived on the tail end of it. "You found some work?" he asked Clancy as he handed me one of the pints.

Clancy's Adam's apple bobbed up and down. "Applying around."

"Best thing," agreed Séan. "Ya won't make a living as a roadie. What ya lookin' for?"

"Anything that pays."

Séan's face lit up. "Why don't ya talk to Brian?"

"That's a good idea," I agreed with enthusiasm. "Why don't you talk to Brian, Clancy? Oh, wait," I added. "You already did that, didn't you?"

"Ach, Fen," said Séan quietly. "Clancy's sorry he did that, aren't ya, mate?"

Clancy looked into my eyes in desperation. "I am. I really am, *Fionnuir*."

"Why don't you's shake and make up?" suggested Séan.

I forced a smile that I knew couldn't possibly reach my eyes and held out a hand. Clancy took it, his palm damp and clammy, fingers like they had no bones.

Séan clapped him on the back. "There now! Prodigal back in the fold again!"

He led me out of Clancy's earshot. "Thought it best if you two made a fresh start, y'know. The others don't need to know about what happened, like."

"Why him, Séan? I mean, why hire him of all people when you know what he did to me?"

Something flickered in his amber eyes. "I know he was a wee shit to say what he did and get you hurt, darlin'. But he had our best interests at heart, y'know."

"Not my best interests, he didn't."

"Well, no - but now he will. Now that yer one of us."

"One of the band?"

He gave me a curious look. "What else?"

I laughed, attempting to cover my blunder. "Yeah, of course. I just wish you'd hired someone else. He gives me the creeps."

"Give him a chance, Fionnuir."

Didn't have much of a choice, did I?

⌘

We had an afternoon recital at St. Malachy's Youth Club that weekend. I liked the traditional gigs. It meant we didn't need a roadie for our equipment so there wasn't the stress of having Paddy or Clancy about. Today had been a sort of 'show and tell' session, where we explained how the instruments worked and encouraged whoever was interested to come up and give it a try.

My nerves nearly failed me when a beefy tough-looking girl grabbed my bow and violin. She treated them like they were a fishing rod and bait about to be cast out into a raging river. That violin had been made by the McCall's in Aberdeen in Scotland, whom my mother claimed were relatives. The bow didn't matter but the violin itself was irreplaceable. I hovered close, ready to snatch them back.

Séan noticed my concern. "Why don't ya sit down, pet?" He pushed a chair into the back of her knees.

I relaxed a bit as she sat. The violin had less distance to fall if she dropped it. Séan caught my eye and winked, making me smile.

The priest descended on us when we were packing up our instruments. I always felt awkward around priests, particularly since I'd seen *The Omen* with Dee when it came out. I had an irrational notion that priests were extra-specially intuitive and could see right through me and recognize me as a fraud.

"Thinking of having an Irish dance evening," he said to Séan, his soft accent sounding like he came from Donegal. "Would you be up to that?"

That sounded like fun. It'd probably be like the *céildh* in Ballyben but without the terrorists.

The others were ready to go and stood impatiently by the door.

"Go you's on," Séan said. "I'll pay you's tomorrow, okay?" He put an arm around the priest's shoulders and they headed toward a little office in back.

"Pint?" asked Declan as we went outside.

I was tempted but I needed to make my check in call. And while I was in downtown Belfast I might as well pop into Boots the big chemist and get some makeup and stuff I needed. I just had half an hour before the shops closed and the center of Belfast shut down for the night.

"Thanks, but need to go shopping. Want to come?"

He looked like I'd asked if I could crap on his head. "Yer all right, love. We'll be in Kelly's if you change yer mind."

Getting the violin through the security gate to the city center was quite a challenge. The guy searching me made me open the case and strum the strings before he lifted it to peer into the f-holes. I cringed when he shook it. With only twenty minutes left to shop, I rushed into Boots only to have to open the case again for their security people. I got what I wanted and queued up to pay. I considered heading to Kelly's Cellars to join the lads, but I really needed to get that call made.

Navigating the revolving security gate to exit the city center, I waited at the curb to cross the road. I could use one of the public phone boxes over there before catching a bus back up the Falls. A familiar figure strode along in front of the City Hall, sans guitar. "Séan!" I called, but the traffic drowned me out. I'd say one thing for him, with his distinctive hair and long leather coat flapping behind him, he'd never be any good at incognito. It looked like he was heading down to where he could hail a taxi up the Falls. If I hurried I could intercept him and we could go together. I took off after him. As I closed the distance between us, I was surprised when he turned left up Great Victoria Street, opposite to where I thought he was going. He crossed over the road at the Europa Hotel and disappeared into their wooden security hut.

The Europa was totally cordoned off with the only public entrance through that hut, where all bags, people, and possessions were treated to intense scrutiny. I'm not certain how many times the hotel had been attacked by now, holding the record as the most bombed building in the world. Yet still it stood, impressive and towering, even if most of the ground floor windows were boarded up for protection.

It wasn't the kind of place Séan would usually go to. Particularly when the rest of the guys were in the more Nationalist-friendly Kelly's. Curiosity got the better of me and I approached the hut where Europa security did not like my violin case any more than the city ones had. They took the case apart, even pulling up the velvet lining to inspect underneath. Satisfied that it really and truly was just a musical instrument they reluctantly let me go through, after making me empty my bag for inspection as well. A short walk from the hut to the hotel's front doors, I strolled as nonchalantly as I could.

Luck was on my side. Once inside I saw Séan with his back to me in the lounge off the lobby to the left. He rested his elbows on the bar as he chatted with the mustached and bow-tied bartender. There wasn't anywhere to conceal myself in the bar to watch, so I walked across the carpeted lobby. Several plush chairs were grouped around wooden coffee tables there. I grabbed the only free one, with its back toward the bar entrance. I felt very conspicuous. The other people sitting around were chatting and enjoying a smoke and a drink. I was the only one on my own. I couldn't sit here and keep looking over my shoulder at the bar - talk about suspicious activity. *I'd* end up being arrested. Remembering an old World War II spy film I'd seen, I dug around in my bag and found my powder compact. One of Mum's old ones, actually. Diamanté stars glittered on the front casing, the gilt worn bare in places with use. An image of Mum dabbing at her face with the little sponge hit me with a jolt. My hand trembled as I did the same, using a piece of cotton wool as the sponge had been lost long ago.

It gave me something to do and I took my time, powdering my tension-moist face into submission. Trying to be subtle, I held the compact so I could look in the mirror over my shoulder like in the spy film. I was sure I looked ridiculous, but astonishingly no one appeared to notice. I periodically poked at my eyebrows or at some imagined smudge on my cheek, and must have reapplied lip gloss about fifty times in the ten minutes I sat there. I was just about to give up when the front doors rattled and someone I knew well stepped into the lobby.

Clancy.

Head down he went straight for the bar. Heart pounding, I clapped the compact shut and dropped it into my bag. What the hell was he doing here? I noticed the people across from me eying me, so I forced myself to relax. I gave it a minute, counting in my head, and then got up. Moving slowly I strolled across the lobby and glanced into the bar. Clancy and Séan sat at one of the tables, heads close together, then both burst into rowdy laughter. Neither spotted me, and I decided to quit while I was ahead. I hurried out and back through the security hut.

I didn't think the conversation had been about me. But I could be wrong. Surely Clancy wouldn't dare say anything more about me - he had too much to lose if his homosexuality was exposed to everyone.

28

Rogue

I had the taxi drop me at the house on Ivie Street. It wasn't until I'd unlocked the door that I remembered my check in call. It couldn't wait. Dumping the violin and bag, I headed straight out to the phone box on the Falls. The telephone company was due to install a phone in the house on Monday, so this would be the last time I could use the call box without raising suspicion.

I pushed in my coins, fervently hoping that I wouldn't get Mike. "This is Banshee."

"Aboot bloody time, girlie!" boomed a voice. I had to jerk the receiver away from my ear.

"Tetley?"

"I *beg* your pardon?!"

I winced. I shouldn't have used his nickname - *any* name to identify him. "I didn't expect you, Sir."

"Aye, no doubt ye didn't. First things first - anything tae report?"

I opened my mouth to say I'd seen Clancy meeting with Séan. But I didn't yet know why and I was afraid that they might insist in bringing Clancy in, which would expose me as the obvious tout. Thanks to Mike and all his lies I couldn't trust them to keep me safe. "No Sir. I'm just watching and biding my time - and doing gigs around the Province." I'd have to watch using that word; only Protestants called Northern Ireland that.

"Anything on Maguire, yet?"

"Nothing. But Sutherland is planning something really big for the band. I'm convinced he wants to use us as a cover for something else. Still working on finding out what."

He cleared his throat. "All right, girlie, enough's enough. Ye've done the job and ye've done it well. Time to get oot of there."

Mike must have sicced him on me. "I can't!"

"Ye can, and ye will. A convoy's on its way doon the Falls as we speak. Just stay where ye are. They're goin' tae arrest ye and get ye safely out of there."

Panic flooded me. I couldn't go yet! Not without finding out what Sutherland was plotting. And a second unbidden thought ran parallel: if I left now I wouldn't see Séan again. The thought terrified me. Proof that I had become emotionally involved like Mike had accused me of. "Sir, you're not on the spot like I am. I have to finish what I started."

"Not your call."

In the distance I imagined I heard the distant thunder of military vehicles approaching. If I didn't do something fast everything would be lost. "Sir, there's no other way," I found myself saying. "I'm so, so sorry."

I heard him bellow, *"Hamilton!"* as I set the receiver down in its cradle. I jerked back my hand as though I'd been burned. What in the name of all that's holy had I just done?

Thrusting my way out of the phone box, in blind panic I dashed across the road and ran all the way back to Ivie Street. A beam like a searchlight flooded the pavement as a door opened. Eileen waylaid me on her doorstep.

"You in any trouble, pet?"

"No!" I answered too quickly, panting for breath.

She gave me a shrewd look. "Come in for a cuppa. You look like ye could use one."

I hesitated. I wanted to run to my house and hide. But if the army convoy came looking for me, what was to stop them kicking in the door again and forcibly taking me out of there? I hurried inside Eileen's and she shut the door. At the kitchen table I surreptitiously used my cuffs to wipe at the sweat beading my forehead.

"You're in a safe house here, love, don't you worry."

I opened my mouth to protest, but a safe house was exactly what I needed right now.

She left me to gather my breath, busying herself preparing the tea and spiriting a plethora of biscuits and cakes onto the table. The enormity of what I'd just done horrified me.

The soles of my feet registered vibration. In these tiny terraced dwellings anything out on the street reverberated right through the floorboards. The unmistakable roar of Land Rover engines approached - my heart went into overdrive. Eileen turned to me and put a finger to her lips. Snapping off the light she jerked the flowered drapes aside. I joined her at the window and side by side we peered out through the lace privacy curtain. Two Land Rovers rumbled by and slowed outside my unlit house. The door hadn't been repaired from their last visit - would they kick it in again? But they didn't stop. The vibration and noise diminished and eventually evaporated as they drove out of sight. I breathed a little easier, but now explanations would be necessary.

"Eileen," I began.

She held up a hand. "You don't need to say nothing, love. As I told ya, this is a safe house. You're always welcome here."

She obviously thought I was involved in some nefarious IRA activity with Brian Sutherland. Not an unreasonable assumption, under the circumstances.

⌘

Séan came bouncing to my door early the next morning. Groggy with too little sleep, I shrugged into my satin gown and went downstairs to let him in. He carried a guitar case in each hand and put one down to thrust an Ormeau Bakery bag into my hands. "Croissants! You'll need to heat 'em up."

"I need to get you a key," I mumbled, trying to wake up properly.

"I've got one." He dug in his jeans pocket. "Here." He produced a shiny new key.

I snapped wide awake. "How long have you had that?"

"All along. Never wanted to barge in on you, like."

Well, that was something, I suppose. At least he didn't use a squad of booted soldiers to kick the door in. Which I had fully expected to have happen at any moment during the night. But the Land Rovers never returned.

Just in case they had I'd taken Mike's poesy ring from my bedside drawer and slipped it back on my finger. If he showed up I could give it back. Hurl it in his face like I wanted to.

I nervously fiddled with it, turning it round and round my finger as I followed Séan into the kitchen. I wanted to demand why he and Clancy had met in the Europa but I couldn't without giving away my spying. "What are you doing up and about so early?" I asked instead.

He shrugged. "Work stuff. You know."

"What work stuff?"

Annoyance flickered across his face. "Band stuff."

"Oh, okay." I concentrated on making the tea. Better not push him.

"Brian's got us a brilliant gig," he continued, relaxing when I didn't insist. "Fuckin' best one yet."

"Where?"

"Portrush!"

I blinked. Just up the road from Dunluce Castle. I hadn't seen it since - before everything went wrong. "When?"

"What is this, the fuckin' Spanish Inquisition? Next weekend. Friday and Saturday."

It didn't take much for his mood to change. I ignored that he'd snapped my head off. "I love the north coast. You ever been to Dunluce Castle up there?"

"Aye, back when I was a kid. Want to go?"

"If we've time, yeah."

His disposition shifted yet again and he smiled, pulling me into an embrace. "Then we will. Anything you want, darlin'."

We took our breakfast through to the living room and sat in our usual places on the sofa. The croissants tasted wonderfully sweet and buttery.

"Go on," he teased. "Ask me again why I'm here so early."

God, I couldn't keep up, he was so mercurial. "Okay, why are you here so early?"

"For Brian."

"What'd he want?"

"Just pickin' something up for him."

I hesitated. Did I dare ask what? I didn't want to piss him off again. I nodded at the guitar cases by the door. "A guitar?"

"No, an AK 47."

"*What?*"

He laughed. "I'm kidding, darlin', you're so gullible. Yes, a guitar. For you." Getting up he brought over the cases. "The fiddle's great and all for the traditional stuff but doesn't work with the modern songs, like."

He unlatched one of the cases to reveal a honey-colored Fender Stratacoustic inside. "Séan, you don't seriously think I could play guitar on stage?"

His eyes darkened. "What is it with you, Fen? Why does everything have to be so fuckin' complicated? All right, if you don't want to pull yer weight, don't. I'll get someone else in who can, at extra cost just for you, 'cos you can't be bothered."

I gaped incredulously. "That's ridiculous, Séan. Of course I'll pull my weight, I'm just not very polished at the guitar." I reached out and he put the instrument into my hands. Resting it on my lap, I let my left hand run along the neck and fingered a couple of chords with my right. "A Fender," I marveled.

My awe appeased him. "Ach, I haggled it cheap from one of the boys at Buggie Baird's." To my blank look, he added, "Harry Baird's shop, ya know? In Belfast? The *only* decent place to get amps and band shit?"

He needn't be so bloody sarcastic, but I kept my thoughts to myself as I strummed a couple of chords.

"That's good, Fen. You'll be fine. All ya need are the set of chords we use. I'll show you. We need to practice a lot of duets, you and me, anyway."

I went upstairs to shower and dress while he got out his electric Fender and made a list of songs he wanted to work on. He'd stored a spare amp in the cupboard under the stairs and got it hooked up. I'm sure the neighbors on either side were fit to be tied by the time we'd worked through a morass of songs, including *Shooting Star* by Dollar, *Don't Go Breaking My Heart* by Elton John and Kiki Dee, and *Summer Nights* by John Travolta and Olivia Newton-John. The last one, I couldn't help thinking about Clancy again, remembering what a crush he had on Travolta.

⌘

Early Friday morning we headed north up the M2 in the van with Paddy at the wheel. I never thought I'd be happy to see him, but if we had to have a roadie I preferred his taciturn company to the strain of having Clancy around. It was a bright, glorious day, what we called, 'exam weather'. While students were stuck doing their O and A Levels, the summer always seemed to peak early. I remember finding it hard to concentrate when everyone else was outside enjoying the sun.

The lads were ecstatic to be heading out of the city. Even Paddy looked more cheerful than usual. It felt like we were going off on a summer holiday rather than working a weekend gig. I also was very glad to get away from Belfast. Ever since I'd hung up on Tetley, I'd been expecting to be snatched off the street and bundled into the back of a Land Rover. I'd purposefully made sure never to be alone. If I had to go out I angled it so Séan accompanied me, and I'd encouraged him to move temporarily into the house while we rehearsed for Portrush.

When we got the first glimpse of the Atlantic Ocean sparkling in the sunlit afternoon, the vast hazy horizon reminded me of when I parascended high over Ballykinlar. I'd sworn to hold onto that moment of joy and freedom no matter how bad things got. The feeling came flooding back now. I wished with all my heart I could go up again - leave the earth behind for just a little while and get a few moments of perspective.

Paddy pulled the van up outside a Bed and Breakfast called 'The Clarendon' on Bath Street, which overlooked the sea. Séan and I had a room on the third floor at the front with an ocean view. Declan, Liam, and Kieran were crowded into one room on the floor below, with both a double and single bed crammed into it. They had a view of a dumpster in the back courtyard.

Kieran narrowed eyes filled with loathing at me. "I used to share with Séan until you came along."

Whiny little git. I retorted, "Oh, so you had sex with him, too?" The others guffawed and Kieran went white, the look in his eyes turning murderous. He grabbed his jacket and slammed out of the room.

"What is his problem?" I asked Séan.

He shrugged. "Don't take it personal, like. He never got along with any of my girls."

Girls, as in plural, I noted.

"He's just jealous," said Liam.

Declan laughed. "Yeah, doesn't like to share."

"Ooh, Séan, I'm free!" cooed Liam, John Inman style, waving a limp wrist at Declan.

I felt Séan tense. "Lay off, guys. That's not fuckin' funny."

Liam dropped the act at once. "Ach, we're only coddin'."

"I wouldn't let no fuckin' fag near me. I'd kill him first."

Oh, Jesus. And Clancy wanted to be our official roadie? Séan would murder him if he knew.

Ever mercurial, he turned to me with a grin. "You want to see your castle we'd better go now. No time tomorrow or Sunday."

My heart lifted. I noticed Liam and Declan didn't ask to accompany us, although I wouldn't have minded having them as a buffer for Séan's mood swings. Séan unlocked the van and I scrambled onto the front bench seat.

"Where did Paddy go?" I asked.

Séan started the van, did a three point turn, and drove past a church onto Main Street. He mustn't have heard me.

"Séan, where's Paddy?" I asked again.

"Ach. Business," he said vaguely.

"What kind?"

"Look, I don't fuckin' know, okay?"

I was getting just a bit fed up with him. "There's no need to snap my bloody head off."

He glared, taking his eyes off the road. "What'd ya say?" We drew dangerously close to the bumper of the car in front.

"Watch the road," I warned.

Séan clamped his foot on the brake and swerved the van to a stop. "Don't you fuckin' tell me what to do, Fionnuir. And stop asking me questions. You're pissing me off."

Chauvinistic bastard. A leftover relic from another century. I just stopped myself from slamming out of the van in a temper. If I alienated him, then everything I'd done so far would be for nothing. A car horn blasted from behind but Séan kept staring at me, waiting for my response.

I swallowed back my anger. "Okay, I'm sorry. Didn't mean to–" What? What word should I use? "*Disrespect* you." Even though he was the one doing the disrespecting.

The hard expression left his face and he put the van in gear, driving onto the coast road. I fumed but hid it, keeping my face turned away as I looked out unseeing over the Atlantic. He could be a complete prick, but then so kind and considerate the rest of the time. I gave myself a mental shake. I was getting in way too deep. Not exactly experienced in the relationship department, I only had Mike to compare him with. Not a very effective barometer.

We passed a signpost pointing to the town of Bushmills. If he'd been in a better mood I'd have suggested a visit to the whiskey distillery. Except, of course, he'd probably only want to tour Jameson's. I should have taken Mike there - maybe have convinced him how much nicer it was than his ghastly Bourbon. *Fuck!* There I went, thinking about him again.

We approached Dunluce from the opposite side from when Mike and I had come so the view wasn't quite so dramatic. But as always, the jagged beauty of the ruins struck me. Séan parked and switched off the engine. I moved to open the sliding door and his hand closed over my wrist.

"I'm sorry, Fen. I don't mean to be a bastard. 'Specially not to you. Forgive me?"

He was absolutely sincere, I could see that. Considering my situation I didn't have much of a choice but to forgive him. "Nothing to forgive."

He smiled and pulled me to him, kissing me so tenderly it was hard to remember why I was angry in the first place. He held my hand as we strolled toward the castle. Try as I might, I couldn't help but think about the day Mike and I had come here. Our first date. I'd been so happy, so full of hope. My only worries then had been that he was a British Army soldier and that we could both get in trouble for being together. Tame compared to my current problems.

But that day Mike had grilled me about Dee's brother's traditional band. That must have been when he first thought of me as a potential recruit. Sadness engulfed me. The whole thing had been a lie, from beginning to end.

Séan and I wandered through the clumps of tourists until we reached the edge of the castle where the kitchens had fallen into the sea. Digging in his pocket he pulled out a cigarette and waggled it at me, pretending to ask permission. I nodded and he strolled off downwind. I perched on what was left of a thick windowsill and basked in the sun, looking out to sea. Far below was where Mike and I had had our champagne picnic. I thought back to how he had reclined elegantly on the rug beside me, looking so handsome he'd rendered me speechless.

The sun's heat was soporific, I must have fallen into a doze. Séan leapt onto the windowsill, making me jump as he whooped out a melodramatic stage cackle. Raising his arms he grasped the hem of his coat so he looked like a great winged vampire bat. He swooped and bit my neck, pretending to suck my blood. His teeth grazing just below my ear gave me the shivers and I giggled. Making a sign of the cross with my fingers, I tried to ward him off. He held fast and we ended up in a mirth-filled heap on the grass. People glanced over at us, some disapproving and others amused.

⌘

The Londonderry Arms Hotel was minutes away as the crow flies from the Bed and Breakfast. But with the one-way traffic system in Portrush, we had to take a convoluted path to get to the front door to unload the van.

Paddy still hadn't put in an appearance and I didn't dare ask about him. None of the others mentioned him either, so it looked like we were on our own to set up. It was to be a strictly non-traditional evening. Just popular stuff that people could dance to. With a pro-British name like '*London*derry' I wasn't surprised. The assistant manager, a man in his early twenties greeted us. He looked a bit untrustworthy, with an affected Elvis-type sneer, and wore a shiny dark green suit.

"It's the first of the summer holiday-maker crowd in town this weekend, so I want you to keep to cheerful stuff that people will want to dance to."

"Got it covered, Mr. Campbell," Séan assured him.

"Just Adrian," he said with an oily smile and left us to it.

"Fuckin' fag," murmured Séan.

Kieran sniffed. "Better not bend over in front of him, lads."

They laughed boisterously and I was glad Clancy wasn't around to hear their ignorant remarks.

⌘

Séan and I stood close together on stage, a microphone on a stand between us. I strummed the guitar as we harmonized: '*If I had words to make a day for you—*'

I almost believed the words as we gazed at each other. I really did feel in love with him when we sang together like this. There was something so intimate and magical about it, as though we were the only two people in the world.

When Séan took center stage to sing *Darlin* by Frankie Miller, the usual would-be groupies congregated, gazing with pleading adoration at him. 'Darlin' was what Séan always called me, so every time he sang the word he'd look round and wink. The groupies shot me death-threat glares, and it gave me a perverse kick to know that I, not any of them would 'score' him tonight.

I boggled as one of them yanked down her lacy red panties in full view of everyone and unsteadily stepped out of them. After an animated conversation with her mortified-looking friend, she came up with a pen and scrawled something on the underwear. Raising them over her head, she snapped them like a slingshot as hard as she could at Séan. They caught on the head of his guitar, hanging flag-like from one of the tuning keys. He waggled the guitar back and forth like he was signaling with semaphore, then removed the underwear between finger and thumb and tossed them over his shoulder. The girl flushed and scowled at me as though it were my fault.

Of late I'd been getting a few male admirers of my own. When we took a break after the first set, a blond-haired guy came up to talk to me, presenting me with a colorful blue frothy cocktail. Séan always accepted any drinks his groupies gave him, so I gladly took it.

"Thank you."

"Not at all," he said with a grin and lifted his beer glass in salute. "So, what's your name?"

"Fen." With this being a British bar I was leery of giving him the full Irish pronunciation.

"I'm Malcolm. What you doing after the dance?"

Séan materialized. "Fuck off, mate. She's with me."

Malcolm's smile vanished. Without another word he peeled away and disappeared into the crowd. I turned to give Séan a challenging look. "I can take care of myself, you know."

He planted a kiss on my lips and grabbed my bottom with both hands, squeezing our hips together. "You're mine, darlin'. I don't want no one messing with you."

His possessiveness made me uncomfortable, but sort of exciting at the same time.

Toward the end of the second set, the manager fought his way to the stage and waited for us to finish before speaking quietly to Séan. Putting down his guitar, Séan mouthed 'phone call' to us, holding his hand up with thumb and finger stretched, and followed the manager out to the lobby.

Phone call - here? The others looked as disconcerted as me. We'd never received one at a gig before.

"Hope it's not bad news," I said to Liam as we trouped over to the table we'd claimed earlier. A healthy variety of pints and shots awaited.

"Hope not," he agreed.

They all lit up cigarettes, so I pushed my chair back a little, for all the good it did, the entire bar already being thick with smoke.

Séan returned and I searched his face for clues. He marched up to the table grinning like a Cheshire cat.

"So, who was it?" interrogated Liam.

"Brian."

"What'd he want?" demanded Declan, when the rest of us sat in mummified dread.

Séan laughed. "Look at you's, expecting the worst. Well, that was the best news ever." He produced a glossy brochure from his inside pocket. "Get that lot moved." We shifted the drinks out of the way and he spread the brochure out on the table. A tourist map of Edinburgh Castle in Scotland.

Liam slapped his palm on the table. "No fuckin' way! This what I think it is?"

Séan laughed. "Sure is."

I looked round at the others. "For fuck's sake, Séan, what is it?"

"We're *only* representing Northern Ireland at the Edinburgh Festival, darlin'. One of four bands at the opening ceremonies."

We sat in stunned silence for a second, then exploded into whoops and cheers. My mind whirled as I tried to grasp the significance of this.

"Fuckin' brilliant, isn't it?" I realized Declan held his pint toward me, waiting to clink glasses.

"Bloody fantastic!" I agreed. Beer spilled onto the map as we all knocked our drinks together, even Kieran.

"Who else is bein' represented?" asked Liam.

"Scotland, Wales, and fuckin' England, of course." Séan wiped the spillage away and we leaned in to pore over the map.

"What about the Free State?" demanded Kieran with a sniff.

Declan cuffed the back of his head. "Since when were we part of de United Kingdom, ya daft fucker?"

Séan leveled him with a look. "Not since the sixth of December, 1922, mate."

Kieran grinned. With a knowing look at Séan he pulled a permanent marker pen out of his pocket. Leaning over the map he scribbled out the word 'Royal' from the Royal Mile that led up to the Esplanade at the front of Edinburgh Castle.

"Quit that, Kier." Séan yanked the map off the table and began folding it up.

Kieran brandished the pen like it was an Arab Jambiya and snatched the coasters from under our drinks. One by one he frantically scored out the 'London' from 'Londonderry Arms Hotel' on them as we watched, dumbfounded. I noticed a man in a Lacoste polo shirt, sitting on a bar stool close by, glaring belligerently. "Stop it, Kieran," I hissed.

"Fuck off, it's *Derry*. We don't want no part of London." He grabbed hold of the bar menu in the center of the table and scribbled out the 'London' on that, too.

'Lacoste' lunged over from the bar and there was a flurry as he snatched the pen from Kieran's grasp. "You got a fuckin' problem?" he demanded, words slurring.

"Go fuck yerself."

Lacoste, unsteady on his feet, jabbed his finger against Kieran's concave chest. "We don't want no fuckin' Taigs in here, ya Fenian bastard."

Oh shit.

In the blink of an eye, Séan grabbed the pointing finger, bending it way back. Lacoste cried out, twisting his body to go with the finger. As one, Kieran, Liam, and Declan snatched up their drinks, jumped up from their stools and backed away from the table. I followed their lead. We'd become the focus of attention in the entire bar.

With a monumental effort Lacoste freed his finger and slashed a fist at Séan, who easily blocked it. I watched aghast as Séan followed through, thwacking a neat left hook in return. The crack of flesh and bone smashing together made me cringe. Blood spattered and a bloody tooth plopped onto the table.

Lacoste stared stupidly at it. When it dawned on him that it was his tooth, he clapped a hand to his mouth. "Fucking IRA Fenian cunt!" he spat from behind his fingers.

We all stared in dread at Séan. He went very still, his facial muscles tight, pupils dilated. "What did you call me?" he asked quietly.

"Jesus, fuck," I heard Liam mutter.

"A fuckin' IRA Fenian cunt, you fuckin' cunt!" Lacoste lisped wetly.

Séan smiled. "That's what I thought you said." As fast and deadly as a grizzly bear's decapitating swipe he laid into Lacoste, his fists a flurry of violence.

I grabbed Liam's arm. "Do something!" Séan'd kill him at this rate.

Liam held up his hands, backing off. "Not me, love."

Lacoste went down, his arms raised as he tried to shield himself. Séan kept pummeling, obviously having no intention of stopping. If the others wouldn't do anything, I had to. I stepped forward to grab Séan's arm.

"Séan, for God's sake!"

My right eye exploded in pain like it had been hit with a hammer. Half-blinded I reeled back, realizing I'd caught the tail end of one of his punches as he drew his fist back. Completely unaware he continued his assault.

I tripped over my own feet as I staggered out of range. Someone steadied me. "Thank you," I murmured, then did a double-take. *Heather* from Finley Manor?

Almost imperceptibly she shook her head in warning and I shut up immediately.

Séan raised a booted foot and kicked the prone Lacoste hard. I cringed. He did it again, and readied for a third kick but the bouncers finally intercepted, thrusting through the crowd and grabbing hold of him. He fought them with the strength of a trapped animal, but they managed to overpower him.

The crowd parted to let the hotel manager through. "Get that psycho out of here," he ordered.

"Fuckin' nancy poofter!" yelled Séan. The bouncers dragged him, struggling and kicking toward a fire exit door to the back.

"The rest of you!" The manager pointed to us. "This way!" He headed for the lobby, followed by the others.

Heather leaned close and spoke quietly. "I'll sort this, Jen. Get out of here."

I'd have to wait to ask why she was here. She kneeled beside Lacoste, helping him to a sitting position. As I turned to go I saw her pushing the hair back off his face and inspecting the damage.

"You're done," the manager told us. "Get your stuff and get the hell out. Don't even think about coming back here tomorrow."

The bouncers returned, dragged our equipment out and dumped it on the pavement. Declan headed round to the back courtyard where he'd parked the van and brought it round. I expected Séan to be with him but he was alone. When I asked him about it he shrugged.

"No sign of him. He'll come back when he's ready, don't worry yer head." He peered at my face. "What the fuck happened to you?" I explained and he gave me a brotherly one-armed hug. "That's why we know better than to get in the way."

Kieran studied me for a moment. "It's an improvement," he said with a sniff.

Declan gave him a shove. "Ach, fuck off, ya wanker!"

We were a forlorn trio, driving the circuitous one-way system through town back to the B&B. My mind whirled. I felt shaken to my very core by Séan's unrestrained violence.

I half-expected him to be in our bedroom in the Clarendon but he wasn't. At the dressing table I inspected my eye in the mirror. It looked dreadful. Swollen and red, already closing up. I dug out the bottle of Jameson whiskey we'd brought along from Séan's bag. What I wouldn't give for a shot of good Black Bush right now. Pouring a hefty portion into one of the two glasses by the sink, I took it to the bed and sat to pull off my boots.

The doorknob rattled and Séan banged the door open, making me jump. He looked at my whiskey. "Pour me a glass."

I hesitated. I decided not to tell him to go fuck himself, but seethed as I poured Jameson into a glass for him. How dare he issue orders as though I were his dogsbody. He roamed the room like a great trapped lion with a red-gold mane. Snatching the glass from my hand, he swallowed the whiskey in one gulp, then shoved the glass back. "Get me another."

My anger bubbled over. "Don't you think you've had enough, after tonight's performance?"

His fist came from nowhere and knocked the glass clear across the room. It hit the wall by the dressing table and shattered. All the heat of his rage focused on me. Fear torrented through me but I stood my ground, choosing fight rather than flight. The defiance infuriated him and he raised an arm to backhand me.

"Don't you fucking dare," I warned, my voice low and intense.

He drew up sharply, and his eyes focused. His arm dropped and to my consternation his face crumpled like a child's. "Ach, Fen. I'm so sorry darlin' - I'd never hurt ya."

Oh yeah? What would you call what he almost just did? He reached out to take me by the shoulders. I stepped back. "Don't touch me."

Anguish distorted his face and then it became a tight, angry mask. He strode to the door and slammed out, rattling the hinges.

I shook all over. I'd never been in a violent domestic confrontation like that before. He really would have hit me if I hadn't stood up to him. Mike's words came back to me, *'What is that saying, about a wolf in sheep's clothing?'*

He'd been right all along. But I wouldn't listen.

The front door downstairs slammed, loud even from way up here on the third floor. Heart pounding, I got the room key and made sure the door was securely locked. And even though it felt like overkill, I dragged the upright wooden chair by the dressing table over and propped it tightly under the doorknob. I didn't know how effective it would be, but it made me feel better. I downed my Jameson as fast as he had and poured another. The bottle rattled against the glass as my hands shook.

Gradually I managed to calm myself and take stock of the situation. Focus on work - that's all I should do. Now that I'd found out that Sutherland had the Edinburgh Festival in his sights, I should find a phone box and call in as soon as possible. Probably right away but I couldn't face it. Tomorrow would be time enough.

The room had no heating and I couldn't tell if I shook from nerves or the cold. I switched off the overhead light and got in bed fully clothed. The mattress sagged horribly and a spring twanged under me. But despite that I obviously fell asleep right away, for when I awoke daylight filtered from behind the faded curtains. I got out of bed to go to the window. Or at least I tried to. The mattress had done a number on me - it took me a moment to stretch out and straighten up.

Drawing back the curtains, a mysterious rose-tipped sunrise bleeding into the cobalt sky beckoned. I couldn't wait to escape this stifling, antiquated room. Stripping off I had a quick wash in the sink, avoiding my reflection. I could now see out of my right eye, but no makeup in the world would cover the horrendous bruising and swelling. Changing into blue jeans and a sweater, I pulled the chair away from the door and found myself running until I was outside. Heading off to the right, I followed a narrow road that led down to a little patch of green, with a sprawling building by the shore. A white sandy beach stretched beyond, disappearing into the far horizon. Heavy winds whipped the waves into a surfer's dream, and mini whirlwinds swooshed the sand as I trailed along the shore. It was completely deserted this early, for which I was glad. Wind flung sand in my face and I fought my way for about a quarter of a mile, turning back when my eyes began to sting. I returned to the green patch and sat on a concrete wall overlooking the sea. The sun had begun to warm the stones and it was sheltered from the wind. Seagulls swooped overhead, their mournful cries perfectly matching my forlorn mood.

My thoughts returned to the night before and I wondered about Heather. What would her report on me say? I was mortified that they'd sent someone after me, and that it had been my roomie at Finley, of all people. She had always inferred that she thought me stupid. This no doubt confirmed it for her. I'm certain she overheard Séan telling us about the Edinburgh Festival, so I needed to report it myself or Mike would think I'd gone native for sure. Hopefully now they'd agree it was right for me to have stayed put, and Tetley mightn't have me shot when he eventually caught up with me. And maybe I'd be able to see the Festival through with their blessing. If that were the case I'd better patch up my differences with Séan fast, no matter how disgusted and furious I was.

As though the thought conjured him I heard the swish of leather and looked round to see Séan approach. Tension coiled within me. What would his mood be this morning? I kept my gaze riveted on the horizon as his booted feet came to a standstill. He put a leg over the wall and eased down beside me, appearing alien and incongruous like a huge raven perched there in his black leather coat. He looked like he hadn't slept all night.

He peered closely at me. "Let me see, Fen." Gripping my chin, he turned my face toward him. "Jesus Christ, I'm so sorry, darlin'. God forgive me, I didn't mean to do that."

"I know you didn't," I assured him, making an effort to placate. "But you sure meant to beat the crap out of that Prod last night."

He rested his elbows on his knees and covered his face with his hands. "It won't happen again, I promise."

"Séan, you half-killed him. You wouldn't have bloody stopped if the bouncers hadn't grabbed you."

His hands dropped and he rested them on his thighs. "I shouldn't 'a done it, I know. He insulted me - called me a fuckin' IRA Fenian cunt. I couldn't stand for that. I'm sorry, Fionnuir."

"Which one bothered you, that he called you a cunt or a Fenian? Or that he called you IRA?"

He gave a bitter laugh. "The Fenian part. I know I'm a cunt."

I laughed but noticed he didn't answer the IRA question. "So, what's wrong with being called that? Particularly a 'RA Fenian?" I sounded like Clancy as I pretended to warm to the subject. "Isn't that what Fenians are, Irish fighting passionately to free the country they love from British oppression?"

Séan brightened. "Aye, I suppose."

"So, where's the insult in that? The 'RA are the best kind of Fenians."

He reached over and took my hand. "You're the best thing ever happened to me, Fen."

I stared at my hand in his, curled within his long fingers. The possibility of him developing feelings for me never occurred to me. I'd only thought of myself, my revenge for the Percy French, not anyone else. It's the innocents like my parents, like Séan who were the ones who got hurt. I gave his hand a squeeze because I didn't know what else to do. He flinched, dropping his hold and I noticed that his knuckles looked in really worse shape than I thought, his nails filthy with black grime underneath.

He got up from the wall and held out a hand for me to take. "Let's get a proper fry-up. My stomach thinks my throat's cut." He put an arm round my shoulders as we headed up through the park toward the town center. "I knew you were mad at me about the gig, Fen, so I squared it with the Londonderry Arms manager."

"We're playing tonight after all?"

"Nah, but he's not goin' to press charges or nothin'."

I raised a teasing eyebrow. "Don't you mean the *Derry* Arms manager, Séan?"

He laughed and pulled me into an embrace, swinging me off my feet. "That's my girl."

29
Full Circle

Paddy showed up at the Clarendon after breakfast. "Mr. Sutherland wants to see you as soon as we get back," he informed Séan.

Séan responded by lighting a cigarette. "No doubt."

I searched Paddy's face, trying to work out where he'd been all night. "You missed the excitement at the gig," I fished. He made a non-committal noise and headed upstairs to wake the other lads.

In the melee of everyone packing up their stuff to put in the van, I stole away on the pretext of popping into the local newsagent's so I could check in and report Sutherland's plan. I'd seen a phone box, only minutes away up on the street above the little park where Séan and I had sat. Let's hope it worked.

I retraced my steps. Lots of people were in the park now. A tinny ice-cream van shrilled *Pop Goes the Weasel*, and every so often I heard distant shrieks from people riding the Big Dipper roller coaster in Barry's Amusement Park up the street. I passed a large group unpacking boxes and setting up trestle tables. A bulky young man spotted me and peeled away to intercept. "Hello." He turned out to be a very masculine woman.

"Hi," I replied, skirting round her.

She thrust a pamphlet at me, her arm barring my way. "You're not alone, you know. We can help. Do you want to talk to someone?"

I blinked. "No thanks."

Concern filled her blue eyes. "Look, we'll have free soup here at noon. At least come and join us for that."

She wasn't going anywhere until I responded. I took the pamphlet. "Thanks, I will."

"Hope to see you later. God bless!"

As I went on my way I looked more closely at the sign they'd set up and saw it was a Presbyterian church group, raising funds for Women's Aid. *Oh, God.* My face burned as I realized she'd thought I was an abused wife with my blackened eye. On the front of the pamphlet was printed *'Is there life after marriage?'* with a photo of a young bride in her wedding dress at a sink, looking miserably at the camera as she washed dishes, wearing rubber gloves.

The phone box had a garrulous woman in her mid-thirties talking into the receiver. I hovered outside, willing her to hurry up. Driven to desperation I leaned on the side of the box and stared daggers at her until I'd intimidated her into hanging up.

"In a hurry?" she demanded belligerently as she came out, then saw my face. "Oh, I'm sorry, dear. Go ahead. Do you need any help?"

Lost for words I held up the Women's Aid pamphlet. She nodded and went on her way. Shaking my head I crumpled the pamphlet into a pocket and picked up the receiver. Pushing in my coin at the pips I said, "Banshee."

"Have you completely lost your goddamn mind?" shouted Mike. "Archangel," he added, an obvious afterthought.

Shit, shit, shit. "Look, before you say anything else I have something concrete to report."

I heard him tapping the end of a pen on a desk surface. "Go ahead." He must have sat forward then, for I heard the chair creak. Immediately it transported me back to those big, draughty rooms at Finley.

"We're going to be one of four bands at the Edinburgh Festival opening ceremonies in August. That's the big gig Sutherland's been planning."

I heard him scribbling furiously. "You're sure?"

Nerves got the better of me. "Of course I'm fucking sure, why else would I be reporting it?" With an effort I moderated my tone. "Séan announced it last night after a phone call from Brian."

"Right." More scribbling. "Anything else?" His voice was devoid of emotion. I could almost see his dutiful military shutters coming down over his arrogant face.

"Nothing. Wait - what was Heather Baird doing in Portrush?"

"Check in when you've more." He terminated the connection.

Fucking arrogant asshole prick. I slammed down the receiver even though he couldn't hear it. So that's how it was. They didn't trust me and Heather had been sent to check up on me. If Séan hadn't completely lost it in the Londonderry Arms I might never have known she was there. I had brought this on myself, I knew that. How could they trust me after I'd hung up on Tetley and disobeyed a direct order?

Fuck it.

Before heading back through the park, I ran to the closest shop and bought some crisps and a big bag of Wine Gums, Séan's favorite candy. A poster Sellotaped to the window proclaimed the upcoming season of summer theater in Portrush. The only one I recognized was Belfast's Belvoir Players who apparently were going to do a comedy called *Sink or Slim*.

Theater made me think of Dee for the first time in a while. Had she continued with her acting career? For all I knew she could be mere streets away right now, in a touring production. I had never been back to the Lyric after *The Shadow of a Gunman*. And I'd never thought to look in the paper to see if her name was mentioned anywhere.

I added the *Belfast Telegraph* to my purchases, then changed my mind and selected the *Irish News* instead. The shopkeeper looked at me askance as I handed over my change. Resisting the urge to explain, I thanked him and hurried back to the Clarendon, avoiding making eye contact with the Women's Aid people.

The boys were smoking, waiting by the van when I showed up. Séan had packed my bag for me and had it in hand. When he saw me he rolled his eyes and thrust it in the back.

"Sorry," I said, out of breath. "Got these for the drive." I brandished the crisps and Wine Gums. Presenting the newspaper to Séan, I added, "And I know how you like to catch up on the news." I could read it after he'd finished.

Placated, he gave me a hug. "My wee darlin'."

The atmosphere as we set off on the two-hour drive back to Belfast was strained, to say the least. Declan, Liam, and even Kieran were in a snit with Séan about losing the gig and wouldn't speak to him. Who could blame them? Séan climbed onto the back bench seat beside me and apparently oblivious, not five minutes out of Portrush, promptly fell asleep. I slid the paper from his lap and unfolded it as quietly as I could. There were plenty of plays listed in Belfast, but I didn't see Dee's name anywhere. I hadn't realized how much I'd wanted to find out where she was, going against my orders once again. What if I did see her? Clancy would know how to contact her. How bad would the danger be if I asked him to? Why would it be any more perilous to see her than having Clancy know my real identity?

The arguments for and against ran like dogs chasing their tails through my mind. My head began nodding and I fought drowsiness. The temptation to rest on Séan's shoulder and fall asleep became too much to resist.

I woke to find him gently shaking me. Rubbing my gritty eyes, I sat up to find that we were already on the outskirts of Belfast. But I woke up with resolve. Like most decisions I've had difficulty coming to, it's usually how I feel about it on waking that persuades me one way or the other. I knew I was going to contact Dee as soon as I could. I justified it by deciding I could not move on in my life in any positive way until I'd put my past - at least this part of it - to rest.

⌘

It was a simple matter to get Clancy to set up a rendezvous between Dee and me. I suggested the Crown Liquor Saloon on Great Victoria Street, just across from the Europa. No one I knew frequented there and it was perfect for a semi-private meeting, with individual snugs and latching doors. She picked the time - three o'clock on Thursday afternoon.

I was a bundle of nerves as I made my way there. That Dee had agreed to meet me at all was great, but I had no idea if she were only coming to have her say at the horrible way I treated her. This was daft. I felt almost more nervous about seeing her than when I went to audition for Séan's band.

Stepping over the Italian tile mosaic of a crown at the entrance, I remembered Dee telling me the story behind it. The people who built the pub were in a mixed marriage of Protestant and Catholic. They'd argued over the Royalist name 'Crown' until the Catholic wife agreed to it, as long as a crown would be placed on the floor so that everyone would walk on it. I wasn't sure how true it was, but it made a good story. I paused for a moment to let my eyes adjust from the bright sunlight to the dim Victorian interior.

"Jen!"

My stomach lurched to hear my real name. I spotted Dee's distinctive beacon of platinum hair and made my way over to the snug at the far end of the bar. On the threshold I hesitated, unsure of myself. She stared back, her face as familiar as my own. Then her lip quirked and she pointed at the table where two shots of whiskey sat untouched. A grin spread across my face. For a second, it was as though the past few months had never happened. Closing the door I slid onto the bench opposite her. Tall walls of paneled wood with stained glass at the top made it like we were in our own private little room.

She gave a guarded smile. "I was beginnin' to think you'd gone and topped yerself, after all."

Now that I was here I couldn't find any of the words I'd rehearsed. "Almost, but not quite."

"I left my Sacred Heart picture for ya. I knew while it was there you'd be safe."

"You gone religious on me, Dee?" I asked to deflect the threatening tears.

She shook her head. "Nah. But things like - what happened - they make ya think."

I nodded.

"What happened to your eye?" she asked.

I touched a hand to my face. The shiner had faded considerably but not enough to be completely concealed with makeup.

"I got in the way of something," I answered honestly.

"Some guy's fist?"

"It was an accident."

I could see she didn't believe me. "So, there is a guy, then?"

"Yes."

"Anyone I know?"

"No." An awkward silence descended between us. I grappled for a safer subject. "How are things back home?"

Her eyes clouded. "I don't go there no more. Nothin's the same since - well, you know. I visit the farm and all, but can't stay there."

"Where do you live now?"

"Bangor. I'm working in a fab wee boutique there."

My eyebrows shot up. "What about the acting?"

"Aye, still doin' that. But it doesn't exactly pay."

I nodded. "So, what took you to Bangor?"

She grinned, her face relaxing. "Remember Gerry?"

I racked my brains. The name sounded familiar.

"He came to the *céildh*," she hinted.

I did remember. He'd spirited her off to the bar just before I'd spotted Mike.

"We're livin' together." She looked abashed. "My Mum'n Dad don't know. They'd kill me." She clapped a hand to her mouth. "I'm sorry, Jen. That wasn't very tactful."

"It's okay. I'm learning to live with the fact that Mum and Dad are gone. Really."

She put a tentative hand on my arm. "I'm so sorry."

The words came at last and I grabbed her hand. "You've nothing to be sorry for. I'm the one who's sorry. You don't know how much - I was horrible to you, I don't know why I took it out on you. Please forgive me, Dee."

She squeezed my fingers. "Ach Jen. I understand. I truly do. I'd probably have reacted the same way."

I stared, not able to take in that she'd forgiven me just like that. I'd carried such heavy guilt for so long and I hadn't needed to. "Who are you and what have you done with Deirdre?" I managed, my voice shaky.

She laughed. "What, you thought I'd rip ya a new one?"

"Yes. I deserve it. God, you're a better person than I ever could be."

"Forgiveness has to start somewhere."

My heart filled with shame. "You talking about the Troubles or you and me?"

"Both."

How right she was. Forgiveness had to begin somewhere. Suddenly I felt about fifty pounds lighter in weight.

She lifted one of the shots and held it aloft. "Fuck the Queen?"

A laugh burst from me and I found I couldn't stop. We giggled like schoolgirls without a care in the world. Through tears I eventually managed to stutter, "Fuck the Pope!"

The Bushmills tasted like nectar. I'd missed it. We ordered another, then got some sandwiches and a couple of beers from the bar.

"You ladies celebrating something special?" asked the barman.

"Yes, life!" answered Dee.

God, it was great to see the same old exuberant Dee. It really hit home just how different I was now. But rather than plunge me into gloom, I felt glad that something had remained untouched by tragedy.

The barman gave an indulgent smile. "Well, there y'are now. Life's a grand thing to celebrate. Pints are on the house."

Dee sparkled with flirtation and leaned over the counter to kiss him on the cheek. "Thank you, you sweetheart."

I wondered if I could ever be that carefree and impetuous again.

"Clancy tells me you're playin' in a traditional band?" she said back in the snug.

I nodded. How much to tell her, I wondered, without compromising my cover.

"Well, I shouldn't be surprised. You were great at Seamus's *céildh*. I just don't–" She trailed off.

"Just don't what?"

"I just never expected you to actually make a career of it, that's all."

I smiled. "Considering I'm a manky Prod?"

She chuckled. "Well - yeah."

"I always envied you being part of something, you know. I never felt like I really belonged anywhere until I joined this band."

She threw me an assessing look. "Why do you feel you belong now?"

"Well, I feel accepted - part of a community in a way I never did before."

"What community's that?"

"Irish, of course!" I answered without thinking. Her startled look brought me to my senses. Too much bloody drink. "The Irish traditional music community, that is," I amended. But it was the same as when I'd told Clancy about loving Séan. My words rang with truth.

"Where you playing next? I'd love to come."

My heart lurched. That wasn't possible. My two worlds must not collide. "I'd love that, but we're not doing anything local until after we get back from the Edinburgh Festival."

"Where?"

I explained.

"Wow!" She clinked her glass against mine. "Clancy never mentioned that! You guys must be really good."

Oh, I ached so much to share it all with her. My thoughts tumbled together - my blossoming but doomed career in the band, and about Séan. How I wished I could ask her advice about my confusion over he and Mike. And tell her how revenge for Mum and Dad was the one constant in my life that drove me to get out of bed every day - yet the conflicting and shameful desire to be part of the society whose terrorists were responsible for their deaths. Oh God. I got to my feet, turning away so she couldn't see my anguish.

"Too much beer," I explained. "Be right back." In the Ladies' I got hold of myself the usual way, splashing cold water on wrists and neck. I now saw why contact with Dee had been stupid. She was from a world I never could never be part of again. As my self-control returned, I realized she'd said that Clancy hadn't told her about the festival. Made me wonder what he *had* told her. I expect not that he claimed to be a British operative. Stupid prick. This might be a good opportunity to see if Dee knew what he was up to.

Back in the snug I remarked, "Clancy's looking well these days, isn't he?"

"Aye, from what I see of him. He's always off doing something."

"Like what?"

"Who the fuck knows? But at least he sees more of Mum. That makes her happy."

"He's spending more time at the farm?"

"So she says, anyway."

"What about Queen's?"

"Your guess is as good as mine."

Had she any idea that he was gay, I wondered. "Any new ladies on the scene?"

"His family'd be the last people he'd tell." She grinned. "What about you and him?"

Oh, if only she knew. "Never going to happen, sorry."

"Yeah, I do get that now." She shot me a crafty look. "Even if you are suddenly one of us."

A Nationalist, she meant. I ignored it. "So, if he's back in Newcastle regularly, does he hang out with Seamus - you know, at Ballyben? At *céilidhs*?"

"Aye. I think Clancy does go with him when he's visiting Mum."

Interesting. Clancy spending more time around Ballyben - and had only started coming around the Falls area. Both established IRA strongholds.

Dee looked at her watch and rolled her eyes. "I have to go, I've got rehearsal at six. The Arts Theatre. For the Belfast Festival coming up in November."

My spirits sank. Time to return to stark reality. "I can't tell you what seeing you has meant."

"To me too. Nothin's been the same since you left."

And it never would be again. We gathered our stuff and she opened up the snug door. I hesitated. I'd better not take the chance of being seen in the street with her.

"I'm not used to all this beer, I need the Ladies' again. You go on, Dee - or you'll be late for rehearsal."

"Okay." We hugged tightly and she turned to go. "Oh, Jen," she said, pausing. "Do you have a phone where you live?" I shook my head. She fumbled in her handbag and scribbled on the back of a used train ticket. "Here's mine. Call me as soon as you're back from Scotland."

I took it from her, slipping it into a pocket. "I will." Maybe after all this was over I might be able to.

⌘

That weekend Curadh was booked for Ballynahinch again - this time the White Horse Hotel. They were experimenting with a live band rather than their usual disco. Probably in competition with the Millbrook Lodge. Paddy had business elsewhere so Clancy was roadie for the night. Kieran had been away somewhere that afternoon and would meet us at the gig.

I got Clancy on his own while we were hauling the equipment into the White Horse. "Thanks for getting Dee to see me."

"Went well, then?"

"Very."

"Are we even now?"

My brow creased. "In what way?"

"We're done with everything not band-related. I don't owe you, and you don't owe me."

"Except our silence, right?"

He laughed without humor. "Obviously."

"Okay, we're even." What else was I going to say?

I followed him into the bar, which looked familiar, although I'd never been in it. These places were all beginning to look the same. The crowds were, too. Séan surprised me by grabbing me, wheeling me round and lifting me off my feet. "A horse came up to the bar and the barman says, 'Why the long face?'" He looked expectantly at me. "Get it?"

"Yes, I get it. Ha bloody ha. Put me down."

He did so. "So, why your long face, Fen?"

I didn't realize my doldrums showed that much. "Sorry, time of month."

His face reddened. "Oh. Right. Wait–" He leaned close. "Thought you were on the pill."

My turn to be embarrassed. I should have thought that lie through. "Yes, but there's a week you go off it every month." He didn't need to know that I didn't do that.

"Ya goin' to be okay?"

"Oh, yeah. Nothing a nice Harp won't solve." I'd never seen a guy blush at the mention of menstruation before. He was an only child, but he must have come across it more than once in his harem of girlfriends and groupies.

"Say no more." He went straight up to the bar and ordered a Harp, which he presented to me.

I felt the urge to toast, 'Fuck the Pope' à la Dee. Seeing her really had been a bad idea.

The evening went well. We played a good variety of popular songs, both slow and fast. The later it got the more slow ones we did, catering to the inebriated, hormone-laden who had 'pulled' and wanted to dance groin to groin. Séan was in fine voice as he sang *Just The Way You Are* by Billy Joel. That usually got the shyest couples on the floor. I wondered what it would be to be like them - to have an uncomplicated life, where coming here on a Saturday night was the highlight of the week.

I became aware that a guy in one of the pairs clinched together was watching me. He stood taller than most of the others, with slicked back dark hair and a mustache. His gaze darted away as we made eye contact. My strumming faltered but I recovered. I'd know those eyes anywhere. What the fuck was Mike doing here? Did he think I wouldn't recognize him with that ridiculous hair and mustache?

And who was he with?

Shit, Clancy might recognize him, too. I knew the little bastard would have no compunction in telling Séan he was here. On autopilot I continued playing, my gaze riveted on Mike. He gave no indication that he knew me, and I felt an angry rush of jealousy toward the blonde girl clasped in his arms.

Séan finally brought the song to a close. We had had another slow one planned but I'd be buggered if I'd watch Mike groping that girl any longer. I felt a ridiculously childish urge to start into *The Men Behind the Wire*, just to piss him off. But in this Royalist area an anti-British song would likely end in a murderous riot.

I leaned close to Séan. "I need the Ladies'," I hissed.

He looked alarmed. "Sure, darlin'. Go on." He grabbed the microphone as I slipped the strap off over my head and propped the guitar against one of the amps. "We're just gonna take a quick break, ladies'n gentlemen. We'll be back in ten minutes with more of your favorites - thank you!"

I fetched my bag from the back of the stage and climbed down to pick my way across the dance floor. Without looking at Mike I passed within inches of him and his partner. Pretending to bump into him, I dropped my bag and a clutter of items obligingly spilled onto the floor.

"Sorry." I stooped to retrieve them.

Mike hunkered down at once to help, gathering lipsticks, tissues, tampons, my powder compact, and dropping them back into the bag. His blonde partner stood over us, tapping an impatient foot encased in high-heeled open-toed shoes.

"Clancy's here," I murmured.

"Got it."

Who's the bleached-blonde slag? I wanted to add. I felt my face flame as I looked into his eyes, so I quickly straightened and slung my bag over my shoulder.

I almost collided with Séan. "Everything okay, darlin'?" he demanded, gaze leveled at Mike.

"Yes, of course. Just dropped my bag." Oh God. My heart didn't know whether to stop or go into overdrive - Mike and Séan, face to face! There was no sign that Séan recognized Mike. To my knowledge he'd never met him. Mike held Séan's gaze, maintaining a polite expression of inquiry.

"He's not botherin' ya then?" asked Séan, bristling for a fight.

Blondie stepped in. "Why would he be bothering *her*? He's with me." Her accent was local but hard to place.

I put my arms round Séan's neck and reached up to kiss him on the lips. "Thank you, my knight in shining armor, I'm fine."

"All right, then." Mollified, he backed off and returned to the stage.

I hurried past Mike and Blondie, and could feel the tension emanating from Mike's body as I passed. I was going to give holy hell about this on my next check in call.

I found the toilets out in the hallway at the top of a short flight of stairs. With only three stalls, girls constantly vied for space in front of the mirror. When I re-emerged to wash my hands I thought I recognized Mike's partner just as she left. Was she undercover with him, or a date? I hated to think of him with someone else, even though I was with Séan. The silver poesy ring glinted as I dried my hands. Did Mike notice I had it on? I ignored the ache at the back of my throat.

I wheeled at a touch on my shoulder. "Are you Fionnuir?" asked a petite girl with brown curly hair.

"Yes."

She nodded toward the door. "Your boyfriend's looking for you."

Jesus, could Mike be any less subtle? I thanked her and headed out to the hallway. But Séan waited there, smoking and leaning against the wall.

"Just makin' sure yer all right, Fen."

"It's only a period, Séan - not bubonic plague."

He pulled me into his arms. "Ach, I know, like. But I worry about you."

As he bent to kiss me I was aware of envious glares from the women passing by. He pressed against me and I felt his arousal. I pulled back. "Are you kidding me?"

He laughed, and I found myself laughing with him. "We'll go straight home after this, darlin'," he said softly. "I'll make you feel better."

The promise in his tone made my stomach flip-flop. I wondered if Mike had seen us, but when we returned to the stage, Blondie and he had gone. I couldn't help but feel hurt and resentful at the thought of her climbing onto the bike behind him and holding him close like I once had.

⌘

Clancy had been out of sight for some time. On stage I asked Séan where he was.

"Ach, he's pickin' somethin' up for me."

"At this time of night? There's nowhere open but takeaways."

"So, he's gettin' us fish and chips for later."

I gave a disbelieving laugh. "Really?"

"Yeah, really."

I let it drop, but didn't buy it. Clancy waltzed in about ten minutes before we were to wrap up. I watched Séan tip his chin questioningly at him and Clancy shook his head.

As we packed up the equipment I commented to Séan, "All the takeaways shut, then?"

His face closed up. "We can stop by somewhere on the way to Belfast."

I wondered what Clancy had not been able to pick up.

The wrap up was quick and easy. The exit door from the disco led right out to the back where we were parked. No steps or narrow spaces to negotiate, but the car park was poorly lit so Clancy backed the van up as close as he could. Kieran's Capri was parked several yards away. Over by it I spotted Séan and Kieran in a heated debate, half hidden in the shadows. The others were still bringing out stuff from the stage so I wandered to the front of the van to try and eavesdrop. The sliding door lay ajar and I leaned inside, pretending to rummage for something.

"Can't fuckin' do it tonight," whined Kieran, adding his usual annoying sniff.

"We have to, mate. Clance couldn't get it. Sure, yer already fuckin' halfway there. It'll save us a trip tomorra." Séan's voice was honeyed and persuasive. "Safer, too," he added. Safer? That got my attention. "Look, Kier, I can't go for obvious reasons. Take Clancy and just do it. You'll be back in two hours max."

Kieran sighed heavily. I heard the click of a lighter. "Suppose." Sniff.

I felt the van rock as one of the lads put something heavy in the back. Straightening, I stepped back and saw Séan hook an elbow around Kieran's neck so could rub his knuckles on his head. "I'll make it worth your while, mate."

Kieran struggled. "You fuckin' better." The glow of his cigarette spiraled as he waved his hand about. "Get the fuck off me!"

Séan let go. "Thanks, mate. I owe you one."

"Deliver to the same place?"

Séan nodded. "Aye. Back door'll be unlocked. Don't fuckin' forget to announce yerself when you open it or you'll get a bullet up your arse, like."

Holy shit. I eased back round the van, grabbed a crate of leads and plugs from the ground and lifted it in. Declan slammed the doors shut and we piled in. Liam clambered into the driving seat.

"Before you ask," said Séan, "Kieran's had a skinful so Clancy's running him back."

I pretended indifference. Liam drove through a low, impossibly narrow arch that led out of the car park and turned left, taking the Belfast Road. I glanced over my shoulder out the back window and saw Kieran turn right. Towards Newcastle.

⌘

The next morning I woke early to find myself alone in bed. I hadn't slept much. From the conversation I'd overheard between Kieran and Séan, there was no conclusion to come to other than Séan was involved in IRA activity after all. I felt ill. I'd been so certain he wasn't.

Rolling over I tried to go back to sleep, but the murmur of voices from downstairs intruded. I snapped wide awake. Who was here? Easing carefully out of bed so as not to make the boards creak, I lay with my ear to the floor. Frustratingly, the voices faded as they moved into the kitchen. The kettle clunked metallically against the sink and I heard water filling it. I crept out onto the landing and crouched at the top of the stairs, straining to hear. Their voices were drowned out by the hiss of the kettle heating up. Then the fridge thunked open and teaspoons tinkled against china.

"You didn't get all of them?" I heard Séan ask.

"Nah, just the one. They were movin' the others." Clancy's voice.

"What did Brian say?"

"He wasn't there but Paddy said no more delays. We've twenty-four hours to get the rest of them or we're up shit creek."

Get what?

"What's the fuckin' hold up, anyway?"

"The army's watching our place closely. It's all shifted over to the abandoned farm next door."

I went cold all over, hairs prickling on the back of my neck. Holy God, he must mean Mourneview! What was 'it' that had been moved there? Guns? Or bomb-making equipment, maybe. Fertilizer - readily available on farms, was a vital ingredient in HME's. The Percy French car bomb had been made with fertilizer. Had *Clancy* and his brothers had anything to do with it? Jesus Christ. A ghastly sweet taste rushed into my mouth. I scrambled up and careened into the bathroom. Slamming the door behind me I got the toilet seat up just in time.

The door clicked open and Séan came in. "Darlin'." He crouched down and gently smoothed my hair clear of my damp face. It took me back to the gig at the Students' Union where he had done that in the bathroom - just before my interrogation with Brian. The thought made me nauseous again.

"What's wrong?" he asked when I'd gained control.

"I must have drunk too much last night."

"Ya didn't drink hardly anythin', Fen." He coughed. "Could it be anything else?"

"Just a hangover."

"No, I mean, could ya be pregnant?"

I blinked. He looked eager, as though he hoped I might be. "No," I assured him. "Sure, am I not just having my period?"

"I haven't seen ya use no tampons or nothin'."

Oh, fuck. I didn't realize he had me under that detailed a scrutiny. "How do you know what I do in here on my own?" I snapped, taking the offensive.

He pulled me into an embrace. "Don't take the hump, darlin'. I just wondered."

"Sorry."

"If ya were though, I'd stand by ya, Fen. We could get married."

I forced a laugh. "I wouldn't wish that on my worst enemy," I joked, and stepped out of his embrace.

"We could, though." He looked so intense and serious.

I grabbed my toothbrush and paste. "Well, I'm not pregnant, so we don't have to." Spitting the puke taste from my mouth, I could just imagine what Tetley would have to say about me being sick on the job, and getting so deeply in with Séan - it wouldn't be pretty. I straightened to find Séan right behind me. He watched my face in the mirror as he imprisoned me in his arms again.

"I love you Fen, you know."

If any more blood could drain from my already white face it would have. He held my gaze. As though jerked by strings, I brought my arms up to grasp his forearms. "I love you too," I blurted. Then I burst into tears.

"Whist love, what's the matter?"

I turned round and sobbed against his chest. I'd opened my mouth to say how fond I was of him and how it was early days yet to talk of love. But then the words just came out. As soon as I'd said them I saw the terrible tragedy of it all. Last night he gave me reason to think he was a member of the IRA. How could I ever love a terrorist? And *his* so-called love was all based on lies and deceit. He thought I was somebody else entirely, and had trustingly offered me his heart. "I'm sorry, Séan. I'm all hormones–"

"S'all right, darlin'. I understand."

I sniffled in his arms for a while longer until I remembered that Clancy was downstairs, probably listening to every word we said. "Did I hear you talking to someone?"

"Aye, I've to do some stuff today, darlin'."

I tore off some toilet paper from the roll and blew my nose. "Need any company?"

He smiled. "Nah, you'd be bored to tears. You tuck up nice and cozy here with a hot water bottle and watch a matinee on telly. Don't go nowhere today - there's fish and chips in the fridge you can heat up for tea later."

"Where'd they come from?"

"Special delivery. I promised them, didn't I?" He planted a kiss on my minty-fresh mouth. "Not sure if I'll be back until tomarra so don't wait up."

He headed out of the bathroom, clattering down the stairs. The front door slammed and I ran to the bedroom to look out of the window. Séan strode alone to the corner, his leather coat flapping behind him. I'd be damned if I'd hang around here all day. I needed to find out what was hidden at Mourneview. Jumping in the shower, I got ready as quickly as I could, keeping an eye on the time. If I hurried I could catch a bus in twenty minutes into Belfast, just in time for the afternoon express to Newcastle.

30

Beyond the Grave

The closer I drew to Newcastle the more my stress level increased. The last time I'd taken this bus had been the day of the Percy French bomb. At Seaforde I prepared for my superstitious first sighting of Slieve Donard. If I saw it I convinced myself the entire mission was bound for success, despite the mess I'd made. There - outlined in stark majesty against the cloudless cerulean sky. I sat back and relaxed for the last few miles.

Standing outside the Newcastle bus terminus it all came back in a horrible rush: Mac's collie ears flapping outside the window of the Land Rover, Mum, Dad and me walking down to the Percy French. I plunged my arms into the backpack, crossed the road and strode down Main Street toward the bomb site. I wore a sturdy pair of walking shoes and had thrown the cold packet of fish and chips into the backpack. Even though it was July, I'd also stuffed my black quilted jacket in there, too. You never knew at the Mournes.

The rubble from both sides of the pavement had been cleared and the areas barricaded up. The gaps in the street looked eerie and macabre, like a massive gray skull missing some of its teeth. A sign on one of the fences showed plans to build some apartments on the site of the Royal Arms pub, and new shop premises where the Percy French had stood. I gripped the wiring that cordoned off where the restaurant's big plate glass window had been. The very spot where I had last seen Mum and Dad alive.

It was time I paid a visit to their graves and said goodbye properly.

With renewed purpose I carried on down Main Street, all the way along the Promenade toward the Bryansford Road. This far down the usual day-trippers thinned out. A couple of kids were trying to fly a kite on the beach. They wouldn't have much luck today without even a breeze. Even the sea looked as still as a pond. From the Bryansford Road it was a three-mile hike on winding mountain lanes to the church, and another half after that to Mourneview.

On summer days like this I'd always craved Ross's brown lemonade to quench my thirst, so stopped into a little newsagent's to buy a bottle before heading up the mountain. Dee would laugh at me, saying there was no difference between the white and brown, but I thought the latter had more taste to it.

When I reached the halfway point to the church I stopped at the eight thousand-year-old dolmen by the roadside. Three huge granite stones had balanced together for all these centuries. Called a portal tomb, apparently. When I stood close to it I felt the same kind of awe that Dunluce Castle gave me. The feeling of something otherworldly, unfathomable and watchful.

Climbing up onto the horizontal top stone as I had done so many times before, I settled down to unwrap the fish and chips. They were congealed and soggy but I didn't care. I could barely taste them, anyway. From atop here I could see a little sliver of the Irish Sea shimmering in the sunlight. I imagined myself harnessed high above under a parachute, drifting - far removed from my worries for just a little while.

The brightness cut out like someone had hit a switch. A few little patters hit my face, then rain torrented. How well I knew the weather on these mountains! With a shiver I took my coat out of the backpack, packed the lemonade and most of the fish supper back in, and jumped down from the dolmen. Slipping on my coat, I zipped it up and pulled the hood over my head. Thank goodness I'd brought it.

I saw the smoke spiraling from the Donard Presbyterian rectory chimney long before the house was in sight. Even on a July afternoon Reverend Scott needed a fire to warm that tomb of a place. I made my way along the uneven stony lane up to the graveyard, each step swamp-heavy. Now that I was here I wasn't so sure this had been a good idea. The ground had settled at the plot, enough for the polished granite headstone I'd asked Mr. Catchpull to arrange. Gold letters engraved on black, simply listing their names and dates of birth and death.

"Hello, Mum and Dad," I said softly. Not that I expected an answer. The feeling of isolation, emptiness and total loss overwhelmed me. Tears mingled with the rain - I wasn't sure I cried because they were dead or because I couldn't sense anything of them here at all.

A bark split the air and Mac came barreling toward me, tail windmilling.

I dropped to my knees in the mud and held out my arms to catch him. He skidded into me, jumping up and bouncing mucky paws on me while he licked the rain and tears from my face. I hugged him so tightly he yelped. I let go and he flopped onto the ground so I could tickle his tummy. He was obviously content and full of life. I felt a little less guilty for leaving him. With everything that had happened since the Percy French, I'd scarcely given him a thought. Poor darling Mac. I had abandoned him just when he probably needed someone the most.

The rain stopped as suddenly as it had started. My heart sank as Reverend Scott emerged from the Rectory and approached. "Hallo there!" he boomed.

Mac leapt to his feet and ran to him, flopping on his back again, and wriggled in ecstasy as Scott bent to rub his tummy. I felt exponentially better. Mac only did that with people he trusted and loved; he was much happier here than I could ever have made him.

"Hey now, old fella," said the Reverend softly, with evident affection. He looked up at me from under his gray, bushy eyebrows. I didn't see any recognition in his eyes - my new haircut, hennaed hair, and whatever makeup hadn't run in the rain apparently disguised me well.

"Welcome," he said with a smile. "Don't get many tourists this far up the mountain."

I didn't answer.

He straightened up from petting Mac and somberly gazed down at my parents' grave. "Terrible tragedy, that family. Both killed in a bombing. And the daughter–" He stooped to scratch away splotches of bird droppings from the headstone and retreated into his thoughts.

"What about her?" I prompted.

He shook his head. "Disappeared after the funeral. Suicide."

I stifled a scoff. I thought Clancy had been jesting when he said that's what everyone thought. I suppose it made sense to them. I'd stormed off in a highly emotional state from the memorial service and had never been seen nor heard of again. Only Mr. Catchpull knew I was alive and was bound by contract to keep the knowledge to himself.

But it could have turned out that way. There was that moment in the farm before the memorial service when I wanted to put Mike's pistol to my head and pull the trigger.

Scott was intent on clearing the headstone of the bird droppings and some moss down the side. I turned away and walked stealthily over the grass and out of the graveyard. I stopped on the lane when Mac caught up with me, tail wagging - hoping I'd take him for a walk like old times. I crouched down to give him one last hug.

"You're far better off here, Mac my darling. You'd hate it in Ivie Street, a good Orange Protestant doggie like yourself." My throat tightened. "I'm going to miss you." I let him go and straightened. "Go on, Mac - go home!" He gave a little whine, head on one side. Desperate to get away before I completely lost my composure and began bawling, I pulled a pretend rubber ball from my pocket and threw it over the stone fence into the graveyard. "Go get it, Macaroni-mutt!" Tail up and wagging, he bounded happily back into the graveyard.

I'm not sure that ditzy old Reverend Scott would remember I'd even been there. Shoving my way through a thin part of the hedgerow, I veered into the adjacent field that belonged to Mourneview. An oft-used secret shortcut in the past - it would save me having to pass within sight of the O'Neill farm. I let myself cry a little for Mac as I followed the bushes around the field, until I emerged on the hillside that looked down over our farm. For a moment my spirits lifted until I saw the neglect. Farmhouse boarded up, yard deserted and grass left to grow high around the walls. Dad's beloved weathercock still perched in solitary splendor atop the barn, but with no one to look and see which way the wind blew. At that moment the breeze shifted and the vane responded, moving with a harsh squeak.

That weathercock had been where it all began. I could see so clearly the sequence of events since that army helicopter uprooted it from the barn. I wouldn't have met Mike if that hadn't happened, wouldn't have had him at my apartment, so he wouldn't have walked out on me, causing me to run home to Mum and Dad to lick my wounds. Then none of us would have been at the Percy French when the bomb went off.

I stopped, knowing the folly of going down this path. All the *if onlys* in this world and beyond weren't going to bring anyone back. Skidding down the hill, I pushed through the tall, damp grass and went into the farmyard. The rain had swept away any evidence of activity, so I couldn't tell how long it had been since anyone was here. Predictably the big sliding door into the barn was heavily padlocked and chained. Heading round to the other side where it backed up against the yard wall, I took off my backpack and stowed it in the dark space between. There was a hole back here that I doubt anyone had discovered yet. Dad had never got around to replacing the broken piece of corrugated iron and had 'temporarily' affixed some tarpaulin over it about nine years ago. It had been almost as long since I'd crawled through. The edges scraped at my arms and legs as I squeezed myself into the barn.

Natural daylight filtered in from high windows and from gaps at the tops of the walls. A sharp mashy scent assaulted my nostrils. I peered through the gloom to see a still bubbling busily in the barn. Relief flooded me and a grin split my face. *Poitín!* So this was what was hidden from the authorities, not bomb-making stuff.

But as my eyes adjusted to the light my worst fears were confirmed - three metal milk churns and several bags of fertilizer lay propped up against the side of Dad's old workbench. On the bench sat an industrial sized coffee grinder. No doubt used to grind the fertilizer pellets into powder. Several gallon-sized containers marked 'diesel' sat on the shelf above the bench, and strewn on the surface of the workbench were thick protective gloves, copper wiring and tape. A clump of car and large flashlight batteries were piled on the other side of the bench on the floor.

I approached the workbench. Holy fuck. An assembled bomb, complete with fertilizer, diesel, and home-made blasting cap sat in a fourth milk churn ready to be armed. A commonly-used kitchen timer sat beside it along with a pile of paperclips.

So. This must be 'the rest' of what Clancy and Kieran were supposed to have got. *Murdering terrorist fuckers.* And Séan was in on it. He'd duped me. Completely and utterly.

I picked up the timer and twisted it around, listening to the ticking as it counted down, loud and ominous in the echoing barn. I'd deal with Séan being a terrorist later. Right now outrage that swamped me - murderous outrage that they'd fouled Mourneview with this evil stuff. As if taking Mum and Dad wasn't enough. They had to taint their memory, too.

I'd been in this fugue-like state before, but this time I had focus. As though my hands belonged to someone else, I observed them reaching for a length of copper wire attached to the device. I lifted up the timer and threaded the wire around it. Unfolding two of the paperclips, I secured them to the timer so that when it reached zero, the wire and clips would create a circuit. I felt no fear. How well my fingers knew how to do this, thanks to taking apart so many mockups at Finley.

Systematically I checked if there was a circuit to the battery, and that a thin wire filament was in place to spark off the blasting cap. Then I twisted the timer to ten minutes. I could put a lot of distance between me and Mourneview in ten minutes. But that left too large a margin for error in the unlikely event that one of Clancy's brothers might happen along and defuse it. I turned the dial to five. Two minutes to place the device and get back out through the hole, and three to get clear of the yard. More than enough time.

But Mourneview - my past, Mum and Dad, my memories of a happier life - if I did this they'd be lost forever.

What was I thinking? They already were.

I carefully nestled the timer against the home-made bomb, the ticking amplified in the cavernous space. Clambering back out through the hole, I caught my sleeve on a rough edge of corrugated iron, pulling me up short. Trying not to panic, I ripped it free, grabbed my rucksack and stumbled across the yard and out to the lane. I slowed, took a breath, and walked down the grassy hill on the house side of the property, where I'd be shielded from the blast.

The air felt unnaturally and eerily silent - not a single bird moved or chirped. My footfalls on the grass were loud and I was very aware of my breathing, in and out. I almost felt the vacuum of air before a deafening boom erupted. Sudden dry heat hit the back of my head. My heart raced but I didn't look back as I heard the crunch of debris plummeting to earth, and the roar and crackle of flames.

⌘

Back in Belfast when I got off the bus I used one of the phone boxes by the City Hall.

"Banshee."

"Archangel. Where are you?" It was Chalki, thank God.

I was sure they had a way of tracing the number, but there was no need for me to lie. "Belfast."

"You anything to do with blowing that farm sky high?"

That didn't take long. "What farm?"

"Don't mess with me, you know what farm. What are you calling for?"

"What do you mean, 'what am I calling for'? To give you a report, what else?"

"Well, pardon me, but I heard you'd gone rogue."

"Oh, for fuck's sake."

He breathed out slowly. "Did I do not my job right? I mean, did they manage to turn you?"

"Of course not!"

"So, what the fuck's going on?"

It felt like he was trying to keep me on the phone. Uneasy, I peered out through the windows. Two Land Rovers sped toward me. I dropped the receiver, leaving it clunking at the end of its wire against the wall of the booth. Shoving my way out, I merged into the throngs of people on the pavement. I didn't know if those Land Rovers were coming for me or not but I wasn't hanging around to find out.

I'd called in because I wanted to tell them about Séan's and Clancy's involvement with the IRA bomb-making equipment. And because of that I was convinced Brian Sutherland must be behind the Newcastle bombing. Upon reflection, I'm glad I didn't have a chance to. If Séan had been arrested, that would be the end of us going to the Edinburgh Festival, and I wouldn't be able to find out definitively about Sutherland. If I wanted to bring the fucker down once and for all, I needed hard evidence on him. Once I had that I'd call in, and Tetley and company could arrest me all they wanted. Shoot me, for all I cared.

It was after eight-thirty when I got back to Ivie Street. At least Séan was away tonight so I'd have some time to get my head together. I felt so bloody tired as I slipped the key in the lock. Before I could turn it the door was yanked open.

"Where the fuck have you been?" demanded Séan.

My stomach lurched and revulsion filled me. *Murdering cunt.* I gained control of myself and pushed past him.

He slammed the door so hard its hinges rattled. "Didn't I tell you not to go nowhere?"

"You weren't supposed to be here!" I hurled my backpack and coat hard at him.

He parried, knocking them to the floor. "What the fuck's got into you?"

I fought back my rage. I couldn't - *mustn't* alienate him if I wanted to see the Edinburgh Festival through. "I just don't feel well."

He grabbed something from the sofa and held it up. It took me a second to realize what it was. The Womens' Aid pamphlet I'd crumpled into my pocket up in Portrush. He'd smoothed it out. "Where'd ya get this?"

"Found it," I mumbled.

"Ya don't need to lie to me, darlin'. I knew you were gone too long to the shops that day. Ya went to talk to these battered wives people, didn't you? About me hittin' you. You know I didn't do it on purpose."

"I didn't talk to them. They were handing these out. I forgot about it." I hated him so much I wanted to pummel him to a bloody pulp and then use a blunt knife to cut out his heart while it still beat. But instead I burst into tears of fury.

"Ach Fen, don't cry, *mo ghra*. Are you sure yer not pregnant, darlin'?"

If I were I'd rip the bastard out with a blunt knife too. I shuddered, horrified. I didn't mean that. "It must be my period. I'm - sorry." The apology almost choked me. He balled the pamphlet up between his palms and dropped it into the trash can by the door, then took me by the shoulders and studied me. "Look at ya - as white as a sheet. You'd no business going out today, Fen." He turned me and propelled me toward the stairs. "Go on, get into yer gown and I'll have tea–" He peered at his wristwatch. "–*supper* ready for ya."

I dutifully climbed the stairs and heard him clanking about in the kitchen, heating something up. How could I endure the days up to the festival?

When I came down he tucked me onto the sofa with a pillow and blanket, and brought a plateful of chicken and chips and a bottle of Blue Nun from the kitchen. "Was goin' to surprise you with this earlier," he said, managing to convey a subtle tone of accusation. He switched on the television and settled down beside me, pouring us both a glass of wine. It was nine o'clock and an old black and white film called *Went The Day Well?* came on ITV. Mechanically I chewed the food but it had no taste and I could barely swallow. I washed it down liberally with mouthfuls of wine until I felt my taut muscles begin to loosen.

Séan pointed at my half-full plate. "Ya going to finish that?"

I shook my head and he claimed it, wolfing down what I'd left. He was such a contradiction. So kind and tender, yet hidden within a streak of easily roused anger and violence. Was he capable of being a terrorist? It didn't seem possible but I'd seen the evidence. How could I have been such an appalling judge of character? But then I obviously always had been, if Mike was anything to go by.

He put the plate on the floor and took hold of my ankles to raise my feet up onto his lap. My instinct was to wrench them away but let him massage my feet and calves. After a while his ministrations began to have a calming effect along with the wine. But no matter how I tried I could not get the thought of him possibly planting the Percy French bomb out of my head. I didn't see how I could carry on pretending that everything was all right with him, without losing my sanity.

I forced it from my mind and concentrated on the film. Although I hadn't been paying attention, I picked up the storyline pretty quickly. It was set in England during World War II. A village had been invaded by German paratroopers, and was betrayed by their village squire, who turned out to be a collaborator.

It struck a chord. "Fucker."

Séan gave me a sideways glance. "Why?"

I hadn't meant to speak out loud. "Well, because he's just screwed over all the people in his life - thrown them to the wolves. Maybe his family too. He's completely betrayed every last one of them."

Séan laughed. "All's fair in love and war, darlin'. He's doin' what he has to do for his country."

"He's a traitor." I couldn't seem to stop.

"Come on, Fen. You've told me outright that ye admire the 'RA for doin' what they're doin' for Ireland. What that man did was no different."

"Yeah, it was. He's opened the way for an *invasion*, not just change and reform. Look, I know it's only a bloody film, but if it were true he'd have been responsible for overthrowing the entire British Empire."

Séan's brow furrowed. "Fuck me, ye sound like a Brit. Don't let Brian hear ya talk like that."

Shit and fuck. "You know what I mean."

"No, I fuckin' don't." His voice rose in anger. "Are you telling me you wouldn't do the same as that man given half the chance? What if you and a 'RA Active Service Unit could get into somewhere like the Houses of Parliament and take it over so Sinn Féin could run the country? What's the difference?"

"The difference is a lot of innocent people are going to die." Like me and my kind if civil war did break out in Northern Ireland.

"Innocent blood has to be shed in any war. It's a legitimate action against British brutality and repression. That's just how it is."

I yanked my feet off his lap. "So, you can justify murder as long as it's for a cause?"

"Darlin', I'm not going to argue with you, given the state yer in, okay?"

I clenched my fists. "Don't you dare take the high road with me."

"What the fuck is this about, Fen?"

I had to know the truth. "I heard you and Kieran talking the other night, outside the White Horse. You told him to deliver something. I know it was bomb-making equipment."

"How d'ya know that?"

I took a gamble. "I saw it."

His pupils dilated. "At the Emerald?" I nodded, keeping my face neutral. He reached over to snap off the television and turned to face me. "Christ, Fen. Don't fer the love of God let on to Brian you did."

"So, you *are* in the IRA. You do plant bombs. You murder innocent people."

A plethora of expressions slid across his face. Fear, realization, anger, and then to my utmost surprise tears welled up and he buried his face in his hands. I watched, astounded.

"I'm glad ye found out, Fen. I didn't want there to be no secrets between us, like."

Calm descended over me - energy flowed through me as I felt in control again. "Tell me everything, Séan."

He wiped a hand across his nose and reached for his coat, which he'd laid over the back of the sofa. "I only did it for Brian 'cos he told me to. I owe him everything. He looked after me when my Ma was murdered by the Brits."

This, I already knew.

He drew out his cigarettes and lighter. "He made it plain all along I owed him, like - he swore me into the 'RA as soon as I was sixteen, even though I didn't want to have nothin' to do with it." He put a cigarette in his mouth and lit it, inhaling deeply.

I didn't make my usual objection to the smoke. "So, he forces you to plant bombs and kill people?" I managed not to sound scathing.

"No, he doesn't force me."

I studied his face, trying to read him. "So does that mean yes, you kill people or no, you don't?"

"Course not, darlin'. You know me better than that."

Did I? But he looked utterly sincere. And now I had more damning evidence on Sutherland. Séan had implicated him, what more did I need? But I wanted more. I wanted to play the festival, a chance like that would never come again. More than anything though, I wanted that evil bastard

Sutherland brought down for good. With no doubt as to his guilt.

Séan studied my face intently. I was at a loss for words so I got up and fetched the ashtray he usually took outside to the back when he smoked. I placed it on his thigh and crouched to pour more wine into his glass. So, he wasn't a killer. I didn't think he could be - but he *was* in the IRA. He mightn't have killed anyone directly, but they had.

He took my hand. "D'ye hate me, Fen?"

I sank to my knees onto the floor so I could look him in the eye. "What for? You said you never killed anyone."

"Fer lyin'."

My thoughts raced. "You did what you had to." Maybe this could work to better advantage than I ever thought possible. "So, Brian's made you be in the 'RA? You wouldn't have joined anyway?"

He took another drag of his cigarette. "No way. But once you're in, you're in for life. There's no gettin' out."

"What if you didn't live in Northern Ireland, Séan? What if you got away from here? You could be in a band anywhere."

Wonder lit his eyes. I realized the thought had never occurred to him. "Leave Northern Ireland? And go where?"

I shrugged. "Scotland? I know you'd hate England."

He reached for another cigarette. "But Brian gets us all the gigs - the good ones."

"After the Edinburgh festival you can get your own gigs, Séan. You'd have your pick."

He sucked hard on his cigarette, blowing smoke out the side of his mouth. "I couldn't ask the lads to leave their homes."

"Yes, you could. They don't have to come if they don't want to. It wouldn't take you any time to start up a new band over there."

"Brian wouldn't like it."

I reached across to retrieve my wine glass and took a sip. "Maybe not, but you're a grown up, Séan. If you want to move to Scotland, just do it. Leave all this bloody crap behind."

He chewed at a nicotine-stained hangnail on his thumb. "Would ya come with me?"

I bit my lip. If only I could make a new start away from here. But with Séan? "I don't know. Maybe. I need to think about it."

His eyes narrowed ever so slightly. "How long d'ye need?"

God, I had to buy a little more time. "How about after the festival?" At least I might be able to think straight then.

"Deal. After the festival it is." He leaned down and kissed me. "I bet Brian'll not object to me stayin' in Scotland, particularly if everything goes as planned."

I kept my expression neutral. "Everything?"

His gaze shifted. "The opening ceremony, y'know."

I swallowed, choosing my words carefully. "Has he something else planned?"

Séan looked me right in the eye. "Like what?"

"Like something for the 'RA. There'll be loads of important people at that ceremony - maybe even royalty. This'd be the perfect opportunity to - well, make some kind of statement, wouldn't it?"

I held my breath as he held my gaze. I could see no deception in him at all. "Ach, no, darlin'. That'd spoil any big plans for Curadh, wouldn't it?"

I smiled and pulled him back into the kiss, cigarette and all. He meant every word. And Brian would need Séan's complete knowledge and cooperation if he'd planned anything dreadful for the opening ceremony. I felt giddy with relief.

⌘

I only saw Brian Sutherland once more before we left. He came to wish us luck during one of the final rehearsals, pressing a wad of cash into Séan's hand. "Treat yourselves to something nice over there, lads." He nodded to me. "And lass, naturally."

"Will you be at the festival too?" I asked him boldly.

He looked amused. "Good Lord, no. But I'll be watching the live broadcast on television, be sure of that." A chuckle escaped him. "Oh yes, be sure of that."

I wondered what he found funny but couldn't ask.

He shook Séan's hand and gave him a hearty clap on the back. "Don't let me down, son."

"I won't, Sir."

That all seemed innocent enough. I'd read every piece of paperwork pertaining to the opening ceremony that I could lay my hands on. There were no special guests named - no one that the IRA would have any advantage in harming. I couldn't even grill Clancy for any information. He hadn't been needed as a roadie for rehearsals and to my surprise we weren't getting one for the festival, either. "Won't we need someone to help us set up?" I asked Séan.

"You read the letter, darlin'."

I had. All we apparently had to do was show up with our instruments and everything else would be taken care of. Our stuff must be delivered to the castle twenty-four hours before the opening ceremony dress rehearsal. 'For security reasons' I noted, and that the concert was taking place in Crown Square inside the castle, not out in the Esplanade where members of the public had bought tickets to watch the Military Tattoo.

I held off on making a check in call, afraid of interference before the festival. There was no terrorist plot to report. And Sutherland wasn't even going to be there.

⌘

Séan and I stood side by side on the quay at Larne, ready to board the Sealink ferry to Stranraer in Scotland. We had cleared security without any bother and waited for Declan and Kieran to get through. Liam had taken the van into the bowels of the gargantuan vessel and would meet us on the ship once we'd boarded.

"Sorry," I heard Declan say to the police officer patting him down, "I forgot to pack me machine gun."

"And yer Semtex and all," added Kieran, next in line.

God, they should have more sense than to crack jokes like that. The officers leveled baleful glares at them and Séan hurried over. "Shut up, you two wankers!" He gave Declan an affectionate cuff around the ears and turned to the officers. "Sorry, Sirs. Don't mind them, we're representin' the Province in the Edinburgh Festival. High spirits and all that, y'know?"

I noticed him using the British term 'Province'. The officers finished up and nodded us on. On board we went straight to the bar and claimed a booth.

To Kieran's horror the metal grill was firmly in place over the bar.

"T'will be open once we're underway," Declan assured him.

Liam came in with a stream of passengers from the vehicle deck and found us. The engines' thrum increased and the floating monolith ponderously chugged out of Larne Harbor. The bar finally rattled open and Kieran and Liam charged over to be first in line. They returned laden with pints, shots of whiskey and a variety of crisp packets.

Declan raised a glass. "*Slàinte!*"

I automatically looked over my shoulder to see if anyone objected. "*Slàinte!*" the rest of the lads shouted and we all clinked glasses.

"To our success," added Séan, catching my eye.

Kieran downed his whiskey in one, slamming the empty glass on the table. "*Tiocfaidh ár lá!*" he bellowed.

It sounded like 'chuckie aar laa' and even I knew it meant 'our day will come' in Gaelic, a Nationalist war cry.

"Shut the fuck up," hissed Séan.

Kieran sniffed. "Well, it will."

The ferry rocked, disconcerting in such a large vessel. Through the windows alternative views of sea and sky rocked in the choppy Irish Sea. My beer sloshed around my stomach and I broke into a clammy sweat. Cigarette smoke fogging up the bar didn't help, and then a scent that I'd normally find appealing wafted close by - fried bacon. A woman carrying a tray with two steaming Ulster Fries on it passed close. The ferry hit a swell and shuddered. She almost dumped the tray over us.

I set my glass on the table and surged to my feet.

Séan shot me a concerned look. "Ya okay darlin'?"

"A bit queasy. I'll get some fresh air."

"Hang on, I'll come with ya."

I gave his shoulder a pat. "Ah no, you're all right. I won't be long."

The deck lurched as I stumbled outside so I held tightly to the handrail. Blustery sea air hit me like a cold shower and immediately made me feel better. Gulping in lungfuls I hoisted myself up a staircase to the upper deck where I could see both bow and aft. All the decks looked deserted. No one sane would brave these swelling waves and battering spray. Pulling up the hood on my coat I braced myself against the railing to watch the distant hills of Ireland recede. Could I really leave it all behind for good? Perhaps. But not while I had unfinished business.

As we drew further away from the shores of Larne, I began to experience something akin to what I'd felt when parascending. A feeling of detachment descended on me as though by physically removing myself from Northern Irish soil, it all appeared less intense - less urgent. The last glimpse of land slid into the misty horizon. Time to look forward. I turned toward the bow and nearly jumped out of my skin. Mike, wearing jeans and a thick, padded anorak stood right behind me. I stepped back and nearly lost my balance against the railing.

He steadied me. "Don't jump, Jen," he said with his disarming smile. "It's not worth it."

"How long have you been there?"

"Not long."

"You could have let me know. What are you doing on the ferry? And don't tell me it's because I haven't checked in."

His expression turned deadly serious. "Well, you haven't. There's something you need to know."

I clapped my hands over my ears. "I don't want to hear it. I know I've fucked up. But I'll come in after the festival. Just let me see it through, that's all I ask."

He put his hands over mine and gently lowered them from my ears. "It's not that, Jen. Heather Baird is dead. Shot."

It felt like all the oxygen sucked out of the air. My chest hurt, I couldn't breathe.

"Her body washed up on Portrush Strand yesterday," he continued. "She was chained to the body of a man. A Protestant. He'd been beaten to a bloody pulp."

A sharp vision flashed into my head of Séan's knuckles, raw and bleeding, the fury that consumed him as he laid into that man in the Londonderry Arms. How he barely controlled himself, almost hitting me before running out into the night.

"That's not all, I'm afraid. The Londonderry Arms manager was found in a dumpster behind the hotel. Also beaten to death."

'I squared it with the Derry Arms manager,' Séan had said that morning. I found my voice. "Do you know who did it?"

He gazed steadily into my eyes. "I think you already know."

Séan's voice intruded from the deck below. "Fionnuir!"

Mike gripped me by the shoulders, his face close to mine. "Pull out of the festival now. Get away from Maguire before it's too late." He slipped away just before Séan appeared at the top of the stairs.

"There y'are, darlin'. I was getting worried."

I stared mutely as he approached. Like an automaton I allowed him to gather me into his arms. "Ach, darlin'. Not a good sailor, are you?"

I couldn't afford to think about Séan's possible role in Heather's horrible death. Not yet. I fought my way out of my fugue. "Doesn't look like it," I heard myself reply.

"I got ya a nice hot chocolate with a dash of Jameson. C'mon back inside - that'll help settle yer tummy." He gently led me down the stairs and into the bar. I meekly let him. As he settled me back at the booth, placing the warm mug of chocolate into my frozen hands, I kept my gaze lowered, focusing on Mike's ring on my finger. I hoped with all my might that he was wrong about Séan.

31
Ferry Me Over, My Love And I

Due to the heaving waves of the Irish Sea the ferry docked at Stranraer about half an hour late. Three hours of queasiness and imminent puking had been quite enough for me. I eagerly led the way down several flights of stairs to find the van below decks.

"I'll take the first shift," offered Séan, letting the others who'd had more drink than he to sleep it off.

Exhaust fumes clogged the deck as engines rumbled into ignition. In no time we trailed the car in front down the ferry ramp into the port town of Stranraer. I huddled up beside Séan, barely taking notice of my surroundings. In my mind I saw over and over the moment I'd left Heather in the Londonderry Arms. She'd insisted I go. But I blamed myself for her death. She'd never have been sent after me in the first place if I'd checked in when I was supposed to.

Séan had the heat turned high and my eyelids began to feel too heavy to keep open. I found myself in the Londonderry Arms kneeling over the man Séan had beaten up. It seemed to take my hand forever to reach over and roll him onto his back. I screamed in panic and horror. He had Heather's face - what was left of it.

"Ya'll right there, darlin'?" came Séan's voice.

I jerked awake. My throat hurt, had I screamed out loud? "Just nervous. About tomorrow."

Rustling came from behind. "What's to be nervous about?" asked Liam. A symphony of yawns sounded as the lads all woke up.

I shrugged. "You know - performing for the first time outside Northern Ireland."

Liam leaned forward and patted my shoulder. "Sure, you won't know the difference in Scotland, they're just like us."

Kieran sniffed. "The Duke of Edinburgh's a bit different."

That took a moment to sink in. My head snapped round to look at him.

"What's he got to do with anyt'ing?" demanded Declan.

Kieran met Séan's gaze in the rear view mirror. "He's doing the opening ceremony," said Séan.

A jackhammer hit me in the solar plexus. "We're playing in front of the *Duke of Edinburgh?*"

"Aye and a few other bigwig toffs."

"But there are no special guests listed. I checked."

"Course there are, darlin'. They kept that under wraps to us minions - for obvious reasons."

"How do you know about it?"

He tapped the side of his nose. "I have my ways."

Kieran sniffed. "He has no fuckin' business bein' there. Should'a had one of Mary Queen of Scots' relatives do the ceremony."

"He is one of her relatives," I answered in automatic pilot.

His beady little eyes hardened. "You a fuckin' Brit?"

"Fuck me, watch yer mouth, Kier." Séan slid a hand into the inside pocket of his coat and drew out an engraved silver flask. "Here, shut up and put something in it."

Kieran took it and unscrewed the cap. The raw stink of *poitín* wafted out and he gulped down a mouthful. "Not as good as yer usual, Séan."

"Ach, we had a mishap with the quality stuff."

I knew he meant the still I'd blown to kingdom come at Mourneview. Kieran handed the flask round. Against my better nature I took a drink and the liquid scorched like fire from the tip of my tongue to the depths of my stomach. I needed a fucking drink, even if it was gut-rotting *poitín*. The husband of the Queen of England would be a perfect target for the IRA.

The flask went round a couple more times until I'd medicated myself enough to pass out again. I drifted in and out of sleep with the Duke of Edinburgh foremost in my mind. I'd been wrong so many times - could I have missed something with Sutherland? I'd seen the bomb-making equipment at Mourneview, and Séan had let slip that a device had been stored in the Emerald. But I'd never thought it could be linked to the festival.

The next time I opened my eyes green hedgerows had morphed into gray pavements, pubs and shops.

"What's in Troon, mate?" demanded Liam.

"Elevenses."

I checked my watch and perked up. A strong coffee would revive me. Rain pattered hard, the wipers scraping two semi circles on the grimy windshield. Séan pulled into Troon railway station car park where a little caravan boasted fresh tea, coffee, and snacks. It looked a bit forlorn in the rain.

We clustered under the caravan's stripey awning, the only customers. Over by the station entrance sat a public phone box. I eyed it, wondering if I should call in the information about the Duke of Edinburgh. Finley must already know about it but if so hadn't shared it with me. I wasn't sure what to do.

"Get me a tea, Fen," ordered Séan and strode off through the rain into the station. I really did resent the way he ordered me around.

"Where's boy wonder off to?" asked Declan.

Kieran shut him down with a sanctimonious sniff. "Never you mind, mate."

We huddled inside the van with our cardboard cups and listened to the rain beat on the roof. Kieran produced a cigarette packet and lit up.

"Séan said no smoking in the van," I snapped.

He blew the smoke right into my face. "Fuckin' get out if you don't like it."

"You little shit." I slid over and opened the passenger door.

He grabbed at me. "Stay where you are, stupid bitch."

"Fuck off." I jumped down from the van and slammed the door. Little creep. I heard Liam say, *'Lighten up, Kier,'* before I began sploshing through puddles into the station. I couldn't go into the phone box. Not with them watching.

Troon station looked just like one of those perfect, quaint little structures you can buy for model train sets. An old-fashioned red-brick Victorian building, festooned with scarlet geraniums in hanging baskets along the platform. The Gents' and Ladies' toilets sat on opposite sides of the waiting room. I crossed over to the Ladies', waiting as a frazzled young woman clasping a newborn in her arms struggled out. I held the door for her and she shot me a grateful smile. About to head in, I felt the vibration of an approaching train under my feet as it rumbled into the station. The shrieking brakes set my teeth on edge as I went to the window overlooking the platform. Voices clamored as people disembarked and crowded into the station. Séan, always distinctive with his red hair and long coat came into view as the mob thinned. A window on the train slid open and a sandy-haired man leaned out of the carriage. With a start I recognized Clancy. Was he roadie for us after all? He spotted Séan and eased a shiny silver-colored guitar case out of the window. Séan stretched up to take it in his arms.

The train thrummed, readying to leave. As it clanked out of the station Clancy offered Séan a salute and a wide grin. Puzzled, I wondered if he were going ahead to Edinburgh to meet us there. Then I realized he was on the western line back toward Stranraer.

Séan approached the waiting room. Not wanting him to know I'd been spying I turned tail and hurried out of the main entrance, almost slamming into Kieran. *Fuck!*

"Where's Séan?" he demanded.

"Toilet, I think," I said quickly and dodged round him. I wanted to run as fast as I could but made myself stride nonchalantly across the car park. The van windows were opaque with cigarette smoke. Both Liam and Declan looked guiltily at me when I threw open the sliding door.

"Séan's his way," I warned. They frantically stubbed out the cigarettes and fanned wildly, attempting to force the smoke out. Kieran and Séan emerged from the station and crossed over to us. The guitar case had a neon yellow *'Jesus Saves'* sticker on the side. Kieran climbed into the driver's seat and scooted the chair forward while Séan secured the guitar case in the back. Liam and Declan watched without comment.

I cleared my throat. "Where'd that come from?"

Séan threw me one of his irresistible grins. "Got it just in case, darlin'."

"Yes, but–"

"Will one of you's drive?" he interrupted and climbed into the back. He patted the seat beside him and I shifted from the front to join him. Kieran started the engine and Declan sat beside him, leaving Liam to share with Séan and me.

I should just tell Séan I'd seen Clancy bring the guitar, and demand to know why the big secret? But I held back. I knew questions made him angry.

He ruffled my hair. "It's my lucky guitar, Fen. Had it delivered to the station when I realized I'd forgot it, all right?"

"I never saw it before."

He chuckled. "I never needed it before."

⌘

When we reached the outskirts of Edinburgh we'd been six hours on the ferry and road. We could almost have flown from Dublin to New York in the same amount of time. Séan used a street map to direct us to the B&B we were booked into. All through the city, flags and banners smothered every corner and post advertising the festival and bagpipe Tattoo tomorrow night. Excitement thrummed though me in spite of the horror of Heather's killing constantly hijacking my thoughts.

At a red light on the main thoroughfare of Princes Street I stared up at the castle high on the hill. It looked like it had thrust its way through a time portal, so stark was the contrast between its medieval outline and the modern city spread below. Dunluce Castle might have looked like that at one time, on a much lesser scale.

"Hey, we're famous!" shouted Declan. He pointed to a poster on a nearby lamppost with 'Curadh' clearly listed.

"Fuckin' A!" whooped Liam, punching a fist triumphantly into the air.

The B&B was just a couple of streets up the hill on Cranston Street. It sat on a corner overlooking Waverly train station, probably one of the original city buildings, made with the same type of brownish-gray stone. Two little turrets perched on either side on the roof, adding medieval character. Kieran parked the van on the tiny curb outside the front door.

"Wait here with the stuff, Jen," ordered Séan. "We'll go on to the castle right after, like."

For once I didn't rankle at his high-handed manner. As soon as they'd disappeared with our bags into the B&B, I scrambled to the back of the van and untied the guitar from where Séan had secured it. The case turned out to be made of aluminum or something and felt cold to the touch. Unclipping the latches, I gingerly raised the lid. Inside lay an electric guitar, also made from metal, a black panel on the front. Nothing extraordinary about it - the standard couple of dials on its face and six large metal tuning keys on the strings. Lifting it out, I discovered the back covered with stickers from various Christian youth clubs. I ran my hand over the case lining, pulling up the black velvet cushioning. I steeled myself, expecting to see the worst. But I found nothing. It really did only hold an innocuous guitar. An obviously much-loved, much-used - *lucky* guitar. Perhaps it had been Séan's first instrument. I imagined him learning to play on it and promising himself he'd use it when he 'made it big' or something. With relief I clipped the case shut and tied it back safely in place. But why such secrecy about Clancy?

The boys returned. Séan handed me a brass church key attached to a plastic tag showing number thirteen. "Here you go, darlin'. Lucky fer some."

Declan claimed the driving seat. We trundled up a long steep hill, which led to the famous narrow cobblestoned road known as the Royal Mile. At the top it opened out onto the castle Esplanade, where a guard halted us at a security barrier.

Séan gathered up all the paperwork and got out while we waited. Huge bleachers sat on either side of the Esplanade. About sixty impressive military bagpipers and drummers in full tartan regalia clustered in groups, talking and smoking. The guard checked Séan's paperwork and pointed across the length of the Esplanade, where another barrier blocked a vehicle entrance on the right hand side of the castle. We navigated our way there.

"Everyone out and unload," ordered Séan.

We hauled the two guitars, bodhrán, and my violin from the back of the van. Amps and electricals were all provided at the concert, along with an electronic keyboard on stage that Declan would play. Séan grabbed the emergency toolbox and big square flashlight that we used at every gig.

A guard escorted us into the security hut. One by one, we presented ourselves for intense scrutiny. First bodily patted down, then swept with beeping wands to detect any hidden metal. We had to empty pockets of change and show them if we had belt buckles. A guard reached into the violin case, making me cringe as he roughly twanged the strings. He tipped the violin end up and peered into its f-holes. I had to dig my nails into my palms to stop myself from snatching it from him when he shook it. He set the violin on the table and pulled the bow from the case. Running his fingers along the length of the horsehair, he set it down beside the violin. Then the tin of rosin rattled as he pulled it open. He plucked the little solid cake out, balanced it in his palm, then dropped it back into the tin. Pulling up the case lining, he thoroughly checked underneath and satisfied, told me I could put everything back.

Séan loomed by my side through the entire thing. I noticed sweat beading his forehead. Why did he insist on keeping that heavy leather coat on, even in August? He must be boiling. Security made him remove it and they examined it thoroughly before patting him down. Then the officer performed the same intensive search on the two guitars as he had with the violin. Everything finally passed muster, and we were ordered to leave the instruments in the hut. They'd be delivered to the Green Room tomorrow.

I clutched the violin to my chest. "I'll keep this with me."

"Sorry," insisted the guard. "It all has to stay together overnight."

"Why?"

He met my gaze square on. "Make sure there's nothing ticking in 'em."

"Your fiddle'll be safe," a second guard assured me. "I'll make sure of it, hinny, okay?" I reluctantly handed it over and he opened the hut door to let us out. "You can leave your vehicle on the other side of the Esplanade by the gate for today, but you'll have to move it when you leave. Strictly no parking there tomorrow."

"No problem," Séan assured him.

"Okay, go park and a minivan'll take you up to Crown Square."

Séan shrugged his coat back on, grinning ear to ear. He slung an arm around me, the leather scent of his coat surrounding me. His body felt like a furnace, damp under my palm.

"God, you're hot."

He laughed. "Aye, I'm hot stuff, darlin'."

I rolled my eyes.

As soon as Declan returned we clambered into the waiting minivan. It took us up the narrow cobblestoned path that led under the Portcullis Gates, such a tight fit I was sure the minivan would be scratched on either side. But the driver knew what he was about and passed through unscathed. He edged slowly up a hill past an array of impressive black cannons that pointed over the city. Apparently at one o'clock every day, one of the cannons was fired - a huge tourist attraction.

We curved round to the left and up toward another narrow gateway. A van with 'Edinburgh Catering' emblazoned on the side was parked there, with a couple of young men removing pallets of crockery from the back. Our driver bypassed the gate and drove around to the left past St. Margaret's Chapel. He pulled up in front of another semi-circle of cannons, separated by a wall from the side entrance to the Royal Palace. Two doors faced us, the bigger one jutting out in a semi-circular tower, reaching up to the roof of the palace. It lay wide open, revealing a stone spiral staircase inside.

"Green Room's joost in there," the driver told us, rolling his r's in a strong Scottish burr. Oh, he so reminded me of dear old Tetley. "But niver mind aboot that today. Go on tae the Square."

My rising spirits plummeted again with the thought of how disappointed Tetley must be with me. Following our directions we walked to the right and under an archway with a recessed portcullis. We approached a stage that had been constructed in Crown Square in front of the steps of the National War Museum building. A weatherproof hanging protected it from the elements, and a fabric screen stretched from the side of the stage out to the archway. Any coming and going between the Green Room and stage would be concealed from the audience. Technicians worked busily around the stage, setting up sound and lights. In the Square we found rows upon rows of elegant gilt garden chairs facing the stage. I hoped the weather would hold as the Square offered no obvious protection against the elements. Groups of people clustered in the front rows. I heard a mixture of accents raised in high spirits and laughter - they must be the other bands representing Scotland, England, and Wales. We filed into the second row, behind a guy in his twenties with a strong Cockney accent. He had an arm around a girl about the same age, and he peered unsmiling at us over her shoulder.

A soft-bodied and flamboyant man in his thirties jumped up onto the stage and took the podium. He wore bright red plastic-rimmed glasses and a light pink scarf wound around his neck.

"Jesus, not another fruitcake," groaned Liam.

A second man, more conservative in jeans and white shirt, handed round a printed list to each band. An amp emitted a piercing whine, setting my teeth on edge. The man on stage visibly winced.

"Hello everyone," he said in a cultured Scottish accent. "I'm Vincent, your concert director. Congratulations on being chosen to represent your country. You've earned yourself a wee mention in the history books."

Séan gave a little laugh and winked at me.

"So tomorrow," continued Vincent, "not only will you have the honor of playing before our illustrious Duke of Edinburgh, you'll be playing to a host of hand-picked VIP's - European dignitaries including royalty, our own Peers and Tatler-readers, and some of the top echelon from the United States."

A murmur rippled through the band members.

"Tatler-readers?" mouthed Séan, shooting me a confused look.

"Tatler Magazine," I whispered. "The toffs read it."

Vincent tapped the microphone. "You the crème de là crème, top traditional musicians of the British Empire, will provide said VIPs with your excellent entertainment until the Duke's arrival to kick off the festival at eight o'clock sharp."

Kieran and Séan exchanged meaningful looks at the 'British Empire' but fortunately didn't comment. I glanced at the list in Séan's hand. Curadh was third to play. He nodded to us, showing his approval.

"Be here for rehearsal tomorrow at two sharp, in the order listed there," trilled Vincent. "Bring your costumes, your make up, your lucky charms - everything you need for the entire day right up to the performance. Once you're in the castle past security you don't get out until after the ceremony." He paused for dramatic effect, regarding us with his hands on his hips. Another sobering reminder of Tetley. "Understood? I don't want to *hear* about it if you've left something at home. *No* one gets out once in. No exceptions." He made an exaggerated sign of the cross. "All right, my children - go and sin no more."

"Pillock," muttered Liam.

"What does he mean, lucky charms?" asked Declan.

"'*They're always after me Lucky Charms,'*" said Séan in an overly exaggerated Southern Irish accent.

The four of us glanced at each other.

Liam shook his head. "What?"

"Ach, it's an ad. In America, like."

"For soddin' lucky charms? They'll buy anything there. Suckers."

Séan cuffed the back of his head. "Never mind. It's like fuckin' corn flakes , ya halfwit. They would've laughed in America."

We filed out of Crown Square under the portcullis and archway. Security directed us through another arch where the seventy Lang Stairs led straight back down to the castle gates. Once down I looked longingly at the cannons and the enticing view over Edinburgh. "I'd like to do some sightseeing."

Séan ruffled my hair. "We'll have all the time in the world for sightseeing after the festival, darlin'."

I suppose he was right. "Okay. And I want to go to the zoo," I said firmly. I'd read they had a fantastic tiger enclosure.

He hugged me. "And so ya shall, Cinderella." We trekked along the cobblestoned road to the Gatehouse and across the dry moat onto the Esplanade.

Liam skipped in front of us as we approached the van. "Who fancies a pint?"

Declan chortled. "I need one after listenin' to that poofter."

"Fuckin' Brit poofter," added Kieran.

Liam chortled. "Don't forget his lucky charms."

"Lucky charms my arse."

Séan held out a hand to Liam for the keys. "I'll drop the van at the B&B and meet you's there. *World's End*, right?"

⌘

We joined the veritable mob of band members surging down the hill to Edinburgh's most famous pub, *World's End*. It was already packed with tourists, tired and thirsty after traipsing round the castle all afternoon. There was standing room only, spilling out into the cobblestoned lane.

"Let's go somewhere else," suggested Declan, eyeing the crowd with distaste.

"How would Séan find us?" I asked.

"Sure, we'll get the drinks." Liam grabbed Kieran and they dove into the multitude.

Declan brushed aside some litter and discarded beer bottles from a patch of pavement so we could sit on the curb. Olivia Newton-John's voice filtered through speakers from inside the pub, warbling *Magic*. My thoughts immediately careened back to Heather and the Londonderry Arms. My mood darkened.

 Declan stared curiously at me. "Ya happy?"

I plastered on a smile. "Why do you ask?"

"Ya were very quiet the whole way here. Everyt'ing okay?"

My heart warmed. Of all of them he was by far the kindest. "Everything's great. I'm just knackered after the long trip here."

Kieran and Liam appeared with the drinks and the four of us perched along the pavement in a row. A lone policeman strolled up the hill and paused to have a word with a group of people sitting on the curb just down from us. They got to their feet but as soon as he moved on, they plonked themselves down again. The cop reached us. Up close he looked pretty young and earnest.

"Ye can't sit there, you're blocking traffic."

"What traffic?" demanded Kieran.

"Shut up," I hissed, clambering to my feet.

Dec and Liam did the same, Liam giving the rebellious Kieran a shove with his foot. "Get up, boyo."

He obeyed and the officer nodded and moved on to the next group. We stayed upright long enough for him to pass by, and like the others, promptly sat back down again.

Sipping my beer I watched the rest of the bands mill about in the street. A growing carpet of discarded crisp packets and brown beer bottles spread over the pavement. The policeman should have been more concerned about this dreadful mess than non-existent traffic. A braying laugh caught my attention. I recognized the English guy who'd been sitting in front of us in the Square. I overheard someone call him Rob. He downed what was left in his bottle of Newcastle Brown Ale and casually dropped it into the gutter. Catching my disapproving look he sneered.

"Can't believe they're letting Paddies play this year. They must be desperate."

His strident accent grated on me. I resisted pointing out that Northern Ireland was British, so technically we'd be 'Limeys'. Didn't think that'd go down too well with the lads.

"We're not Paddies, ya stupid prick," growled Declan. "We're Celts."

Rob brayed again. "Same difference."

Liam snorted and nodded toward the Scottish band members. "Tell that to them. Hey lads!" They all turned. "This knob-head called you Paddies."

The tallest, sporting well-defined muscles, leveled a baleful glare at Rob. "Lookin' for a fight, ye English oik?"

"Fuck off, Scotch berk."

Declan whooped with laughter. "Ooh, that's fightin' talk!"

The Scottish guy puffed himself up. "It's 'Scots' you thick cunt." The two men squared off.

"Party time, folks!" yelled Kieran.

I scrambled up and backed against the wall while everyone else surged forward, crowding round to watch.

"You show 'im, Rob, love!" shouted his girlfriend.

Rob threw a punch. I never saw if it hit home as my line of sight was blocked. Glass shattered on the pavement and a wave of bodies crashed together. To my shock a couple of girls launched into the fray, screeching and pulling savagely at each other's hair. I pressed my back to the wall, utterly astounded. One moment we were all enjoying a nice drink on a warm summer evening, the next all bloody hell had let loose.

Liam cackled like a man possessed. "Scotland the brave!" he howled. "Culloden's revenge!"

Sirens blared in the distance, rapidly growing louder. "Declan!" I shouted. He heard and turned, giving me a thumbs up. Flashing lights in the streets below heralded the imminent arrival of the police. I backed into the shadows of an alleyway beside the pub and managed to melt out of sight. Tires squealed and doors slammed as officers spilled out.

I waited, holding my breath. To my relief Liam, Declan and Kieran joined me in the alley. We charged away from the fracas, emerging into a little maze of courtyards belonging to the shops and homes back there. My heart thumped hard as we took refuge in a tiny square of green grass by a clump of rose bushes. When no searchlights came after us we made our way out of the labyrinth of alleyways. As though we'd been nowhere near the riot we strolled nonchalantly over to Canongate street below the Royal Mile, and down a little side lane that led to our B&B. As we drew close to the front door a shout came from across the street.

"Yo!"

I peered into the darkness and spotted Séan straddling a see-saw in a little children's playground. He looked like a giant March hare, crouching low to the ground with his knees high up. "Comin' for a chinky, mate?" called Liam. "There's a takeaway down the road."

"Aye, Fen and I'll follow you's. C'mere for a minute, darlin'."

Kieran hesitated on the pavement, then dogged me as I crossed the street. "Bugger off, Kier!" Séan said.

Kieran shrugged and took off after Liam's and Declan's retreating backs. Séan stood up as I approached, allowing the see-saw to lower so I could climb on opposite. It had been so long since I'd ridden one I couldn't even remember doing it. Sliding a leg over I crouched and took hold of the pommel with both hands. Even though I expected it, I still giggled when Séan sat back down, his weight careening me upwards. We alternated up and down a few times, grinning at each other like silly kids. When he smiled like that with not a care in the world, I couldn't believe he'd be involved in violence and terrorism. But he was.

My thoughts must have shown on my face for he paused our see-sawing. "What's wrong, *mo ghrá?*"

"What's *mo ghrá* mean?" I asked, hoping to deflect him.

"Yer a funny girl, not having any Irish. Means 'my love'."

I froze, my mind struck blank. "Oh."

"Y'are, you know. My love." He stood, letting me gently down before he lifted a leg over the see-saw and approached. I gripped the pommel so tightly my knuckles gleamed white. He perched right in front of me, prying my fingers free so he could take my hands in his. "What's wrong, darlin'?

You've been quiet all day, like."

There was no holding it inside, no matter how prudent it would be. My words came in a rush. "Where'd you go that night, after you left the B and B? In Portush?"

He raised my hands to his lips and gently kissed them, one by one. "Walked on the beach, thinkin'. 'Bout you and me."

I swallowed. "You didn't - go back to the Londonderry Arms?"

A cinnamon eyebrow raised and he speared me with an intense look. "I squared it with the manager, remember?"

"Yes–" I trailed off.

"Came to a decision that night, Fen. Listen, I've never felt like this about no one before. Yer different to any girl I've ever known and I want ye to be mine. So we'll not go back to Belfast after the opening ceremony. We'll stay in Scotland."

My mouth opened and shut. "What?" I couldn't think fast enough.

"Mate of mine lives in Glasgow. We'll stay with him till we get on our feet."

I gazed into his hypnotic amber eyes. For a moment I was tempted. But sanity prevailed. If I were to make a new life for myself it must be on my terms. And *after* I had done what I set out to do: bring down Sutherland, or my parents and Heather's deaths would have been for nothing. I dissembled. "Séan, we can't just leave everything–"

"Course we can."

"What about Brian? The 'RA?"

"England's just over the border. I can still serve the Cause. Maybe better." His voice grew silky. "You do love me, don't ya?"

My lips felt dry and chapped. "You know I do."

"Then marry me, Fen. Say yes." His eyes clouded over with doubt as I grappled for an answer.

"Séan, this is out of nowhere. I need time."

"How long, darlin'?"

I could not make a decision about anything until the Festival was out of the way. "At least until after the opening ceremony."

"All right, darlin'. Till then."

32
Evil Be To Him Who Evil Thinks

I awoke before Séan the next morning, my right arm numb from me lying on it. It was almost noon, I was surprised I'd slept at all. I'd planned to sneak out to a phone box as soon as Séan fell asleep but I'd gone comatose after my head hit the pillow. Gently extricating myself from the tangle of bedclothes I rested on an elbow to gaze at him. He looked positively angelic, his red-gold lashes feathering his eyes, full lips slightly parted. Only the cloud of fiery hair spread over the pillow gave any indication of the flame that burned within.

My intense stare must have roused him, his eyes fluttered open. Their amber depths sparkled in the sunlight filtering between the curtains. I'd never seen him look more attractive.

Just after one o'clock, the four of us made our way up the Royal Mile to the castle. On the bleachers set up on the Esplanade a police officer used an intensely focused sniffer dog to check all the seats. They were taking no chances, obviously. Séan watched too, shading his eyes with his hand from the sun's glare. As we approached the drawbridge, close to a hundred kilted bagpipers and drummers streamed out from the gatehouse, readying to practice. An impressive army of Celtic warriors.

"Nice legs," I commented. "You lot should wear kilts on stage."

Declan laughed. "No fuckin' way, I'm not wearin' a skirt!"

We entered through the castle gates and climbed the Lang Stairs, accompanied by the discordant wail of bagpipes as they warmed up. They sounded like an angry clowder of cats on heat.

A sign had been pasted to the side turret door of the Royal Palace, reading: 'GREEN ROOM', and along the little wall that separated us from the cannons stood a row of five Porta Loos. A hand-printed 'OUT OF ORDER' sign was stuck onto the far right one.

We found the Green Room up one floor of a spiral stone staircase and through a large doorway. Wood panels covered the lower half of walls that were painted eggshell blue, and a huge fireplace dominated one of the walls. There were darker blue squares in the paint as though pictures had recently been taken down. Probably stored somewhere safe until we'd all gone.

A security guard oversaw our entrance, a walkie-talkie in hand. He hovered by a table in the corner that had been set up with coffee and tea-making paraphernalia. A trestle table also stood along one side of the room, with a wardrobe mirror set longways on top, propped against the wall. For each band's use, five separate areas had been partitioned off with heavy curtains. On front miniature flags from each of our countries heralded whose was whose. It made a colorful display, the Welsh red dragon on green and white, the Scottish white saltire on blue, England's red centered cross on white, and our Red Hand of Ulster under the crown.

Kieran tore it down. "Well, that's fuckin' got to go for a start." Crumpling it into a ball he flung it at the wall.

What a petty little turd. I glanced at the guard but he either hadn't seen or had chosen not to.

Our instruments and toolbox equipment had been placed in a neat pile against the wall in our area. We checked them thoroughly as the other band members trickled in, filling the room with chatter and laughter. Some looked a little worse for wear, sporting evidence from the brawl last night.

Once the security guard had checked us all off on a list he spoke into his walkie-talkie and left through one of the doors at the far end of the room. One of the Scottish band members sneaked over to try the handle, but the door was firmly locked.

Despite the 'NO SMOKING' sign, cigarettes lit up, rapidly stinking the room. I really wished they wouldn't but I couldn't do a thing about it. If this kept up I'd have to start smoking myself as self-defense.

Crackling static overhead loudly interrupted, making me jump. A large speaker was attached to the wall over by the door, next to a printed sign: 'LISTEN FOR YOUR CUE!' Vincent's flowery tones, distorted by static announced, "Rosethorn, you're up for rehearsal. Come to the stage immediately. Rosethorn, you're up."

The English band scurried to gather their instruments and head out. The speaker crackled again. This time Jamie announced, "Thistles, stand by, you're next. Curadh and Dyffryn Gwyrdd, you haven't signed in, yet. Please do so pronto."

Liam looked nonplussed. "'Diffren gwid'? What the hell's that?"

"Us," said a tall guy with long black hair as he passed. He winked at me. "'Green valley' in Welsh."

Séan stubbed out his cigarette in one of the ashtrays on the trestle table and followed him out. The Scottish band got their stuff ready and placed it by the door. We might as well be prepared too, so I retrieved my violin from the top of our pile to tune it.

"What does 'thistle' mean in Scots, d'ya think?" Liam whispered. "'Prickly'?"

I chuckled. "Don't for God's sake let them hear you or we'll have another riot on our hands."

With a laugh he crossed to the hot water urn to make himself a cup of tea. Declan and Kieran joined him and they brought their cups back to our area. I concentrated on the violin until it was in perfect pitch, then laid it on the chair next to me. Liam retrieved his uilleann pipes and Kieran reached past me to grab his bodhrán case. Declan got Séan's Fender, which just left the lucky guitar. I didn't know if Séan intended to play it on stage or not, but I assumed so, considering how much trouble he went to get it here. I knelt down and unclicked one of the latches on the aluminum case.

Kieran slammed his palm on the case, holding it closed. "Don't touch that, ya stupid bitch!"

Angrily I knocked his hand aside. "What the fuck's your problem, creep?"

Pain blinded me and I registered he'd snatched me by the hair. I grabbed his wrist and gripped tightly with both hands so he couldn't rip the hair from my head. He began to drag me out of our area. Helpless, I couldn't do anything other than hold onto his arm with all my might.

"What the fuck?" shouted Declan.

I felt a flurry of movement above me and mercifully my hair was free. My eyes watered as I gingerly put a hand to my searing scalp.

Séan had Kieran by the throat up against the wall. "For fuck's sake, cool it."

Kieran scrabbled at Séan's vise grip. "Stupid cunt almost had that open," he rasped, pointing to the aluminum guitar case.

Séan dropped his hold. Kieran sank to the floor, over-dramatically gasping and hacking.

Séan hunkered in front of me. "Ya'll right?"

I nodded, swallowing hard at the painful lump in my throat. He helped me to my feet and onto a chair at the trestle table. "What's in the case?" I managed. "He hardly went psycho over me seeing a bloody guitar."

"Show's over," Declan told the gawping band members. "Nothin' to see here, folks." He leaned close to whisper. "Always wanted to say dat."

I gave him a weak smile and Liam handed over a cardboard cup of tea. Even though it was weak and lukewarm, I drained it.

Séan leaned down and offered Kieran a hand. They grasped forearms and he hauled the little runt to his feet. "You need to fuckin' hold it together, mate, or yer no use to no one. Hear me?" Then he brought the aluminum case and held it open in front of me. "Just a guitar, Fen, see?"

The speaker crackled and Jamie's voice boomed, "Thistles, you're up for rehearsal. Come to the stage immediately. And Curadh, stand by."

The Scottish band descended on their stuff by the door and were away in moments. Séan put the aluminum case back into our area and took his Fender from Declan. Liam slung the uilleann pipes under his arm, while Kieran gathered his bodhrán and tipper.

I felt numb with shock. Only my smarting scalp laid evidence to the vicious attack. I managed to shake it off for now and focus my energy on the upcoming rehearsal, but I vowed when this day was over, Kieran Lynch would get his comeuppance. I'd see to it. My hands shook as I retrieved my violin and bow. But from rage, not nerves.

⌘

Séan led the way out of the Green Room. The tails of his long coat flapped on the steps as he descended and I had to drop back to avoid standing on them. Why did he insist on wearing it all the time? He was the only one in the castle not dressed in summer-weight clothing.

"Testing, testing. One, two - one two," boomed from within Crown Square as we approached the portcullis.

Only a foot or so of the stage front was visible, the covered walkway blocking the rest. One of the Thistles stood within view, tweaking the keys on his bass guitar before launching into a rock version of *The Skye Boat Song*.

Liam snickered. "That's original."

All four bands had chosen a traditional song that represented our country in some way. I wondered what the English band had chosen? *Rule Britannia* came to mind and I stifled a laugh.

The Skye Boat Song halted abruptly with a screech. Sound problems. We reached the steps at the side of the stage as the Thistles started up again. They sounded really good, they'd be a hard act to follow.

Sound and light technicians worked furiously around the stage and I spotted Vincent and his assistant Jamie in a booth set up at the back of the audience seating. I turned to point them out to Séan and discovered he'd vanished. The Thistles crashed to the end of their song. My ears rang in the sudden quiet.

"Applause, applause, applause," came Vincent's voice through the P.A. "Now, take a bow!" The Thistles obediently moved to the front of the stage and practically kowtowed, looking slick and professional. "Very good. Now, pipers - pipe!"

"Who does he t'ink he is," muttered Declan, "one o'the days of Christmas?"

Two bagpipers who'd been waiting on the Foog's Gate side of the Square blasted into a reel and marched over to stand in front of the stage.

"Thistles!*"* bellowed Vincent over the cacophony, "come off stage right." They unhooked from the amps and headed toward us on the left-hand side. Liam snorted and they drew up short. "Good God, not *house* right!" shouted Vincent. "Do you not know the difference? Other side - *right*, I said!"

They retreated and climbed down the far steps, appearing beside us a moment later via the narrow passage curtained off behind the stage.

"Curadh!" yelled Vincent, sounding more frazzled by the second. "Come up stage left while the Thistles exit."

I hesitated, looking around in panic for Séan.

"Fuckin' go on," hissed Kieran.

"Dear God in heaven, have aliens abducted them?" demanded Vincent.

"We're coming!" I called.

"Well, don't let a bloody truck drive through - get a move on, for the love of God!"

The pipers wrapped up their reel as I led the way on stage. A technician looked at each of us in turn, with increasing impatience. "Who has the guitar?" he demanded.

"It's comin', mate." Declan took his place at the keyboard, filling the air with churchy chords and arpeggios while he tested it. I crossed to the furthest microphone stand at stage right, and Kieran and Liam took the mics stage left, leaving the center one for Séan.

Jesus Christ, where the fuck—

Séan bounded onto the stage. *Thank God.* Moving to his mic, he was met by the scowling technician who hooked up the Fender. Checking the tuning, Séan shot me a wide smile and a wink.

I put my palm over my mic and whispered, "Not playing the lucky guitar?"

"That's for later, darlin'." His voice boomed through the sound system.

"Sorry, are we interrupting?" Vincent's voice dripped with sarcasm.

Séan grinned and leaned away from the mic. "That fella has way too high an opinion of himself - bloody ponce."

The sound check seemed endless but finally Séan counted us in: "One, two, three, four!" and we launched into our updated rock version of *The Foggy Dew*.

> "'*As down the glen one Feb'ry morn, to a city fair rode I*
> *There armed lines of marching men in squadrons passed me by—*'"

A couple of hiccups with the sound later, it finally all came together and we got to play right through to the end. My nerves dissipated. At least until we had an audience out there.

"Applause, applause, applause - very good," said Vincent. "Take a bow." The four of us stepped forward and managed to bow in synchronicity. "Now get off."

"Charming," muttered Declan, making me chuckle.

"Pipers!" called Jamie.

The bagpipes started up again and the two kilted men marched toward the stage. As we exited stage right, Dyffryn Gwyrdd made their way on.

In the cramped passageway behind the stage as the opening strain of *The Ash Grove* in acapella began, Liam pretended to slap Séan on the back of his head. "Where the fuck were you?" he shouted over the singing. "Don't ever leave us hangin' again."

Back in the Green Room we found a couple of waiters in white jackets putting out platefuls of sandwiches, sausage rolls, and little cakes on the trestle table. One looked up as we came in and fixed Séan with a steady gaze before returning to his work. Séan headed into our area. I followed and found him crouched over the aluminum guitar case, opening the lid.

"Will ya get me some sandwiches, Fen?" he asked.

I nodded and retreated to the trestle table, piling a bit of everything on a plate for him. Nerves had sapped my appetite but I made myself eat a couple of the substantial chicken curry sandwiches. The closer the evening approached the more anxious I grew. Not so much about our performance - we'd rehearsed it enough that I knew I could get through it without messing up. The fact that the Duke - *royalty* - was going to be here and I hadn't been able to make a call to report it really worried me. I hoped I was just being paranoid. The IRA had a sort of agreement with Scotland, not to impose terrorism on them as they couldn't afford to alienate any of the Celtic connections. Maybe they hoped to find allies in them, I didn't know. But the more I thought about it, the more unlikely it seemed that the Duke of Edinburgh was in any danger. Still, I wished I could have made that call. My stomach had that ghastly sinking feeling you get when you feel you've done something wrong.

If the Queen were opening the festival I doubt anyone would be representing Northern Ireland at all. We were Britain's profound embarrassment, they didn't really want us part of the United Kingdom but were stuck with us.

I stopped short of slamming my plate down, shocked at myself and infused with guilt. That was the kind of pro-Nationalist sentiment that Clancy would have come off with. I glanced at the aluminum guitar case again. Why would Séan have Clancy bring it and not mention he had? And why did that turd Kieran have such a fit over me trying to open it? It really was only a guitar. I'd checked it again and again, and even Séan had openly shown it to me.

He and Kieran sat close to each other, in intense conversation. I studied Séan's face. Whatever they discussed, he looked strung as tightly as an arrow about to fly. Nerves fluttered in my stomach again. Maybe I should attempt to make that call now. I'd seen a payphone down by the gates. I could sneak down, with everyone busy stuffing their faces. Unnoticed, I left my plate on the trestle table and slipped away.

Just before the Lang Stairs I met a group of kilted men, resplendent in full Scottish regalia, coming from the direction of St. Margaret's Chapel. I paused by the array of cannons in Half Moon Battery to let them pass. A glimpse of Edinburgh through one of the slits in the wall distracted me. The low evening sun both shadowed and lit the city, a Midas-gold sheen tempered with dusky copper. I leaned on one of the cannons to look through the slit, and felt suddenly small and insignificant. Here I was in an alien city, with people I could never really know, pretending to be someone that I wasn't. I'd become adrift. Playing at the ceremony tonight had grown to be the most important thing in my world, and I realized it shouldn't have. Mike and Tetley and everyone had trusted me to do a job - and not only had I failed to do it, I'd put my desire to play at this festival before all my obligations. I'd wanted so much to make something of my broken life, to belong somewhere. All I'd done was ensure I belonged nowhere.

"Fen."

Séan had followed me out. If I'd not paused to look out over the city he would have tailed me down the stairs and witnessed me using the phone.

I smoothed my face of anxiety and turned. "Beautiful, isn't it?"

He peered over the cannon's muzzle through the slit. "Don't wander off like that, darlin'."

Had he seen me watching him earlier? "Just needed some air."

"I need ya by me, okay?"

His hand shook slightly as he reached to pull me close, and I felt his whole body trembling. "You're not worried about tonight, are you, Séan?"

He paused a moment. "Just a bit of stage fright."

That was a first. "We'll do brilliantly," I assured him. "It'll be over in no time."

"Aye. And then?" He fixed me with a steady gaze.

I frowned. "Then?"

"Your answer, *mo ghrá*."

Ice trickled through me. So, that's what his nerves were about. I had purposefully thrust his proposal from my mind. But I was deluding myself for even considering it. I wanted to love him - had almost convinced myself that I did before I found out about the bomb-making stuff at Mourneview. My heart sank like water in oil as I finally acknowledged that I never could. Too many terrible things came between us. Even if we could overcome those, the one thing that would always stand between us - was Mike.

I mentally shook myself. I couldn't afford to think about him now. Later I would. I'd face it all when the performance was over.

"Not even a hint, then?" he asked.

"I'm sorry, Séan."

He kissed the top of my head. "I can wait. Just a wee bit longer, right?"

⌘

The guests began to filter through Foog's Gate for the catered reception in the Great Hall. Declan and Liam joined me to take a peek. I was really curious to see what these hand-picked-invitation-only-toffee-noses looked like. They'd all come prepared for an uncertain summer evening on Castle Hill, dressed in woolen layers. It would probably get pretty chilly after the sun went down and the warmth seeped from these ancient stones.

A clown with a pointed hat and sequined, spangled costume had been hired to keep the few children in the audience entertained. He had a round smiley face painted on, so he didn't freak me out like scary circus clowns with their maniacal droopy expressions. He pretended to drop the red, white and blue beanbags he juggled, and then tossed them one at a time to the laughing kids. He retrieved more from his gargantuan pockets and let them keep the ones they'd caught. Then with great ceremony he handed out little Union Jacks and Scottish pennants for them to wave during the show.

Down on the Esplanade the bleachers were already filling up with people who had come to see the Tattoo, even though it wouldn't start until after the private opening ceremony. I saw a television crew setting up, and the entire castle simmered with expectation and excitement.

High above the stage on the roof of the National War Museum, huge spotlights snapped on. Once evening set in, Hollywoodesque floodlights would stream dramatically into the dark sky. Diagonally across on top of the Royal Palace, another beam highlighted the Duke of Edinburgh's Royal Standard flag on the center turret. On the far side of the square an array of colored theater gel lights pointed gaily at the stage from the control booth.

Séan appeared. He'd evidently been searching for us. "You's lot need to get changed," he snapped. "Like *yesterday*." If anything his nerves were worse. He couldn't stand still and kept clicking his lighter on and off.

Rob from the English band came barreling down the spiral staircase just as we started up. He jumped the last three, forcing us out of his way.

"What're you bloody Fenians doing, lurking down here," he scoffed. "Plotting to assassinate the Duke are you?"

I looked at Séan in alarm. He'd gone deathly white. "Don't rise to the bait," I murmured.

"Go back to the Green Room, all of you's," he ordered through gritted teeth.

Liam and Declan shot each other a look and started up the stairs. I hesitated. "Let it go, Séan. He's an idiot."

"Go on, I'll be right up."

I wanted to grab hold of him, bodily prevent him from following Rob. "Please don't have a fight just before we go on stage!" *And let's not have another Londonderry Arms incident.*

"I said go on!"

His tone brooked no argument. I climbed the stairs, feeling sick to my stomach. He'd promised never to beat anyone up that badly again. At least with so much at stake at the opening ceremony, I trusted he'd control himself. Heather's murder intruded again with the memory of the Londonderry Arms. I made a supreme effort and thrust it from my mind. In less than an hour things would be sorted, I'd give Séan his answer, then get my life and priorities in order. But not until then.

The others didn't take long to change into their green stage gear and peeled out of our area to give me some privacy. Séan had charged me with getting the costumes together. He'd handed me £150 cash and told me to have at it. I'd trawled pretty much every shop in Belfast until I came up with four different tops for each of them, all in the same gorgeous shade of emerald green. Séan had a silky poet shirt that made him look very Byron-esque. Even if he insisted on wearing his leather coat over it, which he probably would, he'd still look glorious. The green set off his beautiful hair to perfection. Declan wore a waistcoat covered in glittering green and white sequins, à la Elton John. I thought he'd be more visible at the back of the stage with all that sparkle and it showed off his toned biceps very nicely. Liam wore a green T-shirt with a circular design reminiscent of the Irish tricolor flag on the front. I thought the flag bit would please him, which it did, and the fabric shimmered like glittering snakeskin. Kieran had been difficult to shop for. I'd found a ludicrous leprechaun knitted waistcoat, which I was tempted to make the nasty wee shit wear but restrained myself. Finally I settled on a V-neck green tunic with intricate white Celtic-type knots on it.

I found my outfit in a charity shop on the Lisburn Road. As far as I was concerned it was the best of the lot. A shimmering taffeta dress with a plunging neckline and wide, swirly hem that I shortened to a miniskirt and buoyed up like a floppy tutu with masses of white netting. It must have been a bridesmaid's dress, for I unearthed a pair of matching satin stiletto-heeled pumps in the same shop.

The taffeta rustled loudly as I slipped into the dress and zipped it up. Then I stepped into the stiletto shoes and took courage. In heels like these I felt invincible. Emerging from behind the curtain I brought my makeup and hair stuff over to the mirrors on the trestle table.

Declan gave a wolf-whistle. "Lookin' good there, Fen."

It was amazing how putting on costumes transformed us all from scruffy band members into professional performers. The atmosphere in the Green Room felt positively electric as all four bands got ready. Maybe like me they just couldn't stop marveling that out of all the bands in their country, they had been chosen as representatives.

Séan appeared at last and slipped behind the curtain. He didn't look like he'd been in a fight.

Vincent turned up hot on his heels. "All right, boys and girls - quiet, please." Everyone obeyed, gathering round. "'*A drum, a drum, Macbeth doth come*'. The time is upon us. Rosethorn, get in place by the stage; we're about to begin. The rest of you, gather yourselves and stand by. Break a leg, all of you."

"What did ye invoke the Scottish play for?" wailed one of the Thistle guys. He had attempted unsuccessfully to cover up a black eye with makeup.

Vincent withered him with a look. "Don't be absurd, boy. This isn't the theater."

"Excuse me." Rob's girlfriend stepped forward. "We've lost Rob." My heart lurched and I darted a glance to our curtained-off area.

Vincent's eyebrows shot up. "What do you mean, you've lost him?"

"He's not 'ere."

I opened my mouth to say I'd seen him heading to the Porta Loos, but stopped myself.

"What we gonna do?" demanded the girl.

Vincent tossed his head. "Do? You'd better find him, and pronto."

Séan emerged from behind the curtain, green shirt on, leather coat back in place, and boots in hand.

Vincent addressed the Welsh band. "Get out there and be prepared to go on first." Spinning on an expensive looking crocodile leather boot he stalked out. Chaos ensued as the six Welshmen gathered themselves and the Rosethorn band members hurried out in search of Rob.

I got up and steered Séan into a chair at the trestle table, making a pretense of brushing his hair. "Did you do something to him?" I asked quietly.

He met my gaze in the mirror, his eyes chilling. "Nothin' the fucker didn't deserve."

Jesus, God. Laying the brush down on the table, I took a step toward the door, my heart heavy with dread.

Séan's arm shot out, grasping my wrist. "Where ya goin'?"

I pulled from his hold, my heels clicking loudly on the bare floorboards. He bent down, scrabbling to pull on his boots. I quickened my step and hurtled down the spiral staircase. Dusk had fallen, and in the darkness I saw the Porta Loo on the far left now had the 'OUT OF ORDER' sign stuck on the door, not to the right.

Several military bagpipers drew near, descending from St. Margaret's Chapel. Two of them branched off and reached the Loos before me. Involved in some shared joke, they laughed raucously. One pulled open the out-of-order door and stopped dead.

"Fucking 'ell."

The other piper looked inside and reacted. Grabbing the walkie-talkie from his belt he jabbered urgently into it. My steps faltered and then I launched forward so I could see, too. A man was stuffed head first into the toilet hole.

Melodious acappella burst from Crown Square as Dyffryn Gwyrdd began their performance. It should have been the English band, but how could they play without their lead singer? As the two pipers grabbed the upended legs and hauled out the body, I recognized Rob even though his head and upper torso were smothered in filthy muck. One of the men held a couple of fingers to Rob's soiled neck, then shook his head.

Séan caught up with me and bodily forced me away from the scene into the shadows by the palace wall.

"Jesus Christ, Séan." I gaped at him, horrified. "What've you done?"

"Nothin'." He imprisoned me with his body, his hands leaning on either side of me. "And if you know what's good for you, you'll do nothin' too."

To my revulsion he was aroused. The violence had excited him and he ground the evidence hard against my pubic bone. Anyone looking on would think we were in a lover's clinch. I tried to shove him away but he slid his arms tightly around me. "Sure, the world's a better place with one less filthy Brit," he murmured.

Bile rose in my throat. His amber eyes had altered, taken on a frenetic, kaleidoscopic look. *Lucy in the Sky of Diamonds.* He was crazy. Why hadn't I seen it before? Totally and utterly unhinged. Over his shoulder I saw more kilted men arrive in a rush. I fought to focus my thoughts. Séan had just casually murdered a man in cold blood. And relished that it had been a British man. With dawning horror I realized that everything he had told me about being forced into the IRA must have been a lie. Delusional. He had to be to claim he was Sutherland's victim when it was clear he was Sutherland's lackey. And he was proud of what he had just done, thrilling in the violence, the killing. Mike had been right all along. Séan *had* been responsible for Heather's murder, and God knows who else's.

I drew breath to shout for help but Séan silenced me, closing his mouth over mine. He thrust his tongue roughly into my mouth, so deep it made me gag. He pulled back and gave a chuckle, his hands manacling my upper arms. *Oh, God - could no one see?* I tried desperately to push him off and my hand knocked against something solid under his arm.

God almighty. "You've - a weapon?" I managed.

"Now, yer going to be a good girl, darlin', aren't ya? You'll see the gig through or I'll put a bullet in yer pretty brain." He kissed the center of my forehead. "Right here. Got it?"

My voice came in a whisper. "You going to kill the Duke?"

"Did ya hear me?"

"Yes." I nodded woodenly, my head spinning. Séan might be able to keep me from raising the alarm right now but the moment we headed for that stage, I'd scream holy hell and have the entire Scottish regiment descend on him like seagulls on a scrap of bread. Shit, there were enough soldiers around to take out an army let alone one crazed IRA nut job with a pistol.

"That's my girl. And just in case ya have any ideas about yellin' for help out there, I'll kill Liam and Declan where they stand, and then you darlin', and then me."

What would that achieve? "You wouldn't."

"Try me, darlin'."

I faked calmness. "All right, whatever you say, Séan. I don't want to know about your plans. I'm only here for the gig, you know that."

The kaleidoscope faded from his eyes. "An' you know I love you more than anything, Fen, don't ya? I'm only doing this for our future."

"Fuckin' Christ on a cross," came Liam's voice, strident with tension. "There they are. We're about to go on stage and not a bloody concern in the fuckin' world."

He, Declan and Kieran had come looking for us, instruments in hand.

"Ferget anything *important?*" demanded Kieran with a sniff, fixing his little hostile rat eyes on Séan. He carried the aluminum guitar case.

"You's can fuck each other later," Liam said. No one laughed.

"Get a cocksuckin' move on," said Declan, thrusting the violin and bow into my hands. "We're on."

33
Requiem

On the other side of the walkway screen the audience clapped along in oblivious pleasure to *The Skye Boat Song*. Through a gap I glimpsed the children's pennants flapping in time to the music. Where the fuck was Security? Distracted by Rob's murder, perhaps. Maybe that's why Séan did it.

He kept a hand clasped on my arm, every sinew in his body taut. He stared intently into the passage that led round the back of the stage. I saw Liam and Declan look at each other, then urgently at Séan. Kieran had vanished.

The Skye Boat Song tumbled to a close and the audience broke into enthusiastic, cheering applause. A reel played as the Thistles left the stage.

Liam picked up Kieran's bodhrán from where it lay on the steps. "Where the fuck's Kier?" he shouted over the wailing din.

On cue, Kieran reappeared, his face pinched and tense. He met Séan's gaze and nodded. Séan relaxed, letting go of me. He grabbed Kieran and ruffled his hair. "Well done, boyo."

Well done, what? What had he done? I glanced over my shoulder. If I ran could I make it out to the Square? But no. No amount of speed outran a bullet.

"Get the fuck up here!" Liam gestured frantically from the stage.

He shoved the bodhrán into Kieran's hands. Séan bent to retrieve the tipper, presenting it to Kieran as though it were a sword. Then he propelled him up the steps, clapping him on the back. Declan followed, handing the Fender to Séan as he passed. Liam stalked on stage, his elbow already working at the uilleann pipes bellows to fill them with air.

Séan startled me by pulling me close. "So, what's your answer, Fionnuir? Yes or no?" His manner gave no doubt that there was only one answer he'd be prepared to accept. Agree to marry him or get a bullet in the head.

A technician gesticulated wildly from the side of the stage but Séan ignored him.

I found my voice. "Yes, Séan." *You insane fuck.* "I'll marry you." My voice sounded hollow and insincere but he bought it.

His face broke into a delighted grin and he swept me onto the stage, landing a playful smack that I scarcely felt on my rear. Like a zombie I got into place in front of the microphone. *God, I hadn't checked if the violin was still in tune. Too late now.*

Spotlights scorched the stage. The front was jam-packed with amps and footlights. I squinted past their glare at the audience in the Square as the bagpipers were wrapping up the reel. I couldn't see any security. An ocean of expectant faces looked back at me. If only they knew a fucking psycho with a gun stood before them.

Vincent's voice flowed silkily from the PA. "And now - for the first time all the way across the Irish Sea from Belfast, Northern Ireland! We're proud to welcome - Curadh!"

Applause broke out, significantly less enthusiastic than for the Scottish band. As though a puppetmaster propelled my arm, I woodenly raised the violin and bow and stood ready. A Union Jack pennant caught my eye in the front row, being waved fiercely by a fair-haired angelic little girl, a huge gap-toothed smile on her face. Séan took his place center stage and dramatically thrust an arm up high. When the applause died he swept it down, cueing Kieran to break into a war-like drum beat on the bodhrán.

What the hell was my cue? This was a nightmare I'd frequently had. Being on stage and not knowing what was happening. On automatic pilot I managed to come in when I was supposed to. As we'd rehearsed a hundred times, I harmonized with him.

> "'While the world did gaze in deep amaze
> at those fearless men, but few,
> Who bore the fight that freedom's light
> might shine through the foggy dew—'"

I almost faltered when I finally glimpsed a security guard. *Look at me. Look at me!* I willed him with all my might but he was intent on scanning the audience.

I thought the song would never end. Eventually we reached the finish, ending on an upbeat. Out of breath I swept the bow into the air, holding it aloft to signal the end. The audience burst into applause, and I heard a few grudging cheers.

Séan looked exultant as we took our bows. I peeled away at once for stage right. I'd dash round the passageway behind the stage and alert Security before Séan knew what I was about. I didn't think he'd carry out his threat to shoot Liam and Declan. At least I fervently hoped not. But he was on my heels immediately and trapped me with an arm across my shoulders, his guitar bumping into my arm. I felt the pistol in its holster against my side.

The others followed hotly and Liam jumped in the air, launching a high-five hand. "Fuckin' A! We did it!"

Declan matched him, their palms slapping together. "I need a fuckin' drink, mate." He let his body go fluid, mimicking melting with relief.

"Last one there's a bollocks."

They raced ahead and out of sight.

Séan clasped a hand to Kieran's shoulder. "Check it," he ordered.

His voice sounded strained and I looked closely at him. *Check what? What the fuck?* Kieran ran ahead and Séan kept an arm tight around my shoulders as we headed out through the fabric walkway.

Crown Square had been cordoned off, blocked by hurdle-like barriers. Soldiers armed with short-barreled sub machine guns guarded them. The Porta Loos were also under guard, the walkway to the Lang Stairs too.

"Fuck," spat Séan, stopping dead.

My thoughts careened at terminal velocity. Dec and Liam were out of immediate danger. I needed to break Séan's vise-like hold on me and run for help. In the distance I heard Vincent's voice through the PA. Back here behind the amps it was muffled, but I picked up 'security threat' and 'Duke's speech canceled'. A wash of relief flooded me. Murmurs of disappointment swept through the audience, and I heard chairs scrape on the ground as people got to their feet.

Séan hustled me into deep shadow where the archway met the palace wall. Sweat beaded his forehead and his grip on me was bruising. My heart lifted with triumph when I realized there was no way he could shoot the Duke now.

We'd been spotted. Two soldiers broke away from the barriers in Crown Square, approaching cautiously.

I swallowed hard. "Let's just walk away, Séan, No one but me knows you have that pistol and I won't say anything." And I wouldn't. At least until the soldiers were in range.

He wasn't listening. His head snapped back and forth as he gauged the distance between the approaching soldiers and the security barriers.

"Hey, you!" called one of the soldiers, north English accent distinctive.

Séan's answer was to wrench the pistol from under his coat. The soldiers went into stand-to mode, aiming their SMG's. Séan's grip on me loosened but before I could break away he forced me in front of him, using me as a human shield. He clasped me to him as intimately as though we were in bed, spooning. The soldiers kept their distance.

"You coward," I hissed, too shocked to be scared.

"This's the only way we might get out of this alive, darlin'."

My head swam. He'd ruined all chance of that. All we'd had to do was stroll back through the archway, find Liam and the others and not draw attention to ourselves. But now? I could only hope to convince the soldiers before they shot us that I wasn't involved. If only I'd made that fucking check in call.

Séan bent his head over my shoulder to check the time on his wristwatch. "We just need some luck on our side."

He let me twist my head back to glance back into his feverish eyes. Finally everything became clear.

Fear shot through me. "The lucky guitar!"

His lips quirked into a humorless smile. "Under the stage, aye."

Blood pounded in my head. A *bomb*. Why hadn't I realized? A bomb under the stage. I thrust the visceral image of the Percy French from my mind and began to struggle in earnest. He snatched hold of my hair and I froze as chilling metal pressed against my temple. My head forced back, a flash high up on the battlements of the War Museum caught my eye. Something buzzed close to my ear. A sharp crack sounded, followed by a dull thud. Séan staggered against the wall, pulling me with him. He'd been shot - a jagged hole erupted in the leather coat at his shoulder. We both stared in disbelief at the wet stain blooming from it.

The pistol wavered. I snatched at it but he flipped it into his other hand and forced it against my head again. With his injured arm he held me fast, his strength unfaltering. Now he was a wounded, trapped animal with me as his only shield.

Wind slapped me in the face, throwing dust in my eyes and whipping my hair banshee-wild around me. A black shape blurred the inkiness of the indigo sky as something unfurled silently from above. I thought I was hallucinating. A surreal white semicircle pulsed overhead. It took me a moment to understand it was the whirring of 'copter blades. I could only see a glittering fan shape as they caught the light from the beam on the palace roof. Four dark, almost invisible figures silently slid down ropes and landed in graceful readiness, like stalking panthers on the cobblestones.

SAS troopers.

"Stay the fuck away!" shouted Séan, desperation or fear raising his voice an octave.

One of the four men pushed the ski mask back from his face. Under the ghoulish camouflage cream I recognized Mike. No time to be relieved.

"A bomb!" I yelled. "Under–"

Séan cut me off, shoving the pistol violently into my mouth. Galvanic shock reverberated through my teeth followed by the tang of blood from a split lip. My throat closed against the metallic incursion, and I tried to resist the urgent gag reflex.

Mike's authoritative voice rang through the courtyard and two of the silent troopers vanished into the fabric walkway leading to the stage.

Thank God. He had understood me.

Searchlights seared the archway, highlighting us.

Mike riveted his gaze on Séan. "Let her go. You're done."

The pistol yanked from my mouth and I gulped in air. Séan held out a wrist, brandishing his watch. "Not done yet, ya fuckin' dumb Yank. There's still time."

Mike produced a Browning. "Not for you." He aimed it squarely at Séan's face.

With a hollow chuckle Séan ducked, hiding his head behind mine. The breath caught in my throat as I gazed down the barrel of Mike's pistol. He wouldn't shoot, would he? He made brief eye contact with me and gave an almost imperceptible nod. My heart hammered, hoping I knew what he wanted me to do. Drooping my head forward, I whiplashed it back with all my might. Sharp pain jarred the back of my head as I connected with Séan's nose cartilage. He reeled back, his hold on me lifted at last. I raised a leg and slammed my stiletto heel into his foot, then jack-knifed aside and threw myself to the cobblestones. I was faintly aware of twisting my ankle as I hit the ground. Seeing how close I'd fallen to the fabric walkway I scrabbled inside to take cover, kicking off my heels.

A crack of pistol fire sent my heart racing. First one shot followed by another a split second later. My insides pitched and roiled. Mike or Séan was dead. Maybe both. Saliva thickened my tongue, I wanted to vomit.

Then I remembered the bomb, the lucky guitar. Focusing, I propelled myself to my feet and staggered to the back of the stage. The space underneath was scarcely high enough to crawl under. No wonder runty little Kieran had been the one to plant the bomb. Cold sweat hit me when I realized the troopers couldn't fit under the stage and had sent in some kind of remote machine to examine the device.

Holy fuck, there wasn't time.

I wriggled my way under the stage. There was just enough room for me to raise my head. Dragging myself over to the open guitar case I craned my neck to peer inside.

Christ, how ingenious. The guitar strings were, in fact, copper wires. The timer, attached with duct tape, had been the volume control knob. How Séan got blasting cap and all here beat me. Thoughts spiraled out of control. I remembered the waiter in the Green Room - the stare he and Séan had exchanged. Fuck, Brian Sutherland had put all the pawns in place on his chessboard a long time ago. He'd been planning this for months. A large square torch battery and four pounds of C-4 sat snugly in the case, ready to level Edinburgh Castle and everyone in it. No doubt courtesy of the waiter, again. And the aluminum guitar case itself made the bomb casing. All brought in under Security's very nose.

A sound intruded, slamming me back to the present. Whirring came from the bomb-disposal machine close by. *For God's sake!* I swung my leg sideways and gave it a sharp kick. The stupid thing clattered and buzzed in futility. Turning my attention to the bomb my stomach lurched in horror.

The timer showed less than a minute before detonation. My response was visceral. I wanted to back out of there as fast as I could, run, run as far away as possible.

Had Mike shot Séan? Or the other way round?

A sob tore free of my lungs. Mike had to be okay. He had to be.

Which fucking wire to disconnect? No time to check for tilt switches or other complications.

The timer ticked inexorably down.

Hesitation means death, came the echo of Colonel Pierce's voice.

Jesus Christ, I had to do something. *Occam's razor* - the simplest answer is often correct. I reached in and took hold of the most logical connection on the battery. I clamped my eyes shut, held my breath and smartly yanked it free. The timer clicked as it hit zero.

A zillion thoughts careened through my mind. Mum and Dad, heads thrown back in laughter over a shared joke, Mac barking and bouncing up and down in anticipation of a walk, Dee and me giggling, getting tipsy for the first time, flirting with boys at a disco - Mike tenderly making love to me, Séan's fiery hair glowing in the sunset - the Mourne Mountains with Slieve Donard as crisp as a Swiss alp in the snow, me parascending above, blanketed in peace and serenity.

But no explosion.

I flopped my head and lay prone in utter, overwhelming relief, my forehead on the cold ground. The bubble of silence around me dissipated, replaced by frenetic chaos. Stamping of running feet, hectic shouting, the throb of rotor blades accompanied by roaring engines and shrieking sirens.

I inched backwards until I felt my torso clear the claustrophobic space. My cramped muscles wouldn't obey as I tried to clamber to my feet. Strong hands closed around my waist and aided me upright.

Mike. It was Mike.

I leaned into him, tears flowing freely down my face.

"It's okay, Jen," he murmured into my hair. "It's over now."

Epilogue
A week later

My gaze kept straying to the door. The café nestled on the corner in a quiet lane just off Newcastle Main Street. I'd single-handedly finished the large pot of tea already, but was reluctant to order anything else as apparently there were no toilet facilities for customers. Bloody Troubles. No more public toilets anymore. We had to learn to hold it.

I wiped my clammy palms on my jeans and managed to knock the teaspoon off the table again. The other three customers in the café turned as one and glared. I'd been clattering stuff to the floor for the last forty minutes.

I'd probably been in a score of cafés just like this one with the Curadh lads, waiting for Séan to pick us up for a gig. Every time I looked up I expected to see him in the doorway, blaze of hair and leather coat. He'd sweep across the café, a smile lighting his face.

I'd never see that smile again. Not that I wanted to. Everything about him had been a lie.

My last sight of him in Edinburgh Castle would forever haunt me. He'd crumpled to a sitting position against the wall with his legs straight out in front of him. The light had extinguished from his amber eyes, leaving them eerily shark-like and empty. His face was blankly serene in death. A tiny dot of blood centered his forehead right between the eyes where Mike's bullet had hit home. It all felt so unreal and far removed from me, like I watched a film. From a distance he looked as angelic as he had when sleeping that last morning.

The café door pushed open and Mike appeared, motorbike helmet in hand. I couldn't believe he'd shown up. My insides flipped. He spotted me and threaded his way through the tables. I could barely meet his gaze when he sat opposite.

"Hi," he greeted.

Struck mute, I couldn't think of a thing to say. I wanted so much to explain, get absolution for the things I had done. My eyes may have been opened fully to understand both sides of the Troubles but shame flooded me. In gaining that understanding, I had gone too far - disobeyed orders, lost my bearing, lost myself. I had been infatuated with Séan, a psychopathic murderer even though Mike had warned me about him from the beginning. I felt tainted. How could Mike forgive me? How could I forgive myself?

"You were right all along about everything," I blurted. "I don't know what happened, why I wouldn't listen to you." My voice faltered and he leaned closer to hear. "I thought I loved Séan. But it wasn't him. It was the band, the belonging somewhere. I think I lost my mind."

"You weren't prepared," he said simply. "That's all, Jen. We sent you in too soon."

"But I've ruined everything, Mike. Us."

Something flickered in his dark eyes. Something that gave me hope. "I did my fair share of ruining long before that, if you remember," he murmured.

He reached across the table and took my hand. We stared at each other for a long moment. Maybe we still had a chance. He ran his thumb over the silver poesy ring he'd given me, squeezed my fingers then let go.

"Sutherland's been arrested," he said, his gaze intent. "Was cozied up at home with his whiskey and cigars, TV tuned into the Edinburgh Festival coverage. Guess he hoped to catch the explosion live."

A thread of satisfaction inched through my veins, then flowered in my heart. I had to swallow back tears of pride and relief. The man behind the Percy French bomb had been taken down at last. I'd achieved exactly what I'd set out to do - I could let Mum and Dad rest in peace now.

"What about Kieran?"

"Kieran Lynch has been implicated. He'll face a few years in jail." He lifted up the lid of the teapot, peered inside then set it back.

Good. The little bastard would have a rotten time being bullied in Long Kesh - I hoped. "And the others?"

"They're clean. We let them go."

That was a relief. They'd known nothing about it for sure.

"Funny thing though," continued Mike. "Clancy O'Neill is nowhere to be found."

I'd almost forgotten about him. He was as guilty as Sutherland and Séan - he'd delivered the guitar containing the bomb.

"You know what?" asked Mike. "You owe me a whiskey."

I raised my eyebrows, a smile spreading across my face. "I do?"

"None of your Irish swill, mind you. Good ol' Yankee Jack Daniels."

I laughed. I didn't care what we drank, but I joined into the spirit of things. "Oh, no, it'll have to be Bushmills."

His lips quirked. "Come on, then."

He got up and held out a hand. I took it as we walked out of the café together. His bike sat just outside at the curb, and I waited as he unlocked the trunk to get out the spare helmet.

Down the street toward the sea movement caught my attention. Someone with sandy hair and a green and white Celtic scarf disappeared round the corner. *It couldn't be!* I dashed over but the figure had vanished.

"What is it?" asked Mike, coming up behind me.

"Just thought I saw someone I know."

"Who?"

"A ghost."

If it had been Clancy, no doubt he'd come find me when he was ready. Then it'd be his turn to face the music. I gave a humorless chuckle, acknowledging the pun.

Mike helped me strap the helmet on. I climbed onto the bike behind him and slipped my arms around his waist. I marveled to hold him close again - I never thought I would. In moments, we were off, the bike roaring down the street. I had no idea where we were going, but as long as we were together, I didn't care.

ACKNOWLEDGMENTS

Leigh Goodison - fellow émigré and literary cohort: for so many years of friendship, moral and professional support. (Not to mention all the *Freixenet* shared whilst plotting.)

Scott Simmons - real time alpha reader and friend: for putting your life on hold daily to give me your immediate and insightful feedback.

Lieutenant Colonel Simon Barry - military advisor: and for teaching me to parachute way-back-when in Ballykinlar.

Thank you to mentor Irene Radford; beta readers Sharon Dunlop, Trenna Landers, Terry McAuley, Bill Johnson, Jim Blythe, Ian Blythe, and Fiona Blythe. For the wee details, thank you to Lynne Vinton, Clare Foster, Liam Collins, June Wilson, Patricia Wilson, Barb Nickels, the ever-patient Neil Shannon, Steve Blythe, Heather McLaughlin, Patrick Wiese, Skip Fuller, Contessa Timmerman, and Gene Paxton. Thank you to Bill Duff, historian, and to Queensmen Russell Wicks, Bob Jones, and Peter Ives. I hope I haven't left anyone out, so many wonderful people were incredibly generous with their time.

And very special thanks to wolf-champion and film producer Kim Guidone for giving me the 'homework' that kick-started the book into gear, otherwise I think I might still be procrastinating.

A bestselling author and editor, Lizzy's published works span many genres, including science fiction, Celtic nonfiction, fantasy, screenplays, and stage plays.

Having grown up in Belfast, *A Song of Bullets* is set amidst the worst era of Northern Ireland's 'Troubles' in the 70's, and based on true events in her life.

She's currently working on a sequel, and also a screenplay based on the memoirs of her great uncle, Ernest Blythe, an Irish journalist, managing director of the Abbey Theatre, and politician who served as Minister for Finance in the Irish government.

Lizzy's career is as varied as the genres she writes. Starting out as a library assistant in a Northern Irish rural town, she moved on to study Theatre Arts and Literature in London, and toured the United Kingdom as a professional actress. Roles ranged from the goddess Hecate in Shakespeare's *Macbeth* to Gustav, the Amazing Dancing Bear in a clown troupe.

www.lizzyshannon.com

The Slidderyford Dolmen, County Down

www.ingramcontent.com/pod-product-compliance
Lightning Source LLC
Chambersburg PA
CBHW030020180626
46810CB00001B/128